About the A

Jamie Pope first fell in love with romance when her mother placed a novel in her hands at the age of thirteen. She became addicted to love stories and has been writing them ever since. When she's not writing her next book, you can find her shopping for shoes or binge-watching shows.

Maya Blake's writing dream started at thirteen. She eventually realised her dream when she received 'The Call' in 2012. Maya lives in England with her husband, kids, and an endless supply of books. Contact Maya: mayab author.blogspot.com, twitter.com/mayablake, facebook. com/maya.blake.94

Approaching fifty Mills & Boon titles, **Dianne Drake** is still as passionate about writing romance as ever. As a former intensive care nurse, it's no wonder medicine has found its way into her writing, and she's grateful to Mills & Boon Medical for allowing her to write her stories. 'They return me to the days I loved being a nurse and combine that with my love of the romance novels I've been reading since I was a young teen.'

Postcards from Paradise

January 2023
Caribbean

April 2023
Costa Rica

February 2023
Brazil

May 2023
Australia

March 2023
Hawaii

June 2023
Bali

Postcards from Paradise:
Costa Rica

JAMIE POPE

MAYA BLAKE

DIANNE DRAKE

MILLS & BOON

First Published in Great Britain 2023
by Mills & Boon, an imprint of HarperCollins*Publishers* Ltd,
1 London Bridge Street, London, SE1 9GF

www.harpercollins.co.uk

HarperCollins*Publishers*
Macken House, 39/40 Mayor Street Upper,
Dublin 1, D01 C9W8, Ireland

Postcards from Paradise: Costa Rica © 2023 Harlequin Enterprises ULC.

Tempted at Twilight © 2017 Jamie Pope
The Commanding Italian's Challenge © 2020 Maya Blake
*Saved by Doctor Dream*y © 2017 Dianne Despain

ISBN: 978-0-263-31899-9

FSC
www.fsc.org

MIX
Paper | Supporting
responsible forestry
FSC™ C007454

This book is produced from independently certified FSC™ paper
to ensure responsible forest management.

For more information visit: www.harpercollins.co.uk/green

Printed and Bound in the UK using 100% Renewable Electricity
at CPI Group (UK) Ltd, Croydon, CR0 4YY

TEMPTED
AT TWILIGHT

JAMIE POPE

To every girl who wears her Blerd status proudly.

Chapter 1

"Have you taken leave of your senses?"

Elias Bradley sat in the chief of surgery's office and quietly listened as she berated him. It wasn't the first time she had done so. He seemed to have a way of getting under his boss's skin.

"You're not even cleared to be back yet, and you get into an altercation with a patient's boyfriend?"

Elias's already injured hand was radiating with pain, a reminder of the scuffle he had gotten into, but he remained silent, knowing it was better not to speak until Dr. Lundy was done yelling.

"How can I make you head of trauma if you act so impulsively?"

Impulsive.

It wasn't the first time he had heard that word used to describe him. Teachers. Girlfriends. Even his own family had said it. But being impulsive wasn't always a bad thing. His rash decisions had gotten him pretty far.

"With all due respect, ma'am. One of the things that makes me a good trauma surgeon is the fact that I think and act very quickly. I saw a man grab a patient and try to yank her out of the hospital before she could be treated. I feel that my actions were necessary and in the end protected that patient from further harm."

He was impressed with how calmly he defended himself. He wanted to scream, *That guy was an abusive jackass. Somebody should have kicked his ass a long time ago.* But he kept that in. Sometimes he did think before he acted.

"You punched him!" she roared. "Hard enough to break his nose, and even if I cared about his face or the potential lawsuit that might be coming, it doesn't compare to how much I care about your hands. What good is a surgeon who cannot operate? Right now, you are a highly paid pain in my behind."

He had never heard the normally proper chief speak that way, but he had never seen her this enraged before, either. "I was only in the hospital to try to make myself useful. Even if I can't operate, I can work in the ER. I can still see patients."

"No, you cannot. I handpicked your orthopedic surgeon and your occupational therapist. They have both reported to me that you are nowhere near able to return to surgery, that even if you weren't a surgeon, that you would need to be on light duty. Working in the ER in the biggest, busiest hospital in Miami isn't anyone's idea of light duty. And taking into account your penchant for championing the abused and less fortunate, I'm afraid I'm going to have to ban you from the hospital until you are medically cleared."

"You're banning me!" He'd never thought it would have come to that. At most he'd thought she would yell at him and relegate him to paperwork, which he would be fine with, because he loved being in the hospital. He loved the sights and the smells and knowing that what he did made a difference. He didn't have much else in his life at the moment. His siblings were all very happily married and busy with their own families. There was no special woman to go home to. His life revolved around the hospital. He ate all his meals there. He slept there much of the time. Hell, all the people he socialized with worked there. He wasn't sure what he would do with himself if he couldn't come to work.

"Yes, you are banned. I have put an alert out to all the security guards that if they find you here, you are to be escorted out. Your swipe card has been de-activated."

"You're treating me like a criminal!"

"No, I'm treating you like an asset that needs to be protected." She took a calming breath. "You are probably one of the most talented young surgeons

I've seen in years, and you are excelling in a difficult, highly specialized field. You want to take over
as head of trauma, but how can I promote you if I
can't trust you to act rationally? Your hand is not
even a quarter of the way healed, and you go and
punch someone. Did you think about your career?
Did you think about the potentially irrevocable damage you could have done to your future?"

The truth was he hadn't thought of it at all. He'd
just acted. That big guy dragging that scared woman
through the ER had made his blood boil. He wished
he could say that if it happened again, he would have
called security or ignored it, but he knew himself too
well. Hand damage be damned. He still would've
knocked that guy on his ass and given him a big taste
of his own medicine.

He had two sisters. He hoped some guy would do
the same for them if they were ever in that situation.

"You have nothing to say to that?"

"Nothing that wouldn't cause you to yell at me
again."

She sighed and shook her head. "Go home, Dr.
Bradley. In fact, leave Miami. You'll be out of commission for quite some time. Do something you
wouldn't normally do. But considering the way you
broke your hand, maybe you should sit in a room and
not move for a couple of months."

A couple of months.

A nauseating twinge rolled in his stomach. He
didn't think he could sit at home for a couple of

months. He was immediately mad at himself again for breaking his hand. He had been doing one of those extreme mud runs with his brother and brother-in-law. He had crawled under barbed wire and had been submerged in a fifty-foot pool of mud. He had even run through fire, only to get tangled in the cargo net. He was on his way down when his foot got caught, and as he yanked it free, the runner just above him lost his balance and they both fell. The other guy had landed on top of Elias as he had put his hands out to break his fall. It was almost a twenty-foot drop.

He had replayed the incident in his mind a thousand times that day, but there was no way he could have prevented it. No way he could have changed the outcome. He had badly broken his hand and wrist, the pain so extreme he had passed out for a moment. He had to have surgery, from which he had yet to heal. His hand had already been swollen and practically immobile before he punched the guy. He was surprised he'd even been able to make a fist. Lord knew he couldn't do anything else with it. But that was the power of adrenaline.

His older brother, Carlos, was a baseball superstar who had been on the disabled list for nearly a year because of a ruptured Achilles tendon. Elias had lectured him about overdoing it, demanded that Carlos rest, acted like the smug doctor he was. But when he was doling out that advice, he'd never thought he would end up in nearly the same situation.

"Get out of my office, Dr. Bradley. You have been working nonstop since medical school. You're a young man. Take some time to enjoy yourself."

He stood up and left the hospital. It wasn't bad advice. He just didn't know how the hell he was going to do it.

Cricket Warren glanced at her phone…again. Only four minutes had passed since she'd last looked, but those four minutes seemed like a hundred years to her. She was seated in the bar area of a small oceanfront restaurant on Hideaway Island, waiting for a ghost from her past to appear. Well…maybe *ghost* wasn't the right word, but she wasn't sure what to call the person she was supposed to be meeting. They certainly weren't friends. They never had been. Just two people who happened to be born to parents who ran in the same social circle.

"Miss? Are you sure I can't get you something to drink?" the bartender asked her from behind the bar. "It's still happy hour for another fifteen minutes. Drinks are half-price. Our special is pineapple margaritas. They come in a pineapple cup. Everyone seems to like them."

Cricket was tempted. She wasn't much of a drinker, but she must look kind of sad sitting in a bar by herself, twiddling her thumbs. "Oh, I probably shouldn't. I'm still waiting for my friend."

"Your friend is late," a man said. He was sitting at the end of the bar with a domestic beer in his hand. His back had been to her most of the time she was there, his eyes glued to some sporting event on the large television over the bar, but she had definitely noticed him. She didn't have to see his face to know he was one of those hypermasculine men whose pheromones filled the air and made otherwise sensible women turn into a pool of senseless goopy jelly. His was broad backed, tall, muscular. He sat up very straight, which Cricket's mother would have appreciated. He wore his inky-black hair in overlong curls, which might have been considered boyish or feminine on another man, but worked on him. He was brown skinned, some beautiful shade that she couldn't begin to describe. And just when she decided that she had better stop cataloging his features, he turned to face her.

Well...damn.

He might be the most gorgeous man she had ever laid eyes on, and a tiny spark of recognition went off in her brain. She had seen this man before, but she couldn't immediately place where she would have met such an extraordinary-looking human.

Maybe in her dreams.

"Yes," she said quietly, hoping he wouldn't hear her embarrassing breathlessness. "My friend is quite late."

"Have a drink. They won't get mad at you. And if they do, they aren't the kind of friend you need."

She opened her mouth to speak but then hesitated.

"I'll buy you the drink. My sister-in-law loves those pineapple things. You should try it."

Cricket was twenty-nine years old. She spoke four

languages fluently and had studied with the best and brightest around the world, but she'd never had a stranger offer to buy her a drink in a bar.

Ever.

But then again, guys never made passes at pudgy girls with two PhDs who were named after bugs.

"Say yes," the man said to her, the corner of his mouth curling in an appealing way.

She swallowed hard and warned herself not to be the awkward person she was ninety-nine percent of the time. "I need to know who I'm saying yes to."

"Elias." He got off his stool and walked over to her, his hand extended.

"Cricket," she responded absently as she took note of his hand. Normally she introduced herself as Cree, because scientists named after bugs didn't usually garner respect, but this time she had forgotten and introduced herself by her given name.

He had recently had surgery. There was a barely healed incision running from his wrist all the way up the palm of his hand and one along his thumb.

"Do you inspect everyone's hand you shake so closely?" he asked. It was then she realized that she hadn't shaken his hand at all—she was holding it with both of hers as her thumb ran along the still-angry incision line.

"You shouldn't be shaking my hand. Yours is swollen. You should wave, or do that head-nod thingy that guys do."

"Would a wink suffice?" He took the chair next to her at the four-top.

"Oh, no. Winks can be kind of creepy, don't you think?"

He smiled at her, fully this time, showing off a set of perfectly white teeth. He became even more gorgeous, if that were possible. "They could be sexy, too. I guess it depends on who is doing the winking."

"And on the winkee. No?"

"I wouldn't find it creepy if you winked at me. Is your name really Cricket?"

"Yes. Like the bug," she admitted with a small sigh.

"That can't be true." He laughed. "Your parents must have thought it was a cute name for a girl."

"No, they thought I looked like a bug, so they named me Cricket. Cricket Moses Warren."

He slanted a brow at her. "Moses as in part-the-seas Moses?"

"I suppose, but I think I'm named for my great-great-grandfather, who was a conductor on the Underground Railroad. His name was Moses."

He winked at her. "It's nice to meet you, Cricket Moses. I am Elias James Bradley."

"Oh, how normal of you to be called Elias James. I suppose your parents were too unimaginative to name you after a noisy, beady-eyed bug and an ancestor of the opposite sex."

He grinned at her. "No, I'm named after a soap actor and my father." He raised his hand to signal the bartender. "A pineapple margarita for my new friend, and another beer for me."

"Friends now, are we? I don't even know one embarrassing thing about you, and you know two about me."

She wasn't normally so chatty with strangers, especially deliciously beautiful strange men, but she was feeling kind of nervous. "You know I just had surgery on my hand and I have very limited movement in it."

"Is that embarrassing?"

"Yes. I work with my hands. I can't do my job now because of it."

"You work with your hands, huh? Are you an MMA fighter?"

"No."

"A football player?"

"No."

"A boxer? Did you hit someone so hard your hand shattered in tiny little pieces?"

"I didn't break my hand at work."

"How did you break it? Freaky sex accident?"

"You're weird." He grinned.

"I know." She nodded, not believing she wasn't censoring herself like she normally would. "I have been my entire life."

"I like it." He looked down at his swollen hand and attempted to bend his fingers without much success. "I broke it doing a mud race. I fell from a twenty-foot landing and then had a 250-pound man land on top of me. My wrist snapped."

"Ouch." She gently took his large, swollen hand

in hers again and studied it. "Your hand should still be immobilized. Judging from the healing of this incision, you're about a month post-op."

He frowned at her. "Are you a doctor?"

"No," she lied—or half lied. She was a doctor, just not a medical one, and according to her mother, her PhDs were little more than expensive pieces of paper. "I just know a little about this."

"Who's this man you are meeting?" Elias asked as the bartender set down their drinks in front of them.

"I'm not meeting a man," she said as she studied the drink she'd allowed him to order for her. It actually came in a hollowed-out pineapple and was very interesting to look at.

"You're not?"

"No." She picked up her drink and took a sip. She found it delightful. "Why would you think I was meeting a man?"

"Because you are a beautiful woman sitting in a bar with a nervous look on your face."

"You think I'm beautiful?" She grabbed his beer and slid it away from him. "How many drinks have you had?"

She was smart. She was creative. She was great at board games, but she had never thought she was beautiful. She tried to look her best. But at most she was pleasant to look at.

"I didn't even have a sip of my second. I wouldn't tell you that you were beautiful unless I thought you were. I like your hair and your mouth and your huge doe eyes."

She tried to ignore the fact that his compliment made her feel warm all the way down to her toes. "That's why my parents named me Cricket. Because of my eyes. They call me Bug."

"Do you mind?"

"I didn't at first, but then everyone in school started to call me Bug, and not in the cute, endearing way my father intended."

He nodded. "That must have sucked."

"It did," she agreed. "I bet you were popular in school."

"What makes you say that?"

"I'm purely judging a book by its cover. You were a jock. You played football. All the girls loved you because you are so perfectly gorgeous." She swept her eyes over him again, enjoying how he looked more and more by the second. "You can hold a conversation, so I'm guessing you weren't just an athlete but participated in something like student council. You were prom and/or homecoming king. How much of that did I get right?"

"All of it," he said with a grin. "But you missed something."

"What?"

"I sang in the choir."

"That is surprising. Did you join to impress girls?"

"I liked to sing." He shrugged. "You never told me who you were meeting."

"A childhood…friend?"

"You don't sound too sure about that."

"I'm not sure I like her. I don't think she likes me, either. She always makes little digs at me. 'I'm seeing the most incredible man. I guess you haven't found anyone yet. I've been promoted at work again. Are you still doing research in that dark little lab of yours? Don't worry, you'll change careers when you get up the courage.' It makes me want to spill something on one of those thousand-dollar handbags she carries around."

"If you don't like her, then why do you see her?"

"I don't know," she said. "It's completely irratio-nal, isn't it? But we grew up together. We attended the same private school. We took violin lessons together. We even have horses stabled at the same barn."

"Horses?"

"Yeah. My guy is old and overweight and his name is Seymour, and hers is this exquisite Ara-bian who wins prizes for his beauty."

"What's his name?"

"Adonis."

He shook his head. "Sounds pretentious."

"It is and he is! He's a mean horse. I bet he makes little catty remarks about the other horses behind their backs. My boy is sweet as pie. Beauty and speed aren't everything in a racehorse." She looked up at Elias, realizing that she was having a longer conversation with him than she'd had with any man that wasn't about science for the first time in years. And he actually seemed interested in what she had to say. Most of her conversations with the opposite sex were purely intellectual, about topics that most people without PhDs couldn't follow. And at times, they bored the heck out of her. Sometimes those men even asked her out, and rationally those men should have been stimulating to talk to. But this handsome stranger with a broken hand made her feel more comfortable than anyone else ever had. "Why are you letting me ramble on like this?"

"I don't know. We're the only two people in this bar. It seemed like we should meet."

Elias was being truthful when he told Cricket he didn't know why he was having this conversation with her. He had been feeling restless since he had been banned from the hospital. Staying in Miami, being around all the sights and smells, knowing that people were being gravely injured every minute, all over the city, and he could do nothing about it, was making him nearly jump from his skin. So he had escaped to Hideaway Island, home of his brother and twin sister. They had been supportive when he told them that he was going to be out of work for some time as he healed, both offering their homes for him to recuperate in, but he couldn't be around them, either.

They were both married. Carlos had a daughter. His twin was still a newlywed and so ridiculously in love with her husband it sometimes made Elias's stomach churn. They were all happy and settled, and Elias felt very out of place with them.

He was the only one of his siblings who was single. He didn't want to get married. In fact, he planned to remain single for years, but when he was with Carlos, he felt…unsettled. Like he was missing out on something. So he had escaped his sister's house and come to the nearby restaurant for a change of scenery.

He had immediately noticed Cricket when she walked into the bar. She was much different from the women he encountered in Miami who lived in slinky dresses with lots of exposed skin. They were overtly sexy.

Cricket was sexy, too. Oddly sexy, in a way that discomfited him. She was not his type at all, but when she walked into the bar that night, his senses went on high alert. He took in everything about her. She wore a short pretty sundress with a bold graphic floral print. Her legs were by no means long, but they were beautiful and thick—the kind of leg that a man liked to slide his hand up and down in bed. Her hair was in loose, almost fluffy curls. It wasn't a modern style. Hell, it wasn't classic or chic or anything, but it suited her. She looked perfectly sweet, with wide innocent eyes and beautiful full lips.

And he had been sitting with her for the past ten minutes, unable to pull himself away.

"Is there any particular reason you are meeting this woman you don't like here tonight?"

Cricket shrugged. "She asked to see me. It's been a while. Said we need to do some catching up. She's probably feeling a bit low about herself and would like to take a few jabs at me to boost her confidence."

"Why do you let her do that to you?"

"She must not be very confident if she has to tear me down to pull herself up. In an odd way, it makes me feel better. If someone that physically perfect has doubts about themselves, then I realize that I'm not so different."

"Everyone feels shitty about themselves sometimes."

"And that applies to you, too?"

"Of course." He nodded.

"Not about your looks. I wouldn't believe someone who looks like you would."

"Are you flirting with me?"

Her eyes widened in surprise. "Am I? I never tried before. I didn't think I knew how!"

He grinned at her again. He was doing that a lot tonight. He felt a little bit like an idiot, but it felt good. He needed any reason to feel good lately. Without the hospital he was feeling lost, empty. For the first time in his life he was idle, and he sure as hell didn't like it. "If you weren't flirting, what do you call it?"

"Being honest." She took a long sip of her drink. "Maybe it's this stuff that's making me extra honest this evening." They both heard the sound of heels clicking on the floor in the distance, and Elias knew that his conversation with this quirky woman was about to come to an end.

"I'll leave you to enjoy your friend. It was nice speaking to you, Cricket."

"I enjoyed speaking to you, too, Elias."

He got up and walked back to his spot at the bar just as a woman rounded the corner. Cricket was right.

Her friend was beautiful. She was tall, with caramel-colored skin and light eyes. Her body was toned, her hair long and ruthlessly straight, highlighted with different shades of blond. She was perfectly made-up and perfectly dressed. She was perfectly boring.

"Hey, Bug!" She smiled brightly. "It's great to see you."

"Hello, Giselle. How are you?"

"Great! Just great." She hugged Cricket. "What a cute little dress you're wearing. I could never pull it off, but you have never been afraid of wearing things you find in the thrift store."

"I didn't get this in a thrift store. I got this in a little boutique downtown. The one you're always talking about."

"Oh." She took the seat across from Cricket. "Do they carry your size there? I didn't think they carried anything over a size ten."

"They do," Cricket said, her nostrils flaring a bit.

"Good. You can carry the extra weight so much better than most people I know. I'm glad they have clothes for larger ladies."

Elias felt his nostrils flaring a bit. He wanted Cricket to tell the woman to go to hell.

"Everyone deserves nice clothing," Cricket responded cheerfully. "So what's going on with you? I know there must be something if you wanted to see me."

"I just wanted to catch up. You are one of my dearest friends."

"Were you working late? That promotion you got must be keeping you busy. You were nearly a half hour behind schedule. But I know you must have been too busy to text me. Us career girls have to really put our noses to the grindstone to prove we're just as good as the men, so I understand your tardiness."

Elias wanted to applaud Cricket. She wasn't a pushover. He liked that.

"I'm sorry about that. I was on a call." She reached across the table and gave Cricket's hand a light squeeze. "So, are you seeing anyone? I'm still with Arnold. It's getting serious! But don't worry, sweetie. You'll find someone someday. Women can have children well into their late forties nowadays."

That was it. Elias left his spot at the bar and walked back over to Cricket's table. He didn't spare a single look at her friend before he took Cricket's chin between his fingers and kissed her full, pouty mouth. He wasn't sure if that was the stupidest thing he had ever done or the best decision of his life, because he felt the immediate spark of sexual attraction in their kiss.

He lifted his head briefly, looked her in the eyes and kissed her again. This time she slid her hand up his jaw and kissed him back a little more deeply than he had kissed her.

"I'm sorry that took so long," he said to her as he slipped into the chair next to her. "I got our dinner reservations moved back another half hour."

"Dinner." Cricket nodded, giving him a conspiratorial grin. "Can't wait."

"Um," Giselle said. "Hello. I'm Giselle, and you are?"

"Elias." He nodded his head but didn't extend his hand to shake. "I'm Cricket's boyfriend."

"Isn't he gorgeous?" Cricket laughed.

Giselle looked stunned. "Uh… I… I—I didn't know you were seeing anyone."

"Well, Elias walked up to me and introduced himself, and I've been taken with him ever since."

"Oh, how sweet," she said, looking and sounding disbelieving. "I'm happy for you." Her eyes narrowed. "Tell me, Elias. What do you do for a living?"

"I'm a trauma surgeon."

"Here on the island?"

"There are very few traumas here. I work at Miami Mercy. I'm on leave right now. I broke my wrist and haven't been cleared to return yet."

"My boyfriend is in pharmaceutical sales. He's at your hospital a lot. Maybe you know him."

"I don't. I don't ever speak to drug reps unless they are bleeding out on my table."

"Where did you go to medical school?"

"Miller."

"You got into one of the best hospitals in the country." She nodded. "Did you meet Bug at a work function?"

"No. It was purely by chance, and I couldn't seem to get her off my mind ever since."

None of those things were lies. If it were any other day, he might not have been there. He might not have even given a second look to Cricket or cared that she was being disrespected by her rude friend. But it wasn't any other night. Tonight he wanted something to take his mind off not being able to work, and he was glad that Cricket was that something.

"So, are you getting serious? Your mother will be pleased, I'm sure," she said rather stiffly. "Who wouldn't love another doctor in the family?"

Another doctor? She'd told him she wasn't one, and he had believed her because he spent a lot of time around doctors and she seemed a little more free-spirited than most of them. But maybe he didn't know as much as he thought he did.

"It doesn't matter what my mother thinks. It only matters that I'm happy, and right this minute, I'm incredibly happy."

Giselle frowned, almost like she didn't understand what Cricket was saying. "I didn't mean to keep you two from your date night."

"You're not!" Cricket said. "Elias wanted to meet you."

"I've heard a lot about you." He nodded as he took Cricket's hand and raised it to his lips. "I want to know all of Cricket's friends."

"That's nice." She stood up. "I'm meeting Arnold tonight, so I have to run. It was good to meet you, Elias. Cricket, I'll call you?"

"Yes. Catching up with you is always fun."

She walked out then, and as soon as her heels clicked out of earshot, Cricket turned to him. "What on earth possessed you to do that?"

"I don't like the way she speaks to you."

"I can handle myself, you know."

"I know."

"You kissed me." She tilted her head and studied him.

"I did, and then you kissed me."

She had soft, plump lips. They were perfect for kissing. He could have just sat down beside her, held her hand and pretended like he was her boyfriend, but he'd kissed her. He *had* to kiss her. It seemed like the right thing to do in that moment. It might have been one of those impulsive moments that his boss was so fond of pointing out. There had been no thinking involved. His mouth just moved toward hers.

"Do you like tacos?" she asked.

He blinked at her for a moment, confused by the change in topic. "Yeah."

"What about frozen custard?"

"The soft-serve kind?"

"Of course."

"Yes."

"Let me wine and dine you," she said with a grin. "Or maybe I should say convenient food and converse with you."

"You are so weird," he said again, shaking his head. "I would love to have tacos and custard with you."

Chapter 2

Hideaway Island was one of those small coastal islands that felt a little bit like paradise wrapped up in a warm blanket. Cricket had spent her childhood in Miami and her early adulthood in the New York area. But she had spent all her summers there on the island. It was how she recharged her always draining batteries, and tonight she felt full of electricity.

There was a beautiful man strolling down the beach beside her. His feet bare, his pants rolled up, his eyes taking in the scenery around them. She didn't blame him. Hideaway Island had to be one of the most beautiful places on earth. Especially at twilight, when the sky was purple and orange and the breeze kicked up and the air smelled like ocean and sweetness and something magical that she couldn't identify.

They had stopped at the food trucks lined up in front of the boardwalk and dined on a bench before they embarked on their stroll. She felt at ease with Elias when she shouldn't. He was a stranger. A stranger whom she had met in a bar! He could be some kind of con artist or murderer. She had already witnessed how smoothly he lied to Giselle about being her boyfriend and a surgeon at one of the best hospitals in the country, but despite all of that, despite all the rational thoughts that were always firing in her head, she liked him. She liked talking to him, being in his large presence. There was something safe about him.

There was also the fact that he'd kissed her tonight. She had been kissed before, but his had been the sweetest, because it had been so unexpected. She didn't have time to worry about her breath, or what he was thinking or how she looked. She had just let herself be kissed. And she had kissed him back. Tingles, warmth and sparks all felt like trite ways to describe how she had felt when he was kissing her, but there didn't seem to be other words for it. All she knew for sure was that she wanted to feel that sensation again, and it was going to have to be tonight.

Before her rational thoughts returned and she talked herself out of having more fun.

"Do you live on the island, or are you here just visiting?" she asked him.

"Visiting. I have family here. You and I met tonight because I needed to escape them."

"Not a wife and kids, I hope."

"Yeah, Serena is pregnant, too. I can't take all her complaining and the kids running around the house like a bunch of wild animals."

Cricket stopped in her tracks and looked up at him.

Elias took out his phone and snapped a picture of her.

"What the hell!"

"I had to get a picture of your face. It was priceless. You're gullible."

"You're a great liar. Let me see the picture."

"No." He slipped his phone back into his pocket. "You might delete it."

"Is it that bad?"

"No. It's cute." He wrapped his arm around her as they continued to walk. It was nice. His body was so large and hard, and for once in her life she felt petite and protected and liked for who she was. "No kids, wife or girlfriend. I'm single. My sister is a newlywed, and there is nothing worse in the world than being stuck hanging out with two people who are in love."

"I could think of a couple worse things."

Elias sighed. "I really like my sister's husband. He's exactly who I would have picked for her."

"But?"

"We're twins. We went to the same college. We

lived next door to each other until she sold her town house. She used to call me every day. We were close."

"You're not anymore?"

"We are, but it's different. Her husband comes first, which he should. But I kind of miss being the first person she tells all her stupid crap to. It used to annoy the hell out of me when she called me just to chat, but it was a part of my day. Now it feels like something is missing."

She smoothed her hand down his back, and he looked down at her with a sheepish grin.

"If you ever tell anyone I said that, I might be forced to kill you."

"Got it. Men break out in hives whenever they think someone might know they have a feeling."

"I'm a manly man," he said, deepening his already-deep voice. "I snapped my wrist and went in to work the next day with duct tape wrapped around it."

"You didn't."

"No. It hurt like hell. I'm pretty sure I started crying and passed out."

She laughed. "I don't believe that, either."

"I just remember my brother cursing and saying something about our mother flying to the States to kill him."

"Your mother doesn't live here?"

"Costa Rica. She moved there after my father passed away."

"Oh." She went quiet for a moment. "I'm sorry."

"Don't be. It's been many years now."

They continued to walk on in silence until they came up to a set of houses that were directly on the beach. "My house is right up there."

"Is it?" He looked at the house and then back at her. "It's nice."

"It is nice. Would you like to see it?" She was inviting him inside. She didn't want this night to end. It had been surreal and comfortable and wonderful, and it wasn't even 8:00 p.m. yet.

"Yes, I very much would."

Her heart beat faster as they walked quietly up the path that led to her beachfront home. She had never done this before. She had never met a man who she was this attracted to, who she wanted to spend so much time with. First dates had always been horrible for her. Awkward. Panic inducing. But she had met Elias by chance. There was no time for her to get worked up, to overthink, and tonight she wasn't allowing herself to think at all. She was living in the moment. Doing what made her feel good.

"Whoa," he said when she let them in.

Her home was beautiful, a gift from her parents, but Cricket really knew it had been her father's idea to give her this house when she finished her second doctorate. It was an overly generous present, but her father adored her and knew how much she loved this island and cherished the summers she had spent there as a child. It was nothing to him to give her this gift, even though her mother was against it.

Cricket, after all, was the heiress to one of the largest tech fortunes in the world.

"I know it's a little sparse right now. I haven't spent much time here until recently."

"Where were you?" he asked, looking around.

"My lab was based in Boston, but I traveled a great deal."

"I heard you say something about research. What kind of research do you do?"

She hesitated for a moment. There was nothing romantic or sexy about her job, but she was proud of her work. Her mother told her she should never be embarrassed of showing off her brain. But the older she got, the more she realized that men didn't necessarily want to date a woman with a bunch of fancy letters after her name. "I'm a medical scientist."

"A PhD?" he asked, stepping closer.

"Yes, I'm afraid I have two of them."

A devastatingly sexy smile crossed his lips. He then grabbed her bag and tossed it aside before he wrapped his arms around her and kissed her again. His lips were open, his mouth wet, his tongue warm. She immediately went slack, and he brought her body closer to his. Large, hard, hot. Those were the only words she could think of to describe him. He smelled so good, like ocean air and aftershave and soft-serve vanilla ice cream. She could get drunk off his scent.

"Tell me to go home," he said into her mouth. "Right now. Tell me to leave."

"I can't. You leaving is the very last thing I want."

"I was hoping you would say that." He pulled her cardigan off and kissed that little curve that connected her shoulder to her neck.

A moan escaped her as his hands slipped up her dress to skim the backs of her thighs. "You're so beautiful," he told her as he hooked his thumbs into her underwear and slid them down. "I want you so damn much."

She sought his mouth again, wrapping her arms around his neck and kissing him with a heat that she had never experienced before. She felt his erection against her belly, and it caused her to grow wetter, even more aroused than she was when he had started all of this. She'd had only one serious boyfriend, one sweet, lovely man whom she would have happily spent the rest of her life with, but he'd never made her feel this way. He never wanted her with as much hunger as Elias possessed.

"Take me to your bedroom."

She took his hand without thinking, and he winced.

"I'm sorry!"

"Don't be. You can kiss it better." He lightly pressed his lips to hers.

"When's the last time you took anything for your hand?"

"This morning. But I'm fine. Don't worry about me."

"I am worried. I need you to touch me all over my body, and for that to happen I need to know you're not in pain."

"If you take me to bed, I promise you the only kind of pain I'll be in is the good kind."

She smiled at him and took his other hand, leading him into her en suite bathroom. It was a luxurious bathroom by anyone's standards, with a huge jetted tub and a rainfall shower. There was a view of the ocean from the window.

"This bathroom is bigger than my bedroom," he said to her in a low voice. "I would like to spend some time in here if we can."

"We can." She went to her medicine cabinet and opened it up in search for a bottle of pain reliever. Some of the contents came spilling out, including her birth control.

"I guess I don't have to wonder about that," he said and then unzipped her dress. She had on the ugliest underwear. A beige strapless bra. Her white cotton panties had been left on the floor somewhere near her front door. She had never thought she would be here in a million years. She didn't even own sexy underwear, but Elias didn't seem to mind at all. He unhooked her bra and with his uninjured hand cupped her breast, squeezing it ever so slightly as his thumb stroked over her nipple.

She swallowed hard, almost forgetting what she was supposed to be doing. But then she remembered she wanted him to have two pain-free hands so that she could experience even more of his pleasure. She picked up the bottle and closed the door to the medicine cabinet only to come face-to-face with herself in the mirror. Only she didn't recognize herself. Her hair was windblown and wild, her mouth was slightly open, her lips pouty and kiss swollen. She was completely naked, and a large fully dressed man was looking at her with such open appreciation that it made her knees weak.

But the most marked change was the look in her eyes. There was arousal there, pure and naked lust. She hadn't thought it was possible to look like that. It didn't mesh with the image she had of herself in her mind.

"Do you see how sexy you are?" he asked as he pulled her nipple between his fingers. She bit her lip as the pleasure took over her. "I can't wait to be inside you. To feel you wrapped around me. I can't help but feel that you are what I need right now."

She trembled. The power of his words alone made her tremble. She took a small step away from him and filled a glass with water and handed it to him.

"Pills now."

"Open the bottle for me."

She complied, but she did it as she walked back into her bedroom, feeling freer and more confident in her body than she had in all her twenty-nine years. "Sit down," she ordered. He did so with a sexy grin that she was growing to love more by the minute. "Take these." She handed him the pills and began to work at the small buttons on his shirt. She knew his body was in spectacular shape, because she felt every hard-muscled line when she was pressed against him.

But now she could see him in all his glory. Beautiful brown skin covering tight abs and a powerfully built chest.

"I like bossy women," he said and set his glass of water on the nightstand before he pulled her closer. "Have I mentioned how incredible your behind is?" He cupped it, his fingers digging into her flesh.

"No, but a lady always loves a compliment." She pulled off his shirt and then pushed him back on the bed. She unzipped his pants and gave him a silent signal to lift his hips. She was growing wetter and wetter with each piece of skin she had revealed. It was something special to have a gorgeous naked man in her bed, one who she knew wanted her, one who was so aroused that she was afraid he wasn't going to fit inside her.

He pulled her on top of him, their naked bodies colliding. He groaned as her breasts rubbed against him. "Beautiful girl…" His voice was husky and breathy. He ran his hand down the length of her back. "Everything you do turns me on. We need to slow this down before I embarrass myself."

"I promise you," she started but trailed off when his lips looked too kissable to pass up, "that you never have to be embarrassed with me."

He rolled over so that he was on top, his body pressing hers into the mattress. "I want to touch you." She felt his heavy erection between her legs. She had wanted to run her hands over it, her lips, feel the weight of him.

"I really want this to last." He kissed her slowly and so deeply that she felt like she was falling. "Talk to me. Tell me something about yourself."

"As a child I had a cat named Sophie. She was fat and orange and I loved her to pieces. Your turn."

"My older brother played baseball his entire life, but I find the sport kind of boring and have only watched the games that he played in." He kissed behind her ear and ran his hand over her hip. "That was a deep, dark secret that you can never tell another soul."

"Juicy. Perfect for blackmailing."

"Tell me something else," he said as she felt him press against her opening, running his head down the length of her lips.

"Deep and dark?" she panted.

"The deeper the better."

She suddenly got overwhelmingly nervous. This had felt like a dream up until now, but he was in her bed, nearly inside her, and she had never thought this would happen. She had all but given up on men. "I have something big to tell you."

He must have heard the panic in her voice, because he stopped what he was doing and rolled them to their sides. "You're married. You share this house with your husband, and he's about to burst in here with a shotgun."

"No! Of course not."

"Boyfriend?"

"Strike two."

"You're not going to tell me you're a man." He

touched her between her legs, slipping a finger inside her to stroke her. "I can tell."

She cried out. "No. I'm a virgin."

"Excuse me?" She was lying to him. She had to be lying to him. Cricket was definitely an enigma. She was odd and brainy and probably leaps and bounds smarter than he was. But she was so damn funny and sweet, and she had the body of a video vixen hidden beneath her cute sundress and prim cardigan.

She was a sex goddess and he was lucky enough to be taken to her bed, and she was telling him that she had never been with a man before? He just didn't believe it.

"You don't kiss like a virgin."

"I'm only one in the technical sense."

"Explain."

"I was with a man for over five years who was born with a defect and couldn't...you know. It was fine, because sex wasn't terribly important to me, and he did other...intimate things to make up for it. But we broke up three years ago and I haven't made it this far with a man since."

"Have you tried? All you have to do is look at a man and he'll want you."

"I want you." She slid her hand up his cheek and kissed him softly.

He wanted her, too, and this revelation should have shaken him, but he was surprised to find that he wanted her even more. To be the first man inside her, to be the first man to have her body like this. "I'm glad you told me."

"You aren't going to walk away right now. It will kill me if you did."

"I'm not walking away. I can't, and I don't want to."

She let out a sigh of relief. He was surprised by her more and more each moment. She didn't see herself the way he saw her. Thick and delicious. So incredibly sexy that it made his teeth hurt. Being with her wasn't just a want, it was a need. For the first time since he had snapped his wrist, he wasn't feeling so damn empty. He stroked between her legs as he kissed her. She moved against his hand, her hips moving in a way that made it hard for him to believe that she was a virgin. He felt bad for her. She was clearly a sexual person with needs that had gone unfulfilled for so long. He felt even worse for that poor slob of a boyfriend. It must be torture to be this close to perfection without being able to have it.

He was going to have her tonight. Things had heated up so quickly between them. He liked to take his time with women. To seduce them. But he was too far gone. He had never wanted another woman so much. He was more than hungry for her. He felt like if he didn't have her, he would die.

Without giving it another thought, he slipped inside her. The noise that escaped him was primal. She was so wet and so hot and squeezing around him so tightly, putting him in extreme danger of coming before he even started.

He forced himself to hold back and not plunge inside her like he so desperately wanted. "Am I hurting you?" he asked through gritted teeth.

"Oh, God, no." She wrapped her legs around him even tighter, taking him deeper inside. "I need more."

He slid a little harder into her, which caused her to cry out his name. He kept his rhythm controlled and firm. He gave her deep kisses as he pumped away; he kneaded her flesh between his fingers, paid careful attention to her body, to what she liked. He kept his eyes open so that he could look down into her face. He wanted to remember this night, every single ounce of it, because he was sure he would never be able to have another night so damn perfect again.

"Elias…" She dug her nails into his back and squeezed around him so tightly that he lost all his control. She was trembling beneath him, her orgasm coming on hard and fast. He came with her, pushing into her one last time before he spilled himself inside her.

"Thank you for this, Elias," she said a few minutes later. "Thank you."

"Thank you for letting me be the man to do it." He kissed the side of her neck before he lifted his head to look down at her. She was flushed and glowing with perspiration and smiling. He had never seen a more beautiful woman in his life, and he didn't want to get out of bed to leave her. "Can I stay here with you tonight?"

"Yes. I would like that. There is nothing in the world that I would like more."

Chapter 3

"You look chipper today," Ava, Elias's twin, said the next evening as they sat on the porch of the house she and her husband shared.

"Chipper?" He frowned at her. "I don't think I've ever heard that word used before."

"Well, it's how you look. You've been down since you haven't been working. I would say that I feel bad for you, but I like seeing you more often. When you're working I get the exhausted zombie version of you."

"Fourteen-hour surgeries will do that to you."

"Did you have fun last night? You met up with some friends?"

"Yeah," he lied, not knowing why he did. He told

Ava nearly everything, but he didn't want to share his night.

He hadn't just hooked up with some random girl. He took someone's virginity and spent the morning making love to her all over again. He *really* liked Cricket, but he wasn't sure if it was because he was in a weird headspace in that moment or if he just thought she was refreshing. If they had met in Miami, he probably wouldn't have spared her a second look, but they hadn't met in Miami, and this was no typical hookup.

He wanted to see her again, to be with her again. But this morning when he kissed her goodbye, he'd made no move to prolong their connection. He didn't ask for her phone number; he didn't suggest they meet up again. He had just walked away.

There hadn't been hope in her eyes, no expectation. She'd just thanked him and kissed him softly and waved him off. He respected that about her. He might have been weirded out if she wanted to turn this one-night stand into a relationship.

But she didn't seem to want to, and he wasn't looking for a relationship, either, but he wasn't sure he could just leave it at one night with her.

"I'm glad you went out. Are you planning to see them again?"

"I was just thinking about that myself. I might head over to Carlos's and stay with him for a few days."

"You getting sick of me already?"

"No…kind of. Yeah, actually. You and your husband kiss so much I wonder how your lips haven't fallen off. Though Carlos and Virginia aren't much better."

"They aren't." Ava smiled. "When you fall in love, really fall in love, you'll find yourself being the gross person you never thought you would be."

"I sincerely hope not."

"You can hope all you want, but when you're with the right person, you can't help it." She looked over to the house next door. "Since Derek opened up a new studio space, we can actually use our house as a house. This place is bigger and we aren't going to be using the one next door. We were planning to rent it out, but I would much rather have you there. You can come and go as you please, and you won't be subjected to my husband and me making out all over the furniture."

"It might be nice to go forty-five minutes without having to be subjected to that, but I don't want you to lose any rental income for me."

"Lose money? Ha! I was planning to charge you double market value."

"I might head back to Miami soon. I was thinking about taking a trip somewhere. Maybe I'll visit Mom."

"You'll last three days there. There are five women in that house. They'll smother you to death."

"They will," he said grimly. His mother and aunts were likely to kiss the skin off his face. But he had to go somewhere, because if he didn't, he would find himself going back to see the woman whom he hadn't been able to get off his mind all day.

Cricket sat at the desk in her office and stared at her blank computer screen. She was supposed to be writing. She had left her job to concentrate on writing her next book. She had doctorates in anthropology and biology, and she had just spent the last ten months in India and sub-Saharan Africa studying small pockets of isolated populations and the illnesses that affected them. She had notebooks full of notes, but today she couldn't make her fingers work with her brain. And it was probably because her head was still filled with Elias. Two days later and it all still felt like a dream to her, so incredibly magical that it had to be unreal.

She had been with Phillip for a long time. He had been incredibly sweet and gentle. He would hold her for hours and kiss her softly. But there was no hope of sex for them. She had been to doctors with him. They had seen the best in the world—no one could help them. She had assured him that it was fine. That the intimacy they shared was enough. And sometimes it was. He would touch her between her legs, using his fingers and his mouth to bring her pleasure. It had been satisfying for her, even though she felt something was missing. After a while they stopped being intimate altogether. He was more like a brother or a good friend, and still she'd been willing to marry him. He'd been the one to break it off. He'd said that she deserved passion and babies and a life he could never give her. She was deeply hurt by it, because she had never wanted kids and passion faded. She had never asked for a different kind of life.

But then she had been with Elias, who was gentle and sweet with her, too, but he was also strong and powerful, and she needed that. He had made love to her that night and once again in the morning. She had stayed in bed that entire day, in her used sheets, not wanting to get up and change them because she didn't want to lose the scent of him.

She kept thinking of how he felt inside her, that slow, hard slide that made her incoherent. Just thinking about him now was making her aroused. There was a persistent throb between her legs that wouldn't go away.

She knew he wasn't looking for a fling or a relationship, but she wanted to see him again, just to spend a few more hours in his strong presence. She simply liked him. She couldn't say that about any other man she had been in contact with for a long time.

Her cell phone rang, and she looked at the caller ID to see that her mother was calling.

Her mother, the brilliant Dr. Frances Lundy. Born into abject poverty in the projects of New York City, she'd gone on to earn a perfect score on her SATs and been accepted to all eight Ivy League schools. Frances had paid her way through medical school to become one of the top cardiothoracic surgeons in the world and the chief of surgery at one of the best hospitals in the country. And to top it all off, she had snagged herself a billionaire. Her mother was the most brilliant person she knew, and Cricket was still slightly afraid of her.

"Hello, Mom."

"How are you, honey? Your father is here. Say hello, Jerome"

"Hello, precious! I miss you. Come write your book here. We'll have so much fun."

They would. Her father was a giant goofball and the most creative person she knew. He'd invented a smartphone that could hold a charge for three days. It was the bestselling phone in history, and that was only in the last ten years. He had over 150 successful inventions to his name. Cricket often wondered how her parents got together when her mother was so by the book and her father was so off the rails. "I purposely didn't come home because I knew it would be too much fun with you. I wouldn't get any work done."

"And here I thought," her mother stated, "that you were avoiding the long interrogation I was going to give you about spending nearly a year in the most poverty-stricken, disease-ridden parts of the world. I worked incredibly hard to make sure you would never have to witness those conditions, and at every opportunity you go back into them."

"My research could help millions of people, Mom."

"I know," she said softly. "If you weren't so brilliant and kind, you would be a sore disappointment to me."

"Gee, thanks."

"We do want to see you. I'll be away at a conference for the next two weeks and then your father will be away, so we are calling to block off a date now."

This was common with her parents, having to schedule dinner a month in advance so they could all spend time together.

It would be a full six weeks before all their schedules aligned, and so they made a date to meet in Miami at her mother's favorite Creole restaurant. She was looking forward to seeing her parents in person. It had been a long time. She had video chatted with them three times a week while she was away, but it had been months since she had seen them last.

She heard the doorbell ring. She glanced at the clock. It wasn't yet 11:00 a.m., and she hadn't been expecting anyone. No one came to visit her on the island. Most of her friends were in academia and lived all around the world.

She opened the door, and her heart jumped. Flipped. Went right from her chest and into her throat. Elias was there, looking absolutely gorgeous and a little unsure of himself.

"Hi." She was breathless. She couldn't help it. She couldn't hide it from him. She'd never thought she would see him again, but he was at her doorstep.

"Hi. I know it's early, but I was hoping I could take you out for lunch today."

She grabbed his arm and tugged him inside without saying anything.

"I should have called. I was going to call, but I didn't have your number."

She smiled. He definitely seemed uncertain in the moment, and it amused her. He was such a beautiful man, with a smile that must have made hundreds of women jump out of their underwear. Yet he acted as if she might turn him down.

It was wildly satisfying to her. She stepped forward, looped her arms around his neck and kissed him lightly on the lips. "You want to take me out, huh?"

"Yes." He smoothed his hands down her back, which she found arousing and comforting. "Very much so."

"Why do you want to take me out? Is it because you want to go to bed with me again? I slept with you before. You have to know how much I enjoyed it." She kissed his jaw.

He shut his eyes. "I like you, Cricket… I just want you to know that I'm not just using you for sex. I took your virginity. That means something to me. It's a gift you can only give once, and I want you to look back on that night and not have any regrets about it."

Her stomach did a weird flippy thing, and she knew in that moment that she had tumbled a little bit in love with him. She cupped his face in her hands and kissed him with everything she had. "My room.

Right now." She slipped her hands up his shirt, feeling his warm muscled back.

"Lunch first." He made no move but kissed her again, his tongue sweeping into her mouth. "I specifically came here to take you out, not to sleep with you."

"It's too early for lunch…"

"We can have brunch instead," he said as he slid his hands down to her behind and cupped it.

"I look a mess right now." She kissed his neck. "I can't possibly leave the house looking like this."

"You look delicious to me."

"I'll need to take a bath. A very soapy, very warm bath. You want to join me?"

"I can't say no to you."

She led him into her bathroom and turned to face him, staring at him for a moment. She couldn't believe he was here. She had been thinking about him, craving his touch, and now he was here before her and that beautiful experience they'd had wouldn't just be a onetime thing that she would only relive in her dreams. But she was going to feel his hands all over her body again, and she almost couldn't stand it.

"What are you thinking about?"

"What are *you* thinking about?" she countered, unwilling to give up her thoughts.

"You."

"Good answer, sir."

"Take off your clothes. I've been thinking about seeing you naked for two days."

She stripped off her tank top and the soft cotton T-shirt bra that she wore beneath it. She didn't know how to be sexy. She had never felt sexy before, but being around Elias had changed her a little bit. She didn't feel like her normal academic self. She felt womanly and sexual and happy. "Your turn."

He peeled off his shirt, revealing his six-pack, and her mouth went dry. It should be illegal for one man to be so damn fine.

"Your turn again," he said to her in his husky voice.

She grinned at him and turned around to wiggle out of her shorts. She heard him groan in appreciation and took it a step further, bending over the side of the tub to turn on the water.

"What the hell are you doing to me?"

She heard his pants unzip and his shoes hit the floor with a thud.

"Don't move." She felt him behind her, and then his hands were on her hips, his erection brushing her backside. She instinctively pushed her behind toward him, and he slipped inside her. She was incredibly aroused. His slow slide inside her felt so incredibly good that she almost blacked out. He shifted their bodies so that her hands were braced on the side of the tub and she was bent over before him.

He pumped into her with fast short strokes that were different from the other two times they'd had sex. She was finding that she liked it, the frenzy of it. The sound of his heavy breathing, the sound of their skin slapping together and her name on his lips. Every hard push inside was bringing her closer to orgasm.

He chanted her name. Over and over again. He was enjoying her, enjoying being inside her body. She'd never thought she would have this feeling, but this man was an unexpected gift. Had he chosen to walk away this afternoon and never look back, she would still be happy. Because he had already given her so much in such a short amount of time.

"Please, Cricket. Please come for me. You feel too good. I can't hold on much longer."

He didn't have to ask, because she felt herself clenching around him, waves and waves of exquisite pleasure carrying her away. Elias let out a guttural moan and spilled himself inside her. After a few moments of recovery, he stood her up straight, pulled her into him and kissed her deeply. "I'm sorry," he whispered. "You provoked the hell out of me, but you're new to sex and I should have waited to make love to you in bed."

"Don't be sorry. I might be new to intercourse, but not to sexuality."

"That was the nerdiest thing I've ever heard a naked woman say," he said with a devastatingly delicious grin.

"I'm a nerd. I can't help it."

"You're the most beautiful nerd in the world."

"You're very good at making a woman feel appreciated." She gave him a quick kiss before she turned away to check the temperature of the bathwater and add bubbles. "I'd bet you end up going home with a lot of women you meet in bars."

"I don't." He shut off the water and stepped inside the large tub. He groaned in pleasure and then held out his hand for her to join him. She leaned against him and shut her eyes.

This was what heaven must feel like. The hot water. The scented bubbles. And Elias's large hard chest and arms surrounding her. "Why don't you take a lot of ladies home?"

"I don't date a lot because of my work."

"What do you do for a living? I don't think we discussed that."

"We did. I'm a trauma surgeon at Miami Mercy."

She stiffened. Miami Mercy? An uncomfortable feeling settled in the pit of her stomach. Her mother was chief of surgery there. She was his boss.

"What's the matter?" He trailed his fingers down her arm. "You don't like surgeons?"

"No, I love surgeons. I just thought you were lying to impress Giselle."

"I wasn't. I broke my wrist and am not allowed to work. My boss banned me from the hospital."

"Banned you?" The question came out more like a squeak. Her mother had mentioned him. She had been exasperated. Young, brilliant surgeon who was stupid enough to break his hand while participating in some foolish activity. Cricket knew it had to be a big deal, because her mother rarely spoke of her work. Elias must have infuriated her.

"Yes. I tried to go back and work in the ER two weeks post-op. I punched a guy I saw trying to drag his girlfriend from the hospital and hurt my hand again. My boss was so incredibly angry with me, I thought she was going to fire me."

Dr. Frances Lundy normally would have, but Elias must be that good. Cricket knew her mother wouldn't give him another chance if he screwed up again. She would fire him if she thought he was a major liability. And she was fairly sure her mother wouldn't like the idea of one of her doctors picking up her daughter in a bar. She wouldn't like it all.

Cricket absently picked up Elias's injured hand and kissed it. "You love your job, don't you?"

"I feel a little lost without it," he admitted to her and bent his head to kiss her shoulder. He loved the feel of her, the way their wet nude bodies fit together. He had been restless this morning after not being able to sleep at all last night. He had been thinking about her, in a way that he never thought about anyone.

Part of him knew it was because for the past fifteen years, he had been working with single-minded focus toward becoming a surgeon. Even before that, in high school, he had been studying, working extra hard to make sure his grades were good enough. And now he didn't have any of that. Not the smells of the hospital, not the thrill of saving someone's life. His days as a surgeon had always been unpredictable, but now his life was unpredictable with nothingness ahead of him. He had spent most of his days trying to figure out what to do with himself. But not now, not when he was with a sweet, beautiful woman who made him wonder why he had gone so long without one.

He hadn't planned on being there today. He'd told his brother and sister that he was planning to head back to Miami. But he had found himself at Cricket's front door instead.

"What compels one to become a surgeon? And don't tell me it's because you want to help people."

"My mother gets a kick out of telling people that I'm a surgeon. I like hearing people call me 'Doctor,' and I love cutting up stuff."

She looked back at him with a slight grin. "All very noble reasons."

"My father is the real reason I became a doctor. He once told me it was his dream to become a doctor. He was ready to go to college when his own father died and he had to take over supporting his family."

"He must have been so proud of you."

"He never got to see me graduate from medical school. He passed away when I was in college. A massive heart attack took him from us unexpectedly."

He didn't know why he felt compelled to tell her this. He never talked about his father's death. His brother and sisters had each handled their father's passing differently. Elias chose never to talk about it. He had been the one with his father that day. The memory of his father's face twisted in agony would never leave him.

Cricket turned completely, looping her arms around his neck and pressing her chest to his. "I'm not going to say sorry again." She kissed him. "Those words never seem adequate enough."

"You're sweet," he told her. He felt like he had known her forever, but in reality she was a stranger he'd met three days ago. But he knew for sure that he liked her. Probably a little more than was healthy. "Turn back around."

"Why? You don't like looking me in the eye?"

"I do, but you've floated to the top and I can see your behind peeking out of the soapy water. It's incredibly distracting."

She smiled and pressed her lips to his. "I like being distracting. It's new for me."

"I have a hard time believing that. You are very sexy. Men must hit on you."

She turned around again, her back settling against his chest. "I spend a lot of time with brainy types like me, and I study how infectious diseases affect different populations for a living. I don't hang out at bars or nightclubs but once I tell a regular guy that I've seen a virus literally eat away at someone's brain, it usually turns them off."

"I would love to do brain surgery. I haven't gotten the opportunity yet. It's on my bucket list."

She let out a soft, almost musical laugh. "You are a very special man, Elias James."

"Thank you." She had a voluptuous figure and large firm breasts that he couldn't believe she managed to hide so well under her clothing. He touched them, running his fingers over them, enjoying the way her nipples went hard as he did.

He was aroused again. He was in a constant state of arousal when he was with her, but it was nice to touch her body for the sake of touching her. It wasn't going to lead to sex this time. That unexpected surge of lust had taken him over, made him snap and take her bent over the tub. He hadn't planned for that when he walked in here with her. He wanted to prolong it, to savor it, to turn her on so much that she was squirming with desire. But she was too sexy, and he couldn't go one second longer without being inside her.

"Tell me about this last boyfriend of yours."

"He was incredibly sweet, kind and gentle. He's a theoretical physicist and an even bigger blerd than I am."

"What's a blerd?"

"A black nerd."

He laughed. "I've never heard that term before."

"Of course you haven't. You are very far from one. You might be the opposite of one with all your muscles and raging testosterone."

"Hey! I like science and math. I'm a doctor."

"No, you're a surgeon, sweetie. They tend to think

that they are truly more gifted and talented than any other doctor, that they do all the hard work while other doctors simply diagnose. There's no nerd in you. You couldn't do what you do without some hefty confidence backing you up."

"You sound like you have something against surgeons."

"I don't!" She turned around to look at him with wide eyes. "I know a few, and most of them think what I do is a joke."

"What you do is important. I can remove a bullet from a heart, but I can't stop a disease from wiping out an entire population. Don't stereotype us all." He smoothed his hand over her stomach, unable to prevent himself from touching her.

"I'm sorry." She sighed. "I should know better."

He wondered who the surgeon was who'd showed her the nastier side of his profession. "Most of the things you said were true. You should hear how we talk about anesthesiologists."

She laughed again. He really liked her sweet laugh.

"You never finished telling me about your boyfriend."

"You want to know about my sexual history or lack thereof?"

"You like sex. You're very good at it. I'm just curious about how you could be with someone for so long who couldn't give you want you needed."

"I told myself that my love for him outweighed my physical needs. I loved his mind and our conversations. And he did touch me when I asked. He would research things that he could do to please me, and he would do them. But I knew those times weren't enjoyable for him. Even if he were physically able, I don't think he would have been that interested in sex. It's hard to face up to the fact that your partner would rather be reading than touching your naked body."

"But you stayed."

"He was the one to end it. He said we were living more like siblings than boyfriend and girlfriend. He was right, but I didn't think I would ever find someone as supportive and loving as he was."

And now you have me, he thought. It alarmed him. He didn't know why that thought had popped into his head. It was insane. He had just met her. So what if he couldn't get her off his mind? So what if she was the best sex he had ever had? "Relationships are hard," he said, more to himself than to her.

"I agree. I gave up on them after that."

"And love and sex and closeness."

They were quiet for a moment. He, too, had given up on love and closeness and sex. His quest to become head of his department had replaced his need for those luxuries. But human contact was important, feeling this close to someone was important.

"Tell me about your past loves," she said to him.

"There's nothing much to tell. My last serious relationship was when I was in medical school."

"What happened?"

"Residency. Hers was in San Bernardino. I stayed in Miami. I think she's married to a plastic surgeon now."

"Fancy."

"I know. Sometimes I wonder if I should have gone into plastic surgery as a specialty. The hours are better. The pay is ridiculous. I could actually buy a house like this and be able to spend time in it. Having a view of the ocean from your bathtub is something I could get used to."

"I thought you were going to say that you wonder what would have happened if you had married her instead."

"No. I liked her enough. But I didn't love her. I haven't thought about her in years."

"One hopes when they leave a relationship that they are forever burned into their partner's memory." She turned in his arms again and kissed him for a long time. "I guess this doesn't bode well for me. Our two-night stand will be a whisper of a memory to you."

"I won't forget you," he said truthfully. "I don't want to."

Chapter 4

That night with Elias had turned into an entire week. One magical week of sex, deep conversations, breakfasts in bed and walks on the beach. They had only ventured out of her house a few times for food and fresh air, but when they did, Elias held Cricket's hand. Their fingers interlocked. It was the most romantic week of her life.

It was the sweetest week of her life.

But he had to go back to Miami, and she had to get on with her life.

She was being honored at a conference in England, and old friends had wanted to see her during her visit. She hadn't seen Elias in a month, and she found herself missing him every day. But the fact that he was her mother's employee never left her mind. She had grown up with a surgeon. She loved her mother, but her mother's career had always come first. She had worked long hours, and sometimes there were entire weeks where Cricket hadn't seen her. Her mother was determined to advance her career and not be seen as just the wife of a rich man. She was working her way to the top, and that meant there was less time for her daughter. As a result, Cricket grew to think of their housekeeper more as a mother than her own. She didn't begrudge her mother or her success. She was inordinately proud of all Frances had accomplished, but Cricket knew she couldn't fall in love with a man who was on the same path. Elias loved his job. He wanted to be head of trauma. He couldn't wait till he was able to go back into the operating room and master another complex surgery. Loving a surgeon was too hard, and she knew that if she saw any more of him, she would fall in love with him. Or rather, even more in love.

It would be impossible not to fall for a man who satisfied every need she had in every way.

Neither one of them had said anything about continuing what they had. It was like they both knew that something so perfect couldn't last forever.

Cricket lay in bed for two days after she returned from her trip. She was feeling run-down. Her stomach was incredibly queasy. She thought it was just jet lag. But she was a frequent flyer and had experienced jet lag before. This was more than that. On her third day home, she dragged herself to the doctor. And now she was sitting in the examination room waiting for her doctor to return with the results.

"Well, Cricket—" Dr. Grey returned to the room with a smile "—you're extremely healthy. You show no signs of infections."

"A virus, then? It doesn't present like a cold or the flu. I wonder if it's a new strain."

"What you have isn't new. It has been happening to women since the dawn of time."

Cricket frowned. "I'm not following you."

"You're going to have a baby."

"Excuse me?"

"Is your period late?"

"Yes, but ever since I got back from Africa it has been irregular. Are you trying to tell me that I'm pregnant?"

"You *are* pregnant. Your ob-gyn will confirm how pregnant you are, but I'm guessing you're about six weeks."

"But I'm on birth control! I have been since I was sixteen."

"Yes, but you were traveling in a lot of developing nations where infectious diseases are very prevalent. You were given a medication as a precaution to help prevent meningitis, tuberculosis and a myriad of other diseases that could potentially be fatal. That has significantly lowered the effectiveness of your birth control."

Cricket stared at the doctor, dumbfounded, for a moment. "I—I—I can't believe it."

She had been foolish. She knew the risks of having unprotected sex, but she'd done it anyway and now she was pregnant.

She was going to be a mother.

"How do you feel about having a baby?"

She shut her eyes. "I'm shocked. Completely and utterly shocked."

"Do you want this baby?"

Her eyes flew open, and she looked at the doctor. She'd never thought she wanted children. She had come in contact with them a lot through her work. She was content to help treat them, but she'd never thought she would have a baby of her own. Something that had come from her that she would be solely responsible for. It would change her life. Change her worldview and her career. Her life would never be the same.

And she found that exciting.

"Yes, I want this baby," she said honestly. "I just didn't know it until now."

There was a knock on Elias's door that evening. His Chinese food had arrived fifteen minutes ago, so he wasn't expecting anyone. Normally he didn't like unexpected visitors, but he was hoping it was one of his friends stopping by, or even one of his siblings. He had been in a funky mood all week after another visit from his doctor. He hadn't been cleared to go back to operating. There wasn't enough strength in his hand yet, and sometimes if he overworked it, there wasn't enough feeling in it.

His doctor had scolded him once again for attempting to go back so soon after complicated hand surgery. The punch he had delivered to that guy had further damaged his hand. He didn't need to be scolded by the woman. He had berated himself enough for everyone. He couldn't work. The only thing he had worth anything in his life was out of reach.

Technically he could start treating patients again. He could diagnose colds, treat broken limbs and rashes. He could work in the ER, if he was dying to get back to work. But that put him at risk of re-injuring his hand, and then there was a chance that he might never get his strength back. His other option was to wait another six to eight weeks and try to strengthen it in therapy. It wasn't much of a choice. He hadn't spent all that time learning his specialty to give it up so soon after he had started. He'd just have to wait. He was a surgeon. That was his life.

But then he opened the door to see Cricket standing there, and he forgot all about his job. She wore a coral-colored sundress with a sprinkling of tiny white flowers on the bust and gold sandals. Her hair was loose in those big fluffy curls that he was so fond of.

She was a sight for sore eyes, and he had missed her. He didn't want to admit it, but he had missed her a lot these past five weeks. There hadn't been one day when he hadn't thought about her.

He felt himself smiling—the first time he had done so all week. He grabbed her arm and without saying a word to her pulled her inside his town house. He shut the door behind her, pushed her against it and kissed her. It wasn't a soft, controlled kiss. He swept his tongue deep inside her mouth, trying to taste all the sweetness that he had gone without for the past month.

"You're happy to see me?" she asked with closed eyes when he lifted his mouth away from her. Her body had gone completely slack against him. She was warm and soft and smelled heavenly.

He had never been so hard in his life.

"Of course I'm happy to see you. Kiss me."

She obeyed his order, and he slipped his hands up her dress, finding her underwear and pulling them down.

"Wait!" She broke the kiss. "Aren't you going to ask me why I'm here?"

"I don't care why you're here."

He sucked her lower lip into his mouth and sank his fingers into the flesh of her behind.

"I have something to tell you," she protested and moaned at the same time.

"It can wait." He freed himself from his pants.

"It can't!"

He crushed his mouth to hers and pushed his hand between her legs, feeling how slick with desire she was.

"You want this as much as I do."

"Yes," she cried.

He wrapped her legs around his waist and entered her in one hard thrust. She cursed and cried out his name.

She was so tight and wet and hot. She felt so good squeezed around him that he couldn't force himself to slow down. There was no finesse to his lovemaking. Just frenzied pumping inside her.

She bit into his shoulder. She dug her fingers into his back. She cried out his name over and over again. She was never shy when they were together, never reserved. That's why he loved being with her so much.

Her body fit just right with his.

Their thoughts meshed.

Neither one of them had experienced this type of high with another partner, and he wasn't sure he would be able to experience it again.

She orgasmed hard, squeezing so tightly around him that it spurred him to come earlier than he wanted. It took his breath away. It made him see stars and forget where he was for a moment. It was powerful sex.

She was here. In his house. In Miami. She had tracked him down. This crazy attraction wasn't one-sided, and he wasn't sure he could just let her walk away for a third time. They were going to have to keep going until the intense spark they felt burned out.

After a few minutes of recovery, he lifted her into his arms and carried her to his couch. He laid her down gently, covered her body with his and kissed her softly this time. A deep, soft, long kiss. The kiss he should have given her when she walked in, before his control had snapped into a thousand little pieces.

"What did you want to tell me?" he asked her when he finally released her lips.

"We're going to have a baby, Elias."

He had heard her. He had looked into her eyes and watched the words fall from her lips, but he wasn't sure he understood.

"What?" He scrambled off her body and sat up. "What?"

The worry returned to her eyes. He had seen it when she walked in the door, but he'd ignored it, because he had been so surprised to see her. He had been happy to see her.

She sat up and pulled her dress down to cover herself. "I'm going to have a baby."

"Are you sure it's *my* baby?"

She flinched as if he had struck her in the face. "I find that question very insulting."

He knew the words were wrong as soon as he'd said them. Of course the baby was his. He had been her only lover. "I know. I'm sorry. I—I just can't get my head around this. I thought you were on birth control."

"I was up until today. I spent a lot of time with infected individuals in developing nations. I was exposed to a myriad of diseases and given medication to prevent contracting anything. They reduced the effectiveness of my birth control."

"So you just found out today?"

"Yes. My GP informed me, and then I went right to my ob-gyn. I'm about six weeks."

Six weeks.

They had met almost six weeks ago to the day. It must have happened that first night.

Elias buried his face in his hands. He was finding it hard to catch his breath.

He was going to be a father.

His life was about to change forever. Irrevocably. He could no longer do things just because he felt like it. He could no longer come and go as he pleased. He could no longer be so damn impulsive, because his decisions wouldn't just affect him. Whatever he did from now on would have an impact on this new little life he had helped to create.

And yet, as scared as he was, the thought of having a child wasn't an unpleasant one.

He had always wanted to be a father. He wanted to be like his father.

Hardworking, loving, always there for his children. And then there was Cricket, who was beautiful and brilliant and sweet. She would be a good mother.

His gut reaction was to blame her. For trapping him. For changing his life. But how the hell could he? They had had unprotected sex. He was a doctor. He knew better! He had always been so careful. Even when he was in his last committed relationship, he had been careful. But not with Cricket. Rational thoughts ceased to exist when he was with her. All thoughts ceased to exist whenever he was near her.

"Are you healthy otherwise?"

"Yes. I had my doctor test for everything. We're both healthy."

"You're keeping the baby. There's no question about that," he said firmly.

"I very much want this baby," she said softly.

He nodded and looked down at her hands, which she held tightly clasped on her lap.

"There's more I think you should know," she said gravely.

His head snapped up. He couldn't think of anything else important that he needed to know right now. He could barely wrap his head around his impending fatherhood. "What else could there be?"

"Have you ever heard of Jerome Warren?"

"The inventor and tech genius."

"He's my father."

It took a full moment for that to sink in. She wasn't just the mother of his unborn child—she was an heiress to a billion-dollar fortune. That wasn't even including the assets of her father's company, which was so successful it was dizzying.

Normally if he had learned that a woman he was dating was an heiress, it would make him pause, but it wasn't Cricket's father that he was concerned about.

"Your father is married to Dr. Frances Lundy. She's my boss. She's chief of surgery at my hospital."

"I know. She happens to be my mother," she said so quietly that he had to strain to hear her. "I should have told you sooner."

"What!" he exploded and propelled himself off the couch. "You knew I worked for your mother and you didn't say a damn thing to me?"

"I didn't know at first."

"But you sure as hell found out when I told you. Your mother already thinks I'm reckless, and now she's going to fire me when she finds out that I got you pregnant. Do you realize how important my career is to me? It's the only thing I have, and you put it in even more jeopardy by not telling me who you really are. She's never going to let me head up the trauma unit now."

"I don't know what to say."

"There's nothing to say now. Six weeks ago is when you should have opened your mouth."

"Would you have stayed away if I had?"

He paused. Would he have stayed away? Could he have stayed away? He wasn't sure. "I don't know. But I would have had the option to." He paced away from her. "I cannot believe this."

"You sound more upset about this than the baby."

"I'm not upset about the baby! You should know me better than that by now, but apparently I don't know anything about you."

"Yes, you do. You spent an entire week with me. I told you everything about myself."

"Except who your parents are."

"You liked me for me! Do you realize how rare that is for me? My father is a billionaire. The entire world knows that it's all coming to me one day, and people treat me differently because of it. The only people I can trust are in my field, because they don't care about the money. But everyone on the outside who knows looks at me as if I have dollar signs on my forehead. But you didn't do that."

"I don't care about your money. I have plenty of my own. And I don't give a damn about who your father is. He could be a postal worker or a garbage collector, for all I care. It's your mother that I'm more concerned with. What is she going to think?"

"I've been trying not to think about it." Cricket pulled her lower lip between her teeth. "I find her terrifying when she's angry. I'm more scared about telling her than I was to tell you."

Elias sat down heavily next to her, his arm pressed against hers. This whole situation was bad. He was beyond angry. His career was in serious jeopardy, but he found her damn irresistible in that moment. He couldn't stop himself from touching her. "She is terrifying," he agreed. "How are we going to break the news?"

"I'm supposed to be meeting them here for dinner in two days."

He looked up at her, and without thinking he said, "Then I guess that means we'll have to get married tomorrow afternoon."

Chapter 5

Cricket caught a glimpse of her reflection in Elias's large bay window as she walked by. They had just gotten back from the courthouse. She was a married woman. A wife. A soon-to-be mother. She had someone else's happiness to consider now.

Elias had insisted that she get a new dress for the day. She was planning to wear one of the simple dresses she'd packed for this trip, but Elias was adamant that she have something new. Something she felt special in.

It would be nice to start our new lives in something new.

She had settled on a blush-colored tea-length gown with a fluffy tulle skirt. It was whimsical and pretty and fit her perfectly. If it were any other day, she might have been overjoyed with it, but it wasn't the type of dress she'd thought she would wear on her wedding day.

But then again, she'd also never thought she would be pregnant and marrying a man she barely knew.

The joy was missing from the day. The hope. The overwhelming rush of love between them.

She couldn't gauge how Elias was feeling, but she was feeling quite low. He had told her that she was beautiful that day. He had given her the most perfect ring. A round diamond set in a rose-gold band that was decorated with delicate flowers, each with a tiny diamond set in the middle. And after they were pronounced married, he kissed her sweetly on the lips, but he hadn't said a word to her since then. Not a single word on the car ride home. Nothing since they arrived back at his house.

It made that little seed of doubt in her mind bloom into a full-blown plant.

She had balked at the idea of marriage when he first brought it up last night. These were modern times. She made more than enough money on her own to support herself and her child. And with her trust fund, she could hire an army of nannies if she wanted to. But Elias had wanted this. And some foolish thing inside her made her want to give him what he wanted.

This is important to me. Family is important to me. Marriage is important to me, and I want to show my child that. I want us to present a united front when our baby comes into the world. I know it sounds old-fashioned, but I need the mother of my child to be my wife.

She relented. If it didn't work, they could both move on, but Cricket knew she would be hurt when it ended. There would be no way to avoid it. She had wanted to marry for love, and she was positive her husband did not love her.

She watched him as he put the paperwork they had received at the courthouse in a wall safe hidden behind a painting. He looked incredibly handsome today. Dashing, really, in a three-piece gray pinstripe suit that formed to his muscular body perfectly.

She didn't know what to do with herself now. She hadn't planned for this. When she came here yesterday, she had planned to just tell him and then retreat to the tiny apartment she kept in the city as he processed the news. But she showed up and before she could speak he was making fast, furious love to her against the door.

Sex was always incredible with him, but last night had felt different. He'd looked so happy to see her. He'd kissed her like he had missed her, and that had given her a tiny spark of hope. But today she couldn't read him. She would give anything just to know what was going on inside his head.

"Thank you for asking the man to take a picture of us. I would have never thought of that."

"I thought we needed to have at least one photo of us today."

"I love my ring." She fiddled with the band. "Have I told you that? I've never seen anything like it."

He just nodded.

"I wasn't expecting it."

"What kind of man would I be if I didn't give my wife a wedding ring?"

"You know, diamond rings weren't given before the 1930s, when a diamond company put out a large ad campaign. Diamonds aren't at all rare and are intrinsically worthless. You would be no less manly if you took your money and put a down payment on a house or invested it."

"Nerd," he said softly. "You took the romance right away with all your facts."

She smiled at him, glad that a bit of the tension was lessened. She was nervous, and when she got that way she spit out a bunch of useless facts. "I'm glad you gave me this ring. It makes the little romantic girl in me swoon."

He nodded again, and she felt so frustrated that she wanted to scream.

"I'm going to take off this suit."

"Oh. Maybe I should take off this dress, too. But I can wait until you're done."

"You don't have to wait. Come on." He led the way to his bedroom, where she had slept with him last night. Maybe *slept* was the wrong word, because she was sure that neither of them had gotten any sleep at all. She liked his place. It was what she would expect from a bachelor doctor.

It was masculine, neat and tastefully decorated with two bedrooms and an office. They could easily live there with the baby. They were probably going to have to live there once he went back to work. She would never see him otherwise. It was something they needed to talk about. It was one of the dozen things they needed to discuss.

He sat on his bed to remove his shoes and socks. She watched him for a moment, still unable to wrap her head around the fact that he was her husband.

"Do you want to go out for dinner tonight? I can cook if you don't. Or we can just order in."

"It doesn't matter to me. Whatever you want." He continued to remove his clothes. His suit coat and shirt, revealing that smooth bare chest that made her lose her train of thought.

"This is not about whatever I want. This is about you and me now and the decisions we make together."

"Really? The past twenty-four hours have felt like it has been all about you and your choices."

"Don't." She came to stand before him at the bed. "Don't you dare put this off on me. I didn't do this to you. I didn't plan this. I wasn't trying to trap you. We're going to have a baby, and you wanted to marry me. If you don't want this, tell me right now. We can get an annulment and I can take my baby to the other side of the country and you'll never have to see us again."

"Are you threatening to keep my child away from me?"

"No! I married you, Elias. If that doesn't tell you

that I want you to be in our baby's life, then I don't know what will. But I won't be the one you take this out on. I won't allow you to ice me out. I deserve better than that. So if you need space from me, let me know. Because I can be happy with or without you. The ball is in your court."

He looked up at her, and there was hurt in his eyes and maybe some fear. She only recognized those emotions because she was feeling the same way, too.

He placed his hands on her waist, pulling her closer so that he could rest his face on her belly, on their unborn child. "I don't want space from you," he said.

"What do you want?"

"Right now?" He spun her around and unzipped her dress. "I want to take my wife to bed."

She wanted to say no, to refuse him and stomp off, but she couldn't. She liked being with him. She liked his scent and the feel of his arms around her. He made her feel good in a way that no one else could, and she knew she could make him feel good in return.

He removed her strapless bra, and she was standing before him in just a pair of nude-colored underwear. "Sometimes I think the only thing you like about me is what's between my legs."

"That's not true at all." He kissed her still-flat tummy, which she found incredibly sweet. "I like other parts of your body, too." He covered her nipple with his mouth, sucking lightly on it. She suppressed a moan. Things always heated up so quickly between them, and she couldn't blame him for losing control because she was right there with him. "You have the most perfect breasts that I've ever seen," he told her right before he switched to the other nipple.

"They're big."

He looked up at her, a little mischief in his eyes. "Do you think that's a problem for me?"

"They were the cause of my teenage insecurities and frustration. I used to wear three bras just to keep them under control."

"Don't do that." He slid his hand up to one of them and squeezed lightly. "You are so damn beautiful. Do you think I would marry an ugly woman?"

"If she was having your baby, yes."

"Do you think I would get an ugly woman pregnant?"

"Yes. If you liked her very much. I don't want to think the father of my child is a shallow man. And you're not shallow. There are so many wonderful things about you. And the ability to make me feel good after I wanted to repeatedly poke you with a fork is one of them."

He smiled at her, a real smile, and the fist around her heart loosened. He stood up and kissed her forehead. "I like what's in here, too." He pulled down her underwear and ordered her into bed.

She obeyed and lay in the center of his big bed under the covers, watching him strip off the remainder of his clothing. She was nervous. Her heart was racing, and she felt like it was her first time with him all over again. Only this time was more momentous, because she wasn't having sex with a man she had just met. She was making love to her husband and the father of her child.

He settled on top of her, the lower half of his body in between her legs. He didn't enter her even though she'd been ready the moment he unzipped her dress. He kissed her. Long, deep, unrushed kisses that made her melt into the bed and took her breath away.

She didn't know what was going to happen between them or if this fragile marriage was going to last, but this moment was nice, this moment she would hold on to and recall when things got tough between them.

The restaurant where they were meeting Cricket's parents was one of the best in Miami. This was no casual dining establishment, and they had to dress the part. Elias wore a navy blue suit and his best pair of shoes, but Cricket was the stunner. She wore a cream-colored lace dress that fit her curvy body like a glove. It was distractingly sexy but still appropriate enough for dinner with her parents.

She was nervous. There was no denying it. He didn't blame her, because he had been dreading this meeting all day. It could make or break his future, but he was more concerned about her at the moment. He took her hand, and she looked over to him almost gratefully. He had no words for her, but he could offer his touch. They had that. If nothing else, they could take comfort in each other's bodies even if it wasn't in bed.

"This is my mother's favorite restaurant," she told him as they entered.

"Mine is the burger joint on Calloway Boulevard."

"Really?" Her eyes widened a bit. "Can we go there after we leave here? I don't think I'll be able to eat."

"Of course. You haven't eaten all day. You need to feed my child."

"I'm too nervous."

He squeezed her hand, and when that didn't seem like enough, he wrapped his arm around her and kissed her cheek.

The hostess showed them to their table. Mr. Jerome Warren and Dr. Lundy were already there. The eccentric billionaire was wearing a houndstooth-patterned sport coat and a teal bow tie. He smiled broadly when he spotted them. Dr. Lundy looked gorgeous but understated in a black cocktail dress. She didn't smile. She frowned in confusion.

"Dr. Bradley," she started. "I had you banned from my hospital, and you track my daughter down to meet with me. I don't know if it's clever or stalker-ish, but you could have simply called. Though it wouldn't have made a difference. I got the report from your orthopedist. You haven't been cleared to return to surgery yet."

"We're not here on account of my career tonight."

He pulled out Cricket's chair before taking his seat beside her.

"Franny," Jerome said, "you sound like you already know Cricket's friend."

"He's not Cricket's friend. He's my top trauma surgeon, who broke his hand doing some ridiculous mud race."

"Those look like so much fun!" Mr. Warren said. "If I were younger, I would do one myself."

"You don't have to be young to do them, sir. My sister-in-law's father just did one with my brother. He had a wonderful time. I'm Elias, by the way."

"It's nice to meet you, Elias. It's an unexpected pleasure."

"What are you doing here, Doctor?" Dr. Lundy stared at him in a way that could make flowers wither.

"Mother, you were right about Elias not being my friend. He's my husband."

Elias hadn't expected Cricket to blurt it out like that, but he was glad she did. It was out in the open now.

"Your what!"

"Congratulations, honey!"

Cricket's hand crept into his, and he locked his fingers with hers.

"We're married, Dr. Lundy," Elias said. "I didn't know she was your daughter when we met."

"You're pregnant, aren't you?"

"Yes," she said softly. "I'm very happy about it. I didn't marry Elias because I'm having his baby. I married him because it felt right."

That comment made him pause. He kept asking himself why he'd asked her to marry him. The words had just popped out of his mouth.

It wasn't love. It couldn't be, and if he were in this situation with anyone else, he wouldn't have asked. But he wanted all of Cricket. Marrying her felt like the right thing to do. He was the first man to make love to her. He had given her a baby. He felt like he needed to be her husband.

"I knew you wanted to be head of trauma, but I didn't think you would stoop this low. You seduce my daughter, get her pregnant and marry her! You thought this was going to force my hand?"

"I don't care if you have a low opinion of me, but your daughter is no naive dupe. Even if I was so evil, Cricket is smart enough not to get pulled in. I want the job, but I knew it was a never a guarantee. I'm a damn good surgeon, and if I could get hired at your hospital, I can get hired at another top institution. Our relationship didn't start with you in mind. In fact, I didn't even know you were her mother until two days ago."

"It's true, Mother. I knew that Elias worked for you, but he didn't know that I knew."

"He was in your home, and he had no clue who your parents were." Dr. Lundy shook her head in disgust. "I thought you had gotten smarter since your college days."

"Don't, Mother. I was seventeen!"

"It was the same story. You told us he didn't care

about who your father was. That he loved you for you, and next thing we know you were trying to cash out your savings account to buy him a car."

"I learned my lesson. I was a kid. Why can't you let that go?"

"Because now you have gotten yourself pregnant. I wish I could trust you, but I can't."

"Enough, Frances," Jerome said in a stern voice that Elias was sure no one else dared to use with Dr. Lundy. "Cricket is our only child, and she is bringing a life into this world. She is a grown woman with two doctorates who has dedicated her life to making the world a healthier place. We are inordinately proud of her, and we're *thrilled* to be grandparents. And if the man she chose to marry is a doctor that you yourself hired, he mustn't be all that bad. Instead of biting everyone's head off, take a moment to see the joy in this situation." He reached across the table and set his hand over Cricket's free one. "I can't wait to be a grandfather, honey. I prayed for you to find happiness. I'm happy for you. Congratulations."

"Thank you, Daddy." She left her chair to hug her father, and as soon as she let him go, she turned to Elias. "Can you take me home? I don't feel well." She swayed a little.

He was out of his seat in an instant, grabbing her and pulling her close to him. "What's the matter, baby?" he asked as she clung to him.

He was worried about her. She hadn't eaten all day because she was nervous about how this evening was going to go. It had gone as badly as one could expect, and he wanted to take her away from here. He wanted to protect her from her mother's vitriol that was partially his fault. If he were any other man, he knew it wouldn't have gone so poorly. But he wasn't any other man. He was her husband now, and Dr. Lundy was just going to have to get over it. Being head of trauma was his dream, but he had a family now. His father had always put them first. Elias was going to do the same for his family. His father would have been disappointed in him if he led his life any other way.

"Can you make it to the car or should I carry you out?"

"You already broke your hand. Do you think I want to be the cause of your broken back? You'll never operate again. No, thank you. I can't live with that kind of guilt."

He grinned. He couldn't help it. He kissed her cheek. He couldn't help that, either. "Let's get out of here."

"Hamburgers," she whispered into his ear.

"Anything you want."

Chapter 6

When they got back to Elias's town house, he ordered her to bed. She wasn't used to anyone ordering her about, and the independent woman in her wanted to bristle. But she was too tired and numb, and frankly it was a little nice to have someone else to think for her when she couldn't manage to herself. He was protective. He might not have married her for love, but he was going to take his duty as a husband seriously.

He had promised her a hamburger, and she thought he was going to run out to get dinner. But a few minutes later, the doorbell rang and he walked into the bedroom with a greasy bag that looked large enough to hold food for a small army of people.

"Smells like heaven." She sighed as she kicked off her shoes. Her lower back was aching in a way that it never had before, and suddenly she felt too tired to eat. "When did you order it?"

"I have an app on my phone. It took less than two minutes."

She struggled to unzip her dress, but then she felt large warm hands on her back and soon his knuckles were pressed against her bare skin as he unzipped.

"Do you want me to get you something to sleep in?" he asked, knowing that most of her clothes were in Hideaway Island, because she hadn't planned to still be here. She especially hadn't planned to marry him today.

"No, thank you. I think I should eat first."

"You should. I was worried about you," he told her as she sat down heavily on his bed.

"Don't be. Fainting and dizziness are a sign of early pregnancy. So is lower-back pain." She propped up the pillows behind her, making a mental note to make sure she got some more for the bed.

"Rationally and medically I know that, but still, when it's your wife and your child, you can't help but worry."

She found his words sweet, but there was still some of that awkward tension between them that had been there most of the day. The only time it had disappeared was when they walked into the restaurant as a united front. But now that they were alone again, it returned.

Part of her wondered if part of him thought she had done this to him on purpose. Women trapped successful men all the time. And ever since he found out that she was hiding the truth about who her mother was, he didn't trust her.

But after tonight, who could blame him?

"I'm going to feed you well tonight." He sat next to her on his bed. Technically their bed, but she wasn't sure if it was ever going to feel like she belonged there. "I'm going to advise against eating like this throughout your pregnancy. But tonight I say we make an exception. We deserve it." He began unloading the bag. "I wasn't sure what kind of loaded fries you'd prefer, so I got buffalo chicken and bacon and just plain old cheese and bacon–loaded fries. There's cheeseburgers in there. I normally get mine with everything on it, but I had them put everything on the side for you because I don't know how you like your burgers yet. There's onion rings. A slice of chocolate cake, a piece of apple pie and I left the milkshakes in the living room."

"I could cry," Cricket said to him. "This is a heart attack in a paper bag, but it's so beautiful I could cry."

"You are crying," he said quietly as he wiped a tear from her cheek with his thumb.

"Am I? I'm sorry. It must be the pregnancy hormones."

"Don't apologize. You're tired and hungry, and we just had a very tense meeting with your parents. It's okay to be upset."

"I feel like we should talk about it."

"I feel like you need to feed my baby first."

He handed her the container with her cheese-burger, and she absently loaded it with every fixing that was in there. "You keep saying *your* baby. You're quite possessive over something that is going to come out of my body in a very painful manner."

"I know." He flashed her that devastatingly gorgeous grin of his. "That's the best part of being a father. All of the glory. None of the excruciating pain."

She laughed, still feeling the tears run down her face. She didn't feel particularly sad, but she couldn't stop them.

"Eat." He leaned over and kissed the side of her face and let his lips linger there. "You'll feel better after you do."

She shut her eyes, willing him to keep his lips on her skin. It reminded her that she was no longer alone in this world. There was a time in her life when she'd never thought she would have a family of her own, and now she was going to have one. It might not be the way she'd dreamed of but it was a family all the same. She had been alone for years. It was nice not to feel that way anymore.

"So you like your burgers with everything on them, too?"

"Not usually. But tonight if you hand me a can of cold gravy, I would pile that on top, too."

They ate mostly in silence with his large-screen television on in the background, but Elias sat close to her, their sides pressed together. She found his presence comforting, even with the heavy silence surrounding them.

When they were done, he removed all of the food from the room, leaving her with just a milkshake.

She knew she should get up and take off her fancy dress, but she was too tired to stand. So she sat on the bed, her hands folded over her belly, and thought about the life growing inside her. The life her mother was very upset about.

It was too soon to know the sex of the baby she was carrying, but she kept thinking it might be a boy. She hoped he looked just like Elias with his beautiful black curls and his strong build.

"Cricket…" Elias gathered her into his arms and held her tightly against him. "I don't like to see you upset."

She was crying again. She hadn't realized she'd started, but the hot tears splashing down her cheeks told her she was.

"She'll come around. It will be okay."

"I'm so happy about this baby. She acts like I'm ruining my life."

"She's mad about me. She thinks I'll ruin your life."

"Any other mother would be thrilled that I came home married to a gorgeous surgeon."

"You think I'm gorgeous?"

She gave him a wobbly smile. "I only have sex with gorgeous men. Makes for better-looking kids."

The corner of his mouth curled. "She thinks I'm using you to get ahead in my career."

"You aren't devious. I know that."

"I'm glad you do. But the truth is, you don't know me that well. I could be a ton of things."

"You don't know me well, either. But you married me."

"I needed to."

Because of the baby. Not because he was fond of her or thought he could love her. He'd married her because he felt he had no other choice. It didn't make her feel very good about their chances in that moment.

"Help me get out of this dress?" She stood up, feeling a little wobbly, and went to his side of the bed. "It's too tight. Can you pull the top down?"

"Yes." He did as she asked, and she couldn't help but notice that he touched her more than necessary while he did. He didn't just pull her arms out of the sleeves. His fingers slid across her shoulders and skidded down her back. The dress was tight on her hips and he had to yank it down, but he took her underwear with it.

His lips grazed her lower back, and every nerve ending in her body screamed for more. "Do you want to have sex now?"

"No. We're both exhausted and full. I just want to touch you."

"But I'm willing." She turned around and looked down into his eyes. There was arousal there. She loved when he looked at her like she was the sexiest thing ever created.

"You don't have to have sex with me because it's your wifely duty."

"I know." She lifted his hand and placed it between her legs, inside her lips so that he could feel her moisture.

"Spread your legs a little more."

She did.

"Kiss me."

She did that, too, and took so much pleasure in it. He just touched, slowly working his fingers in her folds. His pace should have slowed down the climax; instead his gentle touch brought it on quick and hard. She was crying out and breathless, and as soon as she had shuddered for the last time, he stood up, scooped her into his arms and placed her on the bed on her belly. He unhooked her bra, and she was expecting him to turn her over and cover her body with his and push inside her, but he didn't. She smelled lightly scented lotion and then felt his big hot hands on her back.

It was sweet. It was perfect. She felt like weeping again. But she held back. "Talk to me, Elias."

"About what?"

"About us. About anything. I think we have so much to say to each other."

"But where to start?"

"What do you want out of life?"

"I wanted that job. I wanted to be head of trauma. I wanted to eventually head up my own hospital."

"But now?"

"I just want to do the right thing."

"Oh."

"I like Miami Mercy. I liked working for your mother, but if you want me to quit that hospital, I will. I can find another job someplace else. We might have to move out of the state, but I will leave if you want me to."

She was touched by the offer, but she couldn't ask him to do that. She was already holding on to the guilt that she had made him marry a woman he didn't love. She hadn't actually made him propose, but she should have said no, should have stood firm and made him see reason.

"I don't want you to leave." She didn't want to do anything that would make him unhappy.

"This is a premature conversation. I'm still not allowed to go back to work. It will be at least another six to eight weeks."

"You had another appointment since I last saw you. You weren't cleared to go back?"

"I wasn't expecting to be. Wishful thinking on my part. I knew that it was going to be at least six months because of my specialty. I couldn't just fracture my wrist—I had to break the hell out of it. I live my life doing just a little bit too much," he said as his strong hands traveled down her back.

"Comminuted fracture?" she asked, but it came out as a moan.

"Yes." He kissed her shoulder. "Extra-articular displaced." He lifted her hair to kiss the back of her neck. "I've never dated a woman who knew her medical terms so well."

"It turns you on that I know that you broke your bone in more than two pieces?"

"Yes. Your brainy medical knowledge is the reason I married you."

"You married me because you impregnated me."

"That was a very small factor in my decision." He was quiet for a moment as he continued to massage her back. "I don't regret asking you to marry me, you know." It was as if he was reading her mind.

"We've only been married for twenty-four hours. Give it a few weeks."

"You're easy to be with, Cricket."

"I'm sorry about today."

"It was just one bad half hour. The whole day wasn't bad. I like your father," he said, changing the subject as he focused his hands on her lower back. "How often does a man get to meet a billionaire?"

"My father is pretty wonderful. He was born in the Deep South. Poorer than piss and turnips, as he is fond of saying, and then he pulled himself up."

"He is self-made. Just like your mother."

"That's what they have in common. They both made everything out of nothing. She thinks I have it easier than they did, and I do in hundreds of ways, but my life hasn't been easy. I worked hard, too. My mother thinks I have wasted my potential."

"You have two doctorates. You're well respected in your field."

"My mother says while my nose is in a book, real doctors are out actually solving problems."

"And now I get your issues with surgeons. I thought you were just stereotyping us. You were speaking about your mother."

"Yes. I'll stop complaining about my mother now. It must be really sexy to have a complaining, weepy pregnant woman in your bed."

"If you could see what I see, you wouldn't doubt why I have you in my bed."

"Lie down with me," she said to him as she slipped off her loosened bra.

"Okay." She watched him as he stripped down to just his underwear. She knew she would never tire of looking at his body. He was so beautifully built. Her own body was about to go through a massive change, and she wondered if he still would want to touch her after it did. Their bodies were what kept them connected. What kind of marriage would they have when he was no longer attracted to her?

"Take everything off, please."

He slid his underwear down, revealing his manhood, which was nearly fully erect and gently bobbing as he looked at her.

"Let me love you," she said, reaching out to him.

He took her hand and slid into bed beside her. "I don't think I could stop you."

Chapter 7

A week after the revelation to Cricket's parents, they returned to Hideaway Island. Elias had been planning to go back briefly for a family function, but Cricket asked him to stay on the island until he was cleared to go back to work. She had been afraid to ask him, he could tell. He still remembered the look on her face when she approached him. All flustered and adorable.

I—I don't want to interrupt your life any more, but would you mind if—if we lived on Hideaway until you go back to work? Or at least go back on the weekends. If you don't want to go, I could go by myself. But I would like you to come. That is, if you want to.

He'd wanted to kiss her right then, take her to bed

and peel her clothes off and spend a few hours just buried inside her body. But he didn't. He just agreed to go back with her. Elias was never the type of man who had vices. He drank responsibly. He never gambled. He didn't chase after women. But Cricket had turned on something inside him that made him want to touch her. All the time. Be with her every second of the day, and there were a lot of times when he had to hold himself back. Prevent himself from touching her. He didn't want her to think that all he thought about was sex. He wouldn't blame her if she did, because their relationship had started because they couldn't keep their hands off each other.

He still couldn't keep his hands off her, but he liked her, too. He liked her smile and her voice and the nerdy things she said. He liked that she was his and no one else could claim her.

He saved his passion for her until night fell, and then he loved her for hours. There were times when he tried to give her a break and let her rest for a night or two, but she wasn't content to sleep. She would reach for him, or touch him or simply look his way, and he needed to have her.

Needed to.

It was more than a want.

Much more.

"Are you sure I look okay today?" she asked him, worry in her eyes. She'd often seemed unsure of herself during their short marriage. Like she was afraid to upset him. She wanted to make sure he was happy.

He wanted to reassure her, but he didn't know how. He didn't know how to be married, and in the end, he knew it was his job to make sure she was happy, too.

"You're beautiful." He grabbed her hips and kissed along her jaw. He felt her relax a little. "It's just a barbecue with my family. Stop being so skittish."

She wore a short white dress with multicolored sailboats on it and cobalt blue sandals. She had left her hair down at his request. It probably made more sense for her to wear it up in the humid Florida heat, but it was one of those little things she did to please him. She had no idea that she pleased him without even trying.

"They don't know about us," she said, wrapping her arms around him.

"They'll find out today."

"What if they hate me?"

"Why would they hate you?"

"Because I got pregnant and stole you away from all the other eligible bachelorettes on the planet."

"You didn't get pregnant on purpose."

She looked up at him, the worry not leaving her eyes. "I know, but what if they think that?"

"Then I'll tell them you're an heiress and that I married you for your money."

"Good plan." She smiled briefly and then looked up at him for a long moment, her lips opened as if she were about to speak, but she remained silent.

"Tell me."

"It was nothing."

"Tell me," he insisted.

"Kiss me."

He set his hands on her cheeks and kissed her softly. It was a controlled kiss, because he knew if he let himself really kiss her, he would go wild. She was pregnant. She was his wife. He couldn't go around making love to her on the sides of bathtubs and against walls, no matter how satisfying it might be.

"I want to have sex in the middle of the day," she said, shocking the hell out of him.

"Excuse me?"

"I would like to do that sometimes," she blurted out. "A lot, actually. I need you to do it with me."

"And if I'm unavailable, will you get someone else?"

She blinked at him. "Well, I called that gigolo, but he's booked up for the next six weeks. I guess when you're good at your job, everyone wants you."

She made him laugh. Whenever any inkling of doubt crept into his mind, she would say something unexpected that would make him laugh and want her even more. "Lucky for you I'm available."

"Lucky for me."

"I'll make love to you at twelve fifteen."

"Don't tell me when. Surprise me. Surprise me often, if you can."

She had no idea what she was doing to him, giving him this kind of permission to access her body.

He could get drunk off her and happily stay that way for the rest of his life. "Okay." He nodded, not at all sure if other newly married couples spoke to each other this way. "We need to go now."

She nodded and gave him one more kiss before she let him go.

His brother, Carlos, lived on the far side of the island, in a section that was so secluded it felt like part of another country. The landscape was wilder—tall grasses and big colorful flowers lined the ocean-side road that led there. Elias loved the house, especially after his sister-in-law, Virginia, finished decorating it. But it was a little too far away from town for his tastes. He thought he would never be able to survive living outside a major city, but he had agreed to stay on Hideaway with Cricket until he went back to work. He was looking forward to his time on the island with her. He had been feeling stuck the past month before she reentered his life. Now he had been drop-kicked out of his restlessness and into a more terrifying life.

"Elias, is there something you need to tell me?" she asked as they pulled into Carlos's long driveway.

"No."

"No? I'm an heiress to one of the biggest fortunes in the country, and even I have never seen a house this big."

She was right. Her house was nice, but Carlos's house was amazing by anyone's standards.

"I told you that my brother was a baseball player."

"I thought you meant in school."

"You mean you never realized that my brother is Carlos Bradley?"

"I'm sorry," she said in nearly a whisper. "I have no idea who he is."

"Shortstop for the Miami Hammerheads. Played twenty seasons for the same team. He's a legend and one of the most recognizable athletes on the planet. Hell, the president honored him."

"I'm sorry," she said again, looking at her hands. "I don't know who he is."

Elias pulled his car to a stop, threw back his head and laughed. Of course she didn't know who his brother was. She read scientific journals for fun. She barely watched television, and when she did, it almost always was some sort of documentary. It made sense. He had married the only woman on the planet who didn't care who he was related to. It was refreshing.

"Why is that so funny?"

"Because I've had women try to get with me just because my brother is my brother."

"Why? What do you have to do with him?"

"They're social climbers and status seekers. They thought I would lead them to him."

"But you're a doctor. You work at some of the most prestigious hospitals in the country. You're beautiful. They surely wouldn't think your brother was more worthy just because he hits a ball with a wooden stick. You save lives."

"You haven't met my brother yet. Carlos is very good-looking. He's very rich and he's very famous. Most people would consider him the catch out of the two of us. But he's also very married to the love of his life, so women settle for me."

"Some women are stupid." She stepped out of the car, seeming annoyed on his behalf. He was glad for it. It meant she was no longer nervous.

He joined her, and together they made the walk from the driveway to the huge house. It was a Spanish-style mansion, painted a cream color, with a roof made of handcrafted red tiles. They stood in front of the heavy carved wood door waiting for someone to open it. It didn't matter how many times he had been here; Elias was still blown away that someone in his family lived in a place like this. They had grown up working-class, in a tiny three-bedroom house. Their parents had worked two jobs each. They probably all still would have gone to school and made something of themselves because their parents valued education that much, but Carlos had made things easier for them. It was because of his brother that Elias wasn't drowning in student-loan debt. He owed him a great deal, but whenever Elias tried to pay him back, Carlos refused. Carlos didn't get to go to college because he was drafted right out of high school, but he'd wanted to make sure his siblings got every ounce of schooling they wanted. Elias wanted to make him proud, and he really wanted Carlos to like Cricket. Elias wanted his entire family to like Cricket. But in

the long run it wouldn't make a damn bit of difference if they did or not. He had married her. She was
carrying his child. So their opinion of her wouldn't
change a thing.

"Let's not lead with the marriage thing this time,"
he said to her. "We should tell them later in the day.
I don't want to make today about us."

"I don't want to ruin two occasions this month."

"You didn't ruin anything," he said as the door
swung open. His twin sister was the one to answer
it. Her eyes went wide when she saw he wasn't alone.

"Oh! Hi!" She smiled warmly at them. Ava had
been known as somewhat of an ice goddess before
she met her husband. Marriage had mellowed her out.
She was almost like a new person. Elias had always
loved his twin more than anyone else on the planet,
and now he really liked her, too. "I didn't know you
were bringing anyone."

"Who's bringing someone?" Carlos appeared,
holding his now-two-year-old daughter. "Elias?"
Both his siblings were surprised to see Cricket standing with him. They gave him curious identical looks.
He had never brought anyone home. Not since his
first serious girlfriend in med school.

"I know who you are now!" Cricket exclaimed,
looking at Carlos. "I used to see you every day from
my office window in Boston. You're the pizza guy."

"I'd like to think of myself as a fourteen-time all-
star and World Series champion, but yes, I was the
spokesman for Pippa's Pizzas," he said with a grin.

"Cricket had no clue who you are," Elias explained. "I think she's more excited about the pizza connection than the baseball."

"Pizza?" Carlos's daughter said from his arms.

"Not today, baby." He looked at his daughter with pure love that only a parent could give to a child. "We've got good stuff for you to eat." His eyes went back to Cricket. "This is my daughter, Bria."

"Hello, Bria. I love your pretty dress."

"Pink flowers," she said, looking down at her outfit.

Elias saw Cricket's heart go into her eyes as she looked at his niece, and it once again hit him that they were going to have a baby. In about seven months, they were going to have something special that was going to bond them together for life.

"I'm Cricket, by the way," she said, looking up at Carlos and Ava. "It's very nice to meet you. Elias has told me wonderful things about you both."

"I'm glad my brother hasn't forgotten about us. Elias hasn't told us a thing about you. If fact, he has been extremely quiet these past two months," Ava said, looking at him with some annoyance. "But I'm very glad that we are meeting today. If he brought you to meet us, you must be special." Ava gave him a genuine smile.

"Yes. It's nice to meet you, Cricket," Carlos said. "Please come inside. We're just about ready to fire up the grill."

They walked out to the outdoor living room,

which overlooked a huge pool and the ocean. His sister-in-law was with her mother at the table setting out fruit-filled drinks. Virginia turned around and looked up at them and so did her mother. It was then Elias heard ear-shattering, happy feminine screams.

"Dr. Warren! You get over here and give me a hug, young lady," Dr. Andersen said, beaming.

"Dr. Andersen! I'm so happy to see you. You look incredible."

The two women hugged, and the rest of them looked puzzled. "Your girlfriend knows my mother-in-law?" Carlos muttered.

"Very well, it seems," Elias said, watching the two women embrace.

"And did I hear her correctly? She's a Dr. Warren?"

"Two PhDs. Biology and cultural anthropology. She mostly does medical research, but she's an author, too. She's working on her fourth book."

"Oh, yes, Carlos. You have to read Cricket's books," Dr. Andersen said, looping her arm around Cricket and walking over to them. "Cricket studies how diseases affect cultures and relationships. *Mourning in the Developing Nations* kept me up at night. It made me weep. This girl is brilliant."

"If my mother-in-law gives that kind of endorsement, it must be true. I'm taking anthropology this semester," he said to Cricket.

"Are you!" Cricket's eyes widened in excitement. "Please, tell me you like it."

"It's just the intro class, but I'm finding it fascinating."

"I'm giving a lecture in Miami in a few weeks. You must come! I'll be showing slides from my trip this summer to India. I was studying a village of sex workers who were all infected—"

"You were what?" Elias nearly shouted.

"You knew about that."

"Not the sex worker part."

"They were very nice ladies. Most of them weren't more than girls, though."

"I'm more concerned about the men who visit them."

"I was fine," she said, and he didn't believe her.

"I think we need to talk about this some more later." He didn't want her going back there. Hell, he didn't want her going any other place where people were infected with diseases for the rest of her life.

"Cricket's work is important, Elias," Dr. Andersen said lightly. "And I take it by the disapproving tone and the scowl on your face that you two are a couple."

"Yes." He reached for her hand.

"I'll definitely come to your lecture. You want to come with, Mama Andersen?" Carlos asked his mother-in-law.

"Nothing would make me happier."

A few hours later, the party was in full swing. Ava was married to the mayor of the island, and he brought his entire family over. There were a few kids running around and splashing in the pool. Food was abundant, drinks were flowing. There was a nice ocean breeze.

"This is what Dad envisioned when he saw this place," Carlos said from beside him.

"I know. I wish he could be here to see it."

"I think he is."

Cricket appeared in his line of vision wearing a white bikini. She was walking toward him, like she was out of a dream. The only way he could describe her was womanly. Smooth hips, thick thighs and large, lush breasts. He didn't even notice the other women with her until they approached.

Without a word she reached for him, wrapping her arms around him and pressing her curvy body into his. He smoothed his hand down the curve of her back, forcing himself to stop before he cupped her backside in his hands. He was aroused, and he wanted her so badly it hurt. But that's how he felt every minute of every day.

"Tell me I look awful and that you want me to put my clothes back on," she said into his ear.

"I would never say that to you. And if I do, you should leave me. You're the sexiest thing I've ever seen."

She pressed a kiss to his mouth before she spoke in his ear again. "Your brother is very handsome, but you make my heart beat faster."

"Meet me in the house in fifteen minutes," he

whispered. "Down the long hallway on the first floor. Second door on the right."

Her eyes went wide. "No."

"You said surprise you."

"No," she said again.

"Come on, Cricket," Hallie, Virginia's sister-in-law, called to her. "The beach is calling us."

She gave Elias one last shy smile before she went off.

"Can you believe it took us fifteen minutes to convince your girlfriend to leave the house wearing that bathing suit? She wanted to wear a T-shirt over it!" Ava exclaimed. "I didn't think bodies like hers existed in the real world. You should have seen my husband's eyes pop out of his head when she walked by. But how can I blame him? Even I can't stop staring at her butt."

"I'm going to have to agree with her," Virginia said. "That body is spectacular, right, babe?" she asked her husband.

"No comment," he said smartly.

"It's okay." Virginia grinned at him. "You can admit it. I want to paint her nude. It would fit in my next series featuring all-natural bodies." She looked at Elias. "Do you think it would be weird if I asked her?"

"Yes," he said. "Very weird." Virginia was a trained painter, and her pieces sold for hundreds of thousands of dollars, but Cricket was his, and as selfish as it was, he didn't want anyone else to have her.

"I didn't get it before," Carlos said. "She's adorable and smart and I like her a lot, but I didn't get why you two were together. She's not your usual type, but I get it now. Damn."

"Do you like her, Ava?" Elias asked his twin. He held his breath as he waited for her answer.

"Very much so. She's fascinating and very sweet and makes me feel a little dumb, but I could see us becoming friends."

"Virginia?" he asked.

"I'm pretty sure my mother wishes that she was her daughter instead of me, so I'm mortally jealous of her, but other than that I find her charming. She wouldn't happen to be the daughter of Jerome Warren, would she?"

"The guy who invented every gadget in our house?" Carlos asked. "The billionaire?"

Elias nodded. "He's a really nice guy."

"Wait a minute." Ava shook her head. "Didn't you tell me your boss was married to him? You're dating your boss's daughter?"

"No. I married my boss's daughter," he told them.

They all went silent, their faces revealing their shock. He hadn't planned how he was going to break the news, but all day they'd kept calling Cricket his girlfriend. She was more than that. She was the woman he had promised to spend the rest of his life with. She was going to be the mother of his child. His family needed to know.

"She's your wife?" Ava shook her head.

"We met here on the island and I couldn't leave her that first night. And then when I did leave her, I couldn't stop thinking about her, so I saw her again. I stayed for an entire week."

"That's when you told me you were taking a trip," Ava said. "I thought you were in California, but Derek said he was fairly sure he saw you in town."

"He did. I thought I dodged him."

"Why didn't you just tell me that you were seeing someone?"

"Cricket is someone I wanted to keep all to myself."

"So you married her?" Carlos said, sounding disbelieving.

"I needed to be married to her. There's no other way to describe it. I needed her to be my wife."

"I felt that way about Virginia," Carlos said, reaching for his wife.

"We're having a baby, too." He dropped the second bomb.

"You're going to be a father?" Virginia asked in awe.

He smiled. It might not have been the right time, but the thought of being a father made him happy. "Her mother wants to murder me. She thinks this is some plan I cooked up to propel my career forward. I might end up losing my job because of this, but I don't care. I can work at another hospital. I wouldn't be able to forgive myself if I let Cricket slip through my fingers."

He looked over at Ava, who had tears streaming down her cheeks, her chest softly heaving.

"Hey, Elias. I—" Cricket reappeared from somewhere. "Uh-oh. You told them."

Ava flung herself at Cricket and hugged her tightly. "I'm so happy for you. Welcome to the family."

Elias let out a slow breath of relief. His twin wouldn't lie about something like that. He looked at his brother, afraid of his reaction.

"We're happy for you." He smiled. "Mom is going to murder you. But we're very happy for you." Carlos came over and hugged him tightly.

His family was on board, which somehow put more pressure on him. He really couldn't allow this marriage to fail now.

Chapter 8

Three weeks had gone by since Elias broke the news to his family. Outwardly they had been much more supportive than Cricket's mother. Ava and Virginia had stopped by a few times to invite Cricket along for shopping and out to lunch. They were making an effort to include her in the family. It was unexpectedly kind. Their unfaltering excitement about having a new sister seemed genuine. Cricket, who was an only child and had never had many friends, felt warmed by it. But in the back of her mind, she wondered how they truly felt.

Didn't they think it was too soon? That she and Elias couldn't possibly be in love after such a short period of time? That they were bringing a baby into this world and they were still practically strangers?

Those thoughts had to be going through their minds, because they were still going through Cricket's. But neither one of them showed any signs of doubt, because she knew Elias had sold their marriage to them as uncontrollable love, that they couldn't be apart and that their baby was just a happy bonus. Ava told her that she had never heard her brother say anything so beautiful before as when he spoke about her.

But Cricket didn't feel any closer to her husband. They made love every night, more than once. She wanted to be near him. She wanted to touch him. She wanted to look at his handsome face all day, but she kept herself away. She claimed she had to work on her book, which she did, but she wasn't getting very far. She couldn't concentrate on what was going on in pockets of the world thousands of miles away when she didn't know how to handle what was going on in her own home.

She didn't want Elias to think she was clingy. That she had gotten pregnant to trap him. She didn't want anyone to think that, but she was a trained medical professional. She knew the side effects of the medications she was taking. She should have known not to have sex with him without more protection. But she'd never thought he would walk into her world. She'd never thought he would want to marry her. And if she had to do it all over again, she knew she wouldn't change a thing. She wanted this baby. Even though she knew what she was up against. Even though she was sure her relationship with her mother was never going to be the same.

"Hey." Elias came into her office and lay on the couch adjacent to her desk.

"Hey." She spun around in her chair. He rarely came to see her during the day. She knew he was bored here, but she didn't know how to remedy it. She was afraid the only thing that would satisfy him was going back to work as a surgeon.

She remembered how restless and irritable her mother had been when she was out after a knee replacement. She could only imagine how restless Elias was. He was in his prime. He loved to work. Finding ways to fill his time was hard for him.

"Can I come sit next to you?" she asked him, wishing she could be easier around him.

"You can always sit next to me." He sat up, making space for her on the couch. He took her hand when she sat. He locked his fingers with hers, and she felt like she did when she was still a girl, when that first boy made her feel special. "How's the book coming?"

"Not great. I'm a little preoccupied." She touched her belly, which was starting to round ever so slightly.

"Yeah." He covered her hand with his own. "I know what you mean. Have you spoken to your mother yet?"

"No. She texted me last week to ask me about a book, but nothing else."

"Did you really try to buy a car for some guy?"

She'd been wondering when he was going to ask her about that. She was still embarrassed by it. She was supposed to be so intelligent, but she was human and sometimes she did foolish things. "I did. After I bought him sneakers, a leather jacket and basketball tickets."

"Cricket," he groaned. "I don't want to believe that."

"Believe it." She lifted his hand to her mouth and kissed it. "You need a car? How about diamond cuff links. A gold scalpel? I'm your girl."

"Why did you do it?"

"I thought I loved him. I wanted to make him happy."

"You're enough," he said quietly.

But am I enough for you? she wanted to ask, but forced herself not to. "I grew up a little bit in a bubble. I didn't go to high school. My parents hired private tutors to educate me when they thought that traditional schools weren't enough. I went to college at sixteen. I was a pudgy, awkward, insecure wreck, and I was also an heiress and everyone knew it. Then Mike came along, and he was sweet to me. I was so unpopular in school, so unliked, so alone that when someone was nice to me, I jumped on it. I wanted to keep that feeling, and I gave up a little bit of myself to do so. In the back of my head I knew he was using me, but I refused to acknowledge it. It hurts to think about it, to know that I let myself be used. But it's part of my history. It has made me who I am today."

"It's also made you isolate yourself from people. People that would love you just because you are you. My sisters really love you."

She was surprised by his last statement. "What?"

"They want to be your friend. They want to be a big part of our lives. They want you to call them."

"Did I do something to offend them? I didn't mean to. I'll call them to apologize."

"You didn't do anything wrong, but they are your family now. You can trust them. They wouldn't make an effort unless they wanted to know you."

"They love you. They'll accept me because they love you. Because they are nice people."

"Don't keep yourself away because you're afraid of what others might think. Don't be afraid that they don't like you."

"It's not just anyone. I don't care about what strangers think. I care what *you* think. I care about what your family thinks. We both know that if I hadn't gotten pregnant, we never would have seen each other again. What does that say about us?"

"Who cares what it says about us? You *are* pregnant, and *I* choose to spend the rest of my life with you. And I want you to stop being so damn shy around me. I'm not just some guy who got you pregnant. I'm your husband now. And I don't want us to walk around here like we're some damn polite strangers."

"You're unhappy. I knew you were."

"You're unhappy," he countered.

"I'm not! I get nervous around you. I don't know how to behave."

"Be yourself! We spent an entire week together just three days after meeting. I couldn't leave you. I wanted to be around you. I still want to be around you. I married you. I just don't want you to be my wife only at night. Or when we're in public."

"Then stop treating me like I'm fragile!"

"I don't treat you like you're fragile."

"You do! You're so gentle with me when we're in bed at night, and you'll only make love to me in bed."

"You don't like the way I make love to you?"

"No, I don't like it. I love it. I want more of you, and I don't want you to hold back anymore. It makes me feel like you're bored with me."

"Bored with you?" He turned and grabbed her shoulders. "Are you insane? I want you every moment of the day. But you're pregnant and my wife, and I can't go around taking you against walls and doors and on the kitchen floor."

"Who says?"

He was quiet for a long time. "No one says."

"We're going to be parents in less than seven months. We probably won't be able to be together like that when the baby comes. But we have right now, and we should take full advantage of it."

"You're right." He stood up and took her hand. "Come with me."

"Are you going to take me to bed?"

"Nope. The sunroom."

"But there's so many windows in there."

"I know." He grinned at her and led her away.

Elias glanced over to Cricket, who was lying on a blanket in the sand in front of their house. She was wearing a bikini and starting to show, her belly round and adorable. Her body was changing—her hips were spreading, her breasts growing larger—and as the days passed, his attraction to her also grew. It was a life that they'd created growing inside her, and every time he thought about it, it filled him with pride.

He couldn't resist touching her, and he leaned over and sprinkled kisses on her belly. She grinned and ran her fingers through his curls. Things had gotten a little easier between them in the past couple of weeks. They spent a lot of time together. They had dinner with his siblings at least once a week. They made love whenever the mood struck them, but there was still something there between them that he couldn't identify. A wall that was too high for him to jump over. She was still holding herself back from him.

She didn't trust him. Not to hurt her. Not to turn on her. Not to let her down like so many people had before.

He realized how hard it must have been for her growing up the genius daughter of a billionaire and a trailblazer. There was no one like her in her town. No one she could relate to. No one to be kind to her.

She was expecting him to turn into all those people who had let her down before. And maybe he couldn't blame her for being worried about it. If she hadn't gotten pregnant, he wouldn't have seen her again. He would have walked away, gone on with his life. But he knew now that he never would have completely forgotten about her. He would have wondered what had happened. It probably would have been one of the few things in his life that he had regretted.

So why hadn't he gone after her? What held him back?

No one had ever made him feel the way she did. No one had given him such a rush.

Maybe she had every right not to trust him. He couldn't even trust his own feelings for her. And maybe he had every right to hold a little bit of himself back from her, too. Because as much as he wanted to be with her, he didn't share everything with her. If there was a wall between them, she wasn't the only one who had built it.

He had prided himself on being an open man, but there were certain things he couldn't bring himself to tell her. Like how uncomfortable he was not contributing to the household. The house was paid for, she assured him, the bills automatically deducted from her account. There was no need to change it. She had gone as far as trying to give him half the money for their groceries, but he refused it. He felt like a guest there. Like they were roommates instead of husband and wife. It was her house. Her things. But she was his wife and carrying his child. And he wanted to be a husband and father just like his own father had been. He wanted to take care of his family. But if there was one thing he knew about Cricket, it was that she sure as hell didn't need him.

He wasn't sure what to do about it. He wanted her to be happy here in her beautiful home, especially while she was growing their baby. It might not have made such a difference to him if he were back to work, but he wasn't and he had time to think. And thinking wasn't necessarily a good thing.

"Are you really sure you want to go through with this tonight?" Cricket asked him as he rested his head on her belly.

"Making love to you? You already know the answer to that."

"I'm talking about having my parents over for dinner, you knucklehead." She smiled softly at him.

"Yes, I'm sure. Mostly to show your mother that you haven't bought me a Mercedes."

"You won't let me buy you anything," she pointed out. "Not even ice cream."

"Nope." He wouldn't let her spend a dime when they went out.

"But you bought me a locket." She touched the heart-shaped pendant that rested between her breasts. There was one diamond chip in it to represent their firstborn. She'd cried when he gave it to her. "And my beautiful ring. And those slippers when my feet started to swell in the supermarket the other day."

"I wish I could do more," he said, wanting to say more to her.

She was quiet for a long moment, and he wished he could read the expression on her face, but he was unable to. "You don't have to do anything for me."

"I do. You're going to be giving me the biggest and best present that I will ever have."

She cupped his face and pulled him up so that their lips connected. "You are so incredibly sweet sometimes that I don't know how to handle it."

He knew that she didn't know how to be in an intimate relationship like this. She'd claimed her last boyfriend—whom she'd wanted to marry—was sweet to her, but he wasn't so sure of that. The man sounded more interested in his academic endeavors than he did her.

It was no wonder she didn't realize how desirable she was.

"I have to go inside and start getting dinner ready."

"Stay here." She stroked his cheek with her thumb. "You don't have to cook. We can take my parents out for dinner."

"No. We're entertaining like grown-ups." He sat up and tugged on her hand until she was sitting up. "Come help me cook."

"I might burn the place down."

"That's a risk I'm willing to take. Come inside with me," he urged, not wanting to be away from her just yet.

Cricket stayed with him in the kitchen, watching

him cook at first, asking him dozens of questions. It was why she was so smart. Her unfailing curiosity was why she kept learning. Elias admired that about her. But he wasn't content to have her just sit there and observe him. He wanted her participation. He set her to work, chopping and stirring while he made garlic-and-herb-stuffed pork chops with roasted potatoes and string beans. He knew it would take her mind off her anxiousness. All day he had been trying to keep her calm. She still wasn't on good terms with her mother. He hated that and felt like it was his fault, even though he knew it wasn't.

He was determined to make this evening pleasant for them, to prove to his mother-in-law that he was a good husband for her daughter. He also needed to show her that he was ready to take over as head of trauma when the doctor who was currently in that position retired.

His work was never far from his mind. After Cricket, his desire to return to surgery ruled most of his thoughts. His mother-in-law held his career in her hands and he hated that, but he knew he would have to play by her rules if he wanted to win in the end.

The doorbell rang, and together Cricket and Elias answered it, presenting a united front. Her father, Jerome, greeted them genuinely and warmly. Dr. Lundy was polite but cool as she greeted him and gave her daughter a stiff hug, before she released her and studied her appearance.

"You're starting to show, dear."

"I am." Cricket rubbed her hand over her small belly.

"Can I offer you something to drink? We have pinot noir and riesling," Elias said to them.

"We made appetizers, too. Crostini and jumbo shrimp."

"Did you have this catered? We could have gone out," Dr. Lundy said with a small shake of her head.

"Elias made everything," Cricket told her.

"Cricket helped."

"You can cook?" Dr. Lundy walked toward the side table where they had laid everything out and carefully studied it.

"You know I'm good with a knife," Elias replied. "And I have to be the one who cooks in this marriage. We would be living off cheese and crackers if I didn't."

"I don't cook, either, Bug," Dr. Lundy said, looking at her daughter with affection. "My work was more important."

"Yes, for you it was," Cricket said softly. Dr. Lundy raised a brow in surprise. There were other issues between the two, but right now wasn't the time for them to hash it out.

Elias ushered them all out to the patio that overlooked the ocean. There was a breeze blowing, the air smelled sweet, the sun was just going down. Hideaway Island was truly one of the most beautiful places on earth.

Jerome and Elias did their best to keep the conversation flowing, but it was tough. Cricket was mostly quiet, and Dr. Lundy only interjected when she deemed what they were saying important enough to respond to. It was very different from Elias's family dinners, where everyone laughed and spoke over one another. There was a warmth in the air that was hard to describe.

Had all of Cricket's family dinners been this way—just her and her parents and some stilted conversation? The current tension could have been all Elias's fault, but for some reason, he felt that there was something even deeper going on here.

"What are you working on now?" Dr. Lundy asked her daughter, apparently having had enough of the men taking charge of the conversation.

"I'm still sorting through my research for my next book. I'm due to go back overseas in a couple of weeks to do a little more research and speak to some colleagues who are still conducting a study there."

"What?" Elias focused on Cricket. "You're not going back, right? You've arranged for someone else to do your part."

"No. Of course I'm going back. Why wouldn't I?"

"Because you're almost in your second trimester, and flying to an impoverished, politically unstable, disease-infested part of the world is not a great idea."

"But I made a commitment to speak. My research helps the medical professionals treat those people. It's important."

"Our baby is more important than your research."

Cricket stiffened. "Are you suggesting that I don't know that?"

"I'm not sure what you know. You didn't seem to know that it was the decent thing to inform your husband that you were flying out of the country. You didn't seem to know that something like that would bother me."

"I didn't think it would be an issue. I have been working on this project for the better part of a year. You know how important my work is to me."

"Of course it is, Cricket! It's a huge issue. I don't care about your work. I don't care about other people half a world away. I care about you. We are married. You should have discussed this with me."

"There's nothing to discuss. This trip has been planned for eight months, and I can't back out now. You of all people should be sympathetic to my problem. You're a trauma surgeon. Your only goal is to save people's lives."

"You weren't pregnant eight months ago. You weren't *my* wife eight months ago. You can back out. No one will blame you for wanting to put your child's health first."

"I will not be putting my baby in danger by going over there!"

"The reason you got pregnant is because you were taking medication that you didn't fully understand the effects of. I'm supposed to stand here and be silent and let you take some other drug, or be exposed to some deadly virus, just because you have do-gooder syndrome? And it's not just your baby. It's *our* baby, and if you think I don't get a say in everything that happens to him or her, you're dead wrong."

"Cricket," Dr. Lundy said quietly. "He's right. I can name fifteen medical professionals who would tell you the same thing."

"You're taking his side!"

She nodded once. "Jerome?"

"I'm sorry, Bug. I agree with your mother."

Cricket looked shocked. The betrayal she felt was clear. Elias wanted to feel bad about it, but he just couldn't muster it. The thought of something happening to her made him feel like he was choking.

"I don't want you to go, Cricket," he said as calmly as he could manage. "I want you to call them and cancel."

"I'm not a child." The stubbornness set on her face. "You cannot order me around."

"You're right. You're not a child, but you're carrying my child and I'm your husband, and for the past two months we've been doing things your way, but not on this. You are not alone in this world anymore. You cannot just think about what you want now. You must think about us. You must think about our marriage. We can't have a good one if you're only going to think about yourself."

"I only think about myself? Are you kidding me? My every thought…" She stopped herself, probably realizing that this argument was going to get even more heated in front of her parents. "I need to get out of here." She stood up and left the table.

"Cricket, don't go." He reached for her hand, but she snatched it away.

Soon after, the front door slammed, and he was left alone with her parents. He buried his face in his hands. Their first big fight. He looked up at his in-laws, who both were expressionless.

"I'd bet you two are really wishing that I hadn't married your daughter right now."

"No. That's not what I'm thinking," Dr. Lundy said with a shake of her head. "If you hadn't blown up that way, I would've."

He frowned in confusion, not sure he had heard her correctly. "Excuse me?"

"You were right. We agree with you. What more do you want?"

"She's our only child," Jerome said. "You're her husband, and as much as she doesn't think she needs to be looked after, she does. And that's why she fell for you, because you care for her in a way that no one else ever has."

"I'm crazy about her. I can't even begin to explain it."

"Keep being crazy about her," Jerome said. "You won't have any problems with me as long as you are."

It was late when Cricket returned to the house. Just after 11:00 p.m. Her parents were long gone, the house mostly dark, except for the light over the front door and a lamp in the living room. Elias had left them on for her.

He hadn't waited up. He hadn't come after her. He had only called her twice and when she didn't pick up, he sent her a simple text message.

I'm not asking you to come home yet, even though I want you to. I'm not even asking you to talk, but I need to know you're safe.

She didn't know what kind of danger he thought she would get into on Hideaway Island, but the way he phrased his words took some of the steam out of her righteous anger. She was still mad as hell at him and her parents, but she wasn't mad enough to sleep elsewhere tonight. She had thought about sleeping in the guest room, but why should she be chased out of her bed because of him?

He had no right telling her to cancel her trip. No right to imply that she was selfish. She wasn't doing it for herself. It was no vacation. She was going to go because she'd spent the last three years researching those people. Studying their illnesses. Following their treatments, educating their local governments on how to prevent the spread of disease.

Was going to go.

She had called and canceled a few hours ago.

Her child wasn't the reason she was staying home. Now that she knew she was pregnant, she knew how to take precautions. She wasn't going to put the baby in harm's way at all. It was the fact that she had a husband that made her pick up the phone.

You are not alone in this world anymore. You must think about us. You must think about our marriage.

That had gotten to her. She wasn't alone anymore. She'd always had her parents, but she had felt so alone for all these years. Now she was married. She had said yes when she didn't have to. She had made this commitment to be not only his partner, but his wife.

He didn't want her to go. And sometimes she felt like she was more the vessel that carried his child than his wife, but he cared about her. He took care of her, and she'd uprooted his life. She should be able to compromise on this, even though nearly everything inside her wanted to rebel.

She stared at his large slumbering body as she got ready for bed. She wasn't sure how he could look so peaceful sleeping when she was a big ball of angry mess.

She was afraid to let her guard down, to let him closer, because she was afraid that he was going to walk away. Every man she had ever gotten close to had walked away from her. For so long she'd thought it was her.

Part of her still thought it was her.

She slid into bed beside him, her body touching his even though it didn't have to. Their bed was huge. She could have had all the space she wanted, but she pressed herself closer to him because she couldn't help it. Bedtime was her favorite part of the day. She loved their lovemaking. She loved his big hard body, the feeling of safety she got whenever she was with him. She was angry. Hours later she was still angry with him, but that didn't stop her from wanting to be with him.

"I'm glad you're home," he said. "I wasn't going to be able to sleep without you next to me."

"Shut up." She removed her nightgown and climbed on top of him. "You're not going to be able to sleep yet."

"Shut up? You never say that."

"You don't know what I say or who I really am."

"I know. But I want to change that. I want to know you." He was being so damn sweet to her. He had been furious with her earlier. His words harsh. His demands clear. He was asserting his possession of her. She never wanted to feel owned, dependent on any man. She didn't need Elias to survive, but she did need him in her life. She needed him to be happy, and she hated that she needed that.

"I'm going to kiss you." She slid her hands along his jaw. "But I don't want you to enjoy it."

"That's going to be hard," he said with a slight grin.

"I'm mad at you. Don't smile."

He nodded as he pulled her face down to his. He was the one to kiss her, softly at first. A peck, and then a lick across her lower lip. But then his tongue swept into her mouth, and her nipples went even tighter. She wanted to control the kiss. She wanted to control their sex tonight, but she always lost all her thoughts whenever he kissed her like this. Her mind had been the only thing she could count on all these years, but he turned it into mush. He made her feel things that she didn't think she was capable of. And that made her angry, too.

She broke the kiss and looked down at him. His eyes were closed, his body completely relaxed. He looked almost as lost as she felt. "I'm supposed to be the one kissing you."

"So kiss me. I like the way your lips feel on my chest."

"Do you?" she asked him.

"Yes, and on my stomach and...lower," he said with a touch of mischievousness.

"Well, I'm never going to kiss you anywhere again. I don't want you to like it."

"Okay." He ran his hands down her back, stopping on her behind to knead her flesh with his fingers. It was more than arousing, and she didn't know if she wanted him to keep going or ease the persistent throbbing between her legs right then.

He had been very gentle with her lately, despite her assurances that she wasn't fragile. She liked when he could barely control himself. She liked when he was shaking with need for her. "Give me your hands."

He looked at her curiously for a moment but did as she asked, and she placed them behind his head.

"You have to keep your hands to yourself tonight."

"But I need to touch you."

"I'm punishing you." She removed his manhood from his underwear and stroked it. He was already hard. He always was whenever their bodies were close together.

He sucked in a deep breath. "Can't you punish me by giving me the silent treatment instead? I want to touch you."

"No." She looked into his eyes as she rose over him and sank down. He was so large and so deep inside her. She relished this feeling, and it made her think about her ex. He had been right. Ultimately she wouldn't have been happy in a relationship with him, because this feeling was important to her. She and Elias were as close as two people could be, and she wanted to be closer.

She squeezed herself around him. He inhaled sharply and let out a low, deep moan. She felt powerful on top of him. With her body alone, she could give him pleasure, and she savored every expression he made, every sound of satisfaction that escaped his lips.

She rose up again and started to ride him slowly, almost letting him completely slip out of her before she plunged back down. She had her hands behind her on his legs, her thighs spread wide before him. She was putting on a show for him. Changing her tempo when he was enjoying himself too much, slapping his hands away when he attempted to touch her.

She had him gritting his teeth. She would have laughed if it hadn't felt so damn good. Every stroke was bringing her closer to climax—she wanted to prolong it as long as possible, but by torturing him she was torturing herself.

"Go faster," he urged her as he grabbed her hips.

"Don't touch me." She reached for his wrist, but he surprised her by rolling her beneath him. He plunged hard inside her, all his control gone. It was what she had wanted. He'd held out for a long time, but he was a strong man. And that's part of the reason she loved him.

Yes, she did love her husband. She didn't know why she was surprised by that. She wasn't sure when it had happened, exactly. Maybe she had always loved him. Maybe she knew the moment they met that she wanted to end up here with him.

He drove into her hard, their skin slapping together. She knew she was making incoherent noises and digging her fingers into his back, but she couldn't help herself. And she broke, a scream escaping her lips. Elias's climax came moments after hers, and for a long time they lay together, a sweaty mass of limbs.

He kissed the side of her neck and then her jaw and cheek before he pressed his lips to hers and gave her a deep, sweet kiss.

"You enjoyed that," she said to him, still breathless.

"Very much so."

"You weren't supposed to."

"I enjoy everything that has to do with you."

"Stop it! I'm trying to be mad at you."

"I missed you," he said quietly. "I will miss you if

you go away, and I'll worry about you and I won't be able to sleep knowing my family is halfway across the world."

A large hard lump sneaked into her throat. "Why didn't you just tell me that before you got all macho and bossy with me?"

"I was mad. Your wife tells you that she's leaving you—you get mad."

"You could have come with me."

"If you're dead set on going I will, just to make sure you stay inside the protective bubble that I'm going to lock you in."

"I'm not going. I called and canceled."

"I thought you weren't going to listen to me."

"I was tempted to tell you to go to hell, but the truth is, I want you to be happy. And I know that you aren't. I don't want this marriage to fall apart, and I know if I can't compromise with you now, in a few years I'm going to look back and hate myself for not doing something so simple."

He kissed her throat and then buried his face there. "You've been afraid we're not going to make it this entire time, haven't you?"

"Yes, haven't you?"

"When people in my family get married, they stay married. I would feel like a total failure if we couldn't make this work."

"Why did you have to go and marry me? It's so much pressure. It's suffocates me."

"I needed to be married to you."

For the baby, he didn't say, but she knew that's what he meant.

"I'm not sure how to be your wife. Sometimes I don't read people the right way. You have to let me know if I'm doing something that bothers you. I need you to tell me."

"I will. You have to talk to me, too, Cricket. Don't keep yourself away from me. If we're going to fail at this, we need to go down flaming. With everything out on the table."

"Okay." She nodded.

"What can I do to make you happier?" he asked her as he stroked her cheek.

Love me.

She couldn't make herself form the words. They hadn't even known each other for four months yet. It was too soon to expect love. To ask for it.

"I'm not unhappy. But I'm feeling you aren't so happy here. Do you want to go back to Miami?"

"Going back won't change anything. I need to work."

"I would offer to speak to my mother about letting you go back, but I don't think that will help you."

"No." He laughed. "It won't. My brother-in-law told me that the hospitalist at Hideaway Hospital is looking to cut back on his schedule as he prepares for retirement. He wanted to know if I would take over three days a week for him. It's such a small hospital and at most they only have a handful of patients admitted, so he sees patients as a primary care physician, as well."

"What did you say?"

"That I have to speak to my wife about it first."

"Way to make me feel extra bad about not talking to you first about leaving the country."

"That's what I was going for." He grinned at her.

"Take the job. You aren't cleared for surgery yet, right?"

"No."

"I think you'll feel better having something to do. And you get to get away from me."

"That's the only downside to it."

"You're very good." She sought out his lips and kissed him. "We're not fighting anymore."

"Good. Although I kind of like fighting with you."

"Do you?"

"Yeah." He slid his hand onto her breast. "The making up is amazing."

Chapter 9

Elias studied the boy's foot that he was treating. He had taken the job at the hospital, focusing his mind on medicine. Even if it wasn't the kind of medicine he wanted to practice, it was better than not practicing at all.

The kid had a broken big toe. The nail had split in half. The boy had to be in pain, but he looked more sheepish and worried than anything.

"Mrs. Nieves, would you mind running to the vending machines to get Landon a soda while I fix him up?"

She looked up at him with her eyes full of worry.

"Trust me, it will be better for you if you don't see this. Landon is a tough kid. He'll be fine. But we're understaffed. If you pass out, I'm not sure who will treat you."

"Okay, Dr. Bradley." She kissed her son's forehead a dozen times. "Mommy will be right outside."

"I'm all right, Ma. I swear."

Elias waited until she was out of earshot to speak again. "You want to tell me how you really hurt your foot? Because you didn't just stub your toe."

Landon's eyebrows shot up. "You can tell."

"Of course I can tell. I'm a doctor, and I've been ten before. What did you do?"

"Kicked a microwave."

"You kicked a microwave? Why? Were you mad?"

"Nope. I don't know why I kicked it." He shrugged. "It was big and sitting on the lawn, and sometimes I kick stuff just because."

In ten-year-old boy thinking, it was perfectly logical just to kick stuff because it was there.

"Don't do that again, you knucklehead." Elias grinned at him. "Or else you'll be in here every week."

The boy gave him a cheeky smile. "Maybe twice more before summer ends."

"You like coming to the hospital?"

"You're pretty cool," the boy said. "But I get hurt. So do my brothers. My mother said she would put us up for sale, but no one will take damaged goods."

Elias laughed and patched the boy up. He was still thinking about the encounter when he ended his shift at 3:00 p.m. He came home to find Cricket in the kitchen. She was cooking, which shocked him.

"Hey!" He walked over to her and wrapped his arms around her, settling his hands on her belly. "What's this you're doing?"

"Did you know that there are thousands of short cooking videos posted on social media every day? I went online to look something up, and hours later I emerged with a dozen recipes that even I can handle. It's the most excited I've been in years."

"In years? Really?"

She turned in his arms and kissed him. She tasted sweet, like citrus. He wasn't content with just one kiss and took her mouth in a much longer and deeper kiss.

She sighed when he finished and rested her head on his shoulder. "I should have said that I haven't been this excited over anything that hasn't pertained to you in years."

"That's better."

"How was your day?" she asked him.

"Good. Very good," he answered, surprising himself. Six months ago the thought of being a small-town doctor would have given him hives, but he had been taking on shifts at the hospital for the past couple of weeks, and it wasn't nearly as boring as he expected. He was busy but in a different way, and instead of feeling drained physically and emotionally from complex life-threatening procedures, he got a little charge from interacting with his patients. "I just finished treating a broken toe. Kid kicked a microwave."

"Why?"

"Because he's a ten-year-old boy, and that's what ten-year-old boys do."

"Don't tell me that. I'll be a nervous wreck until our child is fifty."

"Didn't you ever get hurt as a kid? It's normal."

"No. I read. It's hard to get hurt when you spend all of your free time with your nose in a book."

"Didn't you have a horse?"

"Do you think I rode him?" She looked aghast. "I brushed him and petted him and told him that he was special even if he wasn't as beautiful as the other horses."

She made him smile. Every day. When she was around, he couldn't help it. Things had been much better between them. She seemed happy. He was happier. This wasn't the life he wanted, he wasn't doing the job he wanted, but things weren't bad. He could live this life.

When Cricket was happy, the entire world seemed to be brighter.

"Whatever happened to your horse?"

"He's here on the island. Where do you think I went when we had our fight?"

"He's here? And you never told me?"

"I thought I did. He's in the most beautiful stable. It's not far from your brother's house."

"You have to take me to see him."

Her entire face lit up. "You really want to?"

"Of course. I married an heiress. I feel like it's your duty to expose me to fancy crap."

"Let's go right now."

"Right now? I thought you were cooking."

"It's all prepared. All I have to do is pop it in the oven when we get home. It will be ready in a half hour."

"Sounds good. Let's go."

"You're not too tired from work?" She looked at him with a touch of concern.

"No," he answered truthfully. For the first time in his career, he didn't come home exhausted. He came home when it was light, to a warm home and a soft woman. But his hand was getting stronger. The occupational therapist he was seeing on the island worked wonders. Elias had worked so hard to become a trauma surgeon. It wouldn't be much longer now before he was cleared to go back. His single-minded dream had been to be the head of his department, but he was married now. They were going to have a family. He wanted to see his children after school. He wanted to have dinner with them. But it seemed impossible to match his career goals to his family goals.

They still had some time, but he was going to have to think hard and figure out how to make things work out for them.

There weren't many perks to being an heiress. She knew that she could give it all up in an instant. But being able to keep her old, slow horse in this luxurious stable was one of them. The stable had a view of the ocean in the distance. Each horse had a designer stall and the best organic food money could buy. There was a lot of land for the horses to roam freely. It was horse paradise, and her old boy was here. Not because she loved horses or even animals, for that matter, but because as a child, she'd been watching a show on some animal-themed network, and she saw him, abused, nearly half-starved, and she had burst into tears. Her father got on the phone, tracked down the horse and gifted him to her for her fourteenth birthday. Seymour had been here ever since, eating all the food he could get his hooves on.

"This is way nicer than anyplace I have ever lived," Elias said with awe in his voice when they got out of the car.

"It's extravagant, but it's the only thing I treat myself to. I just want Seymour to be happy. He was a rescue. His life hasn't always been this good."

"Seymour." She could hear the grin in his voice. "I like it. I'm assuming he's the chunky gray one grazing over there."

"He's not chunky! He's delightful looking." Seymour looked up at the sound of her voice and came trotting over to the gate from his spot in the field. "There's my boy!" She ran her hand down his long neck, and he nuzzled her.

She climbed over the fence to get closer to him.

"Cricket! What are you doing? You could hurt yourself."

"Relax," she said as she hugged her horse. "I'm fine. My boy is so gentle. He knows he's been saved. He's grateful."

"I'm sure he is. But I don't like you climbing things."

"I guess I won't be going mountain climbing tomorrow. Damn." She looked back at him with a grin. "Seymour, come say hello to your new daddy."

Seymour eyed Elias and then walked a step closer to the gate. Elias eyed Seymour back. It was clear that Elias had never been around such a large animal before, but he calmly walked over to him and extended his hand. "Is it like a dog? Do I let him just smell me?"

"You should always approach every animal with caution," she said to him. "But he's a good boy. Just stroke the bridge of his nose."

"I've never been this close to a horse. When my brother was wooing his wife, he rented horses and took her horseback riding on the beach."

"Romantic." She grinned, thinking about her brother-in-law. It seemed out of character for Carlos, but he loved Virginia so much she knew he would do anything for her.

"Do you want me to do that for you?"

"No. You already gave me the most romantic moment of my life."

"Did I?"

"Yes. You made me a pickle, cheese and mayo sandwich and then made love to me like the contents of my stomach didn't gross you out."

He threw back his head and laughed. He had been so much happier lately. He laughed easier. He was more relaxed. He shared what was on his mind. She was loving the life they had carved out here on the island. She never wanted to leave it. But she knew that as soon as he was cleared to go back to surgery, he would go back. He'd worked too hard not to. Then he would be tired and stressed and she would never see him. It would be like being married to the male version of her mother.

She had avoided surgeons most of her adult life, only to end up madly in love with one.

"My wife was having a craving. It's my job to make sure you always have what you need."

She leaned over the pen and kissed him, feeling that love grow a little deeper. There were so many times she wanted to tell him how much she loved him. But she couldn't. Not yet. She didn't feel safe enough to. Not until she had a sure sign that he loved her, too. It was still far too soon to expect it from him.

"I'm having a craving for frozen custard." She kissed him again. "It would make me very happy if we went to get some."

"Your wish is my command." He looked at her for a long moment. There was genuine affection in his eyes. It made her feel warm all over. The butterflies were still there whenever she looked at him.

The rush. The feeling like the cutest boy in school was paying attention to her.

It was utterly ridiculous. She was a scientist. She had two doctorates. She was nearly thirty! But Elias was gorgeous and strong, and he just made her feel things that she hadn't thought were possible.

"Let's head to the barn and feed Seymour a treat before we head home. I suddenly feel the need to get back there."

He gave her a slow smile, and the look in his eyes turned hot. She loved when he looked at her that way. It meant they probably weren't going to make it to the bedroom.

They began walking back toward the barn a little faster than necessary, Seymour moseying behind them. Neither one of them spoke, but there was heat crackling between them.

Elias was on the outside of the pen and she was inside, but she was glad there was a fence between them, because she knew they wouldn't have even made it back to the barn to feed her horse if there hadn't been.

"Can't you make your horse move any faster?" he asked her as they approached the opening to the building.

"He was built for comfort. Not for speed," she said, grinning. She was still looking at Elias when she heard a shout and the loud pounding of hooves. His horrified expression was the last thing she saw before a big, powerful force slammed into her.

Chapter 10

Elias's voice was still raw twenty-four hours later. He remembered screaming Cricket's name. He remembered reaching for her as the horse thundered toward her. He remembered seeing her body fly through the air and then go deadly still. He had frozen, rooted to his spot for a few short moments just paralyzed with fear.

No. No. No. His mind screamed. *Not her. Don't take her. I can't lose her.*

A panic-stricken teenage girl rushed up to him, and that forced Elias to spring into action. He was a trauma surgeon. He could help her. He would not lose her if he could help her.

He got her stabilized on a board the owners had

in the barn, and a few of the farmhands lifted her into the back of a pickup truck. The horse farm was on a deserted part of the island, and they'd get her to the hospital faster than an ambulance would have.

He treated her once they got back to Hideaway Hospital. Checked her vitals, made sure she was stable. Raised all hell until a helicopter arrived and airlifted her to Miami. Her bones were intact, but she had been hit so hard and there had been so much blood. All because an unruly horse got spooked and ran her way.

The staff at Miami Mercy wouldn't let Elias past the waiting room as they rushed Cricket into surgery. They didn't give a damn who he was or how long he'd worked there. But he knew that they were the best team in the state. That they wouldn't let her die, not because she was the daughter of the chief of surgery, but because they were excellent at their jobs.

He was going stir-crazy waiting for word when a strong hand clamped on to his shoulder. Cricket's father was there. His face tight with worry. The man embraced him hard, and it was what he needed. It was like having his own father hug him. He had been missing his father so much lately, wondering if he was okay with his life choices, with the woman whom he chose to love, to marry.

And through Jerome Warren's tight hug, it was like his own father giving him comfort, promising him everything was going to turn out okay.

Elias knew life would lose its brightness without his sunny wife.

But Cricket did pull through. She was the only one to pull through the ordeal. Their baby didn't make it.

He felt horrible because he hadn't once thought about their baby, only his wife.

He was the one to break the news to her when she woke up and reached down to touch her belly. And it was the most painful moment of his life when he heard the strangled wail she released when the news fully hit her.

Their little family had been shattered. She turned away from him when he reached out to comfort her.

But how could he offer comfort? There were no words. Nothing he could say to make things better. So he settled on holding her hand and not leaving her side until she was released from the hospital a week later.

Things weren't the same between them when they got home.

How could they be?

She'd been so excited about the baby. Excited to be a mother. All her future plans had revolved around the baby. All *their* future plans. And now they seemed to have nothing ahead of them. The house felt empty. Elias had suggested that they stay at his condo in Miami to be closer to her parents, but she wanted to come back to the island, to this house on the water.

He had wanted her to go to bed and rest, but

she sat in the sunroom with the door open and just watched the ocean for days. She sat there from sunup to the moment he physically lifted her out of her seat at night and brought her back to their bedroom.

It was nearly a month later when he realized that he needed to do something more to get his wife back to living.

Cricket felt numb. It was the only way to describe what was going on with her. She was absolutely numb. She was wrecked, she knew, but she couldn't describe the feeling as sadness. She was too far beyond that, and now she felt nothing. Not hunger or thirst or pain or anything. She was pretty sure she would have wasted away if it weren't for Elias. He made sure her body healed correctly after surgery. He fed her. He put her to bed. He even bathed her, filling their huge bathtub with hot soapy water and climbing in it with her. He just held her while the water gently lapped over her. His strong chest keeping her upright when she might otherwise have sunk in.

There was one emotion that was still lurking beneath, and it was love. If she hadn't known that she was in love with him before, she knew now. Head over heels in love. Crazy in love, but now she had nothing to offer him.

The baby was the only reason he had married her. It was a boy. They had learned after she miscarried. That child was their only connection, and now he was gone. Elias would be gone, too. Eventually. He was too good a man to leave her right now when she was at her lowest, but he would eventually go and live the life he had wanted before she had gotten pregnant.

About three and a half weeks afterward, she knew she could no longer continue to walk around like a zombie. She got herself up one morning. She dressed herself and combed her hair and made a large pot of coffee, and instead of sitting in the sunroom, she forced herself to leave the house and walk on the beach.

She couldn't remember the last time she had been out of the house. It was probably to head to the doctor for a checkup. It was nice to be outside in the cool morning air. The breeze whipped her curls around, feeling good against her skin. She stood at the edge of the water, the waves covering her feet before they retreated.

She heard her name being called and heavy footsteps behind her. Fear zigzagged through her, and for a moment she was unclear why. She didn't remember the horse running toward her. She only remembered waking up in the hospital to Elias's twisted face telling her that she wasn't going to be a mommy anymore. But she did remember the noise of the hooves beating the ground and Elias's voice screaming out her name.

This time he grabbed her shoulders and pulled her into him. Crushing her against him so tightly it hurt.

"What's the matter, baby?" she asked him.

"I didn't know where you were." He pulled away from her slightly and looked into her eyes. The worry was clear in them, and so was the relief. "You scared me! You aren't allowed to scare me anymore. Promise me you won't."

He was afraid she was going to hurt herself. The thought horrified her. She would never do that to herself, to him. But he didn't know that, because for the past month she'd ceased to be a person.

"I'm sorry." She closed the gap between them and smoothed her hand down his strong back. "I just wanted to go for a walk."

"Let me walk with you."

"Aren't you sick of me?"

"No! I'm sick at the thought of being without you."

Her eyes went wide at his statement, and suddenly the numbness that was a constant companion washed away.

She knew he had been hurt, too, by the loss of their child, but he had also been worried about losing her, which was something she hadn't cared so much about the past month.

She stood on her tiptoes and leaned in to kiss him softly. But he didn't want just a soft kiss. He cupped her cheeks and kissed her harder. It was the first time they had kissed like this since the day of her accident.

"Let me take you out to breakfast," she said when he broke the kiss.

"Are you sure you're up for that?"

"As long as you are with me."

Chapter 11

Two days later Cricket sat in the living room with her parents, a mug of steaming tea in her hands. Her mother had been to the island three times in the past month, which was a lot considering her work schedule. Her father had come twice a week without fail.

They had been so worried about her, and every other time that they had visited, she had been only vaguely aware of their presence. Now she was fully engaged, but it was exhausting. She was no longer numb, but the heaviness was still there and today it was taking everything in her power not to crawl back into bed.

She looked over to Elias, who was sitting in an overstuffed armchair, too far away from her to touch.

She wanted to be sitting next to him, to lean against him. She could have gotten up from her seat to be with him, but she felt that she was leaning on him too much, that it was time to prop herself up. She'd been totally independent before him. She would need to be after him, too.

"What are your plans now, sweetheart?" her mother asked her.

Cricket wasn't sure why the question took her off guard, but it did. "Um... I—I guess I'll go back to writing my book. I shouldn't keep my publisher waiting."

"Maybe you should go back to teaching. There are quite a few excellent universities in Miami, and you'll have to settle there anyway, once Elias goes back to surgery in two weeks."

"In two weeks?" She looked over to him.

He nodded. "I was going to wait until we were alone to talk about it." He gave her mother a pointed look. "I've been cleared. The result of my latest scan came back this morning."

"When did you go to the doctor?"

"The day Ava and Derek came to be with you. I told you I was going," he said gently.

She had heard him tell her that, but she hadn't been listening. "That's right. You did. I'm happy for you," she said, but her voice didn't really convey it. She didn't want to go back to Miami. She didn't want him working sixteen-hour days. She didn't want him to be so driven, like her mother was, but she had no right to feel that way. She was being selfish, wanting to keep him all to herself when she knew that all he wanted to do was reach the top.

"We can talk about this more later," he said to her.

"Why wait?" Dr. Lundy said. "We're here. We can help you two figure things out."

"I think we can figure our lives out for ourselves, Doctor. But thank you." Elias's voice was tight. Her mother had been offering what she thought was helpful advice the entire time she had been there. It was starting to become grating.

"You are married to my daughter, and you do work for me. I think I have a large role in your lives. Maybe you should look at this loss as a blessing in disguise. Now everything won't happen so quickly. You can take time to evaluate what you both really want out of life and your marriage, and you won't have to rush into anything."

"I used to think your ability to separate your feelings from your thoughts made you an excellent surgeon," Elias said, his voice deadly low. "But now I just think you are the most insensitive person on the planet."

Her mother's eyes widened with surprise. She clearly had no idea what he was talking about, how her words sliced through them.

"How can I be insensitive? You now have one less thing to worry about."

"One less thing!" he roared. "That one less thing was the thing we wanted above all else, and if you can't pull your head out of your behind long enough to see that, then we don't need you here. Our loss is not a blessing! Our lives are not lived to please your stupid, impossibly high standards."

"Excuse me?"

"Get out. You can't even see that you are upsetting your daughter. Just go."

"Surely you aren't kicking me out of the house my husband and I purchased for our daughter. As far as I'm concerned, *you* are the guest here."

"You're right. This isn't my home, and it never will be."

He walked out of the room.

"Frances!" Jerome looked furious. "Sometimes you go too far. This isn't your hospital. Elias is no longer just your employee. He's our son-in-law, and if you can't see that he's clearly in love with our daughter, maybe you should get your vision checked."

Cricket sat there reeling. She didn't know whether to go after her husband or yell at her mother. "You wished this on me, didn't you?"

Dr. Lundy looked stricken. "Why would you say such a thing?"

"Why can't you be happy for me when I'm happy and grieve with me when I'm sad? I wanted that baby more than I've ever wanted anything in my life, and you're acting relieved that it's not happening."

"It's not that I—"

Elias came back from the bedroom with a large

suitcase in his hand. Cricket's eyes filled with tears. He was walking out.

How could she blame him?

This wasn't his house, or his dream or his idea of a good life. And her mother had forced his hand. She would walk out, too, just to make the same point.

"Come on, Cricket." He extended his hand to her, uncertainty in his eyes. Without thinking, she stood and took it.

"Cricket…" Her father stood up. "Don't go. This is your home. Both your home. Please, stay."

"I'm sorry, Daddy, but I have to go."

"Cricket," her mother said as she stood. "You can't really be serious about leaving."

"I am. I'm choosing my husband. You can keep the house."

Elias looked over to his wife, who was dozing beside him on Carlos's private plane. It was one of the perks of having a brother who was one of the wealthiest athletes in the world.

Cricket had never asked where they were going. There was no uncertainty in her eyes when he'd extended his hand to her and asked her to come. She trusted him, and it made him love her even more. She could have been upset with him—maybe she should have been upset with him for yelling at her mother and ordering the woman out. But Cricket was with him all the way, and that made him feel better than he had in a very long time.

He kissed the side of her face, unable to help himself. She opened her eyes and looked up at him.

"I'm an heiress, but not one person in my family owns a private plane."

"My brother isn't into cars or shoes or bling. Before he bought his house on the island, he was living in the same one-bedroom condo he had since he was a rookie. The other players started to tease him for being cheap, so he bought a plane to show them. I think he wasn't allowed into the special superrich athlete club until he bought one."

"I knew baseball players made a lot of money, but I didn't know that they made that much."

"My brother invests in things right before they explode into huge businesses. He's gotten me into some of them."

"Things like what?"

"Dating apps. Car services. Health food stores. Even if I never worked as a surgeon, I can take care of you. You can have whatever you want."

"I don't want anything."

"I know, but I have so much I want to give to you."

"You've given me so much already. I feel selfish. Sometimes I wish you weren't so sweet to me."

I love you. He didn't say the words. He couldn't bring himself to in that moment. "You haven't asked me where we were going."

"It doesn't matter. I think I needed to get away."

"We're going to Costa Rica."

"To meet your mother?"

"And my grandmother and aunts." They had video chatted a dozen times or so since they had been married, but his mother couldn't leave Costa Rica because of her mother's poor health. His grandmother was going to be ninety-seven this year. He understood why she couldn't leave her.

"Are we staying with them?"

"No. I never got to take you on a honeymoon. I figured we could take care of that while we're there."

"Elias." Cricket surveyed the scene from their house, and it took her breath away. She had been breathless a lot today. She had spent so much of her time in poor, underdeveloped countries the past ten years that she had forgotten how truly gorgeous the world could be. Hideaway Island was beautiful and tropical, but there was a small-town, homey feeling whenever she stepped foot on it, but here in Costa Rica… She couldn't even describe what she was seeing. She knew they were at a resort. There'd been a lobby with a check-in desk. They had passed a spa, some pools and a few restaurants, but they kept traveling through all of that until they got to a three-story house that seemed to stand alone on a beach. The entire spacious top floor was theirs. Their bedroom led out to a deck that wrapped around the entire unit. There was a gorgeous tiled half-moon-shaped hot tub there overlooking the ocean. But it wasn't just ocean in their view. There was thick lush forest surrounding them and sounds of wildlife that were soothing and exciting at the same time.

"You like it here?" He came up behind her and kissed her shoulder.

"No, I don't like it here." She turned to face him with a slight smile. "I could die here. Right here on this balcony. In fact, bury me in the hot tub. It's incredible."

He looked into her eyes for a long moment. "I missed your smile."

"I'm sorry." She looped her arms around him and leaned against him.

"Why are you apologizing to me?"

"I'm not sure. I just feel the need to."

"I think you should rest. We are going to have the biggest dinner that two people have ever had, and tomorrow you're going to meet the rest of my family. You're going to need your energy for that."

She nodded. "Do you mind if we get in the hot tub first?"

He grinned at her. "I was hoping you'd ask me that."

Chapter 12

"Your home is beautiful, Mrs. Bradley," Cricket said in a quiet voice.

"Don't call me Mrs. Bradley! You are family now!" Elias's mother, Nilda, wrapped her into a big warm hug. "And thank you. It's very hard to please five women, but Carlos seemed to know that this was the right amount of space for us. I could go two days without seeing any of my sisters if I wanted to—and I often do."

"Ha!" Elias's aunt Arsenia laughed. "You talk more than any of us. We hide downstairs just to get away from your mouth."

A bunch of good-natured bickering followed that, which was typical of any get-together with his mother and her sisters. Elias often wished his mother lived closer to him and his siblings, but he could tell she was happier here. After his father died, she'd been lost without her husband. Being on Hideaway Island, where they had spent family vacations, made her feel empty, but her sisters made her full. There was no space for sadness here. And that's why Elias had thought it would be a good thing for him and Cricket to visit.

They'd had a nice day, a ridiculously huge lunch and a trip to the beach, and now his aunts had whisked Cricket away to go shopping in the nearest village. Elias chose to stay at the house with his mother, who had stayed behind to be with his resting grandmother.

"Abuela looks good," he said to her.

"Yes." She smiled. "She has been so excited to have you here. She wishes you would come around more."

"I know. My work kept me away."

"Your work." She rolled her eyes. "I know most mothers would be thrilled with a doctor and a hugely famous professional athlete for sons, but I would much rather you lived with me for the rest of your lives so I can take care of you."

"Pop taught us to be men, to work hard, to take care of our families."

"He taught you well." She nodded. "You really do take good care of your wife."

"What do you think about me being married?

You didn't react the way I thought you would when I told you."

"You thought I would scream and fuss and carry on?" She shrugged. "I wanted to. If your brother or sisters had gotten married like that, I would have. But I knew for you, my workaholic son, to do something so completely nuts must have meant that the girl was special. You love her very much."

"I do."

"You're both very sad."

"No one wanted to be a mother more than Cricket."

"What about you? Did you want to be a father?"

"Of course I did. I still do. But I didn't think about the baby once the accident happened. For weeks I kept seeing the horse slam into her, her body flying as if she weighed nothing. And then she was so still on the ground. I thought she was gone. She didn't respond to her name. She wouldn't move. But then she did. She opened her eyes and said my name, and I realized that I wouldn't be able to take it if I never heard her say my name again. There isn't one big thing that makes me love her. But there are a thousand little indescribable things."

"And you hate that she is so sad."

He nodded. "It's been five weeks. I can't expect her to snap out of it. It's too soon to tell her that I want to try again."

"You want to try again?" She looked surprised. "I had the feeling that this pregnancy was unplanned."

"It was, but that doesn't mean I wasn't happy

about it. I've been making a crib. Ava's husband has been helping me. I was so excited to meet my son, but I still want that chance. I want to see Cricket be a mother. She has so much love to give."

"Have you spoken to her about this?"

"No. We haven't spoken about anything. There were a few weeks when I couldn't reach her at all. Now I'm starting to get little pieces of her back, and I don't want them to vanish again."

"But you can't go around with things unsaid just because you're afraid of what might happen. You are both going through this. You need to go through it together. It's the only way you'll have a strong marriage."

Elias agreed. He just didn't know how to bring it up to Cricket.

Cricket didn't know when they had gotten to the point in their relationship where they could just be quiet and content in each other's company, but they were there. She felt completely comfortable with him. She felt safe. She had been a living, breathing zombie the past five weeks, but Elias had been her constant. He was the first person she saw when she woke up in the hospital. He had raised hell a few times when he thought she wasn't getting treated fast enough. He was her protector, even going to battle with her mother. She wondered why he was so good. So motivated to be that way.

She could attribute it to his mother. To their strong

family bond. He'd been raised to think that men just acted that way. But she wondered if he was tired of it, if sometimes he just wanted to be catered to.

She wanted to take care of his needs, but it was hard to do when he was so self-sufficient.

She picked up his no-longer-injured hand and kissed his palm a few times. He put down his e-reader and gave her a soft smile. "Have I ever told you that I like it when you do that?"

"Kiss your hand?"

"Kiss me in general. You kiss me a lot. When you wake up. When you leave a room. When I hand you something."

"Does it bother you?"

"No! I just told you that I like it."

"You are the most beautiful man that I have ever seen. You give me butterflies, sir. And I can't believe that you are married to me."

"You're a nerd." He pulled her closer, lifting her with his strong arms until she was half on top of him. He ran his hand up the back of her thigh, his fingers toying with the hem of her dress. She felt a powerful surge of lust strike her. She remembered the day of the accident. They'd been rushing back to the barn so they could go home and get in bed. But they never made it there.

They hadn't been together in over a month. They had been in Costa Rica for three days. They had been naked in the hot tub together. They had slept close together in bed, but he never attempted a thing. She had never felt that kind of hurt before. Recovering physically and mentally from her accident. But her body felt all better now, and she knew he had needs, that he was a man who enjoyed sex and it was her duty as a wife to provide him with it. It was also her joy to give her body to him. She never felt better than when she was in his arms.

"You are also the sexiest woman that I have ever met, and I get great satisfaction just being in your presence."

"Stop being so damn sweet to me." She pulled his lower lip between her teeth and gave it a soft bite before she swept her tongue across it.

"Don't start with me," he growled, lust heavy in his voice. "I want to talk to you."

"You want to talk? Now?"

"Yes. I've been meaning to. I don't think we can go on unless we have this conversation."

She sat up and looked into his eyes, which had gone completely serious. "What do you want to talk about?"

"The baby."

"No." She shut her eyes, feeling the tears so close to the edge. "I can't. I don't want to."

"We have to talk about it. *I* need to talk about it."

"But why? It's over. I was pregnant, and now I'm not."

"It's not over. He was my son, and I wanted to meet him. And I think about him sometimes and what it would be like to see him born and who he would have looked like and what he might have become. And sometimes I think I'm crazy, because how could I love someone so much that I've never even laid eyes on? That I never will lay eyes on? But it was the possibility of what he could have become. It's the thought of seeing you loving him. I feel robbed of the greatest opportunity, and if I feel that way, I know you must feel that way, too. To an even greater extent."

"Of course I do! I was just starting to feel him move. Did I tell you that?" She swiped at the tears on her face. They were coming out so quickly that she was blinded. "I was growing this gift inside me. This gift for you. This gift for the world, and in two seconds it was gone and I blame myself for losing it. For screwing up the most amazing thing I have ever done."

"What!" He shook his head. "You blame yourself? What did you do wrong? It was a freak accident that could have killed you."

"Maybe I could have prevented it. What if I didn't take you to the barn that night? What if I jumped out of the way? What if I fought a little harder to keep the baby?"

"Stop it, damn it! There are no what-ifs. You could not have changed what happened. There is nothing that either of us could have done to change the outcome."

"But I want to change what happened. I wanted to give you a baby. Do you know my favorite part of being pregnant was having you touch my belly? I loved it when you pressed your lips to it and talked to him. That was the one thing I could give you, and now it's gone."

"No, Cricket." She was shocked to see tears well in Elias's eyes. "That was not the one thing you could give me. We can have more babies, but if I lost you that day, I don't know what I would have done. There will never be another you. I will never have another wife."

She was waiting for him to say *like you*. But it never came. Of course he would have another wife if something happened to her. He was a beautiful man inside and out. Any woman would want to be with him.

Even now, he could have anyone else he wanted. Now that the baby was gone, it really hammered home that she wasn't the wife he would have chosen. Their child had bonded them together, and now that child was gone. What was left for them? What was it that would keep them together now?

"I feel so terrible."

"I know." He cupped her face in his hands. "But we can be happy again. I want to see you happy again." He kissed her, his eyes closing, his hands pulling her closer.

She wanted what he wanted. To be happy. Being with him made her happy. But she could never be sure if she was enough to make him happy.

"I need you," she whispered to him as she reached for his shirt. "Please."

"Are you sure you're ready?"

She unbuttoned his shorts and slipped her hand inside, stroking his already-hard manhood. "Undress me."

The lust in his eyes made her wet immediately. She was wearing a simple halter dress that he had packed for her. He had brought all her favorite clothes. He'd even packed the scented lotion she liked. He knew her so well. Better than the man she'd spent five years with, better than her own parents. It was one of the thousand reasons she loved him.

She straddled him. He pulled the tie on her halter, tugging down the bodice as he crushed his mouth to hers. He was a master at undressing her. His nimble fingers unclasped her bra. His hands reached for her breasts, cupping them, running his thumbs over her too-sensitive nipples. She gasped at the sensation, and he pulled his lips from hers and looked into her eyes as he took one of her breasts into his mouth and suckled.

She couldn't stop the moan that escaped her lips. She grasped him with one hand as she pulled her underwear to the side.

"Wait," he said to her as she slid down on him. "I haven't made love to you in a month. Let me at least take you to bed." He grunted as she rose up and slid down on him again. "Let me take my time," he said through gritted teeth. "Let me go slow."

"It's too late. Later. You can go as slow as you want later. I need this from you right now."

Chapter 13

"Wake up." Elias felt Cricket's lips kiss their way up his throat the next evening. They hadn't made it out of their rental at all that day. They'd barely made it out of bed. They had missed each other, missed being together like they had been. But it was different now. He didn't think it could be more intense than it was before, but in a way it was.

He was glad they'd talked, glad he understood how she was feeling a little more than before. She had always put so much pressure on herself. She lived up to impossible standards, and he blamed her mother, who had conditioned her to never feel that anything she did was right.

He wouldn't allow that to happen anymore. That's

why he had taken her away from there. Neither one of them needed that right now. They needed to heal without someone rooting against them.

"I'm awake." He wrapped his arms around her, pulling her on top of him. He loved her body, the way her large, soft breasts felt pressed against him. "Did you miss me?" He captured her mouth in a long kiss. "It's your fault I passed out. I haven't worked so hard in years."

"Don't kiss me like that," she said, sighing.

"Why?" He ran his hand up her back. She was clad only in her underwear, and in his opinion that was far too many clothes. He unclasped her bra.

"Hey!"

"What? We're on our honeymoon. The dress code is naked, and you started this."

"We've had more sex in the past twenty-four hours than most normal people should."

"Neither one of us is normal, love. And if you don't want to have sex with me, you should probably keep your lips off my throat."

"I didn't say I didn't want to have sex with you. I always want to have sex with you."

"Good." He rolled her onto her back and slipped off her panties. "Why are we still talking?"

He pushed inside her, finding her completely ready to be loved. He kept his eyes open so he could look down at her as he made love to her. He loved the way she looked back at him—there was love in her eyes. Neither one of them had said the exact words, but maybe they didn't need to be said. They had been through so much in such a short amount of time. How could there not be love between them?

He lowered his head to kiss her as he pumped inside her. She never was one to sit back and let him make love to her. She was always an active participant. She always made his lust spike uncontrollably. She wrapped her legs around him. Squeezed herself around his manhood, scraped her nails down his back. He could barely hold on, but she seemed to like him that way, to the point where he was too far gone.

Lucky for him, she came quickly.

He climaxed with her and collapsed on top of her, a happy, exhausted, sweaty mess.

"That was good," she said, patting his back.

"You always say that."

"I always mean it." She grinned at him, and he felt the strong urge to kiss her again, so he did. "Don't start again. We're going to be late."

"For what? Did you make dinner reservations?"

"No. We're going on a private night tour of the nature reserve."

"Are we?"

"Yes. While you were napping, I went to the boutique and bought all the gear we need."

He raised an eyebrow. "What kind of gear would that be?"

"Nothing heavy-duty, just rain gear and long pants. Hiking boots. A waterproof camera. Bug spray."

"How much did you spend?"

"A small fortune, but nothing is too good for my husband."

"Are you sure you're up to a hike in the woods?"

"Yes. It will be a light activity compared to all the sex." She stroked her thumb across his cheek. "You don't want to go?"

"I do."

"Good, because I was going to guilt you into it. Now get off me. We've got to get out of here."

A half hour later, they were in the middle of the rain forest along with their guide, wearing LED lights on their heads. He had been surprised to see how into it Cricket was. She was an academic. She had spent most of their marriage with her head in a book, but he remembered that right before they met she had spent months roughing it in developing nations, surrounded by poverty and infectious diseases. She was brave, his little wife. She went over the tiny suspension bridges without an ounce of fear, looking down at the forest floor and asking a thousand questions. They saw owls, lizards and frogs on their journey. The only thing Cricket balked at was the large tarantula they spotted. Even Elias was uneasy about that one, but she had buried her head in his back and wrapped her arms around his waist and asked him to guide her as far away from it as possible.

When their tour was over, they lingered outside, slowly heading toward their rental. There was a warm breeze blowing, the sky was clear and dark, and they could see every star in the sky. They stopped at the hot springs, which during the day were full of people bathing. They were empty now. Quiet. The only sounds came from the rushing waterfall and the wildlife singing in the distance. This was paradise. Elias never wanted to leave it.

"Let's get in," she said, looking up at him.

"Do you have your bathing suit?"

"Nope." She gave him a cheeky smile as she set down her bag and pulled off her top. "Do you think that's going to stop me?"

"Cricket." One hot surge of lust hit him square in the pants. He'd never thought it would be possible for one woman to turn him on so much.

"Elias." Her grinned widened. "Take your pants off. You know you want to."

"We can't have sex out here," he said to her as she stripped off the rest of her clothing.

"I know. I'm planning to make you suffer."

He was already suffering. It was painful to feel this kind of need. He took off his clothing, placing it on top of hers and following her into the hot springs. The hot tub was nothing in comparison to this. The water felt different, cleaner, the air was thick and tropical, the surroundings were too beautiful for words, and he was with a woman who had a naughty side that he was growing fonder of by the moment.

"Tell me some nerdy facts about these hot springs," he said to his wife.

"They are heated by a volcano," she started. "This

one is about one hundred and two degrees, give or take a few. Because of the natural minerals, the water is supposed to leave your skin moisturized and refreshed."

He grinned at her. It never ceased to amaze him that someone so smart could look so damn mouthwateringly sexy. She was a pinup. She had the kind of body that was meant to be covered in oil and draped over a sports car, but she was also brainy. And somehow he'd had the good fortune to be placed in her path. "Come here." He sat on a man-made rock bench that was located just in front of a small waterfall. She obeyed his request, coming to sit beside him instead of on his lap like he wanted.

"You're too far away from me."

"I know. I'm afraid to touch you."

"You should never be afraid of that. Come here." He grabbed her hand and pulled her into his arms. Their wet bodies slid against each other, arousing him more.

"We cannot fool around in here. I don't care how clothing optional this resort is."

"Clothing optional? I didn't know that. I just thought you were being naughty."

"I am! My mother would have a heart attack if she knew what we were up to."

"Don't worry about her." He kissed her shoulder.

"I'm not sure how you two are going to get along when you go back to work."

"I'm not going back to work for her. I sent in my resignation three days ago."

"What?" Her eyes went wide. "You love that job."

"Yes, but I can do it anywhere. What I can't do is work for your mother. Especially after what went down between us. She doesn't have a say in our lives. You and I are the ones who decide."

She looped her arms around his neck and held on to him tightly. "You don't have to do this. I'm sure you can work things out with my mother. She didn't mean to hurt us."

"But I saw the look in your eyes when she said those words. When we get back home, I'm going to apply at other hospitals in Miami, and if it's okay with you, I'm going to start looking outside south Florida. I've got contacts all over, including at the Davis Clinic. One of my former teachers is a chief of surgery there."

"That's the best hospital in the country."

"I wouldn't be applying for trauma. Thoracic surgery would become my specialty again. My hours would be steadier. More routine scheduled procedures."

Cricket made a soft noise but didn't say anything else. They were just speaking in what-ifs, but if he got a job there they would have to move to the middle of the country, away from both of their families. It was a lot to ask of her, but they could make their own family, and they could always visit Hideaway Island.

"I won't apply if you don't want me to."

"Of course you have to apply. If you have the chance to work at the best hospital in the country, you should go. I have been there before to work with their microbiologist in their infectious disease clinic. I've never met a group of more brilliant scientists."

"That's good to hear. We don't have to make any decisions yet. I think we should wait until we find out for sure if you're pregnant again."

"Pregnant again?" She looked startled for a moment.

"The doctor did say we shouldn't have a problem getting pregnant again, right?"

"She said I should be fine."

"I think we should wait till we get back to the States before we take a test. But we can get one here, too. Although I'm not sure if we can get an early-response test here."

"How long are we staying here?"

"As long as you want, but I reserved three weeks."

She kissed his shoulder a half-dozen times. "I want to stay here with you the entire three weeks, but I have something to tell you."

"What is it?"

"I'm not pregnant."

"I think it's too soon to know for sure, but we're fertile. You might be."

"No, I really mean that I'm not pregnant. I can't be. I had the doctor give me a shot of Depo-Provera."

"That's a long-lasting shot. The effects can last longer than six months."

"I know. I didn't think you would want to try again so soon. The doctor wanted me to wait eight weeks before trying to get pregnant again, and this just seemed like the right thing to do."

"You know how much I want to be a father."

"You will be a father." She pressed her lips to his mouth. "You will have all the happiness you want, because it's what you deserve."

Even though his wife was pressed against him and she was saying the right words, Elias felt uneasy. He felt like she was disconnecting herself from his life once again.

Cricket had thought that Hideaway Island was her happy place. The place where no pain could reach her and all her memories would be happy ones. But real life had infiltrated her peaceful sanctuary there. She had lost her baby there. Gotten into the biggest fight she had ever had with her parents there. But she had also met Elias there. She'd made love for the first time there. She had truly fallen in love on that little island, and having so much joy and so much pain connected to one place taught her a valuable lesson. Life can reach you wherever you hide.

They were in paradise, she and Elias. It had been nearly three weeks full of deep, delicious lovemaking and fantastic food. She got to be encased in the love of Elias's extended family. She got the chance to be spoiled by his mother. They had all been so kind to her, and part of her never wanted to go back to the States. They could make a life here in paradise, she thought. They could wake up to the sounds of wildlife and look out the window and see nothing but unspoiled rain forests and ocean water so clear and blue that it looked unreal. Elias could easily get a job here, a job with even more prestige than he had back at home. She could spend her days writing and doing research in the medical field at a university. They could have children here and raise them in a different culture.

It could be a wonderful life, and Cricket knew that all she had to do was say the word to Elias, and he would make it all happen. He wanted her to be happy, no matter the cost to himself, and that's why she loved him so much. And that's why she knew she couldn't stay there forever, because it wasn't the life he had dreamed for himself. They had unfinished business back on Hideaway Island. And even though this place was pretty much perfect, she still missed being home. She had spoken a few times to her father, who was truly distraught with how things had gone down before they left. He told her that her mother was upset, but her pride and strong will wouldn't allow her to apologize. Cricket didn't need an apology, but Elias did. He was the one who had sacrificed so much. She needed to find a way to give him as much as he had given her.

She looked over to him. They were lying on the beach at twilight, their favorite time of day. It was completely empty. There was a lovely warm breeze blowing and the sound of waves lapping the shore. Elias was dozing next to her on his lounge chair, a panama hat draped over his face. She had bought it for him. She thought he looked unbearably sexy at the moment, wearing swim trunks and a short-sleeved blue button-up shirt open to reveal his hard chest, which she had a hard time not running her fingers over.

She got up from her chair and plucked the hat off his face, only because she felt the desperate urge to kiss him in that moment.

She should have known he wouldn't let her get away with just one kiss to the cheek. He pulled her down on the chair, shifting his body so that they both could lie there together. He ran his hand over her bottom. At his request she had purchased a white bikini. It was even sexier than the one she had worn that day she spent with his family. She had felt horribly self-conscious in it. But he kept looking at her, touching her. He enjoyed her body. She had spent so long with a man who was uninterested and unable to be sexual—being married to a man who was the opposite of that was making her feel alive in a way she hadn't thought possible.

"You didn't think I was going to let you walk away from me, did you?"

"I just wanted to give you a little kiss."

"You know I can't take the way you look in this bathing suit." He slid his hand to her back and unhooked the top of her bikini. Her breasts came free and he touched them, smoothing his large, skilled hands over them.

"You need to stop that," she moaned.

"Why?"

"We can't do this here."

"Why not? No one is around. We're all the way at the end of the beach."

"Someone could easily walk up."

"Yes." He kissed her shoulder. "But I doubt they will."

"I don't think this chair will hold up to our love-making."

"That, I'll have to agree with." He turned her so that most of her back was touching the chair and he was half atop her, and then his hand wandered to her bikini bottoms, inside to her lower lips. He groaned when he felt her there. "So soft. So wet."

She felt slightly embarrassed by his words, but they caused her to become even more aroused. "You do this to me. Only you could ever do this to me."

"You make me crazy," he said before he took her mouth. "I can no longer think straight when I'm near you."

He slipped his fingers inside her, stroking her slowly but firmly. She knew she should just lie back and enjoy him, but she was unable to be passive when she was with him. She needed to give back to him. She reached inside his swim trunks and took his hardness in her hand. He hissed in pleasure. She worked fast, knowing she was only moments away from explosion herself.

He kept kissing her, those long, deep, breath-stealing kisses that made her feel otherworldly.

Orgasm struck, and she cried into his mouth. He spilled himself in her hand and kissed her one last time before he got up and led her into the warm ocean water. She was topless, but on this resort clothing was optional. She wouldn't have felt comfortable enough to do that if there were anyone else there.

The ocean water was incredibly warm, the waves gentle. Cricket wrapped her body around her husband's, and they just floated together.

"It's going to be hard to leave this place," she said as she kissed his shoulder.

"We can stay longer if you want. There's nothing pressing to get back to."

"Except life. You have a career that I know you must be missing."

"You're more important to me."

"I'm surprised no one married you before I got the chance. You are a very good husband. Have I told you that? You're a better man than I ever could have wished for."

"There was no one that I wanted to marry before you came along."

She'd gotten pregnant. That's why he married her, and she couldn't forget that. She wouldn't have seen him again if she hadn't. "Are you going to apply for that out-of-state job when we get back?"

"Unless you don't want me to."

"I want what you want. It's a simple as that."

"I want to buy the house from your father."

"What?"

"I have a lot of money saved. I've made good investments. My salary is high enough to support us both. I could buy the house from him."

"No, I don't want you to do that."

"Then we can buy a new house on the island together. I know you love your house, but if we buy a new house, we could make it our own. I like the house, but I feel like it's your house."

"It's not my house. It doesn't feel like home without you there. I'm sorry if I've made you feel like a guest there."

"You haven't."

"My father won't take your money. I know he won't. That was his gift to me when I finished my second PhD."

"I won't feel like it's my home unless I have paid something for it. I think he'll understand where I'm coming from if I sit down and have a conversation with him."

"He likes you. I feel like you want to do this to prove something to my mother. You don't need her approval."

"I hurt my hand and then I met you and then we were going to have a baby and then we lost the baby, and everything in my life felt so out of control. I haven't felt that way since my father died. I can control how I treat you. The work I do. How we live. The kind of father I will be."

"You still wish I was pregnant, don't you?"

"Of course I do. Don't you? I want to make a family with you."

"How many kids do you want? We never discussed it. We got married so quickly. We didn't know each other. Sometimes I think we still don't know each other."

"I know you. I know that your favorite color is marigold yellow. And that you love to spend rainy days in bed. Your favorite food is ice cream, and you'd rather eat that than real food. I know that bugs scare you and having fresh flowers in the house makes you happy. I know you want a simple life. And to answer your question, I want a lot of kids, but I'll settle for as many as you want to give me as long as it's more than one."

Life wouldn't be so simple if he went back to being a surgeon in one of the best hospitals in the world. He would work all the time. He would miss out on large parts of their children's lives. He would try to be there. He would love them, but he wouldn't be able to leave his patients behind because his work was too important. And she wouldn't be able to travel the world and work in less-than-safe places, because she knew that she couldn't risk her life when she had children to think about.

She'd been so happy when she learned she was going to be a mother, but motherhood wasn't the life she had planned for herself. She hadn't planned for Elias to come in and change everything she knew about herself.

"How long do you want to wait before we try again?" he asked her.

He wanted to be a father. He wanted a big family. He treated her beautifully. There were times when he looked at her with such tenderness in his eyes that she would swear he was as in love with her as she was with him. But she could never be sure. Life would be unbearable without him, but spending a life with him and wondering if he would be happier somewhere else would be nearly as painful.

"I think we need to put off this discussion for now. We need to know where you are going to work first, and then we can worry about the house and everything else. I don't want to think about the future. I have a few more days in paradise with you, and that's all I want to think about right now."

"Okay." He kissed her lips softly. "That's more than okay."

Chapter 14

They finally left Costa Rica. Left that little slice of paradise and returned to Hideaway Island, which to Elias had once been paradise for them, too. But returning felt much different. It was as if a little bit of the happiness drained out of them as soon as they stepped foot off the plane. It made sense for them to feel that way. They had a lot of painful memories here, business left unfinished.

Elias stood behind Cricket as she let them into the house that was not theirs, but hers. A gift from her father. The reason they had escaped to Costa Rica. Her mother had said that he had been a guest there, and walking back in, he didn't feel any more at home.

This place would never be his home unless he had some ownership of it.

"It feels empty, doesn't it?" she asked as she turned to him once they were in the living room. "It's odd that it feels empty. It was just the two of us before we left, and it will be just the two of us until…" She trailed off, the sadness seeping into her expression.

She said she wasn't ready to try again. She had taken precautions to ensure that there wouldn't be another accident, and he was fine with that. He enjoyed being with just her. In Costa Rica, he had never felt closer to anyone in his life. But he sensed that even though she said she wanted to wait, she didn't. Or it could be something else. Something she wasn't telling him. He had felt a little distance between them the last couple of days. It left a funny feeling in the pit of his stomach. But he forced down his worry. This was a tough time for them. Everything was so up in the air. They just needed time to figure things out.

Things would settle down between them. Elias took a step toward Cricket and smoothed his hands down her bare arms. "I know what you mean. After the way we left here, I'm surprised the locks on the doors weren't changed."

Cricket looked up into his eyes, the worry clear in her tone. "My mother hasn't tried to contact you? She hasn't offered you your job back?"

"I don't want my job back."

"Yes, you do," she said in a fierce whisper. "It's because of me you aren't going back."

"You influence a lot of my decisions, but you didn't make me quit. It was time for me to move on. It's best to keep my family and my career separate. It will make Thanksgivings that much easier."

"If you wanted it back, Elias, I would ask her for you. If you wanted me to, of course. I've never asked her for anything. She would do this for me. She would have to or I don't think I could ever look at her the same way."

"You're worried about me and my job, and I'm worried that I've ruined the relationship between you and your mother."

"You can't ruin what was barely there. It's never been easy between us."

"You should call her," he urged. "Just let her know that we're back and that you're feeling all right." This wasn't sitting well with him. To him, family was everything, and he couldn't imagine a world where he was estranged from his family.

"No. I left with you that day for a reason. I chose my husband over my mother, and she needs to understand that what I do with my life is my business. If she can't respect my choices, she can at least respect me enough to keep quiet about them."

"I know, baby. Your mother wants what's best for you. I just think she doesn't know how to convey that. But we can't go the rest of our lives not speaking to her."

"I'm done talking about this, Elias," she said forcefully enough that he took a small step away from her. "She's my mother, and I'll decide when and how we communicate again." She shook her head, the anger clearing out of her eyes. "I'm sorry. I shouldn't have snapped at you. I'm tired."

"Do you need me to get you anything? Are you hungry?"

She looked at him for a long moment. There was love in her eyes. It was clear as day, and yet he had never heard her say it. He had never said it, either. Something was stopping him, some invisible wall blocking their words.

She closed the distance between them and kissed his cheek. "You don't have to take care of me anymore, Elias. I'm going to go rest for a few hours."

She walked away, leaving him alone and feeling off center. He wanted to take care of her, not because she needed to be taken care of, but because she was his wife and he was in love with her.

The next afternoon Carlos, Ava and Ava's husband, Derek, showed up to welcome them back to the island. They all seemed happy to see their brother again, and Elias seemed glad to be back around his siblings, because he spoke to them for hours, about Costa Rica and their trip and his mother and aunts. Cricket was happy that Elias's family was so close. There was never any stilted conversation. There was never strain between them. They all seemed to support each other unwaveringly.

It shouldn't make Cricket sad that her husband had so much love in his life, but it did. Because even with her inherited fortune and all her education, she didn't have that. She could never have the big family and the overabundance of love.

She had excused herself to the kitchen under the pretense of getting snacks for everyone. She had been gone for over ten minutes now. Slowly chopping veggies for a platter. She had tried to keep up with the conversation as best as she could, but she still felt like an outsider with the Bradley clan, an interloper. Unlike Virginia or Derek, because they had married into the family in love. Cricket had married into the family because she had been pregnant by one of its members, but now that baby was gone and the only connection she had to them seemed to be temporary at best.

She was glad Virginia wasn't here with her baby girl, Bria. That would have made things worse. That would have made this evening even harder than it was. It had been almost two months since her loss. In Costa Rica, she'd been distracted by the lush surroundings, the new experiences, the constant lovemaking with her husband. But back here, she was reminded that her own family was splintered, that her grief was still there right under the surface, that the insecurities about her marriage were too strong to ignore. Elias didn't want to live in this house or on this island. He had a bigger life planned for himself than he was currently living. And she had a career that she was proud of, one that she had wanted to grow—before that fateful night that placed Elias onto her path.

"You need help in here?" Ava asked as she breezed into the kitchen. Cricket had been around Ava many times before, but she still couldn't get over how effortlessly beautiful she was.

"Did they send you to see what was taking me so long?" Cricket tried to inject some humor into her voice. "I need to have these vegetables cut into precisely two-inch pieces. Research says that's the right length for digestion."

"Is that true?" Ava raised one of her perfectly sculpted brows.

"Probably not," Cricket admitted. "I was thinking and kind of got lost in my thoughts."

"You want to talk? Not about your trip or the weather. I mean really, *really* talk."

"I'm fine."

"No, you're not. It's okay not to be, to tell someone that you aren't. There are certain things I can't speak to my husband about. I run to Virginia and spill my guts. Who do you go to when you need that?"

"I don't go to anyone. I don't have anyone like that in my life."

"I can be that person for you."

"But you're his twin. How do I know you two

don't have some sort of freaky twin connection going on? Your thoughts are probably linked."

"Trust me, they aren't. Thank God, because I'm pretty sure we'd both be in trouble if that were the case. Tell me what's going on inside that brainy head of yours."

"You know that the baby wasn't planned. It was something that just happened. And I was happy about it. I had all these plans that suddenly changed when I got pregnant. I was publishing my work. I was traveling the world conducting research. I was teaching at some of the most respected universities in the world. And then I put it all on hold for Elias, for the family I was going to have with him."

"And now that family is gone."

"And now I can't help but wonder if my mother was right. Maybe in its own terrible, tragic way, this was for the best. I lost some of myself in him. I think I might want it back."

Ava's expression was neutral for a moment, but then Cricket saw understanding in her eyes. "You're not sure if you're meant for the quiet life of dedicated wife and mother."

"I love him, Ava. Only God knows how much I do, but he wants a bunch of kids. He wants to be the kind of father you had. He wants to recreate his childhood with our children, but we aren't your parents. Elias is a surgeon, and I lived with a surgeon before. It's three-day shifts and twenty-hour surgeries. It's constant maneuvering to get to the top. And

I'll be alone again. But this time it will be worse, because I'll be alone with children who are barely going to know their father."

"I see your point." Ava nodded. "This is heavy. Have you talked to Elias about it?"

"What am I supposed to say? 'Give up your dream, the thing you've worked so hard to achieve so I won't be lonely'? 'Forget about all those lives you could have saved and stay home with me so we can watch TV together'? I can't say any of those things to him, because I know him too well. He would give them up to make me happy, because he thinks that's what a good husband should do, even if, in the long run, it makes him unhappy. I don't want him to be unhappy. I couldn't live with myself if he were."

"And he couldn't bear it if you were, either."

"What do you think I should do?"

"The thing that's the hardest to do. Compromise. It's the only way to make things work."

They had been back on Hideaway Island for over a week now. Cricket had been very quiet—most days she holed herself up in her office, claiming that she had to write. He knew that she had to write, that she had a book that was overdue, but part of Elias felt that Cricket was hiding herself from him. For some reason he'd thought that they would fall into some sort of routine when they got back, but there was no routine for them to fall into. Everything was so up in the air. Nothing had been settled. Not about her parents, or where they would live. They had no further discussions of their future. They were just drifting along.

Elias had gone back to picking up shifts at the local hospital and seeing patients as a primary care physician to pass the time. He was ready to go back to surgery. Physically. His hand had never felt better, but mentally...he wasn't sure yet. Maybe he was afraid he had lost his passion. Maybe he was afraid of being out of practice for so long, thought he would screw it up. Or maybe he just wasn't ready to leave his wife. They ate dinner together every night. They shared breakfast in the morning. There was nothing too important that happened in the small island hospital that he couldn't pick up the phone and call her when he wanted to.

But if he went back, followed the career path he'd always wanted, this simple, quiet life he had gotten used to would disappear. And yet he had already taken the first steps to being a surgeon again.

"You look very handsome in a suit. I haven't seen you in one since our wedding day," Cricket said to him as she smoothed her hand down his lapel.

"That was a good day." He leaned down to kiss her lips gently.

"Was it? I don't recall either of us being particularly happy."

"I was nervous and scared. I knew my life was about to change forever. How were you feeling?"

"Like you hated me."

"You know that's not true now, don't you?"

She hugged him tightly, resting her cheek against his chest. He felt the subtle sadness in her, and it worried him. "You're my all-time favorite husband."

"Have there been other husbands that I was unaware of?"

"You're the first, but I think I might be one of those women who would like to get married five or six times. Variety is the spice of life, you know. But I'll always have a soft spot for my first."

He grinned at her and smoothed his hand down her back. "Where will I be while you are marrying all these other men? Unless you plan on doing away with me."

"I don't know where you'll be." They had been joking, but there was a seriousness in her voice that he couldn't ignore.

"Are you sure you're okay with me going in to Miami for the meeting with Florida General?"

"You're better than Florida General. It's the worst hospital in the city. If you were hurt, I wouldn't want you to be treated there."

"But I could turn things around, or at least help to."

"You're talented and brilliant and sexy, and they would be lucky to have you. You'll be fine wherever you end up."

"Cricket, I..." He wanted to say that he loved her, but something stopped him. He hoped he had been reading too much into it, but the past couple of days, she'd been talking as if he had plans of going through this journey without her.

Wherever you *end up.* You *have to decide what* you *want*.

It was never *we*. It bothered him, and more than that, he worried about what she saw for their future.

"What is it?" She looked up at him.

"I'm not staying overnight in Miami. I'll be back on the last ferry."

"I'll pick you up."

"This is just a meeting. I don't even know if I want the job. I have a few options. I thought I would investigate this one in case you wanted to stay close to home."

"I want you to go where you'll be happy." She kissed his cheek. "Come on, let's get you to the ferry. You don't want to be late."

Chapter 15

When Cricket arrived back at the house after dropping Elias off at the ferry, she noticed a familiar car parked in the driveway. She would recognize her mother's sleek black Aston Martin anywhere. Part of Cricket wanted to turn her car around and hide out in the ice cream parlor downtown for the next few hours, gorging herself on hot-fudge sundaes until she was sure her mother had left.

But she knew she couldn't do that. For all her mother's faults, she hadn't raised a woman who ran away from conflict. Cricket knew that this conversation had to happen. Realistically she knew she couldn't go on not speaking to her mother. Her family was so small. There was no way it could continue to be fractured.

Cricket got out of her car, but instead of walking inside her house, she walked around to the back and found her mother sitting on the sand just beyond the house. Her shoes were off, her toes buried in the cool sand. It wasn't a side of her mother that Cricket saw often. But she had seen it before. They used to vacation on this island. And there had been one glorious summer when Cricket had both of her parents there for an entire two months. Her mother had hurt her knee in an accident and couldn't work, and her father had decided to take off time to be with them. It was one of the few times in Cricket's life when she'd felt like she had a real family. A normal family that spent time together.

"I thought you said that one of the rudest things a person could do was drop by unexpectedly."

"That doesn't apply to mothers." Dr. Lundy looked up at her. "Mothers are allowed to say and do rude things to their daughters, and their daughters are just supposed to know that their mothers love them and respect them and don't mean to hurt them."

"Hmm." Cricket sat next to her mother. "Is that right?"

"Yes." She was quiet for a moment. "You're really in love with him, aren't you?"

"From the day I met him."

"And he's good to you, isn't he? He quit his job

at my hospital. I've heard he's been looking around the country. I've gotten calls about him already."

"He's a damn good doctor. I hope you recognize that. If he treats his patients anywhere near as good as he treats me, you shouldn't let him go."

"He's not playing hardball, is he? This isn't a ploy to force my hand."

"No, Mom. It's not about his job. It never was. The way you carry on about it makes me feel like you think that somebody like Elias couldn't possibly be in love with someone like me. That I'm so stupid, I would allow this man to get me pregnant and marry me in order to further his career. There are more important things than work. But it doesn't seem that way to you."

"Of course he could fall in love with you. You're beautiful and brilliant. I'm your mother. I don't think anyone is good enough to be with you. You have to admit that this situation was odd. He's my top doctor, whom I banned from my hospital for punching a patient's boyfriend, and then he shows up married to my only child. And you were pregnant. What would you have thought if you were me?"

"We really wanted that baby. Elias really wanted to be a father and—"

"I hurt you both deeply by diminishing your loss. But what I failed to make clear to you is that I have seen how deeply Elias loves you over the past few months. He worries about you. He takes care of you, and when you were in the hospital he was barking out orders like he was in charge of the world just to make sure you got what you needed. He's a good man and a good husband. I'm glad you married him. You can get pregnant again—right away, if you would like—your father and I would be overjoyed to have a grandchild. But now you have this time to spend together. Take advantage of it. Learn how to be together. I had five years with your father before we had you, and I think that time was good for us. We knew who we were and what we wanted out of life individually before we brought you into this world."

Her mother had just said something very deep to her. Cricket needed to know who she was and what she wanted from life, because she didn't think she could ever truly be a good wife to Elias if she didn't.

Elias had gotten out of bed very quietly that morning. He was off to the Midwest for another interview. This time it was a big one. A dream job at one of the best hospitals in the nation. For the past few weeks he had been traveling all over Florida, interviewing for jobs. He had been offered a few positions as head of a department at lower-ranking hospitals. They would keep him fairly close to his family, but he knew that with his long hours and being even farther away from Hideaway Island that he would rarely get to see them. He knew he wouldn't be happy at those places. And if he was going to be away from his family, he might as well be at a place he could be proud to work for, so he was taking this chance.

He had to be on the first ferry out that morning, so he had said goodbye to Cricket last night. They had made love for hours. He hadn't meant to. He had simply meant to kiss her, but that kiss had turned into more and he couldn't stop himself. He couldn't just take her once; he had to take her as many times as he could until they both passed out from exhaustion. He knew that he should have gone to sleep so he could be well rested for his journey, but he had needed her more than he needed the eight hours. The way she had clung to him afterward... It was as if she was telling him that she didn't want him to leave her.

But not once had she asked him not to go. She had been nothing but supportive these past few weeks. She left good-luck messages on his phone. Tucked notes into his suit pockets, encouraged him the way any good wife would. But there was something she wasn't telling him, something she was holding back. He had felt it ever since they got back from Costa Rica, but he couldn't put his finger on exactly what it was.

He walked back into their bedroom, fully dressed and ready to go. He just needed to kiss her one last time before he left. Even though he'd said goodbye to her last night, he couldn't leave without doing that. But instead of finding her curled up beneath the covers, he saw her sitting in her overstuffed armchair, looking out the window. She was wearing a simple sundress, her curls wild, her eyes still sleepy.

"What you are doing out of bed?"

"I thought you had gone already. I was waiting for my lover to come in and ravage me."

He grinned at her. "I still have time to murder a man before I leave."

"I'm taking you all the way to the airport. I booked passage for the car on the ferry. I'm going to be with you until security separates us."

"You don't have to do that. It's out of the way."

"It isn't. I'm planning to spend the day with my father. He's going to make me French toast and then take me to the toy store." She was quiet for a moment. "I need to take you to the airport, Elias. You'll be gone longer than overnight. This will be the longest we've been apart since we got married."

"It's only a couple of days."

"I'm going to have to get used to being alone once you go back to being a surgeon full-time."

"That's not true."

"But it is. I grew up with a surgeon. Your patients will have to come first. I know that. I'm prepared for it."

It would be just like before. Fifteen-hour surgeries. Exhaustion. Shifts that never seemed to end, but he had found huge satisfaction out of it. A huge sense of accomplishment. But now he had a wife whom he found more than satisfaction with, whom he found happiness with. Maybe going back and doing what he loved and being with the woman he loved at the same time would make him even happier, or maybe it would pull him in too many different directions.

In order to give his all to what mattered the most, something else he loved was going to have to suffer.

"Do you want me to stay home? I won't go to this interview. Just say the word and I'll stay."

"No. You're going to go. You're going to be offered this job."

"You don't know that."

"I do. I know my mother put in a good word for you. She's well respected across the country."

"You didn't ask her to do that, did you? I want to be hired on my own merits."

"I didn't have to ask her, and you should know my mother well enough by now to know that she won't do anything she doesn't believe is right. She has worked with you. She knows how good a surgeon you are. You deserve this job."

"I wish you would stop being the supportive wife and tell me what you want."

"That's easy. I want you to be happy. That's all I've ever wanted."

"Kiss me." He took a step toward her, and she put up her hand to stop him.

"I'll only kiss you when we are saying goodbye at the airport. You know what happens when we start kissing. I end up pregnant. You end up out of a job. You won't be blaming me for this one."

"Kissing you is what led me to marrying you."

"I know."

"I wouldn't take back that kiss, even if my life depended on it."

She looked at him for a long moment with so much emotion in her eyes, it nearly took his breath away. "I'm getting my keys and leaving this bedroom right now. Neither one of us will be safe if I don't."

She was right to go, because if he was with her any longer, he would miss his flight.

Cricket's father kissed her forehead the next morning. She had just planned to spend the day in Miami before she headed back to the island, but she couldn't force herself to leave the warmth of her parents' home. Her house would feel too empty without Elias. The sheets would smell of his skin. There would be little signs of him all over the place. She didn't want to face it. Having him and not being able to be with him was far worse than never having had him at all.

"Good morning, princess."

"Good morning, Daddy. How did you sleep last night?"

"Okay. I heard you wandering around last night."

"I'm sorry. I didn't mean to wake you."

"I wasn't awake because I heard you. I was awake because I was concerned about you."

"Why?" She looked up at her father, who clearly was worried. "I'm fine."

"Bug, I know you better than you know yourself."

"I got an email last night from a colleague I used to work with in Boston. He offered me a job. They are starting a new medical anthropology department at the university he heads. He wants me to run it. But the job is in London. I would head up a department in one of the most prestigious universities in the world."

"Tell me what you want to hear from me, and I'll say it."

She frowned in confusion. "Tell me what you think about it. I want you to be truthful."

"If you think I want my only child living on a different continent, you're insane. But I also recognize how big of an opportunity this is for you, and I will be excited for you. Still, this brings up a hundred more questions."

"Like how I can entertain a job offer when my husband is interviewing for his dream job in Wisconsin?"

"Yes, and more importantly, is this job in London that you weren't looking for one that you want to take?"

It was a good question, one that made her pause and think. "I don't want to be just the wife of a surgeon. I want to do more with my career. I want to leave a mark on this world, and for a moment that job offer seemed like an amazing thing, but then I got a text from Elias's sister. She was just checking in on me. She said she would come over if I wanted, because she knows I have a hard time going to sleep without him."

"She sounds like a wonderful person."

"His entire family is wonderful. I don't know how I would have gotten through these past few months without them, and it's made me realize that I don't want to leave Hideaway Island. I want to be close to my parents. I want to be surrounded by family. All the time."

"That's a beautiful thing, Cricket. You need to tell your husband that."

"I will. As soon as he calls me tonight."

Chapter 16

Instead of calling Cricket, like he usually did when he was away on these trips, Elias pulled out his laptop and opened his video-chat app. He had never been this far away from her since they had gotten married. He had never gone so long without seeing her face, and while he had been busy, meeting with the heads of the hospital and touring the massive groundbreaking facility, he missed Cricket. He missed having dinner with her every night. He missed sharing coffee with her in the morning. And he was very aware that all that would change the moment he accepted a position as a surgeon again.

Cricket accepted the call, and seeing her pretty face put him at ease. She was in a pink nightie, her thin cotton bathrobe hanging loosely around her shoulders, and he could see just a hint of her skin, which was sweet and arousing at the same time.

"Hello, my husband."

"Hello, my wife. How are you today?"

"I'm okay. I stayed at my parents' house last night. When I came home, I had a long lunch with Virginia and Ava. We went shopping and then came back to the house and made cupcakes."

"You made cupcakes?" He grinned. Cricket had never baked. She had just started to cook a couple of months ago, out of necessity. She'd said that she needed to learn how to feed their child, but baking was something entirely different.

"Virginia said it was what girls do when they get together sometimes."

"Did you like it?"

"I loved it. I wish she had never shown me how to do it. I'm afraid I'll now have to eat cupcakes at least twice a week."

"I'll help you eat them."

"So tell me how everything went. I've been nervous for you."

"Everything went incredibly well. I thought Miami Mercy had state-of-the-art equipment, but you should see this place. They are on the cutting edge of medicine. The work they do here will change millions of lives. I was honored to even be considered and was blown away that they offered me a spot on their cardiothoracic team."

"You got the job! I knew you would get it." She smiled at him. "Are you okay with giving up trauma? I don't think you'll see much of it there."

"I wanted trauma for the excitement, but here I'll get to perform experimental procedures, try new techniques. I'll be learning from the best. That is, if you think I should take it."

"Of course I think you should take it! We've been through this before. This is an opportunity that you can't pass up. Take the job. I know you'll love it. When do you start?"

"That's the thing—they want me to start immediately. The surgeon I would be replacing is retiring, and he wants me to shadow him and get the lay of the land before he goes. They want me there tomorrow. They will pay for temporary housing and all our moving expenses. I just need you to overnight me some stuff. I was thinking that you could join me early next week."

The happy mask Cricket had been wearing slipped from her face, and the sadness that she had been hiding for the past few weeks was now evident. He had been waiting for it to appear. He knew in his gut that she hadn't been okay with any of this.

"I won't be joining you next week, Elias."

"Then when? The week after?"

"I don't know how long it will take. I've decided I don't want to leave Hideaway Island. I need to be near family. Yours and my own, and in Wisconsin, I know I won't be able to be happy."

"But you just told me to take the job. Do you want me to reject the offer?"

"No, I want you to take it. You have to take it. You'll live there, and I'll stay here. This job will be a huge part of your life, and I don't want you worrying about me or my happiness. I want you to stay there and do what you are meant to do. Do what you would be doing if we had never met and I had never gotten pregnant."

"What about us?"

"Maybe we need to be apart for a while. You need to adjust to your job, and I need to figure out what I'm going to do about my own. I've still got research that I want to conduct overseas. There are still things I want to accomplish, and this might be the perfect time."

What she was saying made sense. Logically he knew that if she wanted to go overseas, this would be the best time for her to do it. He was going to be incredibly busy, not just with surgery but with learning all the aspects of his new job. He wouldn't be able to be with her very often. Because he knew if he took the job here, his pride wouldn't allow him to give anything but his all. But he still felt crushed. Like somebody had squeezed him until every ounce of oxygen had left his body.

This felt like an ending. It *was* an ending, because they both knew they couldn't have a real marriage with both of them so far away and so focused on their careers.

"Is this what you really want, Cricket?" It wasn't what he wanted, but there was no compromising here. One of them would have to give up something major, and he wanted her to be happy.

Maybe being married to him didn't make her happy.

She opened her mouth to respond, but it seemed as if the words stuck in her throat. She said nothing, just nodded once, the tears welling in her eyes.

"This feels bad," he admitted. "A few months ago I was planning the rest of my life, and now we're talking about being apart."

"You wouldn't have married me if I wasn't pregnant. We both know that. I wasn't in your plans. Being a surgeon was in your plans."

How could he argue with that? He had never planned to get hurt, either, or to meet her, or to fall so damn hard in love, but it had happened and he didn't regret a moment of it. But clearly she did.

"I have to go, Elias." She swiped the tears from her face. "But I love you. I was in love with you the day I married you, and I don't think I'll ever be able to stop."

The screen went blank, and he jumped up from his chair. "What!" But she was gone, and soul-crushing devastation bloomed into something that felt a lot like hope.

He picked up his cell phone and dialed her number, but she didn't pick up. His next call was to a taxi.

Elias had called Cricket once. Just once. Then nothing all night. She hadn't picked up the phone the one time he called, because she couldn't listen to what he had to say. But his continued silence said far more than any words could. He was okay with them going their separate ways. And it confirmed what she had expected all along. She had interrupted his life. A wife was the last thing he had wanted. She had given him back his freedom. It was the logical thing to do. It was the right thing to do, but it was the hardest thing she'd ever had to do.

She'd tried not to cry last night, because crying wouldn't change a thing. She had fallen in love. It had been a beautiful few months. She couldn't regret it, because now she knew how well she should be treated. She knew what a truly good man was. She knew what passion and true lust were. She knew it was possible to feel deep, unending emotion for someone, and she'd learned that she was worthy of love. There was no way she could regret this marriage, but she could mourn it. Because she was fairly certain there wasn't another man on earth that she could love more than Elias.

She got out of bed and walked out to the beach to sit in the cool sand. It was early in the morning. There weren't signs of any people. It was peaceful. The sound of the waves gently lapping the shore soothed her. This place was so damned beautiful. She had traveled the world, but her soul kept pulling her back here. This was where she wanted to spend her life. This was home for her.

"You can't just tell a man that you're in love with him and then hang up before he responds."

She turned around to see Elias standing on the beach behind her. He looked rumpled and exhausted, but he was there—and her heart stopped beating. He was supposed to be over a thousand miles away in Wisconsin.

"What are you doing here? You're supposed to be accepting that job."

"I'm here to yell at you. Why the hell didn't you answer my call?" He walked closer to her. "I had to take four connecting flights and travel all night. I haven't had any sleep, and now I'm mad as hell."

"You only called once. I thought it was a mistake. You didn't even leave a message."

"Oh, so you did hear the phone? You just ignored it. And there I was wondering if you had gotten abducted by aliens or kidnapped. I was thinking the worst, and you just didn't want to pick up my call."

"I didn't want to hear what you had to say."

"Why not?"

"I didn't want to hear you let me down easy."

"Let you down easy? Let you down easy! You don't know me at all, do you?"

"I know that you have wanted to be a surgeon your entire life. That you went to medical school to be a doctor because your father couldn't follow his dreams. I know that you never planned to have a wife. I know if you'd had it your way, we never would have seen each other again."

"You're an idiot."

"You're an ass!"

"I'm an ass who's in love with you." He knelt down before her. "Can't you tell, Cricket? Can't you feel how much I love you?"

"I wish you'd told me that sooner. I thought you were just being nice."

"I'm not that nice! Nobody is that nice, Cricket. This is about you thinking you're not enough. But when the hell are you going to get it? When are you going to trust me enough to know that I'm not going to hurt you?"

"When you love somebody as much as I love you, it's scary. I keep thinking that this can't be real. That it's impossible for anything to be this good."

"I fell in love with you that first night we met. We were on the beach. It was twilight, and I couldn't stop looking at you. I only stayed away afterward because I didn't trust my feelings. I thought love at first sight was crap, but I loved you, and then you told me you were pregnant and I knew I had my shot to marry you without you thinking I was insane."

She frowned at him. "I *did* think you were insane."

"But you said yes when you didn't have to, and I asked you when I knew we could coparent without being a couple. I knew being with you was better than being without you. I want to be with you. I want to stay married to you for the rest of my life. I'm in love with you. What do I have to do to prove it to you?"

She had felt the same exact way. Never before had she experienced such a rush of feelings for anyone. She'd never thought that emotions like that were possible. At least not for her. And that's why she made no move to keep their connection going. She thought it was a fluke, and because of that she'd almost lost out on the love of her life. They had almost lost out on each other.

"You came home," she said as tears slipped down her face. "That's enough." She cupped his face and pressed her lips to his. "But what about your career? That's a job of a lifetime."

"You won't be happy there and I won't be happy without you, so it's not a question for me. I need to be where you are."

Cricket closed her eyes. "I feel so damn guilty. That's why I told you to stay! You weren't supposed to come rushing back here and make me love you more. I won't be able to forgive myself if I let you give up this job for me." She opened her eyes. "Call them and tell them there was an emergency here. I'll go back with you. We'll make it work—as long as we love each other, I know we can make things work."

He sat beside her in the cool sand and looked out at the ocean. "There's only one problem with that plan. I called them last night and turned down the position."

"Why did you do that? I could have wanted a divorce. You shouldn't have been so impulsive."

"You sound like your mother."

"You take that back!"

He chuckled and slipped his hand into hers. For somebody who had just thrown away his shot at a dream job, he was awfully relaxed. Happy, even. "I turned down that job because I have a shot at something I want more."

"You're going back to Miami Mercy? Did my mother tell you that she was going to make you the head of trauma?"

"No. I'm going to be working full-time at Hideaway Hospital. Instead of having the people here go off island for surgery, I'm going to operate here."

"Is that what you really want to do?"

"The job comes with amazing benefits."

"Does it?"

"I'll get to have coffee with my wife every morning. I'll get to eat dinner with her when I come home. I'll get to go to my children's soccer games. I get to have a life and be happy. I get to be with the woman I love as much as I possibly can."

"Those do sound like good benefits." She rested her head on his shoulder. "Remind me to send Giselle a thank-you card."

He looked over at her, surprised. "Why do you need to thank her?"

"Because if she wasn't who she was, then you never would have pretended to be my boyfriend and I would have never fallen in love with you that night."

"I think we need to send her more than a card. Maybe a bottle of wine and some flowers."

"And an invitation to our wedding."

"We had one of those already."

"I know, but I think I would like to have another ceremony. Right here on the island in front of our families."

"Nothing would make me happier than to marry you all over again."

* * * * *

THE COMMANDING
ITALIAN'S CHALLENGE

MAYA BLAKE

CHAPTER ONE

FLY WITH THE ANGELS, mio dolce.

Maceo Fiorenti brushed a kiss over the petals of the single long-stemmed white rose, one of the specially cultivated ones imported from Holland that his wife—his *late* wife—had adored.

Carlotta had indulged in that extravagance, despite his gardener vowing he could recreate the genus right here in their Napoli home. She'd smilingly refused, insisting there was something special in having the flowers flown in twice weekly.

Of course Maceo had indulged her little whim. In their nine years of marriage he could count on the fingers of one hand the occasions when he'd said no to Carlotta Caprio-Fiorenti.

Those occasions had been triggered by her misguided attempts to make him into someone other than the man he saw in the mirror every day. A futile exercise to try to sway him from the path his actions had dictated for him. From a future that should rightly exact just penance for his actions. On those occasions, while it had pained him to see her heartache, he hadn't been swayed. How could he, when he didn't deserve a single breath he took, much less any semblance of happiness?

His lips twisted.

It was almost as if in those moments Carlotta had forgotten everything that had happened.

Had forgotten who he was. What he'd done.

Maceo Fiorenti—heir to a legacy he'd had no choice but to safeguard. Cursed with a destiny he couldn't walk away from because doing so would be the ultimate betrayal. He hadn't taken joy in showing Carlotta a glimpse of the demons that drove him. He'd simply reminded her that *he'd* been the cause of her ultimate heartache. *He'd* taken away the *famiglia* she'd held so dear.

There would be time enough to mourn this latest death—and its attendant layers of bitterness, shame and guilt—when he was far away from here.

For now, he had a legacy to protect. And as the sole remaining vanguard protect it he would, even if it took his last breath.

So what if in his darkest moments he questioned just why he was hanging on?

Because your conscience won't let you stop.

Casa di Fiorenti wasn't just his birthright. It was what his parents and his godfather, Luigi, had lived for. Died for. He owed it to them to keep their legacy alive. Even if he was dead inside. Even if he was haunted with the certainty that he would never enjoy a moment of happiness.

He allowed the tips of his fingers to brush one corner of the pristine white-and-gold coffin in one last, lingering caress.

Let go.

Jaw gritted, he released the flower. The heaviness in his heart grew but he pushed it down. He'd refused to acknowledge that this day was coming, that within months of her cancer diagnosis he'd have to face a future of truly being alone. Now he had no choice.

Maceo locked his knees against the ridiculous but serious threat of them giving way.

'Show no weakness.'

They were the words she'd spoken to him a little over a decade ago, when guilt had threatened to eat him alive, to rob him of the strength to rise from the ashes of his life. Words he'd absorbed, branded into his skin until they'd fused to his soul.

A deep breath and the moment of weakness rightly retreated.

He was *Maceo Fiorenti*. And, as much as it had been trifling sport for him and Carlotta to give the paparazzi fodder to gleefully splash gossip within the sordid pages of their tabloids for most of their married life, today wasn't a day for courting notoriety.

Carlotta was six feet under, reunited—as had been her final wish—with Luigi, her first husband, and Maceo's own parents. But for a twist of fate—ironically of his own making—Maceo, too, would be entombed in this family crypt alongside his family.

But he was very much alive. Despite the odds.

'A miracle', the papers had branded his return to the land of the living twelve years ago. Some had even called him *lucky*.

If only they knew the demons that haunted him. If only they had a taste of the guilt and regret that weighed him down.

Minutes passed as he stared down at the coffin. Minutes during which he felt eyes boring into his very skin. Board members. Acquaintances. Strangers. Sizing him up. Attempting to seek out his weaknesses.

They could try all they liked.

Half an hour later, once the *cardinale* had said his final blessing, Maceo turned his back on his family's final resting place and, ignoring everyone present, made his way across the sun-baked graveyard to his waiting car.

His driver sprang to attention, murmuring words of condolence Maceo didn't acknowledge as he opened the door.

Acknowledging them would mean accepting that he was alone in the world. Sure, as Carlotta's widower he would be saddled with a few dozen Caprios, who shamelessly laid claim to him in one in-law capacity or another. But flesh-and-blood-wise, with no siblings or extended family to speak of, he was the sole remaining Fiorenti.

Alone.

He slid into the back seat, plucked the shades from his eyes and tossed them aside. Exhaling loudly, he massaged the bridge of his nose, willing the tension headache away.

'You wish to return to the villa, *signor*?' his driver asked, disturbing the momentary eerie quiet.

Maceo opened his mouth to confirm that he did, but at the last moment shook his head. Why prolong the inevitable? It was Friday afternoon, and most of his staff had been given the day off to pay their respects to Carlotta, but there was work to be done.

And, no, his reluctance to return to the villa in Capri had nothing to do with the empty *salones* and corridors awaiting him, newly devoid of Carlotta's presence.

'Take me to the helipad. I'm returning to the office.'

With a nod, the older man drove him away from his wife's graveside and the crowd of Napoli's high society, all vying to see him do something worth gossiping about.

Maceo barely registered the helicopter ride that deposited him two streets away from the temporary headquarters of Casa di Fiorenti.

When she'd known the end was near, Carlotta had requested to be closer to the Capri summer home she'd shared with Luigi and Maceo's parents. He'd willingly relocated his company from Rome to the sprawling eighteenth-century building overlooking Naples Harbour. The building where, predictably, two dozen paparazzo now waited, rabid, with long lenses and sharp questions the moment they spotted him.

He slid his sunglasses back on, allowed himself the faintest sigh.

'Maceo! What would Carlotta think of you returning to work even before she's in the ground?'

'Maceo, any plans to make your brothers-in-law directors now Carlotta's gone?'

'Maceo, when will you make an announcement about who will fill your late wife's shoes?'

Teeth gritted, he charged forward, leaving his body-guards to deal with the throng. It bemused him that they continued to throw questions at him when he never answered. Did they truly expect him to divulge all his dark, guilty secrets simply because they demanded it? Especially when the games he and Carlotta had played with them had been meant to hide the biggest, most terrible secret of them all?

He shoved at the heavy door separating his empire from the gossip-hungry mob, his gut tightening at the reminder of the other bombshell Carlotta had thrown at his feet a week ago. He had to compliment her timing. She'd known he'd be incapable of challenging her in any way. That because of that heavy boulder of guilt he carried he would grant her wishes, regardless of the shock and fury boiling in his stomach at her news.

But, while he'd agreed to honour Carlotta's final requests, he'd withheld how he intended to proceed. That was between him and the woman he'd hadn't known existed until a week ago.

Luigi had been previously married, albeit briefly, to an Englishwoman. A woman who'd had a daughter. Another secret his parents and godfather had kept from him.

Maceo's gut tightened with fresh bitterness. They'd blithely ignored the *famiglia* they'd purportedly valued and burdened him with honouring their wishes.

More than that, Maceo had also discovered that Casa di Fiorenti, the confectionery empire his grandparents and parents had built thirty years ago, which *he'd* turned into a multi-billion-euro conglomerate, didn't belong wholly and exclusively to him. That a slice—albeit a very small slice, which he probably wouldn't miss if it broke off and fell into the Mediterranean Sea, but was nevertheless *his* by right—

belonged to a faceless, grasping gold-digger, already sharpening her claws in anticipation of a hefty payday.

A woman named Faye Bishop.

Carlotta had kept tabs on her from afar over the years, and reached out in the past few months without much success.

And now Maceo was supposed to tolerate this woman for a stretch of time, fulfilling Carlotta's last wish.

Anger intensified as he stalked into his private lift.

Faye Bishop had dangled a promise to his dying wife she'd had no intention of keeping. Yet she'd found the time to email his lawyers and accept their invitation to attend the will reading next week.

A dark anticipatory smile curved his lips as he stabbed the button for his office.

Faye Bishop might have succeeded in pulling the wool over Carlotta's eyes.

Maceo would savour teaching her a lesson she would never forget.

Faye resisted the urge to glance at the sleek, near-silent clock, gracefully sweeping its way towards noon. For one thing, it would only confirm that just twenty seconds had passed since she last checked. For another, it wouldn't dissipate the weird sensation of being watched.

Although, thinking about it, it wasn't that strange. Every wall in the stunning conference room she sat in was made of smoky glass, in sharp contrast to the shiny clear surfaces of the vast table and chairs, the cabinets and the sci-fi-looking communication system poised in the middle of the table. The smoked glass was most likely a two-way mirror, allowing her to be gawped at and gossiped about without being any the wiser.

Besides feeling a world away from the remote Devon farm she'd travelled from yesterday, Faye knew her feeling of being a fish out of water extended beyond the sensation prickling her skin. After all, she'd put considerable effort into resembling a fish out of water. So, really, she couldn't fault anyone for gawping. In fact...

She aimed a look at the centre of the widest glass wall and smiled.

Imagining she'd startled one or even several people with her *you can't intimidate me* smile, she relaxed as a layer of tension eased away.

The bulk of her anxiety remained, though. It was a different sensation from that generated by the clutch of tabloid journalists downstairs, who'd pounced on her the moment she'd stepped out of the taxi, but just as unnerving.

More than once in the last hour she'd considered walking out.

If only she hadn't answered her phone all those weeks ago. If only she hadn't made Carlotta Caprio that promise. One she now felt obligated to keep after learning of the older woman's death.

You don't owe her or Luigi's family anything. You should leave them in the past, where they belong.

Her smile died. It was too late. Luigi was gone, taking all Faye's bewildered questions to his grave. And now his wife was dead too.

Really, she had no business being here, grasping at straws and hoping that maybe someone had answers for her—

Her thoughts stalled as the door to the conference room sprang open. Her notions of leaving evaporated, replaced by different questions as she froze.

Questions like what the identity of the man who'd entered was—because he looked *nothing* like a lawyer. Sure, he'd aced the ruthless cut-throat demeanour well enough to evoke images of sharpened blades and sharks' teeth. But there was something else. Something barely contained, something electrifying that gripped her and tightened its hold as seconds ticked by.

Seconds during which she was aware she was gawping. With eyes wide and her mouth possibly hanging open. Seconds during which she couldn't summon a single command her brain was willing to follow. Like blink. Swallow.

Slow down her runaway heartbeat.

The fact that this non-lawyer seemed equally fascinated with her was neither here nor there. Faye was aware that she attracted dumbfounded looks wherever she went. Partly because of her eclectic clothing. Possibly because of the profusion of hennaed flowers climbing up her right arm. But mostly because of the uniqueness of her hair.

She was pleased she resisted the sudden urge to reach up and smooth down the silver, lilac and purple tresses knotted haphazardly atop her head, especially when the stranger's gaze rose to rest there.

What she *wasn't* pleased about was her inability to look away. Her utter, almost helpless absorption with him. She shouldn't, *couldn't* be this affected.

Yes, he was indescribably handsome—enough to give every Roman god a run for his money and easily come out on top.

Yes, he commanded the very air around the room, as if harnessing it to power his godlike form and leaving none for mere mortals.

But liaisons and connections with members of the opposite sex, after that single traumatic event with Matt two years ago, had been permanently delisted from her life.

Aware that her whole body was clenched in peculiar expectancy, as if awaiting some sort of trigger to bring her back to life, she attempted to drag herself free of his forcefield.

A throat was cleared, disrupting the charged atmosphere.

'*Signor...*' A man, who thankfully did resemble a lawyer, spoke in low tones from behind the formidable figure.

The formal address was the only thing Faye understood. The rest of the hushed Italian buzzed in her brain as more men filed into the room, leaving *him* at the door, still blatantly staring at her.

The team of four sat across from Faye at the gleaming conference table, each casting surreptitious glances at various parts of her body. Had she not been wholly enthralled by the man who now sauntered forward with an animal grace that belied his towering height and size to settle into the seat directly opposite hers, she might have been amused.

But this wasn't a jaunt to the pub. Or one of those bring-your-own-instrument-for-a-singalong gatherings her mother spontaneously threw when she was lucid.

She was here because Luigi Caprio had left an indelible mark on her, with the kind of familial love she'd never experienced before, then exited her life without explanation, leaving a worse wreck than he'd found and two lives spiralling out of control.

Faye tried to numb herself against the never healed pain, raked open by Carlotta Caprio.

'How very good of you to make it, Miss Bishop,' the man drawled, once he'd settled his sleek, animal-like frame into the chair, his eyes—which she noted were a rich tawny gold—spearing into her.

Unlike his words, his expression was anything but cordial. For some reason this man despised her.

Her hackles rose, along with a bone-deep shame. Dear God, did he *know*? Had Luigi done the unthinkable and shared Faye and her mother's secret with this man? Would he have been so cruel?

Dread crawled across her skin even as she reassured herself that it didn't matter. Once she left this place she needn't set eyes on this enigmatic man, or any of Luigi's kin, ever again.

She raised her chin. 'I made a promise to Carlotta,' she replied.

It was a promise the other woman had had no business demanding of her. And yet she had. And, because of the curse of the unknown that had always plagued Faye, she'd given in.

The man's lips twisted. 'Ah, *si*… A promise to attend a will reading but not to pay your last respects?'

Her spine snapped straight at his contempt. 'For your information, Mr…whoever-you-are, Carlotta didn't tell me she was ill. Not until our last conversation three weeks ago. After that I didn't think it was appropriate to just…turn up. Not when I was a stranger to her.'

'And yet here you are now,' he said, his deep, rumbling voice and disturbingly attractive accent stretching out the words. Deepening their barbed meaning. Thickening their accusation.

Finally her muscles obeyed the commands she'd shrieked at her brain and lent her enough strength to stand. She pushed back her chair and grabbed the hobo bag she'd tossed on the floor beside her. 'Save your accusations. I was already thinking this was a mistake before you walked in. You've just confirmed that I shouldn't have come here. Let's not waste each other's time any longer. I'm leaving.'

'I'm afraid it's not going to be that easy, Miss Bishop.'

Her fingers tightened around the strap of her bag. 'What isn't? And, seriously, are you going to introduce yourself, like a normal person, or is your identity some mystery I'm supposed to unravel to get to the next level of why I'm here?'

More than one lawyer gasped. Her impression of stepping deeper into a minefield heightened as the stranger's gaze swept downwards in a slow, languid journey from her face, her throat, her chest, to rest on the three-inch gap between her midriff-baring pink top and the waistband of her bohemian ankle-length, patchwork skirt. There it rested, partly in disbelief, partly with a sizzling indecipherable look that sent gooseflesh skittering over her skin.

'Sit down,' he commanded after an aeon, his voice barely above a murmured rumble.

Faye couldn't, because the look in his eyes had para-lysed her again. And as he continued to watch her, other sensations crept in, adding to the chaos. Weakness swept through her frame. Her breasts began to tingle, shooting warnings that her bra-less state was about to become glar-ingly obvious.

To counteract that impending discomfort, Faye folded her arms and aimed a glare across the table. 'Why?' she asked, very much aware that his interest had shifted to the inked flowers decorating her arm. That he looked even more... intrigued.

Intrigue didn't last long before his gaze hardened.

'Because I'm about to lay a few facts on you, Miss Bishop. Contrary to what you think you're here for, my revelations will far exceed your wildest dreams. Unfortu-nately for you, those dreams come with strings. Of course once I'm done you can still insist on taking this dubious high road you're posturing about. And should you decide to relinquish your inheritance—'

'My *inheritance*? What inheritance?' Surprise made her voice cringingly squeaky.

'Sit down and I will tell you,' he instructed again.

Shock propelled her legs to obey. She sank into the seat, and in the moment before he spoke again her gaze darted to the lawyers, noting their solemn looks.

'Now, let's pretend you *really* have no clue who I am—'

'I don't. I'm not sure why that's so unfathomable to you, but I haven't the foggiest idea who you are.'

He stared at her for another long, tight stretch. Then he leaned forward. 'My name is Maceo Fiorenti.'

The surname was familiar. Painfully so. She'd blocked it out of her life—albeit unsuccessfully, because of its sheer size and success—because of its association with Luigi.

'I'm assuming that you're in some way connected to Casa di Fiorenti?'

The lawyers exchanged stunned glances.

'You could say that. But I am also… I *was* also connected to Carlotta.'

In her emails, Carlotta had signed off as Carlotta Caprio-Fiorenti. Faye hadn't given the Fiorenti attachment much thought. Now she did, with a peculiar feeling dragging in her stomach.

The man across the conference table was too old to be Carlotta's son, so he could only be—

Faye felt her jaw gaping again and caught herself. 'You're Carlotta's *husband*?' Why did that knowledge send sharp pangs through her chest? 'But you're—' She stopped, bit her lip to cut off the rest of her words.

One masculine brow lifted in mocking query. 'I'm what, Miss Bishop? Too young? A *toy boy*, as you refer to it in your country? Don't be afraid to speak up. You won't be saying anything the media haven't attempted to dissect a million ways.'

Heat flared up her neck, since she'd been about to say exactly that. Carlotta had been in her late-fifties, while Maceo Fiorenti looked at least thirty years younger.

But this wasn't why she was here. Heck, she was still in the dark as to the reason for her presence in this room. With this man who fascinated her far more than she should allow him to.

'Your relationship with Carlotta is none of my business, I'm sure. And now we're properly introduced, perhaps you could enlighten me as to why I'm here?'

'I'm CEO of Casa di Fiorenti and one hundred percent shareholder of this company. Or at least I thought I was until a week ago.'

Faye frowned. 'What does that mean?'

He leaned forward, and every instinct urged her to retreat. She held her ground. Because to appear weak would be to grant him victory.

'It means that my late wife informed me that Luigi—I'm assuming you do know who *he* is?' he drawled.

She steeled herself against the pain that should have dulled after all this time, but curiously hadn't. 'Of course.'

'Meraviglioso,' he said sarcastically. 'My late wife informed me that Luigi had requested that, should he pass away before you turned twenty-five, Carlotta pass on a bequest in her will or when you reached that age. I take it you celebrated your birthday recently?'

Faye nodded absently. 'Three months ago.' Then she caught her breath. 'That's when Carlotta first contacted me. But…why didn't she tell me?'

'Did you give her the chance? Or did you repeatedly rebuff her attempts to reach out to you?' he asked.

She suspected he knew the answer. Guilt flushed through her, but she refused to cower. 'I had my reasons.'

Pain. Betrayal. The stigma of shame that had never gone away. The anxiety of not knowing why Luigi had left and never looked back but had seemingly kept tabs on her.

'No one can love an abomination like you…'

Matt's words echoed in her head, intensifying the anguish. In truth, she'd succeeded in partially silencing the *why* of Luigi's desertion until those damning words. Now she feared she would never move on. Not until she knew if Luigi had felt the same way.

'Ah, but you didn't feel strongly enough about those reasons to stay away because you'd "made a promise", *si?*'

Far from being needled by his determination to get under her skin, Faye forced herself to sit back. To smile and shrug. 'It's obvious you think I have an agenda, so let's dispense with the rhetorical questions and get on with it, shall we? I have…' She made a show of checking the time on the clock before settling her gaze somewhere over his shoulder. From the corner of her eye, she saw his jaw clench. 'I have about half a day's sightseeing before I go back to my hotel.'

Terse silence greeted her. His tawny gaze compelled her. Unable to resist, Faye found herself looking into eyes that held what looked like grief. She couldn't be sure because it had disappeared a second later. What didn't disappear was the guilt that assailed her.

Regardless of what had happened in the past, the anguish Luigi's desertion had caused her and her mother, this man had buried his wife only a few days ago. At the very least she owed him a modicum of compassion.

She opened her mouth, but before she could retract her flippant words he spoke.

'As the executor of Carlotta's will, it falls to me to inform you that, through your stepfather's bequest, you now own a quarter of one percent of a share in Casa di Fiorenti. Signor Abruzzo, kindly inform Miss Bishop what that means in monetary terms.'

One of the lawyers cleared his throat and flipped open a folder while Maceo lounged in his seat, all panther-like grace and piercing eyes, content to stare her down.

The effect of that stare caused her to miss the beginning of the lawyer's heavily accented speech. Forcing herself to concentrate, Faye caught the last of it.

'...at the last financial audit, Casa di Fiorenti was valued at five point six billion euros. Which makes the value of your inheritance approximately fourteen million euros.'

CHAPTER TWO

MACEO WATCHED THE strange creature's full lush lips fall open. Then immediately cursed himself for that unwelcome observation.

Her lips could rival Cupid's bow. So what?

Per l'amor di Dio, she had purple and silver hair! There were other colours in there, too. She was garbed in hippie clothes and one arm was decorated with flowers. Lush lips and dramatically eye-catching figure or not, she belonged on the set of some fairy-tale movie, not in the corporate offices of his billion-euro empire.

So what if her skin was the most flawless he'd ever seen and her indigo eyes seemed almost too good to be true… the most alluring he'd ever looked into?

He'd buried Carlotta just days ago. And, while their marriage hadn't been quite conventional, he owed her the respect of not listing adjectives to describe the shape of another woman's—

'You're joking!'

Her words refocused him. Infused him with the iciness and distance and gravity he should be clinging to— especially now, when Casa di Fiorenti should be his sole occupation.

'Of course I am. Because of course I would choose now, a few days after burying my wife, to make a tasteless joke about her wishes.'

She had the decency to flush. But her contrition lasted only a handful of seconds. 'My reaction wasn't intended as an insult. This really is the last thing I expected.'

'*Is* it? Truly, Miss Bishop?' Maceo didn't bother to hide his scepticism. He didn't intend to hide anything from her. Secrets were what had eroded his family's foundations.

'Yes, it is. *Mr Fiorenti*,' she snapped, her peculiar eyes sparking.

'Then do as you intended before. Refuse it and leave.'

Curiously fascinated, he watched her tilt her head and return his stare. Sunlight danced off the multicoloured strands of her hair and Maceo forced his gaze to remain on her face, attempted to stave off the effect of this woman's presence on his senses.

He'd stopped in his tracks when he spotted her through the glass, certain he was hallucinating. And even after becoming aware that he was drawing the attention of his executive staff Maceo had been unable to move. He'd been stunned at the curious sensations cascading through him— the most startling and damning being the ferocious pounding in his groin. A torrid and wholly unwelcome reminder, today of all days, that he was a man. With primal needs. Needs long and ruthlessly denied because he didn't *deserve* to have them satisfied. Needs denied in order to achieve his goals. To hold on to what his parents had devoted themselves to.

He hadn't survived hell to fall prey to a passing fascination with this pixie-like creature.

'Your lawyers appear uncomfortable with that idea. Why is that, Mr Fiorenti?' she enquired softly, then held up the arm decorated with hennaed flowers. 'Wait—don't answer that. I'll hazard a wild guess, shall I? They're fidgeting because you're not allowed to tell me to do that.' She glanced at the lawyer who had spoken. 'Am I right, sir?'

His lawyer—damn the man—squirmed guiltily. 'That is open to interpretation, but broadly speaking...*si*—'

The blinding, dare-filled smile she'd flashed at the window as he'd stood staring at her from behind the veil of glass—the smile that had stopped every red-blooded employee within the vicinity—curved into view again, complete with groin-tightening dimples, cutting off his lawyer's words.

Maceo's insides dipped in a mixture of arousal and guilt that made his fist curl on the table. Her gaze swung to his hand and the smile dimmed. He frowned, unsure why the look in her eyes disturbed him. He visibly relaxed, but even though her smile remained, it lacked...*something*.

Something he wasn't going to concern himself with.

He leaned forward, eager to get this meeting over and done with. Faye Bishop wasn't the only inconvenience Carlotta had left behind for him to deal with. There was added the nuisance of her brothers.

'The bequest must be administered. But here's the stinger, Miss Bishop. I have the power to add my own stipulations.'

Her smile evaporated completely. 'What?'

'Your reluctance to engage with Carlotta gave her pause. In her will she's given me the power either to make you a very rich woman today or...' He sat back, let his silence speak.

Her lips firmed. 'Or make me jump through hoops for something I had no idea about and didn't want in the first place?'

Maceo delivered a derisive smile. 'Indulge me, then. Get up and walk out. Prove you mean to refuse it.'

He was confident that she wouldn't. No one in their right mind would walk away from such a—

Shock reverberated through him when she rose again. Her indigo eyes effortlessly pierced the layers of his calm until Maceo wasn't sure whether he was breathing in or out. Whether he was going to jump up to stop her leaving or remain seated and watch her go.

The latter.

He most definitely wasn't going to stop her.

She took one step, then another. Despite her tasteless clothes, her grace was unmistakable, and her hips swayed beneath her sweeping skirt with a raw sensuality that made Maceo shift in his seat. And stare.

She reached the door and grabbed the handle. Tension coiled tight within him. Realising his fingers were drumming on the table, he killed the action just as she turned to spear him with a reproving look that would have levelled a lesser man. A man who *hadn't* committed the sins he had and emerged with the demons he fought every day.

'I came here because I thought that after all this time Luigi had provided the answers I've been seeking all these years. I see now it was a waste of time.'

Maceo sent his lawyer a warning glance as the older man opened his mouth. Carlotta's other request, over and above the financial bequest, had been specific—the delivery of a letter addressed to Faye Bishop. He didn't know whether it would provide the answers she claimed to seek, but Maceo knew he would only deliver it when he was absolutely sure of her motives.

'I'm sorry for your loss, Mr Fiorenti. But I hope I never see or hear from you ever again.'

She walked out, leaving astounded silence behind.

'Did she…? Did that really just happen?' one lawyer asked, stunned.

Maceo refused to acknowledge his own astonishment. She had to be playing a game. What she didn't know was that he was an expert at games. He'd been playing them for the better part of a decade with the paparazzi, keeping them distracted so they didn't dig and uncover his family's secrets. The same games he had played with those board members who deemed him weak.

As if on cue, two of his opponents walked in. Stefano and Francesco Castella—Carlotta's older brothers. Maceo's life had taken a fateful turn the night his parents and his godfather had perished, but these two remained a constant reminder that, besides the secrets that had eventually shattered his family, lies and greed were a menace he also had to deal with.

He neutralised his features into a mask of indifference

even as his gaze flicked to the door. What had Faye Bishop meant? What had his godfather done to her?

And how did I not know Luigi had a stepdaughter?

Realising his thoughts were cartwheeling, Maceo pushed the subject of the ethereal Faye Bishop to the back of his mind.

'I didn't realise we were letting in strays off the street these days. Who *was* that curious woman?' Stefano asked.

'She's none of your concern,' Maceo answered, a little taken aback by the bite in his own voice.

Stefano smiled his oily smile. 'Ah, but I'm a board member. That makes everything my concern.'

Maceo swallowed a growl. There was another reason he needed to deal with Faye Bishop. That fraction of a share was the only thing preventing him from having absolute power over the board. However measly, it might be the difference between ridding himself of Stefano and Francesco—who'd made Carlotta's life a living hell until Maceo had stepped in—and enduring their unpalatable presence.

'You're here to discuss your sister's personal affairs. That woman isn't any part of that,' he said.

Stefano shrugged. 'I was simply being civil to pass the time—'

'You don't know the meaning of the word *civil*, so don't insult me.'

Francesco's gaze narrowed. 'Watch your tone, *figlio*. We not only managed this company while you lay incapacitated in a hospital bed and Carlotta was uselessly wringing her hands, we *allowed* you to marry our sister—'

'I was under the impression that decision was entirely *ours*,' Maceo inserted calmly. 'I'm sure that's why we married without informing either of you.'

Stefano slapped his palm on the table. *'Ascoltami—'*

'No. *You* listen,' Maceo interrupted, his patience gossamer-thin. 'Carlotta was too kind-hearted to tell you that she despised both of you. You made her life hell when she married Luigi and you treated her contemptibly at every opportunity until she made you rich. Now she's gone, and I harbour no such inclination. Your positions in this company are secure…for now. Don't push me or your circumstances will change very quickly.'

He rose from the table, itching to be away from this room. He assured himself that the other reason he was so eager to leave had nothing to do with accessing his security team to verify that Faye Bishop had truly left the building.

Casting one last dismissive glance at the brothers, he added, 'Your sister left you some personal effects. I'll leave Signor Abruzzo to apprise you of them.'

He left the room to ringing silence.

One step out the door and he was retrieving his phone. His assistant answered on the first ring. 'Get Security to track down the woman who was just here. Her name is Faye Bishop. I want her back here *pronto*—'

'There's no need, *signor*. Miss Bishop is waiting in your office.'

Maceo slid his phone back into his pocket and told himself the rush of heat through his veins *wasn't* anticipation. Just as he'd dealt with Carlotta's brothers, he would simply deal with another loose end.

With every bone in her body Faye wished she'd had the nerve to keep walking once she'd decided to reject Carlotta's bequest. But…

Pride goes before a fall.

And hers had been one prideful act she'd known, even as it was enfolding, she'd have to go back on. Because, ultimately, this wasn't about her.

It was about her mother.

It was about every woman who needed vital assistance.

Every victim who could use some support to get back on their feet.

She'd made it as far as the breathtaking steel, marble and glass atrium on the ground floor before good sense had kicked in. Thank goodness the receptionist there had accepted her explanation that she had unfinished business with Signor Fiorenti and allowed her to return to the top floor. Surprisingly, she'd been directed to the CEO's office, instead of the conference room, and here she'd been cooling her heels for the last half-hour, pondering the consequences of her hasty decision.

Had she, with a few emotive words, ruined her chances of helping countless women in need? Would the formidable man who had informed her of her inheritance give her the chance to take back her decision?

A hot little tremor shook through her at the thought of facing him again.

Maceo Fiorenti seemed the unforgiving sort who would hold a grudge. Perhaps even enjoy taunting her. Hell, he'd been bristling with rancour before they'd exchanged a word. It was clear he saw her as undeserving of this inheritance. Which meant she had a fight on her hands...

The heavy opaque glass door opened and, as if summoned by her frenzied imagination, he walked in. Faye jumped up from where she'd perched on the edge of the sofa in the vast, dramatically grey-and-glass corner office.

He barely spared her a glance. Crossing the room, he shrugged off his jacket and tossed it towards a sleek-looking coatrack. It landed perfectly, she was sure, but Faye wasn't paying attention to the jacket. Her eyes were riveted on the play of sleek muscles; her mouth drying as she took in the sheer breadth of his shoulders, the sculpted back, trim waist and the hint of washboard abs.

His body was in pristine condition, honed to perfection, with not a single ounce of superfluous flesh on display. Coupled with his height and jaw-dropping features, it was sinful how magnificent he was.

But she wasn't here to admire his physique, enthralling as it was. She was here to reverse the damage she'd done.

She swallowed and opened her mouth, just as he looked up and spoke, his eyes freezing her in place.

'I'm not sure whether to be disappointed at this backtracking or to praise you for the humble pie you're clearly willing to eat by returning.'

So much for hoping he'd let it go.

She forced a shrug. 'You can be both, as long as you hear me out.'

'*Bene*. Let's hear another impassioned speech you don't really mean.'

Faye swallowed her irritation. 'I was too hasty. I shouldn't have said what I said.'

He flicked her a dismissive glance, his lips twisting in faint amusement. 'I have already gathered that much. The question is why did you say it?'

'I meant it at the time. I expected something else when I came here.'

Some small indication that Luigi hadn't found her an abomination. That the harrowing sadness she still glimpsed in her mother's eyes when she was too drugged up to conceal her emotions wasn't the reason Luigi had turned his back on them.

That got Maceo's attention. 'What exactly did you expect from a woman you ignored for weeks?'

'I didn't expect anything from your...from Carlotta.'

Faye wasn't sure why the word *wife* stuck in her throat. Perhaps because she found it difficult to imagine this man married to Carlotta. She grimaced inwardly at the sexist thought. For all she knew they'd been a perfect match, wildly in love.

That curious dart returned, sharper than before. She doubled her efforts to suppress it.

'I wanted to know why Luigi...my stepfather...'

She stopped, unwilling to divulge the depth of her hurt

to a stranger. Even if that stranger had, until recently, been married to the widow of her stepfather.

Faye shook her head. The whole thing was confounding. 'When your lawyers mentioned Carlotta had left something for me, I wasn't expecting it to be shares in Luigi's company.'

His eyes hardened. 'It is a fraction of a single share.'

She shrugged. 'Yes. Whatever...'

'There you go again—pretending you don't give a damn about the fortune that's landed in your lap. You're going to have to do better than this flippant performance, Miss Bishop.'

'It's not a performance. I care about the inheritance, obviously, or I wouldn't have returned. I just wanted something...*more*.'

An expression flickered through his eyes, but he veiled his features with the simple act of glancing down. The avoidance lasted only seconds before he was back to dissecting her with laser-like precision.

'Why now? He's been dead for over a decade.'

She wasn't fooled by his silky tone. Suspicion rolled off him in radioactive waves. Her heart slowed to a dull, painful thud, and she was bracingly aware in that moment of the dark stain she carried. The reason she strove to live her life in light, lest the darkness overwhelm her.

'I thought perhaps he hadn't wanted to say whatever he needed to say to my face.'

Again something intangible flickered in his eyes, lifting the hairs on her nape. Again the look disappeared, taking with it that tiny seedling of hope.

'My godfather was many things, but he wasn't a man who lived in fear of little girls. What do you believe he needed to say to you that he couldn't when he was alive?' he asked.

Faye shook her head, her insides locking tight around her secret. 'That's between him and me. Or not, as it turns out,

since there's nothing besides this fraction of a share you're
so annoyed about.'

Bleak amusement glinted in his eyes. 'You think that's
what I am? *Annoyed?*'

'You certainly don't seem joyful about it—'

'Perhaps because we both know you don't deserve it, and
nor did you do anything to earn it,' he sliced in.

'Whereas *you* have?' Faye wasn't sure why she felt the
urge to needle him. 'Correct me if I'm wrong, but aren't you
the silver spoon recipient of what Luigi built?'

His face hardened into an iron mask, his eyes livid
flames of displeasure. 'Permit me to correct that misconception. My grandfather started this company with one shop
here in Napoli. My father took over when he was twenty-one
and expanded the company into Europe. It was my family's
hard work that got it off the ground. Luigi's contribution
was immeasurable, of course, but he didn't come on board
until much later. As to your assumption that I've merely
ridden on the coat-tails of my forebears—I'll leave you to
discover how wrong you are in your own time. You've already wasted enough of mine. Do you want to discuss how
you will justify your inheritance or waste more time dis-
pensing insults?'

Faye realised just how much she'd wounded his pride
by his haughty expression. Since she knew the company
was now a billion-euro luxury confectionery brand, Faye
didn't need telling that *he* had been responsible for that me-
teoric expansion.

She swallowed and attempted to corral her turbulent
emotions. 'I... I'd like to discuss this. What do I need to
do?'

He regarded her for several seconds and, had she been
invited to guess, she would've said he was disappointed
she hadn't taken a third option and thrown his offer back
in his face. But then that peculiar gleam entered his eyes
again. Almost as if he was relishing this skirmish. And why

wouldn't he? Hadn't she just presented him with the perfect opportunity to exact his pound of flesh for her insults?

With growing apprehension, she watched him stroll around to perch on the corner of his vast glass desk. The motion drew her attention to his muscled thighs, to the high polish of his shoes and to the stern reminder that she was in the rarefied company of one of the world's youngest billionaires. His expression suggested she should count herself lucky that a man of his calibre was giving her the time of day.

He could easily throw her out. Why didn't he? Because he'd made a promise to Carlotta? The wife he'd adored...?

'Miss Bishop?'

She started. His sharp tone indicated that she'd missed a chunk of what he'd said. 'I'm sorry, can you repeat that?'

His lips—comprising a thin upper and a surprisingly full and sensual lower, which alarmingly evoked lustful forbidden thoughts—firmed. 'I invited you, once again, to sit down.'

She frowned. He had a thing about ordering her to be seated. Was it merely a power play or...?

'Am I boring you or are you under the misconception that I appreciate flighty females?' he rasped, his accent thickening with irritation.

'You're aren't—and I'm not. I'm just trying to wrap my head around all of this. Haven't you ever had a bombshell dropped on you?'

Bleakness dulled his eyes before he blinked it away. 'More times that you will ever have the misfortune to encounter, I'm sure.'

She sat down and dragged her gaze from his to the painting behind his desk, pretending to study what looked like a priceless masterpiece as she fought the urge to inform him how wrong he was. How no one in the world should have to bear the burden of the bombshells she'd had dropped on her.

Abruptly he rose, crossed the room and seated himself directly opposite her, forcing her to focus on him. Not that it was any hardship. He was the epitome of a hot flame on a cold, dark night, drawing a hapless moth to its doom. She stared, taking in the vibrancy of his olive skin, the pronounced jut of his Adam's apple and the steady pulse beating at his throat.

An unfettered urge to stroke her fingers over that spot took Faye by surprise, making her swallow a gasp. Maceo's eyes narrowed, then conducted a sizzling scrutiny of his own before resting on her suddenly tingling mouth.

She wasn't sure how long they stayed locked in that tight, breath-robbing capsule. His phone's ping made her jump, releasing her from the spell.

Maceo glanced down for a moment before his gaze returned to hers. The heat had receded, and in its place was cool regard. 'Just so there's no misinterpreting the information, I'll have my lawyers provide you with a copy of Carlotta's will once we're done here. Your inheritance will be handed over at my discretion. And I've decided, Miss Bishop, that you need to appreciate where the money came from. Perhaps once you experience the hard work and sacrifice that went into your windfall, you won't be as flippant about it.'

Faye frowned. 'I told you—that was just shock. It wasn't my intention to cause offence.'

'Then prove it. I am not simply going to hand over the share. Carlotta didn't want me to and, after meeting you, I am certainly not inclined to.'

'What's that supposed to mean—after meeting me? You barely know me!'

The moment he leaned back in his seat she knew her response was what he'd angled for all along. And she'd walked straight into his trap.

'Here's your chance to rectify that, then. Prove that this bequest means more to you than just money.'

'How? Do you wish me to commission a plaque in Luigi and Carlotta's honour? Sign my name in blood? Maybe get a tattoo on my skin?'

He shrugged, as if they were discussing the weather, but Faye instinctively knew his every word so far had been calculated to gain this result.

'Nothing so dramatic. My request is simple. Walk in their shoes for a time. You will stay in Italy, immerse yourself in Casa di Fiorenti. Show a little appreciation for what Luigi spent his life building. When I'm satisfied, you'll receive your inheritance.'

Faye gripped the armrests of her chair, unsure whether to be shocked or amused. His face was deadly serious, and his eyes warned her to plot her next move wisely or prepare to lose.

'I have obligations. I can't just abandon them to come here and jump through hoops for you.'

He shrugged, distracting her with those incredible shoulders. 'Then by all means leave. Carlotta has granted me a flexible timescale of up to five years. Perhaps she believed you wouldn't be so quick to turn up once she was gone? Let my assistant know when you think you'll be available during the next five years and I'll endeavour to make some time in my schedule for you.'

Her fingers dug into the expensive leather as he sauntered back to his desk, opened a file and proceeded to ignore her.

Faye forced her jaw to unlock. 'That doesn't work for me.'

He didn't look up. 'Then we're at an impasse, Miss—'

'My name is Faye. I'd prefer you use it instead of that barbed formality designed to put me in my place—wherever you deem that to be. Believe me, I'm very aware of our differences, and I promise I won't tell if you come down a step or two from your lofty perch.'

He relaxed deeper into his seat, taking a stance that she

was learning meant keener speculation, a deadlier attack. 'What do you do for a living… Faye?'

The effect of his voice uttering her name was unexpectedly visceral. Disturbing enough to double her pulse rate and make her aware of every inch of her skin.

'Why do I think you already know the answer to that question?'

He offered a cunning smile. 'Carlotta mentioned that you spend your time on a farm in… Where is it, exactly?'

Her heart missed a beat, but she fought to keep her expression neutral as she wondered what else Carlotta had told him about her. Had she mentioned her mother at all?

'It's a place in southwest England, in Devon.'

His gaze wandered lazily over her clothes. 'Some sort of hippie commune, I gather?' he drawled.

'It's a little more than that.'

A lot more, in fact. It was a vital place for respite and support. But she wasn't going to elaborate just for him to disparage her. Or, heaven forbid, decipher why it was that her mother lived there and *she* devoted every minute she could spare to it.

'And what do you do there?'

'I'm a social worker by profession, but I currently volunteer there.'

Since her employment contract had ended, and there were no funds to hire her even on a temporary basis, Faye had been offering her services for free at New Paths Centre while she looked for another job. As much as she hated to admit it, Carlotta's bequest would do financial wonders for New Paths and also fund other much-needed centres— a project she'd been pouring her energy into since she'd left university, with little to no success.

'If you're in between jobs, what's the great hurry to return to your *farm*?'

His voice oozed the kind of disdain people reserved for shameless freeloaders. But Faye didn't waste any effort on being affronted. She was used to being judged by her appearance. She stared back without answering. While he remained completely unaffected her silence.

'Perhaps you'd be better disposed to stay if I informed you that your work here *wouldn't* be voluntary?' His thin smile didn't take the sting out of his words. 'Casa di Fiorenti has a reputation for paying its employees well. Even its interns.'

He named a price that made her gasp. And immediately suspicious.

'Are you serious?' With just one month's pay she'd be able to secure her mother's room and board at New Paths for another year.

'That's for a mid-level employee. As Luigi's stepdaughter—'

'I don't want any handouts. Any job I undertake will be rewarded on merit, not because of my connection to Luigi,' she cut in, this time showing her affront.

His smile hardened. 'Believe me, you will work for it. I have no appetite for scroungers. What I intended to state was that as Luigi's stepdaughter you would be required to learn about the company from the ground up, as my parents required of me, preferably with a year at a cocoa-growing facility overseas. But, since you don't have that kind of time to spare, you'll stay here in Naples, where I can keep my eye on you.'

She flushed, the tension easing out of her even as he eyed her mockingly. 'Oh. I see.'

'The most appropriate place for you to start will be in the research and development department. I will reserve the right to rotate your position as I see fit.'

Faye wanted to protest at his assumption that she'd fall in line with his wishes. Or even stay in Italy. But as she glared at him for his high-handedness she knew she wouldn't walk away. Wouldn't squander the chance to make a significant impact.

Her mother's continued care and well-being would be assured at New Paths. And, as heartbreaking as it was to acknowledge it, her mother would probably not even register Faye's absence.

Pain twisted deep and she clutched the armrests tighter to hold it inside.

'No need to look so concerned, Faye. A hard day's work never killed anyone, as far as I know,' Maceo drawled, shattering her anguished thoughts.

She raised her chin. 'Save your insults, *signor*. I'm not afraid of hard work. As a matter of fact, you can put me to work immediately. The sooner I'm done here, the sooner we can be rid of each other.'

The triumphant gleam in his tawny eyes made the hairs on her nape quiver. And, after a beat, he once again helped himself to a scrutiny of her. A shiver flowed down from her neck, encompassing her body with a hot, electric awareness that left her peculiarly breathless.

'Curb your enthusiasm. I cannot, as you say, *put you to work*. Casa di Fiorenti has a professional reputation to safeguard. That includes a strict dress code in which you currently fall woefully short. And, as you weren't planning on being in Naples more than a day or two, I doubt you have the right attire to work anywhere besides your beloved farm,' he stated drily.

Her flush deepened but she refused to lower her gaze. While her taste in clothes was consciously individual, and she appreciated it didn't suit a corporate environment, she wasn't about to turn herself inside out to please this man.

'I'll accommodate your dress code…but only up to a point. I'm not changing who I am to suit anyone.' She gave herself an inner high-five when her voice emerged firm and strong.

His wry, twisted smile suggested he found her comment amusing. 'We're affiliated with several fashion houses. The

HR department will ensure they're made available to you when you've filled out the appropriate forms.'

She tensed. 'What forms?'

Hooded eyes fixed more tightly on her. 'The usual employment forms. That will suffice.'

Faye forced herself to breathe out slowly. 'Is that necessary?'

Maceo's eyes narrowed. 'You must be aware how suspicious that sounds? How large *are* the skeletons in your closet, Miss Bishop?'

'How large are yours?' she threw back. 'You're the one insisting on this unnecessary assessment before you give me what's legally mine. I won't bare my life to you just so you feel better about doing whatever it is you're doing.'

He remained completely unfazed, leaning forward until the wide breadth of his shoulders filled her vision. 'You will give me your word that nothing in your background will embarrass me or my company.'

Ice engulfed her whole body, trapping her in her seat when all she wanted to do was jump up and flee those piercing eyes intent on digging beneath her skin. On baring the dark secrets she'd been forced to live with from birth.

'The only promise I'll make you is that I'm committed and hard-working. You have no right to make any other demands of me. Take it or leave it. But be warned: I won't simply disappear until you decide to honour Luigi and Carlotta's wishes.'

It was a wild bluff and she held her breath, hoping he wouldn't call her on it. He was the billionaire CEO of a staggeringly successful company, with all the clout and power that came with the position. She knew his legal team would chew her up and spit her out without so much as breaking a sweat should Maceo lift that haughty eyebrow to indicate they should do so.

Something hard and seasoned flickered in his gaze, making him appear much older than he was. As if he'd lived lifetimes and possessed harrowing tales to tell. Would those tales have anything to do with why he'd married Carlotta? Or explain that rabid mob of paparazzi downstairs?

Far from retreating from the frenzied curiosity eating her alive, Faye wanted to know more about this man. Wanted to unearth his every secret. Which was a dangerous state to inhabit when she had such deep, dark secrets of her own.

'I don't respond to threats, Miss Bishop,' he said, his words deceptively soft but effectively grounding her.

'I'm simply stating the truth, *signor.*'

'I've discovered "the truth" means different things to different people. I'm certain I'll find out *your* true mettle in the next six months.'

She gasped. '*Six months?* I can't… You can't force me to stay here that long.'

That eyebrow elevated, spelling out just how inconsequential he found her protest. 'I'm not forcing you to do anything,' he returned, far too smoothly. 'You're hardly my prisoner. Feel free to execute another dramatic exit, since you seem to specialise in those.'

'Three,' she blurted. 'I'll give you three months.'

'Four,' he countered immediately, his eyes gleaming with cut-throat anticipation. 'And I want your agreement that your connection to Luigi will only be divulged at my discretion.'

Four months of sacrifice in return for the ability to help thousands who needed it? With clever investment, the money from Luigi's bequest could stretch for years, perhaps decades. And, even while a large part of her remained horrified, and daunted by the thought of spending time under Maceo Fiorenti's laser eyes and dark suspicion, another part of her, emotionally centred on that bruising rejection all these years later, urged her to seize the opportunity.

Staying in Italy might reveal the truth once and for all— that Luigi had turned his back on her because of the stain of her birth that he hadn't been able to overlook. As much as it hurt to admit it, Matt had resurrected ghosts she needed to confront and, if not lay to rest, at least learn to cohabit with.

'Agreed. Four months and my...co-operation,' she accepted heavily.

His triumphant expression almost made her take it back. But he was already moving on. 'And at the end of it, you'll sell your share to me.'

'Or explore all my options and decide what's best for me.'

Burnished eyes held her in place. 'Selling it to me will be best, I assure you. No one else will give you the value I can.'

Why those words sent hot slivers of awareness through her, Faye refused to examine.

'Are we done here?' she asked, in a breathless rush she hoped he wouldn't notice.

Tawny eyes flickered, resting on her in a way that suggested he knew every thought racing through her head.

'One last thing. For the duration of your stay you'll reside at my villa in Capri. That way we won't have to have any tiresome debate about your room and board.'

The sensation of a silken net tightening around her made Faye shift in her seat. But there was no escaping his ferocious regard.

'No, thanks. I'll find my own accommodation.' Her heart sank at the thought of digging deeper into her meagre savings.

Keep your eyes on the prize...

'Did you see the paparazzi when you came in?' he asked, switching subjects.

Frowning, she nodded. 'Yes...'

'*Grande*. That is just a fraction of the press who follow me around on a daily basis. They'd love nothing better than to fixate on a shiny new object like you.'

Alarm dug into her belly. 'Why would they be interested in me?'

'Your arrival here isn't a secret. And you don't exactly blend into the background, do you, *arcobaleno*?'

Faye whizzed through the Italian words she knew, courtesy of that brief and idyllic time with Luigi before it had all turned to dust.

Arcobaleno. Rainbow.

Another more substantial sensation lanced through her. Heavier. Sinking low into her pelvis before setting off sparks in her private places. Sensations she'd smothered after that singular, soul-shredding experience with Matt.

'As far as I'm aware, that type of tabloid attention is reserved for notorious celebrities—so what does that make you?'

'I'm not here to indulge your curiosity, *arcobaleno*,' he replied with thick sardonicism. 'I'm simply giving you options. Take your chances at some cheap hotel with limited security or remain under my protection, where intrusion into your life will be minimal.'

'Why don't we spell out the real reason?' she asked. 'You really want me under your roof so you can keep an eye on me.'

'I will do so regardless of where you sleep, Faye, since I rarely take anyone at face value. It's entirely up to you whether you wish to sleep in comfort or in a hotel, with the constant inconvenience of the press hounding you and the unfortunate side effect of incurring my displeasure should you be tricked into speaking out of turn.'

A tiny scream gathered at the back of her throat. She swallowed it down because she knew in her bones that he'd love nothing better than to see her lose control. To have her confirm his every last preconception about her.

And Faye was sure that when she throttled back her irritation at his high-handedness she would see the benefit too. After all, he was saving her from unnecessary expense— money that could be put to better use elsewhere. But it still grated that she had to force herself to accept his strings-attached charity.

Her nails dug deeper into the armrests, but she froze when his mocking gaze dropped to her telling reaction. Forcing calm into her body, she replied, 'I'll stay at your villa. If you insist.'

He accepted her acquiescence with a simple nod, then reached for his phone. There was a short, rapid conversation in Italian, and then his eyes returned to her. 'My HR director is on her way. She'll get the ball rolling.'

The relief that attacked her midriff lasted all of two breaths before Faye registered that she was being dismissed—that Maceo was now engrossed in a document.

Insisting to herself that she was equally glad to be rid of him, she rose and willed her feet to turn about, dismissing him as easily as he'd dismissed her. She succeeded after several seconds, but it took every ounce of her willpower not to turn around and confirm that the feeling of his eyes boring into her back was nothing but her imagination.

Celebrating that tiny triumph felt essential. Because as she followed an impeccably dressed middle-aged woman out of the office, Faye's instincts screamed that she'd need every bit of ground she could retain when it came to Maceo Fiorenti.

Their battle was merely commencing.

CHAPTER THREE

THE MOMENT HER DETAILS were recorded on the system Maceo received an alert and accessed it. He despised himself for the unstoppable urge he couldn't deny. Far from being disillusioned after an hour spent grilling Faye Bishop, and having his suspicions confirmed that she was indeed only after the money from her share, he couldn't dismiss her from his mind.

He'd dissected her every quietly ferocious look, every word that had spilled from those Cupid's bow lips. He'd even pondered why she dressed the way she did. Why she inked flowers onto her skin. Why she had so little apprehension about irritating him, when everyone in his private and professional sphere went to unspeakable lengths do ensure the opposite. Even rattled, Faye gave as good as she got.

His gaze strayed to the chair she'd occupied, settling on the armrests she'd all but mauled in her bid not to sink those claws into him.

Maceo found his lips curving and immediately killed the action. The last hour changed nothing. All she'd done was spout words in an attempt to make him change his view of her. Anyone could claim hard work and commitment. The proof would reveal itself in the coming months.

Disgruntlement twisted in his gut. Before he'd met her, his intention had been for her to spend only three months at Casa di Fiorenti. So why had he pushed for six? And why the hell had he issued that directive that she stay at the villa?

While he'd been upfront about interest from the paparazzi, he hadn't divulged the fact that it was his own careful game, cultivated to keep them from digging into his family's past and discovering the unspeakable secret his parents and Luigi had moved mountains to hide. And, more than that, his own part in shortening the lives of his family.

Hindsight might be wonderful, but it was also cruel.

In raining judgement on his parents for harbouring the secret that had altered the very foundation of his beliefs, and shattered the pedestal on which they stood, he hadn't stopped to consider the consequence of his actions.

That he'd found out too late.

Now he had to live with the knowledge that his parents' carefully laid plans, their hopes and dreams for themselves and for him, had been destroyed because of *him*. Because of the implacable stance he'd taken when a cooler head and more flexibility might have saved him from this desolate path. The shame and guilt that rightly prevented him from contemplating any semblance of *famiglia*, or even a relationship for himself, were of his own making.

He had no one to blame but himself.

Grimly grounded by that reminder, he clicked open Faye's file.

His eyes narrowed, a tiny bolt of surprise charging through him as he perused her higher education history. She had a degree in sociology and business, achieved at the top of her class. And yet she chose to waste her time on a farm?

Beyond that there was nothing that should have prompted the tension she'd shown over filling in these forms. Yet it had been present.

Maceo paused when he reached her personal details, a hot wave curling though him as his gaze lingered on the marital status box she'd ticked: *none.*

None didn't mean *unattached.*

And it certainly didn't matter to him one way or the other.

He'd deprived his parents and Carlotta and Luigi of life-long relationships, of decades of reaping the benefits of their hard work. Who was he to contemplate his own pleasure? A liaison? Or, heaven forbid, a *relationship*?

Jaw clenched, he dragged his gaze through the rest of the document.

Altogether, her history was unremarkable. And yet Faye Bishop was anything but... She was a deceptive little flame and she burned far hotter than her outward appearance implied. Was that why Carlotta had made him promise to test her before honouring her bequest? Because she'd experienced Faye's uniqueness for herself?

Basta!

He was spinning tales where there were none.

Rising, he strolled to his window, hoping for a distraction. But not even the arresting view could replace a certain fairy-resembling creature with tiny claws, a sharp tongue... and a voluptuous body he couldn't quite erase from his memory banks.

But he hadn't battled the twin demons of guilt and shame on a daily basis without growing calluses. Summoning his iron will, he returned to his desk and for the next four hours successfully dismissed Faye Bishop from his thoughts.

An email from his lawyers confirming that Stefano and Francesco intended to contest their sister's will only roused in him amused anticipation. He'd hoped they would. Now he would ensure they walked away with nothing.

Maceo was contemplating his next move when the knock on his door came. His initial instinct to dismiss the unwanted visitor vanished when Faye Bishop's low, husky voice announced herself.

'Come.' His voice sounded thick, loaded with anticipation. Which irritated him endlessly.

Not enough to rescind his invitation, though.

He sat back and watched her enter, looking as colourful and unruffled as she'd been a few hours ago. *Dios*, she was even smiling—albeit at Bruno, his assistant, who smiled back before, catching Maceo's scowl, he hastily shut the door behind her.

The moment her gaze connected with Maceo's, her smile evaporated. He shifted again, his irritation increasing along with that pressure in his groin as she swayed in that ridiculous skirt towards him.

She stopped in front of his desk. He didn't invite her to sit.

'I'm done with HR,' she stated, after a moment of silence he didn't feel inclined to break.

'The experience wasn't too harrowing, I hope?'

She shrugged. 'It was what it was.'

Maceo just managed to stop himself from sneering. 'A nothing statement that couldn't be more useless if it tried,' he said.

She tilted her head, indigo eyes sparkling with amusement. 'You know, I thought it was just my presence that rubbed you the wrong way, but I'm starting to believe you're just naturally that way.'

A peculiar hollow opened up in his gut. 'And which way is that?'

'Hardwired to be bitter, cynical and just plain unpleasant.'

And guilty. How could he forget the guilt that ate him alive from the moment he woke till oblivion delivered him to his demons?

'I assure you I've never been *just plain* anything in my life.'

'Ah…so you're a special brand of acid rain, ruining the existence of anyone who happens to be caught within showering distance? When you were little, did you have an anti-hero cape, emblazoned with some unique dark lord logo?'

'There was never any need for such a garment. My extraordinariness sufficed. Still does.'

Her eyes widened and her delectable mouth gaped for a second before she caught herself. 'I shouldn't be surprised by that answer. And yet…'

'And yet you are? *Grande.* Know that I have the power and the wherewithal to pull this and any future rug from under you and we'll spare each other any surprises.'

Her amusement evaporated and Maceo felt another niggling sensation—this time disappointment. His exchanges with Carlotta had always been cordial, but spectres of the past and his demons had overshadowed their interactions. His banter with Faye was inconsequential, and yet he'd found himself savouring it the way he savoured the last mouthful of excellent espresso on his sun-drenched balcony before he faced the day.

'Your HR director said you wanted to see me. If it's just so we can hurl a few more insults at each other, then I'll pass. It's been a long day. I'd like to do something else that's not...*this.*'

She flicked her fingers between them in a manner supposed to indicate disdain, but Maceo spotted something in her eyes. Something that echoed his own disappointment.

He was fairly certain—not completely, since he didn't spare it more than a moment's thought—that it was the reason he powered down his computer and rose from his desk. And when he reached for his jacket and shrugged it on, he was aware her eyes followed his every move.

'Where are you staying?' he asked.

She frowned. 'Why?'

'Because you need to collect your things before we head for the villa. Unless you came to Italy with just the clothes on your back?'

Her headshake threatened the precarious knot of multicoloured hair atop her head. And seared him with the burning need to know how long her hair was.

'No. I have a case back at the hotel.'

She named it, and Maceo barely stopped himself from grimacing. It was little above a hostel—unworthy of the name *hotel*.

Si, relocating her to the villa was best. For one thing it would stop any awkward questions as to why Luigi's step-daughter was staying in a hovel once the media got wind of who she was. He ignored the inner voice mocking him for hunting down further reasons for Faye to stay under his roof and headed for the door.

With clear reluctance she swayed towards him, then stopped. Her eyes locked on his. Blazed with an indigo defiance that tripped the blood rushing through his veins.

Maceo knew he should move from the doorway. Astonishingly, his feet refused to obey. For the first time this strange, intriguing creature was within touching distance, and he was wholly and irritatingly rapt with the need to do just that.

Touch. Explore. *Experience.*

This close, he became bracingly aware of her diminutive size. Faye barely came up to his shoulder. And yet her presence filled his senses, taunted him to take a deeper breath of air, to inhale her scent, imprint it on his very being.

Considering the vow he'd taken against experiencing any contentment or pleasure, Maceo knew he ought to feel guilt and shame. But the sensations rampaging through him were neither. This was a sort of…*electricity.*

Anticipation.

Arousal.

Had she been here, Maceo was certain Carlotta would have been amused. Perhaps for once she would not have stared at him with concern shadowing her eyes.

Because—

'Are we leaving any time soon?' Faye demanded, shattering his rumination.

But her bored tone belied the slight flaring of her nostrils and the budding awareness in her eyes that stated she wasn't immune to the charged atmosphere between them.

'After you,' he drawled, not so irritated that he didn't want to test the true mettle of her resistance. But only because it amused him. Nothing else. Certainly not because he wanted her closer. Wanted to decipher just what perfume she wore on her skin. The scent of her shampoo...

Like everything else in your life, she's a temporary fixture. Remember that.

She hesitated for a moment. Then she slipped into the gap he'd created, avoiding his eyes as she passed him and moved into his assistant's office.

Maceo's hand tightened on the door as he took a breath. Then another. Cherry blossom and fresh peaches. An ordinary combination. And yet on her it was a scent he wanted to chase to the source. Linger on and savour.

Dio mio, what was wrong with him? Not even at the age of eighteen, the last time he'd been remotely hormonal around the opposite sex, had his libido wreaked such havoc on his senses. Hell, even then he'd been cynical about the attention he'd received—had known that the power and prestige of his name had largely contributed to the zealous flattery that had come his way.

In the years since becoming CEO that theory had been repeatedly proved. Not even his being married had deterred women. He'd been propositioned on a regular basis. And all it had achieved was a lingering distaste in his mouth, reinforcing his decision that not seeking pleasure of any sort was the right path.

That fortifying goal had been a flaming signpost he'd followed. It had instilled in him a loyalty and fidelity to Carlotta that hadn't caused him a moment's wavering, despite the true situation of their marriage. But now, for the first time, Maceo had experienced a shift in that foundation. Followed by the realisation that he hadn't quite been able to drag his gaze from Faye's smooth skin or the feline movement of her body as she strode away from him.

Basta!

Curtly, he informed his assistant of his plan to work

from his villa office and headed for the lift. He would relocate Faye, ensure she was under appropriate guard, and then forget she existed.

Thirty minutes later, he seriously feared his jaw would snap in two as her phone emitted yet another ping. She ignored it—again—seeming perfectly content to stare out of the window as they travelled to the heliport, her fingers curled around the handle of her small suitcase.

'Are you going to answer that?' he snapped, his gaze shifting to the large bag that held her phone somewhere in its shapeless depths.

'I will when I'm alone.'

Suspicion and intrigue built in him in equal measures, much to his annoyance. 'Don't hold back on my account. Surely any pertinent details I need to know, you've already apprised my HR department of?'

She studied him for a beat, then shrugged. 'Good, then it shouldn't bother you too much. Do we have far to go?' she added, stoking his annoyance further.

'We'll be at the helipad in less than five minutes.'

Her eyes widened. 'The heli— We're going to the villa by *helicopter*?'

Maceo was surprised…and, yes, intrigued…by the curbed delight in her voice. 'That's one of the modes of transport I prefer, *si*.'

'What's the other mode?'

'Speedboat.'

Her eyes grew rounder. Then she frowned. 'I've been on neither. Apologies in advance if anything untoward happens.'

Against his will, his lips twitched. 'Such as…?'

She shrugged again, drawing his eyes to the flowers dancing down one bare, shapely arm, to the delicate bones in her wrist. The tingling in his groin intensified. Grimly, he reeled himself in.

'I'm okay with heights…for the most part…but I don't know if I'll feel sick or not. Is that a thing on helicopters?'

'Motion sickness on helicopters is indeed a thing, *si*,' he rasped. Then watched her pert little nose wrinkle.

'Well, be warned, then. I guess seasickness is also a possibility. If I ever use your boat, that is.'

'I'll bear both in mind and keep the appropriate distance.'

'It's not too late to change your mind about inviting me to stay.'

Immediate rejection of that idea hardened in his gut. 'We will not rehash a matter that is already settled.'

'On your head be it,' she replied, in that tart little voice.

It promised barbs. Ones he felt peculiarly compelled to test, to stroke, to see how deeply they'd cut. It was a sensation that made him relieved to see they were approaching the helipad.

Relief morphed into intrigue when she alighted next to him and stared, stupefied, at the large aircraft that bore his family's logo.

'Good God, it's huge!'

Was it? He'd never given it a moment's thought. These days he occupied himself with safety rather than size, and he employed the best to ensure that no harm came to the things he cared about.

Up until a week ago it had been Carlotta. Now it was just Casa di Fiorenti. His own actions had ensured that.

The hollow ache expanded, the demons beginning to howl in glee.

You survived. Now you're alone. As you should be.

Exhaling around the tightness in his chest, he strove for calm. 'I suppose it is,' he drawled, once again disturbingly compelled by the emotions chasing across her face. 'Is that a problem?'

'Beyond making me think you're compensating for something with the size of your…equipment? Not at all.'

For the first time in a long time Maceo found himself

mildly astonished by a woman's forthrightness. The fact that it brought further acute attention to his manhood and a battering to the vow he'd taken stunned him into stillness.

He clenched his jaw. Pleasure and companionship weren't on the cards for him. And even if they were it wouldn't be with this woman who stared at him, her gaze daring, while the sunlight danced in her rainbow hair and sparked her indigo eyes.

'Forgive me if I've broached a touchy subject.'

Maceo strode toward his aircraft. 'Don't insult either of us. Your patently false tone neither begs forgiveness nor concedes sensitivity. As for the slur on my manhood—I don't feel the slightest inclination to prove you wrong.'

She arrived next to him just as a blush suffused her face. The gaze that had held his so blatantly a moment ago shifted away.

'A word of advice, *dolcezza*. Don't take on the big dogs if you blush so easily. Trust me, I will outlast you on any given day.'

With that, he held out his hand. After a tense moment, she took it.

Maceo helped her into the helicopter and refused to examine why he'd used his direct line to instruct his pilot to take extra care to make the journey smooth. Most likely because he wasn't in the mood for further aggravation from her.

The moment they took off he busied himself answering emails and catching up on further business. Only to glance at her when she gasped.

'Is that the villa?' A sleek finger pointed in the general direction of Villa Serenita.

With a sigh, he slid his phone back into his pocket. *'Si.'*

'It's…breathtaking,' she whispered, her fingers braced against the glass as if caressing his home from afar.

He shifted in his seat. 'A genuine compliment?' he observed drily. 'I'm dumbfounded.'

She didn't respond. It was as if his residence had rendered her speechless.

He took the unexpected moment to see Villa Serenita through her eyes. The circumstances of his life thus far had impressed upon him the need not to take things for granted, the knowledge that one reality could be ripped from him to be replaced by another vastly less palatable but, if Maceo were honest, the place where he laid his head at night had stopped registering in the maelstrom of guilt and shame that had become his everyday life.

Now, as the chopper banked, he looked down at the villa his grandparents had built. The villa his parents had poured their hearts and souls into making a home while harbouring secrets that would shake its very foundation. The place where he himself had taken a stand that had destroyed everything.

'How old is it?' she asked.

Her tone conveyed genuine interest. 'It was a mere shell when my grandparents bought it, over seventy years ago, but the building is over two hundred years old. They kept to the original baroque style, but added their personal touch over the years.'

'And the pink?' she asked, tossing him a look before her gaze was drawn back down. 'Excuse my observation, but I didn't think it was a very…*manly* colour.'

Maceo shrugged. 'It's not a personal affront to my manhood, if that's what you're implying. In fact, I don't think any other colour will do the villa justice.'

To his surprise, she nodded. 'You're right. Now that I've seen it, I can't imagine it in any other shade but coral-pink.'

Was he truly discussing the effeminate colour of the building with this stranger? He gave a sharp shake of his head as the aircraft settled on the ground.

He threw his door open and stepped out, hoping the brisk air would restore some clarity. About to wave her in the direction of his staff and remove himself from her presence, Maceo once again found himself rooted in place. This time by the breathtaking smile on her face.

Had he missed something?

'I survived. Hurrah!' she gushed.

To his chagrin, she affectionately patted the side of the helicopter. He watched the caress, his insides twisting with something close to disgruntled jealousy.

Si, definitely time for them to part company.

'*Bene*. I would have been most displeased had you decorated the interior of my aircraft with the contents of your stomach.'

'No worries there. I haven't had anything to eat since breakfast.'

He frowned. '*Che cosa?* Why not?'

'Because I was too busy answering several hundred questions for your HR manager.'

Before he'd fully registered his actions, he'd caught her elbow and strode with her from the helipad.

'Erm...where are we going?'

'To find you something to eat. Far be it from me to be tainted with a reputation for being inhospitable.'

He took the quickest way to the *salone* closest to his housekeeper's domain and tried to ignore his staff's shocked expressions when he strode into the kitchen.

Giulia, the elderly housekeeper who'd been part of the household since he was a boy, hurried towards him. *'Oh... buonasera, signor! Come posso aiutarla?'*

How could she help him? He stared down at Faye, realised he still held on to her. Registered too, that her skin was indeed smooth as satin, soft as silk. Warm. Supple. *Bellissima.*

'Signor...?'

Madre di Dio.

He snatched in a breath. 'Giulia, this is Faye Bishop. She'll be staying at the villa for the next few weeks. She requires a meal, and then would you show her to the Contessa Suite?'

Giulia was too seasoned to express the surprise reflected on his other staff's faces. The Contessa Suite had been his mother's, just along the corridor from Maceo's own, the Bismarck Suite.

But this too was a turn of events he didn't feel like dissecting.

As soon as Giulia had acknowledged his request, Maceo turned on his heel. He turned back just in time to see Faye gift one of her dimpled, breathtaking smiles to his housekeeper.

'I'm so sorry. I feel like I'm being foisted on you, Giulia… may I call you Giulia?'

He watched as Giulia melted beneath its brilliance before indulgently granting Faye leave to use her first name. Watched his visitor dump her bag on the floor before climbing onto the nearest island stool, leaning forward to rest her elbows on the counter, thereby displaying a larger swathe of creamy midriff.

'Whatever it is you're making, it smells amazing! I might have to beg you for the recipe.'

Aware that he was lingering and drawing more peculiar looks from his staff, since they probably couldn't recall the last time he'd entered the kitchen, Maceo forced himself to keep moving. To banish the far too intriguing Faye Bishop from his mind.

Regardless of the novelty she presented for whomever she came into contact with—and he was beginning to think she'd spun whatever fairy magic it was that she practised around most people, including, unfortunately, Carlotta—*he* was Maceo Fiorenti. A vow of no entanglements in favour of the singular preservation of his family's legacy was his paramount objective. Nothing would sway him from that.

Not even an enchanting creature with the voice of a siren and skin plucked from his most erotic dream.

* * *

Maceo congratulated himself for blocking her out for several hours. Only when every last business detail had been attended to did he rise from his desk and stroll to his liquor cabinet. Drink in hand, he should be satisfied, and yet something niggled. A sense of elusiveness. Of loss...

His fingers tightened around the glass. *Si*, he missed Carlotta. He missed her laughter, especially during their occasional dinners, when he hadn't worked late into the night. He missed those moments when she'd so doggedly tried, and briefly succeeded, to pry him away from his demons. That was the reason he hadn't been able to use her favourite west-facing terrace since her death.

But that wasn't the source of his restlessness.

The puzzle unravelled itself in a flash of relief. Pico. Carlotta's eight-month-old cockapoo. Maceo hadn't seen him since he'd got home. While the dog had been unmistakably dejected in the days before and after Carlotta's death, he unerringly hunted Maceo down within minutes of his return home.

Except today.

Icy dread invaded his stomach. His merciless condemnation of his parents' and Luigi's actions had resulted in the very worst-case scenario, leaving him alone with only his demons for company. Surely the cosmos wouldn't be so cruel as to visit his transgressions on a defenceless dog in a bid to ensure he was truly alone in the world?

No...

Nothing had happened to Pico.

Not so soon after Carlotta.

Even he drew the line at the thought of such a turn of events.

Besides, the staff would have informed him if something untoward had happened.

Still, unable to shake the feeling, Maceo set his glass

down. Exiting his office, he enquired after Pico from the first staff member he came across.

The young girl smiled. 'He was playing in the garden with Signorina Faye the last I saw him, *signor*.'

Certamente. Why had he assumed she wouldn't commandeer yet another being the way she'd wrapped his staff around her dainty little finger within minutes of her arrival?

Realising his mood was slipping again, and that his footsteps had drifted perilously close to the extensive gardens in search of her, Maceo veered about.

He'd had enough of Faye Bishop for today. Tomorrow would be soon enough to set out the precise parameters of her presence in his life. And they certainly wouldn't include dragging things that belonged to him under her spell—especially the one creature that had kept him from feeling completely unmoored.

CHAPTER FOUR

FAYE TURNED HER FACE up to the sun, taking a deep breath as warmth seeped into her bones. In this early witching hour, before the staff descended on the villa to begin ensuring it and the grounds remained in pristine condition, she liked to steal away and find a large rock near the private beach to watch the sunrise.

In the three weeks since her arrival she hadn't quite decided whether she loved the inside, with its stunning baroque architecture and soul-stirring paintings and masterpieces, or the outside, where a combination of tranquil gardens, awe-inspiring stone terraces and gorgeous landscaped grounds resided in beautiful juxtaposition with the churning sea beating itself relentlessly against the stone cliffs.

So far, she'd counted two dozen corridors and archways leading to intriguing courtyards, alcoves and neat little private gardens, each with its own unique mosaic or pedestal or fountain. Everywhere she turned she felt like a child, waiting to discover the next adventure.

In the first few days, when the staff had been open and forthcoming, she'd discovered that not only had Maceo's family lived here, Luigi and Carlotta had also made Villa Serenita their summer home, shortly after joining business forces with Maceo's parents, Rafael and Rosaria Fiorenti.

Faye wanted to dislike this place where Luigi had found happiness. Yet with each new discovery Villa Serenita worked its magic deeper into her soul.

But of course, there was the obligatory serpent within paradise.

Her thoughts reeled back to the morning after her arrival. Maceo had summoned her into his office at Casa di Fiorenti and laid down rules she'd apparently already flouted in the few hours she'd been under his roof.

First, she wasn't to distract the staff with unreasonable requests or overfriendliness. Second, she had free run of the villa but wasn't to grill the staff about its history or past residents. Third, and most importantly, Pico, the gorgeous puppy with chocolate eyes who'd stared at her so soulfully from his place on the kitchen floor that first evening, was off-limits. Never mind that the dog had taken to following her around wherever she went, stationing himself beside her seat at mealtimes, obedient, but irresistible enough to tempt small treats from her.

Faye had been perfectly content to flout that particular rule until Maceo had stopped her two days later, by simply keeping Pico in his private wing. Since then, her enquiries about Pico had met with guarded smiles from the staff.

It was clear Maceo was possessive about his dog. But Faye had weightier things on her mind. She was no further forward in discovering why Luigi had abandoned her so abruptly. Whether he'd believed he was doing her a favour by callously rejecting her and then, like Matt, pretending she was invisible. Matt had ignored her whenever he saw her on their university campus after she'd been foolish enough to reveal her secret.

The picture she'd found in the library a few nights ago, of a much younger Luigi and two other men, had thrown up even more questions.

One of the men was clearly Maceo's father; the resemblance was unmistakable. Equally striking was the third man's likeness to Luigi. But, while the unknown man was laughing in the photo, Luigi and Rafael remained serious. Borderline angry.

Rafael Fiorenti's expression was a familiar one she'd glimpsed on his son's face, but Luigi's expression was alien to her. Which drove home just how little she'd known her stepfather and her complete unawareness of the man named Pietro, according to the inscription on the back of the photo.

Who was Pietro? And why hadn't Luigi mentioned him in the two years he'd lived with her and her mother in Kent?

Because back then, every time you begged for stories of his homeland, he deftly changed the subject...

The ploy hadn't registered all those years ago, but it shuddered through her now. Pain gripped her again, threatening to settle inside her. Faye smothered it, dragging herself to the present. Namely, her meeting with Maceo this morning.

Initially it had been slated as a two-week evaluation, but Maceo had cancelled every meeting except today's. She remained on tenterhooks as to whether this meeting would go ahead but, judging from the butterflies buzzing in her stomach, Faye instinctively knew today was the day. So she couldn't afford to ponder the identities of mysterious strangers in photos.

With a sigh, she pulled her crimson sweater tighter over her pyjamas and made her way back through the garden. Letting herself into the villa by way of the large pantry and kitchen, she was met by the sight of Giulia, sliding a tray of pastries into the giant oven.

'*Buorngiorno, signorina. Signor* has asked for breakfast to be served early in the Salone Bianco. He wants you to join him.'

She froze in surprise. 'Really?' Maceo had yet to invite her to dine with him, either here in the villa or at work. In fact, he'd pointedly avoided her in both places.

Giulia nodded. '*Si.* He wishes to have breakfast in half an hour.'

So the third degree was starting at the breakfast table?

She summoned a smile for Giulia and hurried to her room. She whizzed through her shower on automatic, only forcing herself to concentrate when she walked into the dressing room that was three times the size of her Devon bedsit.

Three weeks on, Faye still couldn't quite believe her suite's opulence or size. Even more unbelievable was the personal wardrobe that had arrived by the boxful the morning after her arrival. When the HR director had informed her she was entitled to a new wardrobe as part of joining Casa di Fiorenti, Faye had expected to be handed a small allowance and pointed in the direction of the nearest high street boutique. Instead, what seemed like the contents of entire haute couture showrooms had arrived at the villa via speedboat. She'd chosen the designer who most suited her taste and returned the rest.

Now, she selected a deep lilac knee-length dress, a fuchsia belt she'd embellished with embroidered flowers, and added the matching brooch handmade by her mother. The pops of colour eased her nerves, but her insides still quaked slightly as she stepped into her shoes, grabbed her bag and left the suite.

The Salone Bianco lived up to its name in sun-splashed resplendence. The only thing that *didn't* gleam white was the gold marble edging the walls of the octagon-shaped room. Every piece of furniture was white, including the lavish dining table, at the head of which sat Maceo, his head buried between the pages of an Italian newspaper.

He didn't remain that way for long.

Faye's throat dried as he slowly lowered the paper and speared her with dark tawny eyes. '*Buorngiorno*. I'm glad you could join me,' he drawled, his voice low, deep and maddeningly invasive to her senses.

She'd only caught brief glimpses of him in the past three weeks, and for the life of her she couldn't drag her gaze from the play of sunlight on his hair, and his broad shoulders and impressive biceps, to which his pristine shirt eagerly clung.

Several superlatives jumped into her brain, but the only one appropriate enough—the only one that effortlessly fitted him, as if coined especially for him—was *magnificent*. He was wasted, merely sitting at a breakfast table when he could've graced the cover of Italian *Vogue* or *GQ* or some other plush magazine strictly dedicated to cataloguing unique male beauty.

If you were into that sort of thing.

Which she wasn't.

So why was her breathing jagged? Her insides going into free fall with each second she spent staring at him? Why, amongst all the adverse emotions cascading through her, was there...*anticipation*?

The sensation irritated her enough to make her reply crisp. 'Was it an invitation? It sounded remarkably like a summons.'

His gaze swept leisurely down over her dress. It lingered at her hips before returning to her face. Faye couldn't quite read the look in his eyes, but whatever lurked there made her blood run hotter.

'If pretending will stop either of us from getting indigestion, then by all means I'll play along. Thank you for accepting my invitation to breakfast. Please sit down, Faye,' he said.

Her breath caught in her throat. The sound of her name on his lips still evoked such sensuality she wanted to request...no, *demand* he say it again.

And what was that if not utter madness? Hadn't she learnt her lesson with Matt, the one time she'd dropped her guard enough to contemplate an experience resembling normality, only to be ruthlessly reminded that she was *nothing* like normal? That she was an abomination?

The reminder dredged up pain, but it also grounded her enough to ignore the cocked eyebrow that was telling her she risked humiliating herself by her deer-caught-in-the-headlights stasis. With stilted movements, she pulled out a chair and sat down.

'Coffee?' he offered smoothly.

'Tea, please. Thank you,' she tagged on, determined to wrestle some civility into this meeting.

A butler glided forward, poured her tea and then, after offering a platter of fruit and an assortment of breakfast meats, melted away.

Silence throbbed between them. Maceo was seemingly content to devour one cup of espresso after another while perusing his paper. At last, with perfect timing, just before she gave in to the urge to fill the silence, he spoke.

'You've spent a few weeks now at Casa di Fiorenti. What's your verdict? Do you still consider it the very heart-beat of the monster that deprived you of your stepfather or have you revised your opinion?' His voice dripped cynicism.

Despite the unfair assessment, she found herself flushing, because there was a kernel of truth in his words. Luigi had been in her life for only two years, but they'd been formative years that had given her a glimpse of what a family could be like. Maybe she would have got over his leaving them if she hadn't been confronted with Casa di Fiorenti confectionery and the memory of his desertion with every supermarket she'd walked into. That ever-present evidence had done nothing to heal the hurt of her loss, but she'd tried to cope with it. Until Matt.

She tried for a diplomatic answer not steeped in anguish. 'I never considered it monstrous. I just—'

'Wanted so very much to dislike it?'

She shrugged, sipped her tea to delay answering. 'Maybe.'

'And now?'

She couldn't hold back the truth. 'So far as I can tell... it's not so bad.'

'Damned with faint praise,' he said drily. 'Tell me what you really think, Faye.'

Again her name on his lips sent a frisson down her belly, and then shamelessly between her thighs. 'Why? What does it matter?'

He didn't answer for a long spell, drawing her attention

to his face in a vain attempt to see behind his enigmatic façade. 'Because I made a promise.'

The answer was unexpected enough to widen her eyes. 'You did?'

He gave a brusque nod. '*Si.*'

'To who?' she demanded, her heart beating for a different reason.

'Who do you think?'

'Your...your wife?' Why did that word continue to lodge a dart of unease inside her? What did it matter to her one way or the other that he'd been married?

Because thinking of him belonging to someone else unsettles you.

And not because of Carlotta's connection to Luigi.

He shrugged. 'For some reason she seemed to want you to form a good impression of the things she cared about.'

That surprised Faye. 'She said that?'

His eyes speared into hers before they flicked away. 'She said many things. I'm yet to conclude if they were the result of facing her own mortality or what she truly believed.'

She gasped. 'How can you say that? Who are you to decide?'

'If not someone in a unique position to sort fact from fiction without the inconvenience of frothy emotion, then who?' he bit out.

'And you would dishonour her by discarding her wishes as you please?'

His face hardened, his eyes growing flat and hard. 'She trusted me to do the right thing because she knew I wouldn't be swayed by...what do you English call it?...*flights of fancy.* And that trust is what I will honour.'

She bit her lip to stop another hot, condemning retort from slipping out. She even tried to eat, despite her throat threatening to clog. After a few bits of toast and scrambled egg, she set her cutlery down. 'If you want me to form a good impression then why instruct your staff to stop talking to me?'

Faye wasn't aware of quite how much his edict had hurt until she blurted the question. He froze, his eyes turning that unique tawny shade and filling with an icy fury that sent shivers down her spine.

'Because there's gossip and there are facts.'

'Do you trust your own staff so little?'

Again he shrugged. 'Carlotta was beloved by everyone, and they're in mourning. I didn't want you to be swayed by superfluous emotion.'

'And you? Aren't you in mourning?'

His face closed up. 'My emotions are none of your concern.'

'Are you sure? I think your emotions directly affect our interaction. You can't seem to look at me or speak to me without attaching unsavoury labels. Which is curious, because I've discovered a few things about you, *signor.*'

'Have you?' His tone was bored in the extreme.

'For someone who demands propriety from others, you certainly like notoriety. Some would even think you've gone out of your way to court it.'

Faye could've sworn he stiffened at her remark; that something resembling wariness twitched in his face. But he shrugged. 'My relationship with the paparazzi is—'

'None of my concern?' she finished, smiling mockingly.

'Exactly so. Carlotta found baiting the media amusing. So I indulged her.'

'Why?' From what she'd read about Carlotta, the woman had been the epitome of class and poise. Faye struggled to picture her dallying with the tabloid press.

'Because it was either let them continue to print hurtful things about her or control the narrative by giving them something specific to print,' Maceo replied, then looked almost bewildered by the truth he'd divulged.

'So it was all a game to you?'

'Isn't life one form of game or another?' he queried cynically, but she saw the muscle ticking in his jaw, his fingers tightening on his cup.

There was more to this than merely taunting the press for laughs.

The picture she'd discovered in the library, now tucked into a book on her bedside table, rose to her mind. But instinct warned her now wasn't the time to ask about it.

Faye shook her head, her insides tightening with bitterness, sadness and shame. 'Not to me. To me life is very real and very serious, *signor.*'

His gaze rose to linger on her hair, then the bright spots on her attire. 'And yet your outward appearance implies otherwise.'

'Don't judge me because I prefer not to dwell in sombreness, like you.'

To her utter surprise, he smiled. It didn't reach his eyes, of course, but the startling radiance of it was enough to make her forget to breathe. When she did suck in a breath, his gaze fell to her breasts.

A different sort of atmosphere charged the air. Like the start of a firework display in the far-off distance, growing closer, more seismic, by the second.

It was the same sensation that had permeated their interaction in his office three weeks ago. One steeped in sexual awareness that still made her hot and restless and twisty inside, especially at night, long after she'd gone to bed, curiously fighting sleep until she heard the distinct sound of his helicopter landing.

That maddening awareness had driven her to her bedroom's arched windows once, to catch a glimpse of him. She'd regretted it deeply when Maceo had caught her in the act, halting mid-stride as he crossed the lawn. For an eternity he'd stared up at her, paralysing her in place with those piercing eyes, before icily dismissing her and sauntering into the villa.

'I don't hear your denial that this is all camouflage for what you're really like underneath the...gaiety.'

Faye was glad she'd set her cutlery down because she'd have dropped it and given herself away as a mini earthquake moved through her. As it was, she took the altogether cowardly option of not meeting his gaze, unnecessarily straightening her napkin as she willed her panicked heartbeat to slow.

Because the truth was, she *was* hiding. Covering up the dark stain of her existence. Tuning out the dark, menacing voice that declared her circumstances would never be normal. That the formation of intimate bonds, physical or emotional, while carrying the burden she did was impossible.

Matt had proved that with his raw and callous rejection.

'Once again we seem to have avoided the subject at hand. Or did you really invite me to breakfast to discuss my wardrobe?'

He stared at her for a beat longer, then sat back. 'I'm meeting with my R&D department today to discuss your evaluation. This is a chance for you to warn me of any... irregularities.'

Returning to firmer ground, she smiled. Learning how Casa di Fiorenti went about selecting new flavours for their exclusive brand had been enlightening. And unexpectedly thrilling. 'Thanks for the heads-up, but I'm not worried in the least about my performance.'

'*Bene.* I hope that "performance" holds up under more rigorous scrutiny next Saturday.'

'What's happening then?'

'Casa di Fiorenti holds a pre-summer party for its top executives and their families, and its business partners. Two hundred people will spend the afternoon here at the villa. You will be required to attend.'

'But... I'm not an executive.'

'No, you're not. But while I'm perfectly happy for you not to attend, it was one of Carlotta's wishes for you see the *famiglia* side of the company. The party is a tradition she started. We haven't missed one in twenty years.' There was a definite bite in his tone when he used the Italian word, but again his face was devoid of emotion.

'Why did she want me there?' Faye asked, something tugging in her chest.

'I can't answer for her. But you will attend. And while you're there you will ensure nothing you do or say brings the company into disrepute.'

Faye bristled. 'Am I allowed to even speak at all, or shall I pretend to be mute?'

'We agreed that revealing yourself as Luigi's stepdaughter will be at my discretion. I'm simply reminding you to weigh the options and be prepared to deal with the outcome should you decide to out yourself.'

She couldn't help but wonder if this was another test. A way to discover whether she was worthy of the gift Luigi and Carlotta had bestowed on her from beyond the grave. But, again, while she'd have loved to throw his invitation in his face, attending this party might deliver the answers she sought.

'I'll be there. And I'll do my best not to disgrace the family name.'

For the briefest second his fists balled. Then eased. 'That's all I ask,' he replied mockingly.

He rose, caught up the bespoke jacket draped over a nearby chair and shrugged into it. The act of watching him don his jacket held her immobile, heat swirling in her belly.

'Are you coming?' he drawled, staring down at her.

'What?'

He glanced pointedly at his watch. 'Your evaluation is scheduled for eight a.m. Do you plan on being there?'

'I... Of course.'

He stepped close to her chair and Faye scrambled up, unwilling to be disadvantaged by Maceo towering over her.

Flustered, she nudged her chair back with a little too much force and stumbled.

The sequence of events was swift and dizzying. With lightning reflexes Maceo caught the toppling chair with one hand and her waist with the other as she tottered on her heels. Then, in direct contrast to the preceding moment, the world stilled.

Faye wanted to ignore the sizzling intensity of the hand holding her, the thawing of his cool tawny regard, the heat fluttering in her chest and the flood of hot awareness through her veins.

She could do none of the above.

Without uttering a word Maceo Fiorenti commanded her body, her speech, the very air she breathed. Or the air she *couldn't* breathe because he'd commandeered that too.

Fierce eyes stared down at her, as if he was trying to see beneath her skin. Had his hand just tightened on her? Had he drawn her closer? Or was it all in her fevered imagination?

As a child, she'd foolishly stuck her finger into an electric socket. That was nothing compared to the sensation coursing through her now as Maceo tugged her closer. The look in his eyes was no longer indifferent. Or dismissive. His eyes smouldered with a definite fire. One that promised consumption. *Annihilation.*

And, far from shying away from it, denying the sort of danger that could destroy her, for a suspended moment in time Faye yearned to embrace it. To *feel* that electric shock. Experience that burn.

That insanity was the reason she raised her hand with a compulsion she couldn't deny, caressed the swathe of skin just above his collar where a vein pulsed, then brushed her fingers against the chiselled perfection of his jaw to the thin but characterful scar halfway between his chin and his mouth. She lingered, explored, while her heart banged hard against her ribs and electricity consumed her from temple to toes.

Maceo inhaled sharply, his gaze dropping to her mouth before darting back to her eyes, his look of hunger so intense she gasped.

The sound forked between them, alive and demanding.

With an Italian curse steeped in gruff denial, Maceo stepped back. His gaze turned from shocked to censorious as he dropped his hands. *'Per al amor—'*

He cut off his own words and whirled away from her.

'I… I'm sorry. I didn't mean—' It was her turn to curb her words. Because she had meant to touch him.

'I'm not sure what you think you're playing at, Miss Bishop, but I'd caution you against trifling with me. Under any circumstance.'

His voice was a hundred blades, slashing her to shreds. Death by a thousand warnings when one would have sufficed.

'Just so we're clear, I don't mix my business with pleasure. *Ever.*'

That final word was icily bitter. She gripped the edge of the table to steady herself against curiously searing disappointment. 'But I'm not your business, am I? I'm Luigi's. Carlotta's by extension. To you, I'm a temporary burden, thrust upon you. You could be rid of me immediately, but are choosing not to. Which begs the question: which one of us is the glutton for punishment in this scenario?'

'I have never taken the easy way out in anything, and nor do I intend—much as it'll give us both satisfaction. As for your little…indulgence just now, you will ensure it doesn't happen again.'

But Faye knew it hadn't been all her. She'd seen the hunger in his eyes. Felt the pressure in his touch. His very male reaction against her hip.

'Then do me a favour. Next time let me fall.'

He looked momentarily confused. *'Che cosa?'*

'You stopped me from falling just now. Next time, if

you're not certain you won't blow things out of proportion, keep walking.'

He seemed stunned by her response. Faye was certain no one had dared speak to the great Maceo Fiorenti that way in his life.

He took his time sliding the single jacket button into its hole, for all the world completely unaffected by the turbulent little incident. Back under rigid control, he inclined his regal head towards the door. 'I will bear that in mind. Shall we?'

The journey to the jetty where his speedboat waited to ferry them to the office was conducted in tight silence. One Faye used to wrestle her senses back under control. By the time she stepped aboard and hurried to the farthest plush seat, she could draw half a breath without fruitlessly chasing Maceo's scent of citrusy aftershave and disgruntled man. She could even avoid glancing his way for several seconds at a time. Pretend his tall, imposing body *wasn't* continuing to wreak havoc on her senses.

She breathed a sigh of dubious relief when they entered Casa di Fiorenti twenty minutes later and he was immediately set upon by his assistant. But even as she scurried away she knew the reprieve wouldn't last. Nevertheless, she locked herself away in the restroom, under the guise of fixing her slightly windblown hair, desperately attempting not to relive those moments in the dining room, as she needlessly straightened her clothes and prepared herself for the grilling to come.

Sure enough, the moment she sat down in the same conference room where she'd first met him, Maceo proceeded to dissect everything she'd learned in the past three weeks. When the head of the department repeatedly assured him that she was in no way slacking in her duties, Maceo turned those tawny eyes on her.

'Tell me the most important thing you've learned so far, Miss Bishop,' he tossed at her.

They were back to *Miss Bishop*, were they? Why did that send a dart of hurt through her?

'I can't speak for all departments, of course, but Signor Triento is an excellent leader. He trusts his staff to deliver on their goals without being a tyrant about it. I'm especially pleased with my assignment to help come up with new flavours for a limited-edition Christmas collection. I already have a few ideas.'

Alberto Triento beamed at her, before a glare from his boss swiped the smile away.

'I wasn't aware we were giving interns such leeway,' Maceo groused, his eyes narrowing on Alberto.

The older man shrugged. 'There is nothing wrong with testing new talent. It might come to nothing. Or it might bear fruit. We won't know until we explore, *si*?'

He invited agreement, but Maceo's gaze grew colder before, as if he'd grown bored of throwing his weight around, he dismissed Alberto.

Faye knew better than to assume he was done with her too. 'So, did I pass muster?'

'Try not to get carried away with the novelty of it all. And bear in mind we test hundreds of flavours every year. Very few make the cut into production.'

'But I get to eat chocolate as part of my job. I'm failing to see the downside to that!'

He pursed his lips, as if her observation had irritated him.

'Why the R&D department?' Faye asked in the silence that followed.

He paused a beat before answering. 'That was Luigi's department. It became Carlotta's after his death. She was an effective marketing director, but Luigi won her over to his side and she grew to love discovering new products.'

Grateful for that morsel of information, Faye felt a lump rise in her throat. 'Thanks for telling me. It sounds like they had a lot in common?'

Eyes that saw far too much rested on her. 'You really knew so little about your own stepfather?'

It sounded like an accusation. But she was still a little too wrung out after that breakfast incident to indulge in another skirmish.

She shrugged. 'We lost touch when he returned to Italy.'

The gleam in his eyes said he wasn't buying it. 'Italy is hardly the other side of the world. How old were you when he left? Thirteen? Fourteen?'

'Eleven.'

Some people experienced life-changing events that lasted a moment. She'd experienced two years that had given her a glimpse of what a true family looked like. Luigi's complete silence after leaving her and her mother had thrown everything into question—including her own worthiness. Learning of her mother's harrowing secret and her own genesis had thrown up further questions.

It had been a burden she'd resigned herself to living with.

Until Matt's declaration.

Until Carlotta's persistence had opened the box she'd strived to keep shut.

As much as Faye despised the need to confront her emotional wounds, she knew it was part of the arduous process towards gaining a semblance of sanity, including exorcising the ghosts of Luigi's desertion.

She took a deep breath. 'He turned his back on me when I was a *child*. So why should I have made any moves?'

Dark shadows flicked over Maceo's face. 'Perhaps he had his reasons?'

Pain seared deeper. 'Everyone has their reasons. Perhaps he should've been man enough to explain his to me instead of—'

'Instead of…?' Maceo coaxed icily.

'Doesn't matter now.'

'I beg to differ. You seem overly…emotional.'

'And you pride yourself on having no emotions at all. So why do you keep pushing me?'

'Contrary to your belief, I care about Luigi and Carlotta's memories. I push you as a warning to you not to consider soiling them.'

'You care so much about Luigi that you married his wife?' she blurted, before she could stop herself. Then knew immediately she'd gone too far.

He grew statue-still, perfectly emulating the marble masterpieces that littered his homeland. 'Don't stray into territory you don't understand.'

What was there to understand? And why couldn't she leave it alone?

'Enlighten me, then. Surely I'm not the first person to wonder at your...*interesting* match.'

He surged upright, and despite his calm breathing his eyes blazed volcanic fire. 'This meeting is over. You may leave.'

She took her time to gather her papers, stand and face him across the conference table. 'Of course, *signor*. But before you accuse me of prying, remember I'm trying to find out about my stepfather. And you factor into that. So tell me what I want to know. Or don't. But I'm not leaving Italy until I have a few answers of my own.'

Including to that mysterious picture someone had hidden between the pages of an obscure book.

Faye Bishop was well and truly underneath his skin.

Distancing himself from her, as he'd done these past three weeks, had simply thrown up more questions. More intrigue. He'd hoped the evaluation meeting might provide clarity. Or, if he was being completely truthful, expose glaring flaws that would justify his assumptions about her.

Alberto Triento's fawning over his newest employee proved there would be no help from that source.

As to what had nearly happened at his breakfast table...

That unbridled heat…that *hunger* he'd never experienced before… That continued insistent tingling in his very being…

Her fingers had been on his face, on that scar no other human had dared to touch, the scar that served as a daily reminder of what he'd done…

Maceo shoved a hand through his hair and resisted the supremely uncharacteristic urge to fidget. Which was laughable. Except laughing was the very last thing he felt like doing.

No, what he found himself reverting back to, with uncanny and alarming frequency, was wondering what she would have tasted like had he succumbed to that fevered urge and kissed her…

He sat down, resisting the urge to rise again.

He was Maceo Fiorenti. He didn't fidget and he didn't pace. The vow he'd taken in that hospital bed to deny himself of everything he'd robbed his parents of had held true for the last decade. So why was he being tested now?

I'm not sure what your game is, Carlotta. She's insolent, ungrateful and far too colourful to be taken seriously. Not to mention nosy to the point of rudeness.

Then why are you here?

Maceo heard her amused voice so distinctly he wouldn't have been at all surprised to find Carlotta right beside him on this marble bench set before the family mausoleum, with her signature bright smile and that perfectly plucked eyebrow arched in sweet mockery.

The fresh flowers he'd instructed to be delivered gave off their sweet scent even while reminding him that the scent of cherry blossom was sweeter to him these days. Ever since he'd caught a certain woman's scent and been unable to divorce himself from it.

That scent had filled every corner of his being at his breakfast table, when he'd almost lost his mind. Almost, but not quite. He'd stepped back from the brink of that insanity.

Shame, Carlotta's distinctive voice mused.

Maceo glared harder at the memorial in front of him. 'I should finish this now,' he said aloud. 'Today. Hand over the inheritance and the letter and be done with it, no?'

Silence greeted his question. He grimaced, knowing he wouldn't take the easy route. He'd made a vow to the woman who'd put her own grief on hold in order to help him secure his legacy. Without his word, what was he?

The reminder he carried with him everywhere burned against his breastbone. With not quite steady hands he reached into his pocket and pulled out the piece of paper, despite the fact that every line was seared in his memory.

It was a replica of the framed one he'd discovered amongst his parents' belongings and now kept in his bedside drawer. A joint lifelong 'to do' list, scribbled on a cheap restaurant napkin, back when his parents had been engaged. Maceo ran his gaze down the list, his chest tightening at the last abrupt tick. The vice intensified as he forced himself to read through every item his parents hadn't been around to tick off.

Because of him.

He'd deprived them of it. It was only right he stuck to *his* vow of deprivation.

Returning the note to his pocket, he stared at Carlotta's plaque.

'She's prying where she shouldn't be,' he said aloud.

Then do something about it.

The words seeped into his bones with a simplicity that stunned him. Rather than keep his distance, he needed to keep a closer eye on Faye. He might despise secrets, but allowing her to pry, to risk airing his family's dirty laundry wasn't an option.

He brushed his fingers over Carlotta's name, his stomach churning with guilt and shame as he flicked his gaze over his parents' memorial.

You should be here. Or I with you.

He bunched his fists, fighting the ever-present battle not to be drawn into that dark hole. He had a duty to perform. And when it was over...when nothing stood between him and the chasm...what then?

He veered away from the question and his monumental guilt and headed for his Alfa Romeo, parked behind him in the private cemetery.

'What do you mean, she's gone *clubbing*?'

The very word tasted wrong on his lips, and he wasn't surprised when his assistant shot him an apprehensive look.

'I believe it's someone's birthday in her department. According to the email, they're going to dinner and drinks, clubbing afterwards.'

Maceo had no valid reason for the haze that passed over his eyes. Or the sharp sting of disappointment that trailed behind it. Perhaps it was because for the first time in recent memory he'd put work to one side. He'd been prepared to subject himself to dinner with Faye, perhaps even answer a few of her questions. Only to find she'd made plans that didn't involve him.

He snarled at the snide inner voice. He had a *right* to be disgruntled. He was her boss.

'Have my car brought around and alert my pilot. I'm leaving.'

'*Si, signor.*'

To his credit, Bruno didn't express surprise at Maceo's uncustomary early exit from the office. He jumped into action, leaving Maceo simmering in unsettling temper.

He was still seething after a solitary dinner, an unremarkable stroll through the gardens with a very solemn Pico and his first nightcap. He refused to glance at his watch, although the opulent antique clock in his study did an adequate job of telling him it was close to midnight.

The sound of a water taxi propelled him to the French doors. From that vantage point he watched Faye step onto the jetty with a grace and agility that wouldn't have been remiss in a ballet dancer. She turned towards the driver as he handed her something. It took a moment—and a peculiar tightening in his gut—to realise it was her shoes.

She laughed in response to the driver's words, one hand lifted to tuck back a swathe of lilac hair in the fluttering breeze, the other clinging to her shoes. The carefree spectacle, for some absurd reason, tripped his irritation into fury.

He made the journey from study to jetty without recalling having moved.

Extracting his wallet, he shoved a handful of notes at the driver and barely heard the man's effusive thanks.

'Did you have a good time?' he asked Faye, aware of the ice dripping from his voice. And not caring one little bit.

CHAPTER FIVE

SHE WHIRLED AROUND and the smile slowly drained from her face.

This day of firsts continued to pummel him. Because, absurdly, Maceo felt a dart of regret that she was no longer smiling.

'Yes, I did,' she murmured. 'And before you give me a hard time—'

He waved her away. 'You don't need my permission to come and go as you please.'

Wry astonishment flared in her eyes. 'I beg your pardon, but have you tried telling that to your face?'

A smile tugged at his lips, despite the irritation bubbling in his veins. Staring past her to the disappearing water taxi achieved the desired effect of restoring his disgruntlement. 'A heads-up would have been nice.'

Her lips pursed. 'So you could give me a hard time about it before I left?'

'So I could've cancelled the plans I made for dinner.'

Her eyes widened in shock. Maceo chose not to be insulted.

'I... You wanted to take me out to dinner?'

'Not out in public, no. I thought we could have dinner together here at the villa.'

Her long lashes swept down. 'Oh. Well, since you've been treating me like an unwanted guest for the last three weeks, dining with you was the last thing I expected.'

He frowned. 'You exaggerate. I've treated you in no such way. And I have it on good authority that your every wish has been catered for.'

Because he'd instructed it to be so. He had affluence to spare, after all, and at the end of this he wanted her amenable to selling that share to him.

Is that all you want?

He ignored the question as she sighed. 'I'm not about to get into another argument with you, Maceo. Or, heaven forbid, offer my views on the way you host guests in your home.'

A rush of heat through his veins stilled him for a moment. And then he brutally dismissed it. There should be nothing *pleasing* about her using his name. She'd invited him to use hers, after all. Yet he yearned to hear her say it again. Perhaps even moan it when he explored that lush lower lip of her with his fingers? His lips?

Dio Santo, what was wrong with him?

His hand went to his breastbone, blindly seeking the list. The *reminder*. But it was still in his jacket, discarded in his study. Much as he was discarding his vow—

No. Never that.

He dropped his hand as she walked past him and headed for the house. Again he felt that maddening compulsion to follow, to let his gaze wander over her, take in those long, supple legs and slim, delicate ankles.

'Was there a particular reason for this dinner?' she threw at him over her shoulder.

For an unguarded moment he wanted to toss back a petty retort that if she'd wanted to find out she should've let him know her plans. Thankfully, the moment passed.

'I was struck by a sudden generosity and decided to answer a few of your questions over a good meal.'

She'd started to climb the steps leading to the terrace, but she stopped and pivoted, her movements entrancingly graceful. 'You were going to tell me about Luigi?'

Her eyes glowed in the dark, luminous and expectant. Torrid heat built within him, flaring until it engulfed his whole body.

'Perhaps. I hadn't quite made up my mind.'

She tilted her head, indigo eyes narrowing. 'Do you take pleasure in toying with me, Maceo?'

The very thought of trifling with her sent a heavy pulse of arousal through him. *Dio*, he either needed to find a different sort of entertainment or to have his head examined.

'You missed your chance to find out.'

Sumptuous lips pressed together. 'How do I even know this dinner plan you claim to have had is the truth? Maybe you're trying to make me feel bad about something that didn't exist.'

'Do you feel bad about *anything*?'

She stiffened. 'What?'

He summoned righteous outrage, hoping it would erode this…this *lust* that insisted on confusing him. 'You had a chance to get your answers from Carlotta and you denied her. Do you feel bad about that?'

She simply stared at him. Bold and seeking. And for the first time in his life Maceo felt the strangest inclination to back down. Look away.

'What happened to you…?' she murmured eventually.

Ice cracked his spine. 'What?'

The light in her eyes dimmed. 'Never mind. I'm wasting my breath.' She started to walk away.

Without stopping to consider the wisdom of it, he reached out and captured her elbow. 'Clearly you have something on your mind. Let's hear it,' he invited silkily. 'A nightcap, perhaps? Maybe that will make you more civil?'

Her eyes shadowed, then dropped away. 'I don't drink. Never have.'

'Any particular reason why not?' he asked.

'Because a clear head is important to me.'

'What a peculiar answer.'

She shrugged. 'You find me peculiar already. What's one more thing?' She pulled away, and with searing reluctance Maceo let her go.

In the *salone*, he strode over to the drinks cabinet, poured mineral water with a dash of lime and held it out to her. She took it, but made no move to drink.

'So, is clubbing your ideal sort of entertainment?' he asked, feeling his reluctance to be done with her eating deeper into him.

'I can take it or leave it.'

'And the R&D team? Can you take or leave them too?'

'What *is* this, Maceo? You've gone from warning me against even breathing in your presence to outright socialising with me?'

Maceo ignored her scepticism. If he was to get her onside to claim that share, he needed to tread carefully. 'Ask me what you want to know about Luigi,' he invited, giving up on making small talk he didn't care about.

The glass trembled in her hand. She tightened her fingers, lowered her head. 'Did…did he ever mention me?'

Maceo shook his head. 'I didn't know you existed until a few weeks ago.' The revelation still grated—badly. *So many secrets…*

Hurt darted across her face and he watched her slowly stroll over to the sofa. She sat down, looking a little lost as she stared into her glass.

'I suppose that means he never mentioned my mother either?' she asked.

Despite her efforts to conceal it, he heard wariness in her tone, saw the way she avoided his gaze.

His hackles rose. 'No, he didn't. Neither did my parents.'

Certainly they had never told him the full story. A story with layers he might never uncover now everyone involved had perished.

He couldn't keep the bitterness from merging with the guilt that churned through his stomach. He'd pushed for transparency and all he'd been left with were ashes and a life of desolation. Because how could he dare to grasp for anything resembling contentment when he'd deprived his own parents of theirs? When each time he looked in the mirror he experienced the guilt of being alive?

'If it's any consolation, I was kept equally in the dark for most of my life. And I detest secrets.'

The last declaration was to gauge her reaction. Sure enough, her gaze shifted away from his.

'Some secrets are better off staying in the dark,' she murmured, so softly he wondered if she'd realised she'd spoken aloud.

He laughed, the sound dark and hollow even to his own ears. 'Only those who seek to justify their subterfuge believe that.'

Her eyes reconnected with his and he was disconcerted by the dark turbulence swirling within. 'Not everything is black and white, Maceo. Some things are out of your control. Some secrets have the power to rip families apart.'

Dio, he knew that too well!

'Only if you let them fester. Cut out the rot and what is left will be enough.'

Long moments ticked by before she glanced away. 'When did Luigi and Carlotta meet?' she asked, returning to the subject she seemed obsessed with.

More and more Maceo was convinced that whatever she was hiding was embedded in her past with Luigi.

'They met when she joined the company. According to those who were around, it was so-called "love at first sight".'

Her lips twisted, and Maceo wanted to applaud her for not attempting to conceal her reaction with inane statements.

'Am I a bad person if I say I wish they hadn't met?' she asked in a hushed voice. One that reluctantly touched him.

'No.'

She started at his unexpected answer. Then ploughed ahead. 'He was the only father I'd ever known.'

'And he turned his back on you. Do you intend to hate him for ever?'

Again, she didn't rush to deny the emotion, and the raw

pulse of her anguish touched something dead inside him, threatened to rouse it.

'Maybe not. But he left us before he met Carlotta, and I hate not knowing why.'

'Some uncertainties you have to live with.'

'Would the great Maceo Fiorenti accept something like this and just live with it?' she asked.

The weight of his guilt pressed down hard. He'd pushed, created discord, and then lost those dear to him before he'd had the chance to make amends. 'No, he would not.'

That sat between them for a minute. And Maceo didn't exactly detest the sense of kinship that flowed between them.

'How did he die? The newspapers mentioned a car accident...'

He forced a nod, memories crashing in despite his efforts to hold them at bay. 'It happened in Milan. They'd just landed the biggest deal for the company yet. They threw a party to celebrate.'

'They...?'

A muscle ticked in his temple and his blood felt icy cold. 'My parents were in the same car as Luigi and Carlotta. Luigi and my parents died instantly.'

She gasped. 'And Carlotta? Was she badly hurt?'

'She was thrown from the car before impact and hospitalised briefly, but as you know she made a full recovery.'

'At the drinks tonight, someone mentioned you'd once been in an accident too,' Faye said.

Maceo refocused to find her frowning at him.

He tensed. 'I'll give you a free guess as to how I feel about office gossip.'

She shook her head. 'It wasn't gossip. They assumed I knew.'

He straightened from where he'd been lounging against the fireplace. 'Have you had your fill of information about Luigi already? You must have if you're inclined to indulge yourself in asking about me.' He used the silky tone Carlotta had fondly referred to as his *'il inferno'* voice as he sauntered towards Faye, not bothering to hide his displeasure about this new subject.

She'd clearly read his expression accurately, and he watched as a shiver coursed through her. He lifted his glass to his lips to hide his dark satisfaction at her reaction. Of course that all went away when she licked her bottom lip, leaving a wet trail that thickened his blood, left him with an instant raw need to be the one licking that plump flesh. Sucking it into his mouth. Tasting the hell out of it...

'I thought we were just making conversation,' she said.

'No, *cara*,' he drawled. 'But if you want something *else* to occupy you, I can think of much better things than to discuss me,' he offered.

She jumped up, and mineral water spilt over her fingers. Maceo took the glass and set it down. When he faced her again, she took a step back.

'What...what do you think you're doing?'

Si, Maceo. What are *you doing?*

He wasn't breaking his vow. He was simply...

'Satisfying your curiosity,' he said. He lifted a hand and trailed his fingers over her smooth jawline.

Again she shivered. 'No, you're not. You're...annoyed. And you're using this...whatever this is...to hide it. Why?'

He shrugged. 'You have an overactive imagination, Faye. I'm doing nothing except paying you back for indulging yourself with me this morning.'

She snatched in a breath. 'I thought you said it must never happen again?'

'No need to panic, *cara*. Nothing has happened yet.'

'And nothing will,' she blurted.

No, it wouldn't. Because his path was set. No pleasure. No liaisons. No *famiglia*.

But nothing said he couldn't teach this creature a lesson for toying with him. For making him...*want*.

He breathed a curiously satisfied sigh as Faye remained still, allowed him the freedom to experience her silky skin, to feel the blood rushing beneath her pulse that was slowly turning her pink with desire.

The hunger that had taken hold of him since that morning intensified, rampaging through him like a wild animal. Slowly he nudged her chin with his thumb, tilting her head up to his.

'Why the hair colour?' he asked, finally giving in to his curiosity.

'Because it makes me happy.'

Such a simple answer. And yet so alien to him that he froze. When had he done something for the simple reason of pleasing himself? Not since before he'd woken up from hell and found himself inhabiting a nightmare.

'And the henna tattoos and the unconventional clothes? They make you happy too?' he pressed.

'Yes,' she murmured, subtly leaning into his touch.

Maceo didn't think she was aware that she was doing so. Dark satisfaction flared higher within him.

'Life is dreary enough without helping it along with boring clothes.'

'Such a simplistic thing to say,' he answered, but in some deep, dark part of him he acknowledged that he was…endeared to her.

Temporarily.

Faye Bishop had layers he couldn't afford to be sidetracked by. Not when he sensed there were secrets she strove hard to hide.

She shrugged. 'I am what I am.'

He indulged himself in another stroke of her skin. Felt her tremble and his own groin pulsate in response.

'But you're not, *cara*, are you? There is much more hidden beneath, isn't there?'

'I'm not sure exactly what's going on here, Maceo…'

He stepped closer, breathing her in. 'Say my name again,' he commanded.

'Why?'

'Because it pleases me.'

Shame slammed into him at the admission. But he didn't...couldn't...take it back.

'Do you always get what you want?' she asked.

'No, I do not. If I did my family would still be alive.'

The starkness of his answer froze them both and he saw the beginnings of softness in her eyes. He wanted to lap it up and at the same time reject it. He did neither. He simply continued to caress her, the hypnotic forbidden thrill of it seeping deeper into his blood.

'I'm sorry you lost them,' she murmured, with genuine sympathy in her eyes.

He inclined his head, accepting the words but then dismissing them before they wound themselves around places he would swear weren't vulnerable.

She opened her mouth again. And against his better judgment and every vow—perhaps because he was suddenly wary of her expertise in confounding him—he stalled her by the most direct means available to him: lowering his head and kissing her.

This was by no means his first kiss, but it was his first since that moment he'd opened his eyes to a whole new world. A world where his parents were no longer alive. A world where guilt and cruel might-have-beens resided.

One simple touch of her lips and Maceo's senses detonated in an unrelenting force so potent and yet so pure it sent him reeling. She moaned, and the sound only intensified his hunger. Her sweet, supple body swayed into him. He wrapped an arm around her waist, drawing her closer. A gruff sound was unleashed from him as her softness moulded to his hardness.

It was as if he'd been uncaged.

He drank her in, delving deep into her mouth to taste

every inch. And how sweet she tasted. Adolescent experiences he could barely recall evaporated from his mind for ever, replaced by this new, mind-bending sensation threatening to overwhelm him.

Faye's scent. Her taste. The soft firmness of her body. All eroded his greatest asset—his control. But even as he assured himself he could wrestle it back, he was also admitting to himself that he'd never felt want like this.

His marriage hadn't been a traditional one. Only he and Carlotta knew their truth. So his need was particularly acute as he fisted Faye's hair, helped himself to another taste of cherry blossom and the pure woman in his arms.

And he would have kept on sampling and indulging if reality had not seeped in like a dark, icy storm.

Was he really doing this? Blithely discarding his vow for the sake of this foolish *temporary* temptation? When the last thing he deserved was *any* form of serenity?

With a control he wrestled extremely hard for, he broke the kiss.

Eyes wide, breath panting, Faye stared up at him, a look of horror slowly etching her face. 'I'm not sure exactly what that was, but—'

'I can spell it out for you or give you another demonstration if you need pointers?' he said, infusing his voice with nonchalance he didn't feel. Maceo had no intention of losing himself like that again, but she didn't need to know it.

She shook her head, sparking an irrational irritation inside him as the look of horror remained on her face, despite feeling a similar sensation at himself.

'I don't want pointers, thank you. What I'd like is to go to bed—if this little game of yours is over?' Without waiting for an answer, she hurried towards the door.

Maceo followed, the decision he'd made at the mausoleum earlier rushing back to him. *Keep her close...safeguard my parents' legacy.*

He watched her climb the sweeping stairs, her bare feet

and shapely legs sparking renewed hunger inside him. At the top of the stairs she paused, one hand on the banister, the other clutching her shoes.

It was as if that compulsion in him had reached out and snagged her. Slowly, she looked over her shoulder, eyes watchful. Saying nothing.

Maceo allowed the silence to pulse while thick, dangerous emotions sizzled between them. Then he delivered his final volley. The one he'd savoured with far too much anticipation while he'd awaited her return.

'Just so you know, from Monday you're moving departments.'

She inhaled sharply. 'Excuse me?'

'You can continue your little assignment for R&D, but it's time to switch things up a little. You'll be working directly with me. Who knows? You might catch me in a mood to answer a few more of your questions about Luigi.'

She stared down at him, her mouth working although no sound emerged. Maceo wanted her to storm back down and tackle him about his announcement. To accuse him of dangling the carrot of Luigi to get what he wanted.

Hell, he wanted a great many things—things that should shroud him in shame and guilt. Because even now his lips tingled. He resisted the urge to touch his fingers to them by lifting his glass and draining the last of his drink, his eyes never leaving her face.

Perhaps she saw his internal battle and deemed it wise to maintain a sensible distance.

Maceo wasn't sure how long they stayed like that, locked in a silent war of unwanted arousal. Faye with her sexy shoes dangling from her fingers, her graceful body arched towards him and her indigo eyes unable to detach from his. Him with the animal need that rampaged through him threatening to leap out of control. Only his vow, battered but stalwart, held him in place.

Eventually she nodded jerkily, her tongue darting nervously over her lips. 'Fighting you on this isn't worth my time. I guess I'll just have to count the days until this is all over. Right? Goodnight, Maceo.'

He didn't respond, because every fibre of his being was locked in a battle to stay where he was and not race up the stairs after her.

Not even the discovery half an hour later that Pico had vanished again and was most likely ensconced in Faye's room was enough to shift him from his study.

Winning this skirmish with her was what mattered.

And he intended to win each one.

It was just a kiss.

Funny how, with every forceful repetition of those five words, the weaker their reassurance became. Five days later and what should have been a deep dive into the cocoa and sugar production reports Maceo had asked her to read barely registered. The effect of that kiss—and her feeble insistence that it had had no profound effect on her—resurfaced again and again to shatter her concentration.

Faye stifled a frustrated growl, kicked off her shoes, rose from the sofa where the reports were strewn and stretched her limbs. But as she strolled to the window of her new office next to Maceo's she darkly acknowledged that stiff limbs weren't her problem.

Her problem was *that kiss*.

Her problem was the dark magic of Maceo's ferocious passion...how easily he'd overcome her resistance.

Most of all her problem was her own stunned realisation that whatever had gone before was nothing compared to the thrill of what she'd experienced.

He'd kissed as if he desired her. As if she mattered. As if he would have expired if he hadn't devoured her.

Because he doesn't know!

And she, momentarily forgetting every valid reason why

she shouldn't...*couldn't*...give in to such base emotions, had yearned for more with every cell in her body.

But when the reminder had rammed through the fog of her desire and brought her to her senses, Maceo had seemed just as stricken as she felt.

Because he'd only recently buried his wife...

There it was again. That stinging sensation. It was almost as if she was...*jealous*. It was irrational. And shaming. Because with every day spent in this place she learned that Carlotta Caprio-Fiorenti had been just shy of a saint. She'd been devoted to Luigi, and then to Maceo. She'd possessed a deep sense of family—as evidenced by her brothers' prominent positions in the company.

Had that been the drive behind Carlotta's effort to reach out to Faye despite her less than warm reception? The bite of guilt was damning and unwelcome. Perhaps because through all of this turbulence she'd still held back from asking Maceo about that picture. About Pietro and who he had been to Luigi and his parents.

She hadn't come across anything else about him, despite scrutinising the countless Fiorenti and Caprio pictures displayed all over the villa, and secretly searching the library from top to bottom for another hidden picture.

A frustrated sound bubbled up from her throat.

'The reports are that challenging?' a deep, sardonic voice said from behind her.

She spun around, a small gasp leaving her lips. Maceo stood in the centre of the room, a solid, riveting figure who made it impossible to acknowledge anything else in the vicinity. With the sun long set, and only a couple of lamps illuminating the interior of her office, the play of light and darkness lent him an even more enigmatic aura, triggering a sort of hypnotic absorption that made her heart thump faster as he filled the room, taking up vital space and oxygen.

'Not at all.' She strove for equanimity and breathed a sigh of relief when she achieved it.

His head tilted a fraction, that assessing gaze zeroing in on her vulnerable spots—which she was discovering were many when it came to this man.

'Then what's the problem?'

'Nothing I can't handle,' she said with false nonchalance. Because he was coming closer, and her gaze was doing that thing where it remained glued to him no matter how much she tried to resist.

Maceo didn't have the same problem, evidently. His gaze veered away to skate over the papers, then the shoes she'd abandoned some time in the last hour. For some reason his eyes remained riveted on the red-soled heels for charged moments before, sliding his hands into his pockets, he re-directed his scrutiny to her.

'Pick two,' he threw out, a deep throb in his voice.

Faye dragged her gaze from the play of dark blended wool over his strong thighs. 'Two...?' she echoed, in an alarmingly husky voice.

He jerked his chin at the reports. 'Are you up to date on the sustainability projects with our growers?' he asked, instead of answering her question.

'Yes.'

She was stunned by what she'd read. She'd dealt with enough supposedly community-minded companies in her bid to secure funding for New Paths and similar women's shelters to know that not all conglomerates were willing to spread their wealth. But Casa di Fiorenti went above and beyond in supporting the farmers whose products it bought. Free grants and sharing resources had increased profit on the ground level—an unprecedented outcome that had seen its competitors scrambling to save face by emulating the multi-billion-euro company.

'And?' Maceo prompted, alerting her to the fact that she'd got lost in the wonder of it all.

'And whoever had the idea to give the farmers the tools

they need to increase their output deserves a medal. Several medals.'

A wry smile ghosted over his lips. 'You have Luigi to thank for that,' he said, approaching her where she stood.

Warmth and bewilderment twisted through her. 'He did this?'

Maceo nodded. 'He set the ball rolling long before it was fashionable to give without expecting something in return.'

Then why? her heart screamed. Why had he shown such kindness and consideration to others but deserted her and her mother so heartlessly? Had their damage and stigma been too much for him?

Faye barely managed to stop herself from making another sound—this one an echo of the pain ripping through her. Instead, she focused on the conversation, aware of Maceo's incisive eyes fixed on her.

'But you kept it going? These labs set up to provide vital technology to help the farmers were put in place only a few years ago.'

'It made good business sense to keep on enabling them to self-sustain. But the legacy is Luigi's.'

Faye wondered if he'd come here to tell her this. Since Friday night he'd been dropping tiny morsels about her stepfather into their conversations. On Monday he'd told her Luigi had backed his father against the board's resistance to hire their first female CFO. Tuesday he had revealed that Luigi and Rafael had been childhood friends from their first day in kindergarten, and that Luigi had taken Maceo on his first sky-diving adventure on his sixteenth birthday—much to his parents' dismay.

While each revelation was a dagger to her heart—because the evidence was stacking up that Luigi had withheld crucial parts of his life, and ultimately left because of her and her mother's shortcomings—Faye had begun eagerly anticipating these visits and revelations from Maceo.

Was it because she hardly saw him otherwise? Because a secret, entirely foolish part of her hoped for a repetition of what had happened on Friday night, even though she knew it was a dangerous, insane route to take?

She pushed the intrusive questions away. 'Thank you for telling me. I'm still not sure whether it helps me or not.'

He stared at her contemplatively before he answered. 'I'm merely providing the information. What you choose to do with it is your decision.'

A knot of bitterness slipped past her guard. 'But you're only telling me the good bits. Not whether he ever let you down. Did he ever lose his temper? Make a bad decision?'

A flicker resembling pain dulled his eyes before he blinked it away. 'Luigi was flawed, like most people. Would my recounting his mistakes make you feel better?'

Yes.

She bit her tongue, suddenly self-conscious, and retraced her barefoot steps to the sofa, aware with each one how small she was in contrast to Maceo's towering frame. How dishevelled and worn around the edges she looked compared to his immaculate appearance. Under the lamplight his hair gleamed, neat and pristine, his tie was perfectly knotted and his *GQ*-cover-ready Italian designer shoes were polished to within an inch of their life.

To occupy herself, so she didn't gawp at him some more, Faye picked up the nearest document. 'You wanted me to pick two—but you didn't say two what.'

'Two production sites you'd like to visit, to see for yourself the work Luigi started,' he said.

The words ignited something peculiar that burrowed beneath her skin and sparked her blood. And as they sank in she forgot she wasn't going to stare or appreciate the masculine perfection as he drew closer.

She met his potent tawny gaze full-on and momentarily lost the ability to breathe. 'I… What? You want me to visit a production site with you?' she parroted.

He stopped an arm's length away and shrugged. 'It's a twice-yearly opportunity we organise for our employees. The last one was two months ago, so this will be a special trip with just the two of— *Cieli sopra!*'

The sudden tightness of his voice, charged with powerful emotion, made Faye's heart miss several beats. Puzzled, she followed his gaze, and flames stormed through her as she caught sight of what had snagged his attention—the bra she'd discarded an hour ago in a fit of frustrated discomfort. She'd thought she'd shoved the frivolous bit of lingerie deep into her bag, but apparently it had been dislodged when she'd kicked off her shoes.

Now Maceo stared at the bright red scrap of lace as if it personally offended his every sensibility. His hand darted to the breast pocket of his jacket, before veering sharply away as if stung.

'Do you make a habit of disrobing in the office?'

His voice was hoarse, throbbing with a beat that resonated deep inside her pelvis.

Faye nudged her bag with her foot. All that achieved was to drag the bra into clearer view. 'I… Of course not. It's after hours. I thought you'd left. That I was alone.'

She chanced a glance at him, and discovered that for some reason her response had made his eyes blaze even fiercer.

'And my presence is the only reason you'd keep your underwear on?'

Despite her burning face, she glared at him. 'I didn't mean that and you know it. Don't twist my words, please.' She surged forward with cringe-worthy gracelessness and tucked the bra out of sight, excruciatingly aware of his laser focus boring into her.

'Are you done here?' he demanded tightly.

She nodded stiffly. 'Just about.'

'Good—then you'll leave with me.'

'Oh, please. This isn't some period drama. You don't

need to protect my honour.' Especially when her very origins were severely questionable.

'Perhaps not. But I find myself needing to ensure that no other man sees you like this.'

The low, terse revelation, writhing with possessiveness, detonated between them, rendering them both immobile and unable to do anything but stare, aghast, at each other. Or at least Faye was certain that was how she was looking at him. Because the stormy emotions coursing through her made her want to fling herself at him, regardless of the words coming out of his mouth.

'Chauvinist, much?' she snapped.

He let her indictment bounce off his broad shoulders without so much as a wince. 'I care very little about how I appear, *cara*. I care very much about returning you to the villa, *pronto*, before you take off another item of clothing.'

Faye got the impression that he wasn't going to budge from her office. And, much to her dismay, she discovered she *wanted* to go with him. Wanted to remain in his company despite the wild sizzle and crackle between them. Despite the fact that her body was still caught in a maelstrom of sensations, the epicentre of which was the super-sensitive budding of her nipples and the flames licking through her pelvis.

Despite every inch of him proclaiming the danger of remaining for one more second in his company, she slipped her shaky feet into her high heels and caught up her bag. 'Okay. Let's go.'

He caught her wrist in his large hand and led her to his private lift. Downstairs, as if he'd commanded it by telepathy, the few employees working late stayed well clear of them. When they reached his speedboat, Maceo barely acknowledged the pilot's greeting.

He planted himself in front of her, shielding her from the view of his driver, his wide body blocking out the worst of the breeze. He continued to keep hold of her arm, his gaze never once straying from her face.

'So…your choices?' he asked stiffly after a minute, barely raising his voice.

She looked up. His gaze caught hers and held it captive. Breathless, she watched it linger, hot and hungry, on her lips before dropping to her chest.

A shocking phenomenon occurred just then.

Far from folding her arms to hide his effect on her, Faye retained her pose, felt her breasts suddenly heavy and needy, her hands dangling by her sides as she sorted through her thoughts to answer his question. *Choices… Site visits…*

'Oh…um… St Lucia. And Ghana.'

He nodded. 'We'll leave this weekend—after the party.'

Under different circumstances she would have reeled at the novelty of everything that had happened in the last few weeks—her inheritance, the luxurious splendour of the villa, the job she found herself enjoying more with each day…hell, even her new clothes. But, while she'd known from the first that Maceo Fiorenti was a formidable man, the almost conceited way he wielded his power continually left her slack-jawed—not that he'd noticed, since he pretty much did as he pleased with little regard for anyone else.

'How long will we be gone?' she asked, struggling to handle yet another twist in this roller coaster.

His gaze sharpened, his sensual lips momentarily flattening. 'Ten days—perhaps more. Already missing your clubbing friends?'

'Believe it or not, I do have people who're interested in my travel plans.'

His hard look eased. 'Your parents?'

She sucked in a breath, then reminded herself that Maceo didn't know her history. 'My mother.'

'And your father? Is he—'

'Not in the picture. Never has been. Never will be,' she insisted, but that sickening sensation gripped her gut so tightly she had to force herself to breathe carefully through it or risk giving herself away.

She didn't notice that goosebumps had broken out on her flesh until his hands slid up and down her arms in a contemplative caress. A different sort of shiver assailed her then, almost but not quite nudging that sickening feeling aside.

'Such a strong reaction—'

'And entirely none of your business,' she injected forcefully, hoping he'd drop the subject.

Thankfully he did, although his gaze raked her face repeatedly before he lifted a hand to tuck a coil of runaway hair behind her ear.

Perhaps it was relief and gratitude that made her turn into his touch. Or perhaps she'd taken complete leave of her senses tonight.

Whatever it was, she gasped when he cupped her cheek, his hand hot and possessive and electrifying enough to make her pulse race faster.

'Faye?'

'Hmm?'

'A body as sensitive as yours shouldn't go unarmoured,' he rasped, his voice low and deep and entirely too dangerous, too *intimate*, for her peace of mind.

A very feminist part of her bristled. 'Because any unwanted attention I receive from the opposite sex will be entirely *my* fault?' she challenged.

One corner of his mouth twisted mirthlessly. 'Because whatever male you eventually belong to will find the idea of you in this state—when he can't do a single thing about it without causing scandal—completely maddening. Enough to risk him committing indecent crimes.'

Whatever male you eventually belong to...

Part of her wanted to laugh. The other part, that had retreated, horrified and bruised, from Matt's callous condemnation, writhed in fresh anguish. She would never *be-*

long to anyone. Because no one would ever see beyond the stain that marked her.

'Thank you for your concern, but you needn't worry it'll ever come to that,' she said.

Primal fire brimmed in his eyes for heart-pounding seconds. Then his hand stroked over his jacket pocket again, his expression growing a touch bewildered before his features shuttered.

He kept hold of her. Helped her off the speedboat when they arrived at Villa Serenita. Tersely dismissed the staff who approached. And when she refused dinner, on account of having already had a light supper in her office, he walked her to her bedroom door, where he bade her a low, charged goodnight.

But not before his laser gaze rested one last time on her bag. On her hair. And finally on her lips before, turning abruptly, he strode away.

Leaving her with the bewildering sensation that she'd narrowly escaped a seismic event.

CHAPTER SIX

FAYE TOLD HERSELF it was entirely coincidental that the silver-threaded white bohemian dress she chose on Saturday was designed to be worn braless. She wasn't tempting fate— never mind one Maceo Fiorenti.

Since their intense interaction on Wednesday he'd reverted to ignoring her existence, not even dropping by to dangle morsels of information like he'd done the previous days. Work-related communications, including information about their trip to St Lucia tomorrow morning, had been transmitted via Bruno.

It was also Bruno who'd informed her of the smart-chic dress code that had prompted her dress selection for the party.

All day the villa had been a whirlwind of preparation. From the vantage point of her mosaic-tiled terrace she'd watched staff stringing fairy lights into the cypress trees dotted around the grounds, landscapers primping every inch of the gardens until the roses and poppies seemed to bloom brighter, and long tables with pristine silverware being set up at various corners of the grounds, gleaming.

Thirty minutes ago the first of the guests had started arriving. She'd head downstairs just as soon as she'd calmed the turbo-charged butterflies in her belly...

She started as a firm knock sounded. Blowing out a nervous breath, she slipped gaily coloured poppy-shaped hoop earrings into her lobes, put on red platform heels, then crossed to the door.

Maceo stood on the threshold, much as he had on Wednesday night, but with a much more measured look. Which changed when he took in her attire. He looked... thunderstruck. A terse Italian expletive was ejected from between his lips, and one hand crept up to his nape.

Faye watched his every reaction with something like lightning in her veins. Then, equally enthralled, she watched him wrestle every scrap of emotion under control, until only a smouldering fire remained in his eyes.

'Are you ready?' he enquired, his voice nowhere as smooth as normal.

'Provided I pass muster, yes.'

The look he levelled at her threatened to burn her to a cinder. 'You are well aware of just how you look, *signorina*. Far be it from me to pile even more compliments on your beautiful head.'

Her insides dipped alarmingly. She would have responded with a offhand remark had he not held out his arm to her. Mildly stupefied, she took it. Let him lead her down the hallway towards the stairs.

'Have you given any further thought to selling me your share?' he asked, with a flippancy she was sure was fabricated.

'Was that why you came up to my room? To make inroads into getting what you want?'

Why that made his jaw clench, Faye had no idea.

'I always get what I want, *arcobaleno*. It's simply a matter of timing.'

'Yours or mine?' She strove for a waspish tone to defuse the pleasure moving through her at his endearment.

His lips twisted sardonically. 'Mine, of course.'

'You know I'm tempted to refuse to sell to you now, just on principle, don't you?'

'But you'll give it the careful consideration it deserves and conclude that you're far too sensible to do that, *si*?' he queried mockingly.

'Just for that, I'm inclined to string you along for the foreseeable future.'

His face hardened. 'Tomorrow is never guaranteed. Remember that, Faye.'

Thrown into a pit of uncertainty at the sombre warning, she remained silent.

When they arrived on the terrace he nodded curtly, then turned away as several dozen guests approached him. A blessing in disguise that allowed her to blend into the background, she told herself.

Snagging a glass of tonic water, she made small talk with the guests who spoke English, and smiled through her halting Italian with those who didn't. When Alberto spotted her and wove his way towards her, Faye sighed in relief.

He designated himself her guide, introducing her to everyone in their vicinity until her head spun from trying to recall names.

She was helping herself to a delicious bite of lemon chicken when Stefano and Francesco Castella approached. Thus far she'd had no personal interaction with Carlotta's brothers, but she'd seen them around the office…noted their calculating glances.

They reached her, and she saw Maceo's head jerk up from where he was engrossed in conversation across the terrace. Narrowed eyes flicked from her to the brothers, returning to hers for several moments before he looked away.

Despite their inconsequential small talk, Faye sensed the Castella brothers were assessing her, probing her for weakness. Beside her, Alberto stiffened at each seemingly casual phrase they uttered. And she sensed the many glances Maceo threw her way while the brothers lingered.

When they eventually left, she frowned at Alberto's sigh of relief.

'What was all that?' Faye asked, slowly expelling a calming breath.

'Nothing you should waste your time on,' Alberto reassured her, although his faint frown indicated otherwise. 'Those two are…*drammatico*.'

Faye bit her tongue against pressing for further elaboration. This was a party, after all. Although judging by the thunder on Maceo's face when he glanced her way her once more, enjoyment wasn't high on his list.

* * *

Not for a single moment in his life had Maceo been so racked with indecision.

Stay close or retreat.

Give in to her demands or pretend she didn't exist.

Every course of action reaped the same outcome—the intensifying of that hunger that had taken root within him, awakening needs he'd suppressed because seeking pleasure of any kind was an insult to his parents' memory.

But since that kiss he'd been bracingly reminded that he was a man. With a man's needs. And Faye was very much a woman. A woman with a great many secrets that might very well prove detrimental to him. To the legacy his parents had died safeguarding.

But a woman, nevertheless.

Out of sight or in his presence, wearing one of her outrageous outfits with that *arcobaleno* hair, she *haunted* him.

He sucked in a slow, steadying breath. Which immediately betrayed him by arriving with her delicate scent. He attempted to concentrate on the conversation he was having, although he didn't need much brain power to glean that it was skewed towards another sycophantic display.

Faye would never stray into sycophancy. She's probably never even come across the word.

She neither cared about impressing him nor elevating herself in his eyes, the way every other guest here strained to. And, despite his less than subtle statements on Wednesday night, she hadn't condemned him to the primitive, sexist junkyard where he probably belonged.

Whatever male you eventually belong to...

Santa cielo! There had been no other male in his thoughts besides himself when he'd uttered those ridiculous words. And, *Dio lo aiuti*, he'd felt every one of them in his very bones. Had experienced a hot, powerful throb of primal possessiveness that had made him question his sanity.

The same sensation had assaulted him when she'd opened her door to him earlier, wearing a dress that had shredded his control. Only a desperate summoning of that framed list, that soul-shaking vow, had stopped him from succumbing to his savage hunger. He didn't *deserve* relief of any kind. Especially not with Luigi's stepdaughter. Although he was beginning to suspect Carlotta's hand in this new and singular torment he was currently experiencing...

Maceo was aware he was fast reaching the end of this particular rope. That soon he would throw another log into the inferno he battled each day. One he suspected might well test his very mettle—

'Is everything satisfactory, *signor*?' asked his Latin American senior executive.

Maceo unclenched his jaw long enough to deliver an excuse tempered with a stiff smile, before removing himself from the tedious conversation.

Instantly, husky laughter reached his ears...curled around his senses, held on tight and demanded attention.

Faye.

With a compulsion he deeply resented, he glanced across his landscaped gardens. There she was, surrounded by a clutch of admirers.

Telling himself he should be satisfied that Stefano and Francesco had made themselves scarce didn't work as his feet propelled him to her. As the bare expanse of her smooth back dissected by the thinnest of twin straps made him swallow a groan.

To their credit, her admirers dispersed as he approached, leaving them alone in the shadow of a cypress tree. The sun hadn't quite set, and the encroaching gloom before the lights came on perfectly suited Maceo's mood.

'You have a face like thunder again,' Faye murmured. 'Tell me... Your dislike of me—it goes beyond your role as executor of Carlotta's will, doesn't it?' She raised defiant eyes to his.

Dio mio, she was truly fearless. And somehow he couldn't find it in himself to be annoyed by it any longer.

'If you must know, I detest people who expect handouts for doing nothing. But perhaps in your case there's valid cause to give you a pass.'

Her mouth dropped open. 'There is?'

He shrugged. And before she could respond to the words he hadn't intended to speak, he ploughed ahead. 'What were you discussing with Stefano and Francesco?'

Her eyes widened, knowledge dawning in their indigo depths. 'They're the reason for your hang-ups, aren't they?'

Partly.

'Answer the question, if you please.'

She sipped her drink leisurely before she answered. 'They tried to be coy about it, but I think they were prying into what I am to you.'

'And?'

'And I didn't give them the satisfaction of an answer. I reckoned if you want them to know, you'll tell them.'

Her unexpected loyalty stunned him. *'Grazie.'*

'What did they do? And, before you deny it, know that I have eyes, Maceo.'

Why did his name on her lips thrill him so? And why wasn't he telling her to mind her own business?

'Besides making Carlotta's life a misery at every opportunity?' he said.

She frowned. 'Carlotta? I thought this was about you. It felt...personal.'

Although for the life of him he couldn't decipher why, he found himself elaborating. 'After the accident, they and the rest of the board members tried to take the company away from her. They pulled every trick in the book, from declaring her incompetent to manipulating her grief. They even attempted blackmail.'

'Then why are they still here, employed by Casa di Fiorenti?' *By you*, her tone suggested.

'Because she was kind-hearted. To Carlotta, family meant everything.'

His neutrality failed when he heard the rough edge of guilt and bitterness in his own voice.

'You don't share the sentiment?' Faye observed.

Secrets he wished he didn't possess clawed at his insides. 'Not when that family is intent on doing you harm, no.'

'The company was yours too. Didn't they come after you?'

'I happened to be...indisposed at the time.'

'Indisposed?'

His lips twisted. 'The small matter of being in a coma and unable to defend myself.'

She paled and sucked in a sharp breath. 'You were in a *coma*?'

Maceo was surprised the office gossips hadn't already divulged that information.

'Oh, my God, Maceo...'

Did she know she'd clutched his arm? That her grip tightened by the second? A throb of guilty pleasure beat through him along with the shame, because he liked her touch far too much to tell her. To remind himself why he shouldn't allow it.

'How—' She gasped as enlightenment arrived. 'You were in the same accident?' she whispered.

'*Si*, I was.' Something moved through him—an awakening of that deep pain. That profound regret. And the guilt. *Always the guilt.*

'What...? How did you survive?'

He shrugged. 'According to witnesses, I was thrown clear too, before the car went off the road. I wasn't as lucky as Carlotta, though. I suffered head injuries and slipped into a coma.'

One he hadn't come out of for over a year.

Her breath emerged shakily. He wanted to devour it. To absorb every ounce of emotion she could spare, hoard it like a miser for those dark days ahead when the reality that he was truly alone threatened to drive him insane.

Did he deserve even that? No, he didn't. And yet he couldn't help himself.

'Does your heart grow soft for me, *cara*?' he queried, yearning for another morsel to take his mind off his bleak future.

She exhaled, another shaky breath that drew him like a siren song. 'I'd be heartless not to feel for anyone who goes through something like that.'

'But I'm not "anyone", am I, Faye?'

Several expressions chased across her face, charged by the dark magic that weaved around them. 'No, you're not. But you deserve the same consideration.'

Her attempt to put him in his place unsettled him. 'Is that all I deserve?' he pressed, giving in to the urge to stroke that smooth, silky cheek, to brush his thumb over lips that tasted as sweet as he suspected heaven tasted.

He knew he should stop. Knew he was letting himself down. But, *mio Dio*, this woman made him weak. And he'd been fighting for so long…

He'd never attributed any lofty connotations to his sexual circumstances. The decision he'd taken over a decade ago had been rooted in loyalty and the need to honour his parents' memory. He'd vowed not to chase pleasure or contentment when his parents lay dead because he'd acted as judge, jury and executioner.

Nothing had changed. His demons raged as virulently as ever, demanding his continued sacrifice. So why was denying himself now so challenging? Why, for the first time in a decade, did he want to fall short of his own goals?

'I'm not sure how…what you mean…'

'Aren't you?'

'Maceo…'

He parried. She retreated.

Their silent little dance had led them behind a larger

cypress tree, farther away from curious eyes. Capturing her soft nape, lowering his head and taking those luscious lips with his in that moment felt deliciously simple. And yet life-altering in a way that shook through him.

She moaned and clung harder to him. The sweet sound of her whimper tore a reciprocal sound from within him—a vocal manifestation of the hunger clawing through him. A hunger *she'd* stoked from the first moment he'd set eyes on her. A hunger he knew deep in his bones would be just as tough to wrestle as his demons.

Later. When this temporary madness had eased.

He nudged her against the tree, exhaling in satisfaction as her soft curves moulded to him. It was almost as if she had been made for him, if one believed in such whimsy.

He most certainly didn't. This was simply a combination of chemicals, aligned to trigger base instincts. Nothing more. He would walk away as soon as this insanity was dispensed with.

He spiked his fingers into her hair, angled her face up for a deeper kiss. A deeper taste.

And felt her hands on his chest.

Pushing him away.

Maceo levered himself away, disbelief dripping ice and reality into his veins, reminding of where he was. *Who* he was.

'Stop. I… I can't,' she said, her voice husky with arousal but firm enough to push him back another step.

While he'd been lost in her allure the lights had come on. A metaphor for his shameful actions, perhaps? Too late, his hand drifted to his breastbone. But of course he'd left the list in his bedroom. Because he didn't want to be reminded of it? A deeper shame crawled over his skin as the answer arrived in the throbbing of his groin.

'Maceo?'

'Hurry along then, *bellissimo arcobaleno.* Consider your reprieve granted.'

Her eyes widened and her lips worked as if she would object. But a second later she turned her back and walked away. Leaving him in a far greater torment than he'd wrestled with only an hour ago. Because, as he'd suspected, even the simple act of watching her walk away challenged his every vow. Threatened to erode the foundations of the belief that had guided him so steadily for a decade.

His turmoil was nowhere near battened down when he rejoined the party and played host with forced alacrity. And when the last guest had departed and he went upstairs, not towards his own suite but in *her* direction, he told himself it was because he needed to face this new demon head-on.

His knock was loud and rough, echoing the sensations inside him.

She opened the door wearing another concoction of bright colours, this time a thigh-skimming nightie that left the expanse of her long, magnificent legs on display.

Maceo swallowed a thick sound he was sure stemmed from this woman's torment of him and watched her wide indigo eyes latch defiantly on to his.

'Is there something you need, Maceo?'

Diavolo, si. He wanted this madness to end. *Pronto.* He wanted his belief in the promises he'd made to remain unshaken, to accept his solitary state, to remain the sole survivor left behind to honour the sacrifices of his family.

He most certainly didn't want his head crowded with thoughts of this woman. To be tortured with elusive glimpses of what stepping off the path he'd chosen for himself might look like.

So he forced his hands to remain at his sides, his shoulder braced against the doorjamb as he cast an indolent eye into her suite. 'Pico. Where is he?'

She blinked in bewilderment. 'You're here about the dog?'

'*Si. My* dog. Whom you've commandeered for far too long. Where is he?'

He gave a low whistle. From behind her shoulder, fully ensconced in her bed and looking infinitely content with his lot, Pico raised his head. He proceeded to eye Maceo warily, warning him not to ruin his good fortune.

Maceo was both ashamed and irritated by his intense jealousy of his pet.

'He's comfortable where he is,' Faye stated—as if Maceo didn't have eyes.

'That may be so, but I recall giving specific instructions that you were to stay away from him.'

She huffed in annoyance. 'Are you *really* here to tell me off about Pico?'

With a compulsion he couldn't resist, he reached out and stroked the irresistible smoothness of her neck. 'Yes,' he answered truthfully. Gruffly. 'But there's another matter that needs attention...'

His hand caressed lower, to the sweet juncture where her neck met her shoulder.

She shivered, but remained bold. Ferociously staring him down. 'Is there?'

'*Si*, and I think you know, Faye. You know that I can't seem to fight this need to taste you again since I discovered once wasn't enough,' he said, aware that his voice was almost accusatory.

His candour seemed to disarm her, if only for a moment. But he gloried in that second when her skin flushed and her lips parted. When her breathing grew rapid and beneath the satin sheen of her nightgown her nipples pebbled.

'And I think you want to taste me too.'

'What do you want me to say to that?' she asked.

Her eyes grew heavy as he stepped into the room, but she didn't retreat. Her fire only beckoned him, pulled him to his doom.

'Deny me, Faye,' he growled, lowering his head because he couldn't *not* draw closer to the perfection of her lips. Couldn't *not* inhale the sweet scent of cherry blossom and arousal blooming from her. 'Perhaps it's best for both of us if you do.'

He had no intention of indulging in immersion therapy, but perhaps sensory deprivation was what he needed. All the same he held his breath, his insides churning with something close to trepidation. Because suddenly a *no* seemed like the worst possible declaration.

Fire sparked from her eyes. 'You've decided I'm to be your next plaything when you don't even like me. Why should I make this game easy for you?'

He bit back a grim smile, stroked his fingers over the soft skin at her throat, revelling in the rush of her pulse beneath his touch.

'You're mistaken about a few things. For starters, *playing* is the last thing on my mind, *arcobaleno*. Secondly, there are a great many things two people can indulge in without the prerequisite to *like* each other.'

A shocked little laugh left her lips. 'Are you serious?'

He looked her square in the eyes, tempted to show her the demons he was ignoring for this stolen moment. 'Exceedingly. You want me to prove it? Tell me right now, Faye. Do you *like* me?'

Her lashes swept down for a moment, then her eyes clashed with his once more. 'Answering that one way or another will give you an unfair advantage.'

He laughed, to his own surprise registering that he was enjoying this exchange. Perhaps immersion therapy was exactly what he needed. Because holding back from devouring her was crucifying him.

'The only one with an unfair advantage is you,' he said.

'Why is that?'

'Because right in this moment you hold all the damn power. Take it, Faye, if you dare,' he taunted.

Her eyes narrowed. Then, with an aggrieved hiss, she launched herself at him.

Maceo speared his fingers into her soft, silky hair, tugging her none too gently that last vital inch into his body. Then he walked her back soundlessly across the carpet towards the wide, inviting expanse of her rumpled bed.

With a groan torn from his soul he devoured her, teeth, tongue and lips sampling every inch of her mouth. Giddily, he felt her hands on him, equally exploring, equally urgent. Demanding everything he wanted to give.

Absently, he heard a tiny affronted yelp, then a thump as Pico relocated himself to the floor.

Maceo's smile of triumph was lost somewhere in the deep kiss he demanded from the warm, tempting woman beneath him. The woman whose secrets and shadows should repel him, whose very presence in his life should reinforce his pledge but instead was shattering it.

Besides his vow, the other reason for his turbulent emotions rammed home.

Diavolo, he didn't like to think of himself as special, but he knew that, despite the circumstances, his situation was unique. A thirty-year-old male without a single true sexual experience belonged in a museum. Or in the depths of some faith-based tome. Not strutting about wearing Italian silk and juggling the challenges of a billion-euro business.

The more reality trickled in, the more the possibility of Faye cracking the titanium shell of his vow grew. Until experiencing his *first*…experiencing *her*…was all that occupied his mind.

Another thing he was discovering was that when Faye was in his arms the demons quietened. He wasn't idiotic enough to believe they would recede indefinitely. But the temporary respite was…intoxicating. Enough to make him yearn for it.

He would pay the price for his selfishness later, when the true depths of his desolation came crashing in. But for now…

'For what it's worth, *cara*, my coming here wasn't an easy decision,' he drawled against her swollen lips.

She stiffened instantly, and he wanted to curse himself to the darkest depths of hell.

'Thank you for that. But—'

'Let me take a wild guess. It won't be happening?' he said.

The dryness in his voice could have started a brush fire. But it was nothing compared to the clamouring in his head as his demons rushed back, mocking his desperation to escape.

'No, it *won't*,' she stressed, pushing at his shoulders.

It didn't help that her voice shook. Or that uncertainty wavered across her face.

But little by little, her resolve hardened. Maceo saw it and despised it, because he was jealous of his inability to feel the same way. To stop himself from reaching out for more when he didn't deserve it.

More than a little bewildered, he laughed under his breath. Perhaps this was another hard lesson he needed to learn.

'Pico stays with me,' she stated, her chin once again tilted in defiance as he rose from the bed and paced away from temptation.

Dio mio, her ferocity sparked a fire inside him. One he wanted to burn in. 'And who are *you* to dictate such a thing?'

'I'm the one he comes to when he misses his mistress. I'm the one he follows around, despite your unreasonable orders. The one he knows will give him the affection he needs.'

Jealousy seared harder, as did the chasm of desolation inside him. 'Did you ever stop to think I have valid reasons for those orders? He'll most likely grow attached to you, believing you will fill the void, when that couldn't be further from the truth. You have experienced what it feels like to be abandoned, if your emotional outbursts about Luigi are to be believed. And yet you would visit it upon another creature?'

Her keen eyes rested on his face. 'Are we talking about Pico or you, Maceo?' she demanded softly.

That peculiar trepidation tightened his chest. He opened his mouth, intent on a brusque denial. But it died in his throat because he was aware that some of his words might stem from a place he didn't like to examine very often.

'You think you know me that well?' he asked gruffly instead.

'You've lost your family in hard circumstances. If I were you, I'd be devastated too. And I'd be terribly afraid of getting attached. To anything or anyone. But—'

'But nothing. We're not talking about me,' he interjected, alarm bells clanging because she was hitting far too close to home. 'We're discussing Pico.'

Hurt wavered across her face before her chin rose higher. 'He'll adapt.'

'Will he? Or is that another foolish wish? A way to absolve yourself of guilt because you might be leaving a scar on a recently bereaved soul?'

Dio mio, could he hold a starker mirror up to himself?

Her gaze dropped before boldly meeting his. 'You say that as if he won't have you when I'm gone. Surely having more people to love is better than having none?'

That shell inside him fractured again, leaching needs that would betray his parents' memory. But, as hard as he tried, Maceo couldn't find the strength to seal it. 'Be very careful, Faye.'

He expected her customary feisty response, but a look that closely resembled sadness shrouded her face. 'I will be, Maceo. I always am.'

She turned away. Dismissed him.

Maceo left her room, leaving his triumphant dog behind, and puzzled for the dozenth time why another encounter with Faye Bishop had left him feeling as if he'd grappled with a cyclone and lost, when only recently he'd vowed to win...

CHAPTER SEVEN

IF CAPRI WAS a cool and sophisticated haven, St Lucia was a sultry, tropical paradise.

The lush vegetation, exotic birds and the sheer profusion of colour seemed almost too good to be true. But then for the last handful of weeks Faye had felt as if she was living in a lucid dream. One of heightened emotion and intense drama, mainly in the form of the man seated next to her in the air-conditioned Jeep with tinted windows, his eyes shielded by a pair of designer sunglasses as they drove away from his private airstrip.

The long flight from Italy to St Lucia had been surreal in itself. Because of course she'd been introduced to another level of affluence in the form of the Fiorenti private jet, equipped with every item of luxury imaginable. And, whether she'd been ensconced in the living area or—in a futile bid to come to terms with the previous night's episode with Maceo, during which she'd skated even closer to danger—retreating to an area that had turned out to be Maceo's personal cinema room, the flight attendants had been a discreet glance away, ready to cater to her every whim.

Not that she'd been tempted to request anything beyond refreshments. She'd been entirely consumed by their interaction from the night before.

Was still consumed by it.

Whereas Maceo seemed to harbour zero qualms about how things had ended.

There'd been no censure, just a long, sizzling, assessing look at the breakfast table. Since then she'd caught him staring contemplatively at her. It wasn't so much as if he was trying to work her out. It was more an inkling that he was already halfway to plundering the heart of her secret.

But from the moment they'd taken off, the powerful CEO had resumed his role. He'd been all about Casa di Fiorenti business, apprising her of their itinerary, which included sailing to two plantations via his yacht. She'd questioned the use of that mode of transport, to be curtly informed that it was so he could travel and work at the same time.

A part of her envied his skilful ability to proceed as normal, while the major part revisited the incident in her suite for the hundredth time.

Yes, she'd disgracefully jumped him. And, yes, the torrid kiss had been sublime. But Faye had become increasingly preoccupied with the conversation *after* she'd pulled the brakes.

The subtext had seemed…monumental. The look on Maceo's face had been an arresting tableau of regret, guilt, pain and fury. Just what had happened to him? And why couldn't she put the incident out of her mind?

As if triggered by the unasked question, his laser-powered gaze flicked to her and she realised he'd spoken. 'I'm sorry, what?'

One sardonic eyebrow lifted. 'We have arrived. I'd leave you to your daydreaming, but I don't think you'd appreciate the heat once I turn the engine off. So…are you coming?'

'Of course I'm—' She looked past him to the structure they'd parked in front of, and was thrown into yet another realm of awe.

'Dear God, do the Fiorentis do anything approaching normal?'

'I don't quite catch your meaning,' he replied, plucking his sunglasses off to slip them into his pocket.

Her gaze darted back to him, her face flaming when she realised she'd spoken out loud. Brazening it out, she flicked a hand at the jaw-dropping house basking in the late-afternoon golden sunlight. 'I mean this…this impossible dream of a house.'

'I take it you like it?' he enquired drolly.

She snorted. 'That's like asking a racing car driver if he likes speed.'

One corner of the mouth she'd become intimately acquainted with last night lifted, lending him a rakish, almost boyish look that softened the dark edges of his demeanour. Heat swirled through her belly as two things struck her—firstly, that she'd never seen him truly smile, and secondly that she was terrified to contemplate the damage such an expression from Maceo would cause a woman.

'Then I hope it'll tempt you to exit before this vehicle turns into a furnace.'

He alighted, and then, to her surprise, came around to open her door. The teasing smile was widening, triggering a curious mixture of excitement and despair, which intensified the moment she stepped out and inhaled his scent.

Memories of that scent on his hard body plastered passionately against hers immediately took centre stage in her thoughts, then reeled forward through graphic possibilities of what might have happened if they hadn't stopped.

'I've lost you again. Should I be offended? Or flattered?' he asked.

'Flattered?' she echoed hazily.

'Your expression gives you away. But, truly, there's no crime in reliving a unique moment.'

'You must be speaking metaphorically, or something, because I see no crime whatsoever in calling a halt after a foolish decision.'

To her absolute dismay, he smiled with genuine amusement. It utterly transformed his face. A true fallen angel with a wicked streak. His smile promised all sorts of devilish delight. Faye felt her jaw dropping and scrambled to right that wrong.

'We're two level-minded adults, *cara*. With needs that

seem programmed to lead us in one direction, whether we wish to go or not,' he rasped, his voice a little rough and a lot disturbing.

'What's that supposed to mean?'

Why on earth was her voice quivering? She wasn't some quaking maiden. She had one experience and its devastating aftermath to her name. And a vow to ensure no more were added to it.

A vow she'd almost broken last night.

A vow she risked now, standing here in the shadow of Maceo's towering frame, getting lost in the accented timbre of his voice and the spellbinding paradise around them.

'It means, whether we like it or not, this thing needs to be addressed.'

Despite his conceited demeanour, there was an edge to the words, indicating that perhaps he wasn't as sanguine about it as he wanted to be.

The hair trigger that demanded she answer with another denial pushed words to the tip of her tongue. Maceo halted them with a simple slide of his forefinger over her lips.

'We really should go inside. I'd hate to see this exquisite skin of yours suffer under this sun.'

As if on cue, a thick drop of sweat slid down her throat and over her clavicle.

His gaze zeroed in on it and Faye felt every inch of the bead's slow trajectory in the rapt expression on his face. Hunger clamoured through her as his nostrils flared. The tip of his tongue glided over his inner bottom lip and Faye experienced it deep in her pelvis, in the hot and needy core of her womanhood.

Move.

She sucked in a desperate breath and dragged her gaze away, only to lose it when his hand slid down her arm to capture hers. Firmly he led her up wide stone steps, through grand oak double doors into a marble-floored foyer with a giant floral centrepiece that gave off sweet perfume through the airy space.

There they were met by a clutch of household staff, who introduced themselves and immediately offered refreshments.

With a cold glass of fruit punch in hand, Maceo shifted into host mode and offered to show her round.

From high-ceilinged rooms with plantation-style shutters that opened out onto exquisite terraces, to a twenty-foot-high pavilion just beyond the main house, fashioned for intimate dining, and a sparkling turquoise pool, every corner of the mansion was breathtaking.

Halfway through the tour Faye kicked off her platform heels, sighing when her feet touched cool stone paving. From a shaded patio, Maceo pointed out the majestic backdrop of the Pitons and the Caribbean Sea. And as her gaze rushed over all that beauty she spotted the sleek yacht moored a quarter of a mile away from the private beach.

It was multi-decked and sizeable, without being overly ostentatious. And yet it sent prickles of awareness skating over her skin. Every space she'd occupied with Maceo so far had offered a sense of freedom—albeit a false one, because Maceo could occupy her space and thoughts even when he was miles away. The yacht, however, seemed...*intimate*.

There was that word again. Creeping far too often and relentlessly into her thoughts.

'Does the inside please you as much as the outside?' Maceo asked when they returned indoors, with that low, deeply disturbing note still in his voice.

Feeling unsettled, she examined his expression for an insight as to the subtle changes in their skirmish. There was no mockery. But there was a quiet, intense emotion she was afraid to decipher.

'It's magnificent,' she answered, simply and truthfully.

He nodded with satisfaction, then straightened from where he'd draped his streamlined body against a wall.

'*Bene*. The housekeeper will show you to your room. If you need anything just let the staff know.'

Abruptly he turned away and started to walk off.

'Where are you going?' she blurted.

He paused, then shot her a droll look. 'I'm attempting, perhaps for the first time since we met, to leave while we're not at each other's throats. I think the term is to quit while I'm ahead, *si*?'

Faye was shaking her head before he'd finished. 'Surely we can find a way to coexist and be...?' She stopped, because she couldn't quite find a term that described what not being in conflict with Maceo looked like.

Pleasant? Peaceful? *Affable?*

Words far too tame for the high-octane friction that existed between them.

'Without...?' he pressed, one eyebrow quirked in amusement.

She threw exasperated hands in the air. 'I don't know. But I didn't fly halfway across the world to be left twiddling my thumbs because you're attempting to be...whatever version it is of yourself you're being right now. At the very least can we call a truce on hostilities?'

That smile returned, played at his lips while he stared at her. 'Very well. If that is what you truly wish. Take the remainder of the day. Relax. Work some of the jet lag out of your system. We'll reconvene at some point tomorrow?'

A knot of tension eased inside her and she realised she'd been holding her breath. Because she'd needed that reassurance of when she'd see him again. *Dear God...*

'Sure. Okay.'

With a far too cunning smile, Maceo walked away, leaving her feeling as if she'd walked into another of his silken traps.

The housekeeper arrived to escort her upstairs, relieving her from dwelling on her thoughts. Faye smiled as the older woman informed her with quiet but deep pride that they were in the much sought-after suburb of Soufrière. That she'd worked for the Fiorenti and Caprio families—in her dream job—for over twenty years.

This prompted Faye, just for a moment, to consider asking her about Luigi and Pietro, before dismissing the idea. All she'd be doing was inviting speculation.

In her opulent suite, her clothes had been unpacked and neatly put away in the large dressing room. French windows led onto a sprawling terrace and Faye's breath caught all over again at the magnificent view.

Once the housekeeper had pointed out every luxurious amenity in the bedroom and sky-lit rainforest-themed bathroom, she smilingly enquired about Faye's dinner plans.

Torn between asking about Maceo's plans and remaining oblivious, she settled for a quiet dinner on her terrace. The view was too stunning to waste. And a few hours to get her head straight wouldn't hurt either.

Dinner was a superb seafood salad, washed down with another fruit punch, after which Faye returned to her suite, took off the scarlet linen jumpsuit she'd travelled in and indulged herself for far too long beneath the powerful jets of the shower before sliding between seriously comfortable sheets.

She woke the next day to a message from Maceo that he would be in conference calls all morning and that she had the day to herself.

Faye refused to examine why the message left her hollow inside.

After a lazy breakfast, she powered up her laptop and re-read every report about Casa di Fiorenti's St Lucia operation. Then she fired off an email to Alberto with some new flavour ideas.

Feeling her concentration wavering after that, she gave up, and slipped into a sun-yellow bikini and matching beach dress with a long slit that fell to her ankles.

Barefoot, she went downstairs to the pool. After confirming the time difference, she plucked her phone from her bag. She hadn't spoken to her mother in a few days, and although she wasn't worried about Angela Bishop's wellbeing, she was suddenly dying to hear her mother's voice.

Her call connected a minute later.

'Hi, Mum? Are you okay?' she asked, when a soft, mellow voice answered.

'Of course I am, Faye. Why wouldn't I be?'

A lump rose in her throat at the clear, lucid response. Her mother was having a good day.

'I'm glad to hear it. What have you been up to?' she asked, reclining on a lounger.

For the next twenty minutes Faye lost herself in her mother's everyday life at New Paths, tossing in a few vague anecdotes of her own. But behind their exchange was the pain and sadness that always lingered.

Faye wasn't aware she was crying until she felt the wetness on her cheeks. She struggled to pull herself together. The last thing she wanted to do was upset her mother with her silly tears.

She waited for a natural break in the conversation, then ended it with as much enthusiasm as she could muster.

She'd just tossed her phone onto the table beside her when a shadow loomed over her.

'You're distressed. Why?' Maceo demanded tightly.

Faye blinked, struggling to get her emotions under control as he sauntered closer. 'It's nothing.'

'I beg to disagree.'

She pressed her lips together. 'I thought we weren't meeting until later. Why are you here?'

He held out a glass and she realised that he'd come with refreshments.

'It's hot out here. I thought a drink might help,' he stated, his gaze tracking her face. Yesterday's easy humour was nowhere in the eyes that shamelessly dissected her expression.

She accepted the drink while trying to hide the feeling of vulnerability his presence elicited. 'Thank you.'

He claimed the lounger next to hers, his gaze never leaving her face. 'Tell me, or leave me to form several probably wildly inaccurate conclusions,' he said, with a deceptive softness that didn't hide his intent.

Faye dropped her eyes to her glass and then, fighting weakness, boldly returned his gaze. 'Or you could leave it alone?'

'We seem to have this conversation quite a lot, no?'

'Because you have no qualms about prying, but only deliver information *you* promise when the mood takes you.'

Was this a test? Was getting her to open herself up to him one of the requisites of fulfilling his duty as executor? Or was it something more?

Faye didn't ask, because suddenly she was terrified to find out that his interest was merely a means to an end...

'My mother,' she blurted, then pressed her lips together, stunned by her own response.

'She is unwell?'

She shook her head. 'Far from it. She's in a brilliant mood.'

He frowned. 'And this causes you distress?'

To say any more would be to reveal far too much, so she remained silent.

Of course Maceo wasn't going to be satisfied with that. 'She lives with you on this farm?' he pressed.

'Yes.'

'Perhaps I'm rusty on the mechanics of family relationships, but verifying that she is well and healthy should be a cause for contentment, should it not?'

Faye scrambled to get her emotions under control. 'It is. I am. I'm not even sure why I am crying.'

His tawny gaze turned sceptical.

'Can we change the subject?' she asked, with a touch of desperation.

'Of course. You want to discuss your favourite subject, perhaps?' His silky words held a definite edge.

Faye nodded, uncaring that she was traipsing from one dangerous territory into another.

He remained silent long enough for her to wonder if he'd changed his mind. Then, 'Has it occurred to you that you're searching for answers that are right in front of you?'

'How do you mean?'

His nostrils flared briefly. 'Perhaps Luigi left you for your own good?'

Pain lanced through her, but she pushed past it. 'Would you leave it alone? Without knowing whether your parents loved you or not?'

His face tightened, his jaw clenching for a moment before he released it. Lifting his glass to his lips, he took a large gulp before setting the drink aside. 'I know they cared for me. To the best of their ability.'

'What does *that* mean?'

Jaded, faintly bleak eyes pinned hers. 'Does anyone really love completely? Or is there an inherent selfishness in us that guarantees we'll always hold back? A fear of disappointing others, perhaps?'

'Did you not love Carlotta? Was that not enough?' she asked, plagued by a need to know.

He tensed, his eyes boring deeper into her. 'How you pry, *cara*. And yet you are such an expert at withholding.'

Faye lifted her chin. 'Is that a yes or a no?'

'Does it matter to you if I did or not?' he parried.

That curious tightening in her chest—the one that strangled her each time she imagined him and Carlotta together—produced a response she wished she could take back the moment it escaped. 'Yes.'

His eyes narrowed. '*Perché?* Why? You wish to know if I am capable of those deep and meaningful emotions you seem inclined to attach to everything?'

His derision stung, but she didn't back down. 'What if I do?'

'Then I would caution you to brace yourself for disappointment.'

Her heart lurched alarmingly, echoes of Luigi's desertion stabbing at her. 'Because you're incapable of love?'

He remained silent for another long stretch, and then he shrugged. 'Because life has a tendency to give you what you want while depriving you of what you need. As to your question... Luigi was Carlotta's first and only love. I went into our marriage with both eyes open and therefore I wasn't disappointed.'

'Not expecting something doesn't mean you're not hurt when you're deprived of it,' she pushed, her mind racing with different interpretations of his answer.

Was he bitter because his love had been unrequited?

Faye bit her tongue against asking and broke his gaze, suddenly unable to withstand its ferocity. She discarded her glass, prepared to rise.

He stopped her by the simple act of caging her legs between his, leaning forward to place his hands on either side of her hips. She didn't feel trapped. More compelled to stay put simply by the hypnotic effect he exuded.

'Are you fleeing because my answers don't satisfy you?'

'I'm not. Weren't we just making conversation?' She tried for a light tone and failed miserably.

'Hmm... I had the impression you were trying to *understand* me, *cara*. The question is, why? We are going to part in a few weeks, are we not?' he demanded, a touch of acid in his voice.

'You're right. We are. And I'll never have to think about you again.'

Perhaps the shadows in his eyes were a trick of the sun, but the tightening of his sensual mouth wasn't. 'Keep telling yourself that, *arcobaleno*.'

'What's that supposed to mean?'

'You are under my skin. The same way I'm under yours. There's no escaping it.'

His voice was sandpaper-rough, perfectly pitched to burrow deep inside her, to places she'd closed off after Matt. And yet he seemed to with effortless ease.

Silence fell between them as his words sank in.

From nowhere, a pulse of potent feminine power flared through her. 'It's just our unique circumstances,' she said.

He shrugged. 'Perhaps.'

One hand moved, tracing the skin where her dress had parted, from mid-thigh to knee, before sliding his hands behind her leg. The sensation was shockingly visceral, enough to draw a gasp.

'If it helps, I don't like it any more than you do.' Before she could respond to that curiously bruising declaration, he continued, 'You think you will forget me that easily, Faye? When you can't even remain within touching distance without your every sense clamouring for me?'

Heat washed through her as his fingers kneaded her flesh. 'I'll take care of how I feel. Feel free to do the same for yourself.'

He didn't respond immediately. Instead his eyes conducted a slow, thorough journey, landing in places that highlighted her breathless state, her helpless reaction to him. She knew her nipples were pebbled against her bikini. That a fine tremble had seized her since he'd laid his hands on her. Her fingers were locked hard into the cushions of the lounger just so she wouldn't reach for him.

'And what way is that? Do be kind and share, *per favore*,' he rasped.

Retreat. Regroup. Anything but sit here, tormented by the need to touch him.

Too late, he saw her struggle. Stoked it.

'Do it,' he encouraged thickly. 'Touch me.'

'No,' she said boldly. Then ruined it by trembling.

That drew a wicked smile from him. And the smile grew

the longer she remained seated, weakening her further when he leaned in until his lips were a whisper from hers.

'You're not a coward. Take what you want. Set us both free.'

She drew in a desperate breath, inhaling his potent scent until every pore of her being was filled with him. Slowly his smile disappeared, replaced by a stark hunger that threatened to eat her alive.

How had they got here?

The answer was terrifyingly simple.

They *always* ended up here. As if an invisible force controlled them.

But she wasn't a passive passenger, without any say or control in her destiny. On the contrary, faced with temptation such as she'd never known before, her willpower had pulled her though when things got out of hand.

'We're going to part in a few weeks...'

His words echoed in her head, intensifying the tightness in her chest and the hollow in her belly.

Perhaps it was the need to eradicate those feelings that made her react. Perhaps her foundations had been badly eroded when she wasn't looking.

Whatever.

With a rough, unbidden little sound, torn from her throat, Faye wrapped her arms around his broad shoulders and closed the gap between them.

Maceo permitted her free rein for all of five seconds, and then he was pulling her into his lap, disposing of the sundress in two easy moves to leave her clad only in her bikini. He reclined on the lounger, dragging her along his body until she was sprawled on top of him. Then he wove dark magic around them.

Words tumbled from his lips as he tasted her with a ferocity that left her breathless. Moaning, she threw herself into the embrace, the knowledge that this exploration was finite, that some time very soon she would be back in Devon with her mother, memories of Capri and St Lucia a distant dream, sharpening the need to absorb and hoard every second of this experience.

She gasped as Maceo flipped them over and dragged urgent hands down her body. Cupping one breast, he flicked the nipple expertly until it peaked, then groaned under his breath. Searing pleasure darted from the point of contact to her core, making her slick and needy and desperate.

Against her thigh she felt his potent power and shivered.

'I want you. I will have you,' he grated against her throat, the sound so raw and deep it was as if he made the oath to himself.

It burrowed deep inside Faye, and the next shiver that coursed through her, while deeply pleasurable, arrived with a warning. Because for a nanosecond every cell in her body had screamed *yes*.

Yes to opening herself up to another devastating rejection.

Yes to putting not just herself and her innocent mother in humiliation's way but Maceo, too.

Because hers was the sort of stigma that could never be washed away.

She'd been selfish once upon a time, had sought solace when she should have kept her secret. She still bore the emotional scars from that.

Matt had only been a fellow university student, but Maceo was Luigi's godson—part of a family her stepfather had treasured and chosen over her mother and her. And, while the knowledge seared pain into her soul, after weeks in his domain she understood why Luigi had made that choice.

Maceo had impeccable pedigree, and despite his tragic circumstances he had become a powerful, dynamic CEO, revered for his intellect. A man who'd elevated his family's business to international renown and success.

How could that compare to her, a nobody, *an abomination*, with a deep, terrible secret?

If she gave in now, even if her secret remained buried

for her lifetime, knowing she'd stained him would be unconscionable.

She started to pull away.

He caught her chin and stilled her retreat. The action left her with very little choice but to stare into intense tawny eyes alight with passion.

'You are thinking of denying me. Denying *us*. *Again*,' he condemned, with a quiet, deadly rasp.

'I... I have to.' The words were torn from her soul.

'The only reason you *have to* is because something holds you back,' he announced arrogantly. His eyes narrowed to laser slits. 'Your HR forms suggested that you are unattached. Is that a lie?'

'You read my HR forms?' she asked, momentarily distracted before his firm touch focused her back on the electric present.

'I'm CEO,' he stated imperiously. 'Now, answer the question. Do you have a lover, Faye?' he breathed, his voice a volcanic rumble as his gaze flicked down to where they were plastered together, chest to chest.

'What? No! If I had a lover I wouldn't even *start*!'

He breathed out slowly. Then, like an approaching tsunami, the hunger in his eyes intensified, growing possessive, blazing with a fire that threatened to turn her every objection to ash.

She knew it was a mistake to keep lying there, feverishly urging her mind to do the right thing when her body was moulded to his.

'*Allora perché?* Why?' he asked throatily, his gaze searching her face as if he would draw the answer from her very skin.

Absurdly afraid that he would achieve that goal, Faye scrambled off the lounger.

'Why?' She repeated his question. 'Here's a question for *you*. Why are you acting as if this is somehow written in the stars? This is not inevitable. Far from it. I don't want you. I don't want *this*.'

The words were flung out with wild, desperate intent—to make them *both* believe it. But all they achieved was drawing Maceo's narrowed gaze, laser beams searching even harder.

'Lie to yourself all you want, *cara*, but don't insult me. We may not be "inevitable", but have you considered that the one way to be rid of this…this *follia* is to get it out of the way?'

She shook her head. *Retreat. Regroup.*

Finally heeding her own advice, she took a few steps back.

Seeing her blatant retreat, Maceo stilled.

They stayed that way, locked in a churning whirlpool of emotions. Every cell in her body screamed at her to close the gap between them once more. Give in to the *follia*—the madness. But how could she while still keeping him in the dark about her secret?

Torn, she turned away. 'I'm going for a swim. In the sea. I may be a while, so you'll have all the time you need to forget this ever happened.'

She snatched up her dress and her bag and hurried away, with every step feeling his eyes boring into her back. She'd nearly reached the stone steps leading down to the beach when his voice stopped her.

'Faye.'

He was close. Far too close.

She didn't look back, terrified in case that face, that body, the heady knowledge that all that determination was focused on having her, swayed her into doing the unthinkable.

'Nothing has changed. I'll see you at dinner. And rest assured that we will visit this subject again. For my own sanity I'll want a better answer than the flimsy ones you have given me so far.'

His words should have been her cue to refuse his dinner plans. To come up with an excuse to stay in her room.

But even that proved impossible. Because on her return she discovered the staff were packing up her luggage.

Her slightly hysterical demand as to why prompted a response in the form of a short, succinct note from Maceo.

Change of plan. We set sail tonight before sunset.
We won't be returning to the villa for a few days.
Maceo.

They were visiting the plantations early? Was it because he wanted this trip to be over as soon as possible or because he had another strategy up his sleeve?

The urge to refuse rose again, but only for one futile second. She'd accompanied him of her own free will. Protesting now would be counterintuitive to everything she wanted to achieve. And, while she'd learned a few things about Luigi, one question still needed an answer. Tonight would be the perfect opportunity to demand it.

Besides, wasn't this fractious subject the perfect tool to ensure they didn't stray into dangerous territory? Because when they were discussing Luigi they kept their hands off each other. But then weren't they equally adept at directing every subject back to this impossible attraction between them?

Not tonight, she vowed.

The declaration rang hollow, so she busied herself selecting a dinner outfit before all her belongings were spirited away. Then, with nothing to do but while away the hours, she indulged in a long, luxurious bath.

Inevitably, evening arrived, and she stood on the jetty, waiting to be ferried to the yacht.

She ran nervous fingers over her dress, wondering if she was overdressed. *Too late.* The off-the-shoulder chiffon dress in shimmery ombre colours that progressed from white at the bodice through shades of blue and purple to end in a dark mauve at her feet would just have to do. Besides simple silver hoops in her ears, she'd forgone jewellery, letting her free-flowing hair provide the protective layer—albeit a laughable one—she badly needed.

The seventy-metre yacht was ablaze with golden light, a gorgeous streamlined vessel made more awe-inspiring by its perfect reflection in the glass-smooth water. Each second they grew closer, and Faye's mouth grew drier.

'Nothing has changed...'

'For my own sanity...'

Maceo's words pounded deep and hard inside her until she could hear nothing but his deep rasp, the dark promise in his voice that would surely be her doom unless she employed every self-preservation tactic she could muster.

She was taking calming breaths when the tender drew up alongside the yacht. A steward helped her onboard and led her through stunning reception areas and hallways decorated in gleaming champagne, gold and bronze accents and up several staircases to the main deck.

There, Maceo waited, leaning against the railing with his profile turned away from her as he sipped from a crystal glass. A lightweight sand-coloured suit complemented his pristine white shirt, both colours drawing attention to his vibrant tanned skin and sculpted features.

The steward discreetly melted away, and Faye took a moment to arm herself against the onslaught of sensations Maceo never failed to elicit. She managed two full seconds before his head whipped in her direction, burnished gold eyes zeroing in on her. He searched her face for several seconds, before conducting a slow, tortuous scrutiny of her body.

'Buona sera, Faye,' he finally rasped, leaving his position to stride towards her. 'You look sublime.'

'Thank you. I think I read somewhere that yachts and heels don't go together. Do I need to take my shoes off?'

Her question invited extended scrutiny, from her feet to

her hair, where it rested for an eternity. 'You may do whatever pleases you,' he murmured silkily, before reaching past her to pluck a fruity concoction that was ready and waiting on a silver tray.

Faye took it from him, sampled it and almost groaned as decadent flavours burst on her tongue.

His lips twitched. 'Good?'

She nodded. 'Very—thank you.'

Maceo nodded towards the railing. 'Come, let's catch the last of the sunset before it's gone.'

Considering his final words to her that afternoon, Faye wondered if this was the first stage in another devious skirmish. But, unlike during his assessment of her, now Maceo's face gave nothing away.

Deciding to accept his invitation at face value, she kicked off her shoes and accompanied him to the railing. The evening would probably turn fraught at some point anyway, on account of the picture tucked away in her clutch bag.

The reminder made her shiver, drawing his sharp gaze.

'Are you cold?'

'No, just… It's nothing.'

Like her, he seemed to accept her response at face value. He started pointing out stunning landmarks to her, and Faye realised the vessel was moving. She cast one last look over her shoulder at the villa, the sense of leaving safety behind dripping apprehension into her veins.

'No need to look so alarmed, *cara*. You will be returned safe and sound.'

'Would you confess if you intended the opposite?' she teased.

Her attempt at humour misfired when his face hardened. 'You have my word that I will always be truthful with you, Faye,' he stated, with such gravity she felt the power of it deep inside.

'Thank you,' she replied, praying he'd lend credence to his words before the evening ended.

After a charged moment he nodded, then slid effortlessly back into host mode. Almost in perfect synchrony, they sipped their drinks as the sun disappeared in a ball of gorgeous flame into the sea.

Then Maceo led her one deck below, to where an elaborate dinner table was set out for two.

The vichyssoise starter was perfect, the poached salmon with grilled sweet potato equally mouthwatering. But what struck Faye most was how much she was enjoying this less intense Maceo. How his infrequent but jaw-dropping smiles curled around her senses, warming that cold, dark place where fear and isolation lived.

She knew it was temporary, that the knot would be back in its rightful place in a few hours. But banishing that warmth was the hardest thing she'd ever done. So she let it linger, lull her into a place of comfort. Just for a little while.

Too soon the plates were cleared, the after-dinner coffee drunk. Nervous over what was coming, she refused Maceo's offer of a nightcap and went with him into another stunning salon, this one partly shielded from the cool night breeze.

He sat down next to her, arms spread over the back of the sofa, his stance deceptively relaxed even though she sensed he was anything but. Hooded eyes speared her.

'There's something on your mind.'

It wasn't a question.

Faye swallowed. 'You said I could trust you to be straightforward with me.'

He tensed, eyes narrowed. *'Si,'* he affirmed.

Trepidation drummed wildly in her belly, but she reached into her clutch bag.

'Good. Here's your chance to prove it.' She held out the picture, aware her hand was shaking, but knowing this felt too big for her to be distracted by that weakness. 'Who is this man?'

CHAPTER EIGHT

At first he looked puzzled, and then, deciphering exactly what she held, his hand jerked off the back of the sofa to curl around hers, his features turning dark.

'Where did you get this?' he growled, thunder rumbling in his voice.

Every cell in her body quivered. 'Does it matter? I have it.' She pointed to the third man in the photo. 'And I want to know who this is.'

He dropped her hand as quickly as he'd grasped it. 'Why the curiosity?' he asked, clearly deflecting.

'Why do you think? Because he looks a little like Luigi. Is there a family connection?' she probed when Maceo remained statue-still, his features taking on the formidable look that had terrified her during their first meetings.

But she wasn't terrified any more. He'd lowered his guard in varying degrees since then, shown her enough facets of himself to prove he was human. He hurt and mourned, hungered and smiled, even if in a more elevated realm than most.

She waited him out, watched him rise from the sofa, pace to the railing, his gaze settling heavily into the middle distance.

'*Si,*' he confirmed finally.

She waited for more. One minute. Two.

'That's all you're going to give me?'

Tension gripped his whole frame. He exhaled slowly before turning to face her. 'Every family has a black sheep. Pietro was the black sheep of the Caprio family. The dark secret no one liked to talk about.'

Faye swallowed. She knew all too well what he meant. She was the dark secret of her own fractured family. Most likely the reason Luigi had left and never returned.

'But who was he to you? To Luigi?'

He shoved his hands deep into his pockets, rocked on his feet once. 'He was Luigi's fraternal twin brother.'

Faye gasped. 'His *twin*?' Her stepfather had had a close sibling and never bothered to tell her?

'Don't be taken in by that. Being twins didn't mean they automatically shared a special bond. *Dio*, they didn't even remotely share personalities. They were as different as night and day.'

'In what ways, specifically?'

Maceo's expression shuttered. But she hadn't come this far to be deterred now.

'Tell me, Maceo. Please,' she pleaded softly.

A faint shudder shook through him and his face softened momentarily before hardening again. 'It is exactly how I have said. You may believe your circumstances to be different, but the Luigi I knew was a fair man, a man of integrity and honour. Whereas Pietro was…not. He was irresponsible and callous and unkind. He drank too much, drove too fast. He did everything to excess.'

'Those are unpalatable characteristics, sure… But that's not why you're reluctant to discuss him. There's more, isn't there?'

He uttered a potent expletive in Italian, his fingers stabbing into his hair. 'I would prefer it if you would leave it, Faye.'

She shook her head. 'We've been dancing around this subject for weeks, Maceo. You give me just what you think is enough to keep me quiet. But it's not enough. It hasn't been from the start. But that's on me. I realise now that I wasn't ready to hear everything. I'm ready now—for better or worse. Please.'

'I'm not unsympathetic. But must we do this tonight?' he pressed, a peculiar note in his voice as his hand drifted to his breast pocket.

About to respond, Faye frowned and looked around. She'd

been too nervous earlier, or perhaps too cowardly, to admit it to herself. Now she did. Everything—from the lighting to the dinner setting, the sheer magnificence of the scenery to the soft music piping through invisible speakers—pointed to one thing…

Seduction.

Her eyes darted back to him, to the fire in his eyes. 'Maceo…'

Bleakness tightened his face. With a heavy, resolute sigh, his hand dropped. 'Perhaps you are right,' he announced grimly. 'Let's stop dancing around this. You want it all, *cara*? Well, have the whole sordid feast. Then I will be free of this.'

Was that how he saw her? As an obligation to be dispensed with?

Something moved through her. Profound and seismic. Alerting her that something fundamental was about to change. Perhaps in what he was about to tell her. Perhaps in other ways she was too scared to contemplate.

Faye's fingers twisted in her lap as he prowled forward in that far too masculine and animalistic way to reclaim his seat next to her. He started to reach for her hand. At the last moment he froze, his face tightening as he reversed the action.

Faye's heart sank, her insides hollowing with unnerving alarm. Words of protest rose to her lips, but his next words saved her from disgracing herself.

'Pietro was the snake in what should've been a peaceful paradise. He was the reason I was at odds with my parents in the year before they died.'

The dark pain in his voice was palpable.

'What happened?' she asked.

'For years they knew he was up to no good. But, irrationally, they believed he was redeemable simply because he was Luigi's blood. They gave him chance after chance, including a position at the company—which he shamelessly abused by misappropriating funds until the board voted him off. By the time I was a teenager they'd decided the best way to deal with him was to set him up with a monthly allowance and mitigate whatever damage he caused by paying off the paparazzi and bribing whoever needed quieting to protect the family from disgrace.'

Faye swallowed down her distaste. 'Did that work?'

Bitterness twisted his lips. 'Of course not,' he rasped. 'They'd simply handed him another tool to torment them with. And he exploited it. The drug-taking and drinking worsened. He gambled away a fortune using the Fiorenti name. At one point it seemed all my father and Luigi were doing was retaining lawyers to stop the negative publicity Pietro was landing them with.'

His jaw clenched tight.

'Two months before they died I heard them discussing how to tackle the latest problem. He'd been drinking in a bar in Buenos Aires and got involved in a brawl. One of the brawlers was later the victim of a hit and run.'

Ice slithered down her spine. 'Was it Pietro?'

'He was suspected of it, but there was no concrete proof. The biggest deal Casa di Fiorenti had ever landed was on the brink of being sealed. They couldn't afford even the smallest hint of scandal.'

Faye could guess where the tale was heading. 'So they made it go away?'

'The victim survived and they talked themselves into taking no action because there was no proof, instead of making Pietro face his deplorable ways. Again. He got off free of blame because he was *famiglia*.' Maceo all but snarled the word. 'Right before my eyes, I was seeing him turn the two men I looked up to into the kind of men who would pay victims of a crime to stay quiet so an irresponsible *idiota* could continue wreaking havoc.'

Clarity brought a sympathetic ache to her heart for what Maceo had suffered, and regret for reopening old wounds.

But she hoped that reliving events he'd probably never discussed before might help him overcome them, maybe even heal in a way she'd never been able to.

'They were your heroes and they let you down. But you're not the sort of man who would just let it go. What did you do?'

'I spent months rowing with my parents over it. The event that night they died wasn't just to celebrate landing the deal. It was also meant to clear the air between us. At least, that's what my mother hoped.'

'But?'

His tawny eyes grew haunted and his lips thinned into a bleak line before he answered. 'But then I discovered that they'd silenced another Pietro incident just that morning. So I hurled judgement at them. Threatened to remove myself from their so-called *famiglia*. Basically uttered words I never got the chance to take back.'

She placed a hand on his arm, as if it would stop his self-flagellation. 'Maceo—'

'The last thing I said to my father was that I was ashamed to be his son. Those were the words he took to his grave.' He sliced his gaze towards her, his whole body bristling with pain, regret and fury.

She leaned in closer, sliding her hand higher up his shoulder until she encountered the cool skin of his nape. 'I'm sure they weren't.'

He slashed her a mocking look even as he angled his body towards hers. 'You're sure? Because you have personal insight into the afterlife?'

She let the mockery slide. 'Because he'd have to have been a fool not to realise you were speaking from a place of love and concern. And I don't think he was. Sounds like he was just caught in an impossible position.'

He laughed. 'It wasn't impossible. On the contrary, it was very clear-cut to me back then.'

'Why? Because you'd walked in their shoes? Felt the

pressure of pouring your heart and soul into a company only to risk it burning into nothing?'

His eyes turned to burnished slits. 'Why, *cara*, you sound like you condone their actions. I take it that means you don't hate Luigi quite as vigorously as you did when you arrived?'

Faye shrugged even as she scrambled to reclaim the foundations of her fortress before the sympathy pouring from her completely eroded it. 'I'm merely trying to help you see things from another angle. You just said *"back then"*. Somewhere deep down you know differently now, don't you?'

He shrugged, but his gaze swept away.

'If you regret judging them, then perhaps you should consider forgiving yourself.'

'Just like that?' he rasped bitterly.

'What's the alternative? Carry this emotional baggage for the rest of your life?'

He swallowed, his hand once again straying to his pocket. 'Yes,' he said finally. But in the shadows of that response she caught a trace of uncertainty.

'Maceo, why do you keep doing that?' She indicated towards the hand on his chest.

He stiffened, his hand bunching before it dropped to his thigh. 'It's nothing I wish to discuss.'

The hollow inside her grew, but she ignored it. 'Can I ask you something else?'

He gave a stiff but regal nod.

'Did Luigi or your father make any provision for Pietro in their wills?'

He frowned, then shook his head. 'No.'

'Doesn't that tell you something? I was nothing to Luigi and he left me potential millions, but he left nothing to his own twin?'

His frown deepened. 'You weren't nothing to him. Clearly you made a huge impact.'

'Did I? Then why didn't he tell me he had a twin brother?'

Bitterness returned full-force. 'For the same reason he tried to suppress Pietro's activities. The obsessive need to keep secrets,' he railed.

Faye stiffened as terrifying reminders of her own secret crashed in. Registering that her hand was still on his nape, she started to withdraw it.

With lightning reflexes Maceo captured it. Eyes on hers, he planted a kiss in her palm, then laid it on his thigh, trapping it there with his hand.

'You know everything now. Every last squalid Fiorenti and Caprio secret. And I thank the heavens for it, because I've grown tremendously bored of the subject,' he drawled thickly.

She forgave the blatant lie so she could fight the disturbing urge to explore the taut, muscled thigh flexing beneath her palm, the male fingers trailing over her wrist and up her bare arm. She shivered when they lingered in the crook of her arm, then watched, terrifyingly fascinated and intensely turned on, as her skin prickled with desire. Even her goosebumps chased after his touch.

'I made a vow years ago, Faye. Sworn over my parents' graves.' He placed a finger over her lips when she opened her mouth to ask what it was. 'It's private. Do you understand?'

She nodded jerkily, her heart racing. Sadly, she understood more than most.

'Your arrival has thrown that vow into chaos. I've decided my only option is to break it. For a while. For my sanity. The consequences be damned.'

Those last words were arrows to her chest. 'No. Maceo, you can't—'

'I can. I will.'

Implacable words forged in steely decision. She knew she couldn't sway him from it.

A curious little sound left her throat as his fingers danced over her left clavicle.

'Yesterday I wanted to taste the sweat that collected right here. For hours afterwards I could think of nothing else.'

The raw, hotly rasped words sucked the breath from her lungs. In an instant treacherous little fires ignited inside her. They stung her nipples into hard, needy points, poured heat between her thighs until she could barely sit still.

Maceo's hand dropped to her waist, dragged her closer, and he caught one earlobe between his teeth. 'From the moment you walked into my office I've been dying to know how long this river of hair runs. Now I know,' he continued in that electrifying monotone, 'and I will wrap it around any limb that takes my whim while I drown in the sweet scent of cherry blossom. And you will let me,' he growled into her ear.

'Will I?' she returned, even as desire pooled in her belly.

'Basta, arcobaleno. Basta,' he chided. 'Let's not fight any more. We've exhausted every subject beneath the sun except this one.'

They hadn't tackled one vital subject. *Her.*

Now she knew more of his past, the surer she was that any connection between them, physical or otherwise, would be an unforgivable mistake.

There was one other subject guaranteed to stop him, and although the feel of his warm lips trailing over her skin nearly stopped her from naming it, she closed her eyes and said, 'Carlotta.'

He stiffened. Against her neck, she heard his harsh breathing.

'I really must commend you for your exceptional ingenuity in summoning these roadblocks, *arcobaleno*,' he breathed as he pulled back.

The pained derision in his voice suggested he was referring to an entirely different sort of blocking.

She shrugged. 'I can't dismiss her.'

He nodded, smoothing a finger almost thoughtfully over her lower lip. '*Bene.* Let's get this over with too.'

He withdrew his touch and she had to clench her belly to stop herself from diving after it.

'I went into that coma as a child. I emerged a man. The company was in serious trouble. Board members were furiously power-grabbing and Carlotta's brothers were intent on seizing my birthright. I couldn't let that happen.' Tawny eyes darkened, inner demons swirling within. 'I faced several months of physical rehabilitation, while she tried to gain firmer ground from where to fight the board. With our shares split under different names we were in a precarious position. It made sense to join forces. We married simply to stop the company from falling into the wrong hands when it became clear that was the only choice.'

'So it was a marriage of convenience?' God, was that *hope* in her voice? Had a part of her not yet accepted the folly of feeling *anything* for Maceo?

He nodded, trailing his knuckles down her cheek. Barely leashed hunger briefly flared to life. 'Exactly so. A platonic marriage that benefited both of us once I was out of rehab.'

She gasped. '*Platonic?* You mean you…you didn't…'

'Share her bed? No, I did not.'

She stared at him, her breath caught in her throat. 'But you were married for almost a decade.'

Piercing eyes hooked into hers. 'If that's your way of asking whether I sought pleasure or release elsewhere, the answer is no,' he said, with the gravity she recognised now.

Faye believed him. From the start he'd seen her as an inconvenience thrust upon him. She wasn't someone he needed to impress or concoct stories for in order to win her over. She was nowhere near the strata he inhabited.

He could have any woman he wanted…

'Why me?' She blurted words she'd had no intention of uttering.

He lounged back against the cushions, eyes burning with that fierce, dangerous light as he gave a low, self-mocking laugh. 'You think I haven't asked myself that same question? There are easier conquests out there than you, *bellissimo arcobaleno*.'

'Then—'

Swiftly, he lunged for her, every trace of humour gone as he threaded his fingers into her hair. 'No, *tesoro*. My patience is exhausted. I won't be indulging you with a lesson in chemistry. Your eyes haven't stopped devouring me since you stepped aboard this boat. You want this, so I can only conclude that you wish me to beg. Is that it? You want me on my knees, pleading for the chance to make you my first?' he growled.

Then he stiffened.

Faye gasped as his final words dripped into her hazy brain. Before she could question him he slanted his mouth across hers in a blinding, possessive kiss, devoured her lips as if he wanted to make her forget what he'd just said.

But despite the glorious sensation of experiencing his kiss she felt his confession throb between them, lending a sharper bliss that came from wondering if this was new to him too. No, he was far too adept at kissing. Far too adept at *everything*.

Just when she feared every cell in her body would fling itself into the cauldron of mounting desire, Maceo eased away. They both struggled for air as he plastered his forehead against hers, his breathing rough and choppy.

'*Santo cielo*, that wasn't how I intended to announce that. Hell, I didn't plan on divulging it at all,' he half snarled.

But he had. And with each passing second the shockwaves intensified.

'How…?' she asked in quiet awe, selfishly seizing another minute to put off confronting her turbulent emotions.

'I discovered very early that my status in life attracted a certain breed of parasites disguised as friends. I was jaded by the time I hit the ripe age of fifteen. Toss in Pietro's unsavoury exploits and their effect on my family and—'

'You didn't want even of a hint of his character associated with you?'

One corner of his mouth twisted. 'I was no saint, *cara*. I might not have performed the ultimate act, but I indulged enough.'

Jealousy spiked her insides. 'Then the accident happened?'

He nodded grimly. 'I was eighteen when it occurred. I didn't emerge from my coma for a year. Through it all Carlotta stayed by my bedside, fighting pressure from doctors and her own brothers to pull the plug. And that was before eighteen months of rehabilitation.'

Fresh sympathy poured through her, and against her better judgement she cupped his jaw. 'Oh, Maceo...'

He kissed her palm. 'Rewarding her with my loyalty and fidelity felt like a small price to pay.'

Honourable words, but she sensed there was more. He was holding something back.

'But it wasn't small. It was a huge sacrifice. Perhaps too big in some respects, even in the name of protecting Carlotta and your family's legacy?'

He tensed again and rose, striding stiffly away from her. 'What do you want me to say? That I didn't feel I had the right to live a happy and comfortable life when my actions had driven my parents and my godfather to their deaths?'

She gasped. 'No! Why would you believe that?'

'Because it's the truth! I was quarrelling with my father, yet again, when he lost control of the car. My words had driven my mother to tears and caused my father to lose concentration. He drove the car off a cliff, resulting in horrific carnage that, by some cosmic twist, I somehow survived. So tell me, Faye, should I have risen from my hospital bed and immediately sought oblivion in a woman's arms?'

His voice was a tableau of raw pain and self-loathing. She jumped up, every cell in her body yearning to reach for him. 'Of course not. But that doesn't mean you can never forgive yourself—'

'I don't deserve forgiveness! I deserve nothing but the misery I have brought upon myself.'

She froze. 'Then why…? *I'm* the reason you're breaking your vow?' she breathed in shock.

He appeared thunderstruck. Then he drove his fingers through his hair, throwing it into sexy disarray. He paced away from her, shoulders heaving as he inhaled, then he charged back, spearing her a narrow-eyed look.

'We've digressed. Yet again.' His tone suggested he was at the end of his rope.

Faye knew she couldn't put it off any longer. 'I want you, Maceo. But I can't have you. And you can't have me.'

A muscle leapt in his cheek. '*Ripeto*. Repeat that.'

'Please—'

He held up a halting hand. 'You plead understanding for something you haven't explained.'

She folded her arms around her middle to stop the cold seeping into her veins from taking hold. 'You're better off not knowing! Please trust me. I don't think your first time should be with someone like me.'

His nostrils flared. 'Why not?'

'Because you'll regret it.'

'That tells me absolutely nothing. Do better.'

'I'm…damaged.'

He turned still as stone and his skin lost colour. 'How?'

She couldn't form the words, so she shook her head.

'No,' he refuted icily. 'You don't get to hold back now. Secrets and subterfuge shattered my family. Whatever it is you believe you're shielding me from, I want it out in the open.'

Ice shrouded her heart. 'You don't. Please, Maceo. I'm not worth it.'

He gave no quarter. 'I will be the judge of that—not you. Tell me.'

She darted her gaze across the deck and beyond, for a wild moment wondering if she could throw herself overboard, swim away until the waters sucked her under. Because surely oblivion would be better than the unshakeable knowledge that she would prove him wrong? That nothing could compare to the repugnant truth she'd guarded so zealously since Matt's heart-wrenching reaction?

'Look at me, Faye.'

Breath shuddering, she met his burning gaze.

'There's no escape from this.'

The sharp edge to his words made her wonder if he meant it literally. Had this been his plan all along? Bring her aboard his magical yacht, set a scene straight from a spellbinding dream and… And what? Show her what she couldn't have?

If so, he'd succeeded. She'd delved beneath the formidable exterior to the heart of the man. And what she'd discovered made her yearn harder for him than before, when this had been purely a physical reaction.

And, because she'd seen him, she owed him the truth buried in her heart.

Her heart dropped to her churning stomach as she forced out words. 'Twenty-six years ago my mother lived in London. She was training to be a nurse, but worked part-time as a waitress. She preferred working the posh parties because they paid better.' Faye dragged her hands up and down her arms to stop the shivering. 'One night she stayed late to clean up and…and one of the male guests attacked her. He…he tied her up, blindfolded her and assaulted her.'

'Mio Dio…' Maceo whispered on a stunned breath, then stepped towards her. 'Faye—'

'No! Let me finish. Please.'

His fists bunched but he nodded.

'The attack was traumatising, and she dropped out of

school. Three months later she found out that her rapist hadn't just taken from her. He'd left her with a permanent reminder.'

She forced herself to meet Maceo's gaze. She knew what was coming and she refused to hide from it.

'He left her pregnant. With me.'

Maceo's face drained of all colour as a wave of visible shock washed over him. Before it could take full hold, before the accompanying horror, disgust and, worst of all, that nanosecond of weighing up which way to go—whether it was worth bluffing his way through his revulsion or fully revealing it—she turned and fled.

'Faye!'

His voice was a firm command she didn't intend to heed. Absurdly thankful that she'd discarded her shoes earlier, she flew down the stairs. From their tour, she remembered the staterooms were on the lower deck and made a mad dash for them, desperate to put a solid locked door between her and Maceo.

Halfway down the carpeted hallway she lunged for a familiar-looking door, her heart banging against her ribs when she heard his footsteps behind her.

Safely inside, she turned to bolt the door.

One long arm thwarted her, followed by his large, immoveable frame as he filled the doorway. Faye chose the safer option of backing away from him. Of looking anywhere but into a face no doubt filled with horror and revulsion.

She sucked in a desperate breath when the tips of his polished shoes appeared in her lowered eyeline.

'Faye. *Cara*—'

She jerked away from the hand rising towards her. 'Don't touch me. I don't want you here. I don't want your pity. Or your morbid curiosity. Or whatever this is!'

His hand dropped. 'Explain to me why I am the focus of your anger,' he invited, with a quiet calm that perversely ignited her anger. Anger that made her forget she wasn't intending to look into his face. Into eyes that stared back at her with stomach-hollowing ferocity.

'Because I warned you and you didn't listen!'

His head tilted with mocking arrogance. Then he had the audacity to nod in agreement. 'True. You warned me that you were *"damaged"*.' He had the gall to use air quotes. 'That I would "regret it". Oh, and something about you not being worth it. Have I got everything?'

'No!' she railed. 'You haven't adequately described your disgust. The horror I saw on your face!'

Mockery and arrogance fled and his face assumed the formidable façade that made lesser men quake in his presence. 'Of course I'm horrified. No woman should have to endure what your mother went through.'

'You…' She stopped. Sucked in a stunned breath as his words sank in.

'Any man who harms a hair on a woman's head isn't worthy of the name. Any *bastardo* who does what was done to your mother is a deplorable waste of space who deserves to be thrown into the darkest pit,' he condemned, flames roaring in his eyes.

Faye shook her head, unable to comprehend his reaction.

'As for what you believe should be my reaction to *you*…' He dragged a hand over his jaw, bewilderment flitting over his face. 'Why would you expect me to blame you for something you had no control over?'

Old flames of humiliation and shame washed over her. 'It's never stopped most people in the past.'

'Who?' he snarled.

Her heart twisted. 'Someone I was involved with… briefly. He called me an abomination.' Among many other things.

His nostrils flared. 'Then he too was a despicable idiot. And I believe I warned you before that I'm not *most people*.'

She wanted to laugh hysterically. Of all the times to remind her he was extraordinary!

Her insides rumbled, as if the tectonic plates formed of every negative emotion she'd suffered because of the circumstances of her birth were attempting to shift. Simply on the strength of his words?

'Why are you trying to convince me that this isn't… That you're not…?' *Completely and utterly nauseated by me?*

He sighed. 'It seems that, like me, you need re-educating, *cara*.' His voice was firm, yet gentle.

The rumbling intensified. Faye shut her eyes and tried to calm the roiling. When she opened them he was closer. *Much* closer. Breath-robbing gravity pinned her in place.

'No child should have to bear the burden of the circumstances of their birth,' he said. 'Or permit those circumstances to get in the way of what they want.'

Her head spun. She felt turned inside out. She'd been convinced this would go so differently. And now…

Now she needed a moment—*several* moments—to think.

'Can you leave, please? I'd like to be alone.'

'I'm afraid I can't oblige you, seeing as you are in *my* bedroom, *mio dolce*,' he drawled.

Heart leaping into her throat, she spun around.

Sure enough, she was confronted with unapologetic masculinity. Masterful decoration and effortless sophistication created by a man who knew what he wanted and expressed it in his surroundings. Bold greys blended with dark bronze highlights. There were sharply angled shapes and edgier art than she'd seen in any of the Fiorenti properties so far, displayed on the walls and cabinetry. But the massive bed she'd somehow missed when she'd stumbled into the room was what really gripped her attention.

As she stared at it, dumbfounded, the atmosphere in the room shifted. Morphed and thickened with a different vibe that catapulted her blood through her veins at triple speed. She didn't need to turn to know he was watching her. She knew the instant he started towards her. Because a raw and primitive drumbeat started at her core and spread like brush fire through her.

She heard the rustle of clothes and pivoted to find him tugging off his jacket. With casual ease, he tossed it over a nearby seat.

'What are you doing?'

'Making myself comfortable.'

He kicked off his shoes, then walked past her to the bedside table, where he slid off his sleek wristwatch and set it down.

Somehow those small, intimate, everyday actions were enough to set off several more blazes inside her. She stood there, mesmerised, as he slowly strode past her, positioned himself behind her and cupped one shoulder with his hand. The other lazily threaded through her hair, caressing, shifting, until to her breathless astonishment it was suddenly a loose rope, wrapped around his wrist. Only then did he lean in closer, align his head with hers so his lips brushed her ear.

'*"I want you, Maceo."* Your words,' he reminded her thickly.

His heat engulfed her. 'There were other words too.'

'*Si*, spoken when you laboured under a misapprehension,' he pointed out. 'One that made the gross error of assuming I would choose anyone less than an exceptional woman to experience this with.'

Faye's core melted, reshaped itself into a form she wasn't quite prepared to examine. Not when her every sense was fully under his control, a raw lump of willing clay, yearning to be moulded into any shape he desired.

'Do you believe I'm that woman?' she asked. She needed to know. To be absolutely sure.

He hesitated for one heart-rending moment. Then, 'In this moment, when you're all I can think about, taste, smell, *crave*? *Si*...' he responded thickly, gently tugging the rein he'd made of her hair, exposing her neck to the thrill of his wandering lips.

The drugging desire that swelled through her was almost enough to make her disregard his words.

Almost.

But *'in this moment'* lingered—a tiny but unmissable blemish for a person who'd lived her life intimately familiar with stains. And on top of that he'd made a vow…one whose full details she didn't know but could guess. Both were searing reminders that this thing had a very limited shelf life.

She twisted in his arms with a whimper, to confront her desire full-on.

He tilted her head back, stared deep into her eyes. 'Tell me you want this, *mio dolce*,' he breathed.

'I want this,' she whispered, urgency powering through her.

He didn't waste another second before he slammed her body into his.

Several salacious facts buffeted her at once. She was doing this—truly experiencing a sexual encounter without shame or secrets for the first time in her life. He wasn't repulsed by her. He'd chosen *her*. No matter how temporarily, Maceo wanted her with a fever that blazed in his eyes.

His hand trailed over her hip to flatten in the small of her back. He tugged her closer until she felt the bold imprint of his manhood. She gasped, tried to pull back when she registered his impressive size. He kept her prisoner in the circle of his arms, his eyes raking her face.

'Stay. Feel what you do to me,' he urged, his voice gritty with rough desire.

Feminine power ploughed through her. With almost unnerving abandon she rose on her bare tiptoes and pressed her breasts into his chest.

He shuddered, and then he was kissing her with the kind of savage hunger that powered those tectonic plates inside her, shifted the centre of her axis just that little bit more.

And yet it warned her there would be ripples long into her future. Long after she'd left this...*him*...behind.

Faye suppressed the thought. Moaned as his tongue curled around hers. Trembled when his teeth nipped at her bottom lip in a carnal sampling that left her reeling. She might have one experience to her name, but Maceo was the true connoisseur. Within minutes she clung to him, every sinew weak with need.

One strong arm banded her waist and lifted her off her feet. Long strides placed them in front of the bed. Slowly he slid her down his front, hissing out a breath when her softness moulded against him.

He raised her arms above her head, caught them in one hand and held them there, in preparation for their own unique dance. His gaze fused with hers; he slowly tugged at her zip and her dress fell to her waist. A firm push and the soft material pooled at her ankles, leaving her in only tiny lace panties.

Without breaking their locked gaze, he linked their hands, palm to palm. '*Mio Dio*, but I'm going to take my time with you,' he vowed, in a gravel-rough voice.

And she was going to expire—she was certain of it.

He kissed her. Surprisingly softly considering the passion that bristled from him. Heart-stopping. Poignant.

Faye felt tears prickle at her eyes. He pulled away again and she sucked in a shaky breath as he spun her around to face the bed. Slowly, excruciatingly, he traced the outline of her body from wrists to thighs. Then he followed the caress with his lips, down the column of her spine.

'*Il mio bellissimo arcobaleno,*' he rasped against her skin. My beautiful rainbow.

Faye felt beautiful. Almost...*treasured*.

She knew she was getting carried away, but she couldn't help it.

When he placed one hand in the small of her back and nudged her, she teetered forward onto her hands. Firm hands removed her panties, feathered caresses up the inside of her thighs. Before she could draw breath Maceo parted her in the most elemental way, tasting her with a voracious kiss that weakened every atom in her body.

'Oh, God!'

Shocked pleasure sizzled up her spine as her night of firsts continued. His tongue wrung bliss from her, and when she climaxed he was there to catch her. To hold her close as he drew back the sheets and placed her in the middle of the bed.

Then he made her wait as he finished undressing. A man fully comfortable in his own skin, he stood tall and proud, content to stare down at her with savage hunger while she fought the urge to squirm with the renewed need flaying her.

Slowly he prowled onto the bed, positioned himself over her so she was caged in his arms. He kissed her in slow, languorous strokes, as if he had all the time in the world.

'I feel the need to make you come again,' he delivered hoarsely.

'Because you like seeing me lose control?'

'Because it's the most beautiful thing I've ever seen,' he growled, then flicked his tongue over one nipple.

Need clamouring through her, she arched her back, presented her other breast and revelled in his unfettered shudder as he accepted her offer.

He teased and tormented her. And just when she imagined she'd go out of her mind he reached for a condom. After sliding it on, he grasped her knees.

'Show me where I crave to be, Faye,' he pleaded gruffly.

Knowing she had him under her spell, even if only for a brief time, filled Faye with a heady power and worthiness she'd never experienced in her life. Every ounce of self-consciousness evaporated as, watching his rapt, breathtaking face, she parted her thighs.

Maceo inhaled long and deep, hectic colour scouring

his cheekbones as he stared at her feminine core. Then his fingers slowly brushed her flesh. '*Dio mio*, you're so soft,' he rasped thickly.

Faye reached for him, unable to stem her need. 'I want you *now*, Maceo.'

He parted her wider, settled between her thighs. 'Then tell me you're ready, *tesoro*.'

'I'm ready,' she whispered.

In one smooth thrust, he slid into her.

Maceo felt as if his heart would beat right out of his chest. He'd stepped off the path he'd designated for himself, a path that already burned beneath his feet, because of the woman beneath him. Her scent. Her smile. Her very *uniqueness*. In that moment, embedded deep within her, he was sure he could search the whole world and never find another close to Faye Bishop.

But he didn't need to. The woman who quieted his demons was right here. Her tightness was welcoming him in ways he'd only dreamed about. Now he understood why men went to war over sex.

He bit back a groan as she gripped him tighter. As she squirmed.

'Please, Maceo,' she begged.

His vision hazed. He fought for control, noting the tremors shaking the fingers he used to smooth back her hair. He traced her brows, her cheekbones, her nose and the bottom curve of her trembling mouth.

'Hush, *bella arcobaleno*. I've waited a long time for this. Allow me a moment to savour it.'

She stilled, her eyes glazing with a look he wanted to distil and devour on a daily basis. Long after they'd parted ways. Long after this moment of madness had passed and he had recommitted himself to his vow.

Exhaling, he stole another minute. But soon the sensation got too much. He moved. Then groaned as sublime pleasure pulsed though him. The pure magnificence of it merely evidenced why he didn't deserve it.

'That doesn't mean you can never forgive yourself...'

He pushed her tempting words away. Concentrated on her.

She squirmed again, making his breath catch. '*Santo cielo*, you're exquisite.'

Words fell from his lips as he stroked in and out of her. Perhaps this transcendent moment was exactly what he was meant to experience? So he could truly appreciate it and make amends? For how could he suffer if he didn't truly know?

Maceo thought a lot of things as the woman beneath him cried out in release. As soul-stirring pleasure overtook him. Most of all he thought about how bleak his life would be after this. And wondered how the hell he was going to survive it.

But perhaps he didn't need to?

CHAPTER NINE

HE REMAINED AWAKE long after Faye fell asleep, treacherous thoughts weaving through his mind. With a few defiant sentences she'd struck a match that now blazed high, illuminating the dark spaces of his beliefs. The girl with the rainbow hair had offered a different perspective he'd refused to consider before.

Marriage and family were still out of the question. But perhaps he didn't need to remain trapped in the shadows with his guilt and regret. Maybe he'd been spared for a reason...

Dared he reach for it?

No. Because the kernel of alarm he'd experienced when she'd shown him Pietro's picture had only been diminished because of the enthralling experience that had followed. In the aftermath its drumbeat grew again, demanding attention.

He pulled Faye closer, running his fingers through her hair. Her serene post-coital expression drew a very male, satisfied smile from him. The experience had shattered him, and he was certain it had shattered her too. And as much as desire was already reawakening, urging him to relive the event *immediately*, Maceo denied the need.

The subject looming at the back of his mind couldn't be ignored. But that didn't mean he wanted to dissect it with Faye.

Too much had happened tonight. He wasn't ashamed to admit he needed a reprieve. Reprieve in the form of sex would be ideal but, glancing down at the sleeping woman in his arms, he knew he needed a different avenue.

With a sigh of regret, he slowly extricated himself from her. Her murmured protest prompted a smile, which disappeared as he headed into his bathroom.

Powerful jets cleansed his body, but they did nothing to allay the growing certainty that Luigi hadn't married Faye Bishop's mother under normal circumstances. The connections were too strong to deny, and the possible reasoning behind Luigi's first marriage very much pointed to the actions he knew his godfather would have taken.

More secrets in the name of protecting the *famiglia*.

More covering up of the misdeeds of Pietro Caprio.

But even as Maceo's suspicions hardened he couldn't help but speculate—with the benefit of Faye's own words in his head now—if there hadn't been a best-case scenario behind the act. Whether Luigi hadn't acted with the well-being of his family at heart.

For the first time since his teenage years Maceo could almost accept that explanation without rancour.

The woman in your bed did this for you.

There was no mistaking Carlotta's voice in his head, prompting him down another path. Had this been her intention all along? For Faye to throw doubt on his goals? And what of him? What was *he* supposed to do for her besides hand over her inheritance and the letter that still burned a hole in his desk drawer? A letter that might well answer a few of his own questions, never mind hers?

Regardless of Carlotta's expectations, Faye in his bed was a delightful bonus, and the thought triggered a predictable reaction in his body—one he welcomed simply because it stopped him thinking of Luigi and Pietro. Of their possible connections to Faye.

Tomorrow. The day after. Perhaps even next week would be time enough to chase the answers he sought.

Aware he was hiding, taking the easy way out, he straightened abruptly from where he'd leaned against the tiles.

And then, like a breathtaking rainbow emerging from the stormy clouds of his thoughts, Faye appeared in front of the fogged shower screen. She looked a touch tentative, then she smiled.

During their encounter in bed he'd surprised a few expressions on her face—enough to convince him that while he might be marking his first true experience, she was almost equally unschooled. The thought triggered a primitive pulse of satisfaction. Against every better judgement, he reached out and drew her into the shower.

Her gaze swept hesitantly over his face before meeting his. 'Are you sure you want me in here? You looked as if you had the weight of the world on your shoulders just then.'

He slid his hands over her silky skin and cupped her delicious bottom, allowing himself the reprieve of completely pushing the subject of Pietro to the back of his mind. 'Not the whole world, *cara*. Just one small dilemma.'

'Which is…?'

She slid her arms around his neck and he bit back a hiss at the effect of her nipples grazing his chest.

'I was debating how long I should allow you to sleep before waking you.'

'Then it's a good thing I only needed a ten-minute power nap.'

Maceo felt his smile widening. Even that strange lightening in his heart didn't surprise him. He'd experienced sublime physical intimacy for the first time in his life tonight. On top of myriad shocking revelations. What was one more ground-shaking reaction?

'Is that a challenge to my manhood?'

She reared back. 'What?'

'That sounded suspiciously like a complaint for not adequately wearing you out.'

She blushed and, *Dio mio*, he wanted to taste every shade of it.

'If that's the case you only have to say the word if you want more.'

Her delicate nostrils quivered, but her gaze was bold as she stared into his eyes. 'I want more, Maceo.'

What are you doing?

He sealed her in his arms, ignored the inner harsh, demanding query and gave her more.

Until he shattered from head to toe once again.

Until her cries filled his ears and warmed parts of him he'd been convinced would remain stone-cold for ever.

Until the only thought that remained in his head as he carried her back to bed was how quickly he could seek oblivion in her arms again.

He continued to ignore that inner voice and they continued to shatter one another in the sun-filled days that followed.

Unsurprisingly, Faye had quickly gathered a clutch of admirers when they'd arrived at the first plantation. Her genuine, almost childlike enthusiasm, her capacity to learn and her unabashed interest in every facet of the production that went into a Casa di Fiorenti confectionery box endeared her to his employees instantly.

Like Pico's slavish devotion, her fan base only grew with each subsequent encounter and now, on their sixth and last day in St Lucia, he watched from his vantage point on his private beach as she charmed the employees he'd invited to a Caribbean-style barbecue.

Despite the intoxicating reggae beats that epitomised the party mood, Maceo remained...*off.* He wasn't in the mood to search for the reason behind his disgruntlement. But, deep inside, he knew the irritant had something to do with the woman who flitted from group to group—barefoot, of course—wearing another concoction of bright clothes that made her blend in perfectly with her exotic surroundings.

At this precise moment she was chasing after the exuberant child of an employee, her unfettered rainbow hair arcing behind her. She disappeared behind a palm leaf cabana, and Maceo dropped his gaze to stare broodingly into his rum punch.

Enough with this cat and mouse game. Until recently he'd been a man who didn't shy away from challenges. A man who stuck to his vows. Yet here he was, evading emails from his R&D director.

It turned out that, while they'd been exploring St Lucia, Faye had been collating ideas for new products and sending daily reports to Alberto Triento. The man was rapturous over the quality of work Faye had produced. Enough for him to question why Maceo hadn't offered her a permanent position at Casa di Fiorenti.

What irked Maceo was that he'd contemplated that very idea. Faye had a degree in business, after all. And her social skills were exemplary. So why was she wasting away on a farm?

Which brought him to his next problem...

The discreet investigation he'd initiated the morning after their first night together had already borne fruit. Most of which, while not conclusive, pointed in the direction he'd hoped they wouldn't.

He tightened his jaw as his demons howled.

More secrets.

He sucked in a grim breath. Faye should be told, of course. But what if it was all a huge coincidence? What if Luigi *hadn't* gone to England purposely to seek out Faye's mother? What if—

His gut tightened as soft, warm fingers slid over his nape. Inhaling sharply at the pulse of pleasure that burst to life inside him, he glanced up.

Faye stepped in front of him, another hesitant smile playing at her lips. 'Any reason why you're so grumpy at your own party?'

'Perhaps because I don't like parties?'

She tilted her head, her long hair swinging over one shoulder. 'And yet you keep throwing them...' she mused.

He shrugged, not quite seeing the point in divulging that *she* was the reason he was throwing this one in particular, after overhearing her express sadness that she wouldn't see the plantation workers and their families again. Why her mournful expression had triggered him into having his privacy disrupted for the better part of an afternoon he chose to ignore, in favour of pulling her into his lap.

She came with a willingness that smothered a layer of his disgruntlement. And when she leaned into him he refused to name the sensation powering through him. Although it closely resembled...*elation*.

'It's our last day on the island. I thought it appropriate to mark it in some way,' he said.

'There are many ways to celebrate. You picked one that involved all your employees. Are you trying to hide the fact that you *like* to give back?'

He lowered his head until their foreheads touched. 'Give me an hour or two and I'll show you just how much I can give back,' he suggested gruffly.

She laughed, and the sound transmitted itself straight through his blood into his chest.

She started to rise. His grip tightened on her convulsively.

'Maceo...?'

Thoughts crowded his head—the uppermost one being the fact that he needed to come clean. About his suspicions over Luigi and Pietro. About his investigations. About the letter.

But until he was absolutely certain, why risk causing her hurt by raking open old wounds? Why alarm her unnecessarily if all this turned out to be false?

'Go. Enjoy yourself. But be warned that I intend to throw everyone off the beach in an hour. I wish to be alone with you.'

She blushed, and another pulse of pleasure unravelled inside him. She was truly a sublime novelty. Enough for him to silently extend himself a little more time to explore the uniqueness of it all.

'Okay. I'll go and warn them, so they're not completely horrified when it happens.'

'*Grande.* Go,' he instructed, then countered his command by pulling her close and slanting his mouth over hers.

Maceo didn't care who saw. She was his. For now. Until he did his duty.

Her soft moan brought that peculiar lightness to his chest once more. He tugged her closer, kissed her with a boldness that announced to every male in the vicinity that she was his. When he was thoroughly satisfied that he'd made his point, he released her.

She scrambled away from him with a dazed look. In that moment, temporarily satisfied with his world, and the knowledge that whatever his report brought he would deal with it adequately, Maceo raised his glass to his lips and drained the punch.

'You're brooding again.'

Faye immediately hated herself for blurting out the observation. It wasn't as if Maceo was ever overly talkative. But she couldn't ignore the fact that he'd grown increasingly laconic over the last few days, prompting her need to discover why earlier at the party.

She'd walked away with no answers, just a kiss that had left her insides shivery. Hours later, she was no further enlightened.

Was he bored already? Had their chemistry fizzled out so soon for him?

The dismay thickening in her gut didn't shock her. She'd sensed this coming, but foolishly buried her head in the sand.

'Tell me about New Paths,' he said abruptly. 'How long has your mother been there?'

She froze as tiny ice droplets slid down her spine. 'Why?'

His stare was level. Almost neutral. 'You think I shouldn't be curious about where you come from?'

'Um…no, I guess not.' She tamped down her nerves. 'What do you want to know?'

Their conversation over the past few days had been thrilling and engaging. The kind that effortlessly went on long into the night and kept her rapt, to the extent that she feared how attached she'd become to the time she spent with him.

And that was before their lovemaking. Just thinking about *that* drove sensations through her being she couldn't comprehend. Faye understood the basics of chemistry, but *this* was entirely unfathomable to her. Had Maceo not confessed his uninitiated status she would never have believed it. From that very first time he'd leapt into another stratosphere. To say he was insatiable was an understatement.

Their second day onboard the yacht he'd pulled her into his arms right on the top deck and calmly freed her from her bikini. Her shocked laughter had elicited a dark chuckle in response, followed by, 'I have more than a decade of sex to make up for. And you, *dolce bellissimma*, are so very responsive. How can I not have you like this?'

Every touch, every kiss, every wicked look from his flame-filled eyes surged through her, taking her from one peak to another.

'Am I losing you?' he murmured now, a knowing tone in his voice.

Heat crept up her neck as she recalled that, while their conversation had skirted the outside edge of personal, it had never strayed this close to her past.

'Mum's been at New Paths for over twelve years.'

'So you grew up there with her?'

She shook her head. 'I only spent school holidays with her. The rest of the time I was away at boarding school.'

His eyebrows rose. 'Boarding school?'

'Yes. The school I attended had a special programme. Every year they picked five students to attend a top boarding school. I was lucky enough to get a place.'

'Perhaps luck had nothing to do with it,' he murmured, that pensive look in his eyes again.

'What do you mean?'

He shrugged. 'Your intelligence is exceptional. I'm willing to bet that alone earned you a place.'

Faye wasn't sure why the compliment didn't quite hit the sweet spot. Why it made the back of her neck tingle.

In the next moment he relaxed in his seat again. 'Alberto has been singing your praises.'

Her heart leapt with delight, her befuddlement fading. 'Really? He's been alarmingly quiet about the emails I sent him.'

'To me, he's been positively exuberant,' Maceo retorted drily.

Delight ballooned and she laughed. 'Sneaky man.'

'Si...' Maceo responded indulgently. He set down his glass, his eyes resting on her with that intensity that made her aware of every inch of her body. 'He even suggested I should give you a permanent position in the company.'

Her insides somersaulted in a mixture of alarm and something else she wasn't ready to name. 'I... Why would he do that?'

He shrugged. 'Your contribution has made an impact. Perhaps he sees an asset that will benefit the company.'

Asset. Benefit.

Being discussed in such cold business terms should put her off. And yet... 'And you? Do you concur?' she asked, despite her glaring recognition that the question bordered on the personal zone.

Having sex with him because she wanted to was one thing. Casually inviting him to give a verdict on her worthiness to his business, when her future couldn't include him, was an open invitation to pain and misery.

It terrified her enough to say, 'You don't need to answer that.'

'I don't? Why not?' he invited.

His eyes bored into her, as if trying to divine her thoughts.

'Because I'm leaving in a few weeks.'

'And if I took Alberto Triento's advice and offered you a job? What would you do, Faye?' he queried softly, in direct opposition to the fire burning in his eyes.

Faye was stunned by how much she wanted to say yes. To rearrange every silly dream she'd harboured for the sake of remaining by this man's side for a little longer.

The power of it robbed her of breath, before she forced common sense in. 'I'd say don't let him influence you into making a hasty decision.'

Several seconds passed as he stared at her, his eyes darkening several shades. The brief flaring of his nostrils signalled his displeasure, but in the next moment he shrugged.

'Perhaps you're right. I shouldn't rearrange my life for a novelty.'

The words stung, as they were meant to, reminding her of other words.

'I made a vow...'

He'd said those words just a handful of days ago. She'd blinded herself to them, and to the contemplative looks he'd slanted her way since, when he thought she wasn't paying attention.

Faye fiddled with her water glass, growing anguish twisting her insides.

She started when he abruptly rose from the dinner table beneath the pavilion in the villa. Tonight he wore dark trousers, paired with a midnight-blue linen shirt that did wonderful things for his olive complexion. Two strides and he was before her. Her body clenched in anticipation as she stared into his eyes, acknowledged the ferocious passion etched into his face.

When he grasped her elbows and tugged her up, she rose to join him. There was a sizzling edge to his passion that intensified his lovemaking, she'd discovered to her delight and dismay, and she was very partial to it.

'You've spent the day charming my employees. Now I think it's time for you to shower *me* with your attention.'

He swung her into his arms and strode away from the pavilion, through the villa—mercifully devoid of staff—and up the grand staircase into his suite. There, he took his time to slide her down his body, ensuring she felt her full effect on him.

Before her feet had fully touched the floor he was winding her long hair around his wrist, a practice he'd grown rabidly attached to. The act triggered an equally visceral reaction within her, and before the coil of hair was fully wrapped around his wrist her core had shamelessly dampened, throbbing with a needy drumbeat that made her breathless.

Maceo didn't kiss her immediately. He simply examined her with quiet intensity. Gripped by an urge she couldn't fathom, she hooked her fingers into the space at the top of his open-necked shirt and pulled it apart.

'Santo cielo!,' he swore under his breath, his nose flaring with wicked arousal, right before he lowered his head and bit her bottom lip. 'More,' he demanded gruffly.

She kissed his throat, trailed caresses down his sculpted chest, and then, growing bolder, nipped his firm skin. His breath hissed and he shuddered.

'More?'

'Si...' he growled thickly.

Faye lost all sense of time and self. She devoured him as if it was their last time. As if he was the last meal she would ever consume. Something had happened during their conversation and it had slid a layer of edgy unease between them. She couldn't pinpoint the cause, yet she felt it. It fed her urgency, and when Maceo stumbled back against the wall she fell on him, a ravenous creature she didn't recognise.

Thick, provocative words fell from his lips as her eager hands undressed him. When he was completely naked, a virile god arrogantly demanding worship, she fell to her knees. A glance up showed his rapt, savage expression.

Vibrating with feminine power, she took him in her hand

and wrapped her lips around him. A tortured groan rumbled from his throat, fuelling the fire of her passion. With her tongue and her lips and her hands she feasted on him until his knees buckled. Until he pulled away with a tortured, *'Basta, per favore.'*

One hand urged her up. The moment she stood he reversed their positions and pinned her against the wall, a formidable, virile male in control. One thick arm wrapped around her waist, he settled himself between her thighs, his eyes fixed heatedly on hers, and thrust into her.

Her primal scream bounced off the bedroom walls. It was followed by a series of needy cries, which he answered with overwhelming vigour. Locked together, they feasted on each other until sweat slicked their skin, until their breaths were fused into one life sustaining stream, until it all culminated in a mind-melting release that shook her very soul.

Maceo followed swiftly behind, his powerful body shuddering in her arms as he let go.

She was still floating when he carried her to his bed, when he slid them both between the sheets and pulled her close. But, as much as she wished for oblivion, Faye found herself awake long after his breath had evened out in deep sleep.

Her eyes darted in the darkness as she struggled to rationalise what was happening.

Dismay deepened as the answers she'd held at bay smashed through her barriers.

Everything that had happened between them from the moment she'd arrived in Italy was beginning to make a devastating sort of sense. This was never going to be an emotionless interlude. Even without the sex, Maceo had affected her on a deep, visceral level.

Gradually, that irritating little niggle she'd felt at the dinner table unveiled itself.

She didn't want to leave Italy. Not just yet. And it had nothing to do with her stepfather or Carlotta or anything she'd learned so far.

She wanted to stay because of Maceo.

The thought terrified her more than anything had terrified her in a long time. And yet still she stayed in his arms. And when he woke an hour later and slanted her that brooding look in the dark she melted straight into him.

Because her foolish heart didn't know any better.

Ghana was sublime. A sprawling metropolis in parts. A verdant jungle paradise within half an hour of leaving the capital, Accra. Sitting just above the equator, it was humid during the day and cool in the evening. But what took Faye's breath away was the sudden majesty of its thunderstorms. They arrived with tremendous force, shook the world and drenched everything in sight within seconds.

From her vantage point in the world's most spectacular tree house, in the middle of the Ashanti Region's jungle, she marvelled at the green lushness around her. Everywhere she looked cocoa trees swayed with gentle grandeur for miles, in the rich landscape she'd explored twice over since their arrival two days ago.

Faye had learned every little thing about the precious cocoa bean—especially the new variety of rose-pink bean that was setting the confectionery world alight. But, more than that, she'd collected samples of the indigenous fruits of Ghana and intended to add them to Alberto's collection.

Thoughts of returning to Naples brought apprehension. Somewhere between St Lucia and Ghana, Faye had talked herself into letting this thing ride out in its own time. It might end tomorrow. It might end the day she left Italy. The only certainty was that it *would* end.

Maceo hadn't mentioned the job offer again. And, as much as she told herself she was fine with that, her chest tightened every time she contemplated her inevitable departure.

In other ways, her emotions had been soothed. Maceo's insistence on Luigi's integrity had left her with the belief that her stepfather hadn't forgotten about her. She only wished he'd found time to explain his desertion in the years before his death.

But dwelling in the past was futile. She didn't begrudge him the happiness he'd found.

Would she find a love like that some day?

Her heart lurched when her thoughts immediately zeroed in one specific figure. A strong, formidable Italian who, as if she'd summoned him by thought alone, now slid his arms around her waist.

To disguise his effect on her, and to stop herself thinking that in mere weeks she would leave and possibly never see him again, she jerked her chin at the spectacular theatre of the raging storm. 'I've never seen anything like it.'

'*Si*, it's magnificent, isn't it?'

'The foreman, Kojo, says it can last several weeks.'

Maceo's chin nudged the top of her head. 'It's why I prefer to come at this time. If I had to choose between thunderstorms and the mosquitoes in the latter months of the year, I'd choose this.'

Faye smiled, even though she remained a mess inside. 'Are you saying you're afraid of a few mosquitoes?'

His lips twisted in a half-smile. 'I prefer to battle opponents that don't sneak up on me in their attacks,' he said.

Before she could respond his arms dropped, and he walked back into the tree house.

Made up of two large, opulent rooms, divided into living and sleeping areas, it was built into the branches of a giant wawa tree, with the actual walls of the tree house made of the same wood. Locally made rugs covered the floors and walls, and an embroidered throw with a cocoa theme covered the king-sized bed. Off the side of the bedroom was a rainforest shower and bathroom, and adjoining the living room an alcove with a large desk that Maceo had commandeered.

Faye watched him go, rubbing her arms to stop the cold shiver that had nothing to do with the rapidly cooling temperature. She stopped herself from following, and on impulse headed into the bedroom. She hadn't checked on her mother since leaving St Lucia, and for some unknown reason she felt her heart lodge in her throat as she dialled her number.

She hadn't decided when to tell her mother about her inheritance. They hadn't spoken about Luigi, the man she'd been so briefly married to, in years, and Faye wondered sometimes if her mother had succeeded in forgetting him. Regardless of that, Faye knew she'd have to tell her eventually.

The call crackled, and when her mother came on the line it grew progressively patchy. Eventually Faye gave up, with a promise to call back, and looked up to find Maceo leaning in the doorway. Even though she'd revealed her darkest secrets to him, she still tensed. Had he overheard her conversation?

'I didn't mean to disturb you,' she said, trying to read his face.

He shrugged. 'I came to suggest you wait until the storm is over because the connection will be bad.'

She nodded. 'I sort of got that.'

His gaze dropped to her phone. 'How was your mother?'

Her tension increased. 'I couldn't really tell. I'm hoping she's the same as when we spoke in St Lucia.'

His eyes narrowed. 'What's her general state?'

Pain lanced through her. 'She has good days and bad days.' It was an adequate enough answer. And yet she found herself elaborating. 'The assault was traumatic in itself, but the real trauma came when she found out she was carrying me. I think that completely broke her mentally. I was oblivious to her deep trauma for years before she got help.'

He walked into the room, his hands leaving his pockets to hang by his sides. 'You were a child. How could you have known?'

'I was old enough to see how hard she took Luigi's leaving. She got so bad we were both assigned counsellors. I was too young to grasp exactly what was going on half the time, but I knew that she was suffering. About a year after Luigi left her counsellor suggested New Paths as a permanent residence. It was a whole new experience for her. Most of the time she thrives there, but every now and then she has a relapse.'

Maceo flinched and his expression turned almost furious. Just as he had on the balcony, he turned away abruptly.

Her stomach hollowed. 'Sorry if that was TMI. Not everyone wants to know the messy details.'

He turned back to her, his eyes burning. 'On the contrary. I want to know everything.'

The firm assurance brought a lump to her throat. Swallowing, she nodded. 'New Paths has a high success rate with alternative therapies. Mum's is a combination of medication, art and music therapy, specifically designed for her. That's the kind of therapy I want to do eventually,' she confessed quietly.

Enlightenment fired in his eyes. 'That's what you intend to use your inheritance for?'

'Yes,' she stated boldly. 'You probably think it's not—'

'I think it's highly commendable. Luigi would be proud.'

Tears prickled at her eyes. 'Do you think so?'

He nodded, his eyes gentling in a way that suggested he wasn't as unaffected as she'd imagined. They stared at one another, jagged understanding throbbing between them. Then another crack of thunder attempted to shatter the tree house.

She jumped. Maceo chuckled.

The atmosphere was broken. And when he returned to his desk a minute later Faye couldn't help but accept that she'd slipped just a little bit further down that slippery road where her heart was in even more danger.

CHAPTER TEN

IT WAS A little terrifying how returning to Capri felt to Faye like coming home. Perhaps the feeling stemmed from never having had a true home, her mother's mental fragility and resulting anxiety having left her in a state of flux.

Those two years spent with Luigi had been her closest to stability and 'home'…

Pico's over-exuberant greeting merely deepened the sensation of homecoming. And that night, when he scratched at the door for entry into Maceo's bedroom—where he'd insisted she moved—she smiled at Maceo's put-upon expression.

'I'm under no illusion that he's pining for me,' he said.

'Will you let him in, please?'

'I suspect I'll have to—or else listen to him whine all night,' he growled, before rising to open the door.

A thoroughly pleased Pico rushed in, but when he attempted to jump onto the bed Maceo whistled sharply. 'He can stay for tonight, but I refuse to have him on our bed.'

Her heart squeezed, then banged against her ribs in foolish reaction to his words. Under the guise of petting Pico, Faye ruthlessly tried to bring her feelings under control. Which turned out to be a futile task because, a moment later, when Maceo tugged her into his arms, the cascade of emotion smashed her fortitude to smithereens.

In the following weeks Maceo continued to whittle away at her foundations until Faye accepted that when she eventually left she would be taking an extra suitcase full of heartache with her. Because her feelings for Maceo had long passed the *just sex* they were supposed to be indulging in.

To stop herself being totally overcome by her staggering emotions, she attempted to place a professional distance between them—first by requesting a return to the R&D department, and then by demanding that they keep their physical relationship between themselves.

Maceo grumbled, but when she refused to back down, after a twenty-minute debate, he grudgingly gave in, before pulling her beneath him in bed with the instruction to put him in a better mood—a task Faye was all too delighted to perform.

Day after day, she was discovering tiny new facets of her lover.

Maceo could be gentle when required, was extremely generous to his staff, and without fail, visited his family's memorial every weekend.

On the third weekend after their return she asked to accompany him. He hesitated for a fraction of a second before holding out his hand.

An hour later she stood beside him, tears prickling in her eyes as she paid her respects to the only father she'd ever known, silently accepting that she would never truly know all the answers.

There was one question she hadn't yet asked, though.

She tried to ignore the lingering distance she felt from Maceo as they left the cemetery. But, just as when they'd been in St Lucia, she felt that small pebble of unease chafe, its presence looming larger with each day.

'I've never asked about Pietro's whereabouts… I'm assuming the two of you aren't in touch?'

Maceo stiffened, and the hand gripping hers tightened. 'No,' he said tersely.

He said nothing more. Faye pulled at his hand till he stopped. Looking into his face, she glimpsed a caginess she'd never witnessed before.

'Maceo, what is it?'

His lips thinned and his jaw clenched before he answered. 'He died of a drug overdose in Malaysia, three years ago.'

She gasped, her gaze swinging back to the family mausoleum. Maceo shook his head. 'He left instructions to be cremated wherever he died. I didn't attend the funeral.'

He resumed walking and after a moment she joined him, aware that the distance between them was widening. But she was leaving in a few weeks. Reminded of how Luigi had left her with questions, Faye swore she wouldn't let Maceo do the same.

They had no dinner plans the following Friday, and, as had become her habit, when she finished work she took the lift to Maceo's floor.

Bruno was nowhere in sight. About to knock on his door, she hesitated when she heard voices.

With a grimace, she lowered her hand, recognising Stefano's and Francesco's cold tones. She'd stayed clear of them since the party at Villa Serenita, and wondered about why Maceo kept them around, considering the obvious friction between them.

She shrugged mentally. Luigi and Maceo's parents had accommodated Pietro, despite his deplorable behaviour. It stood to reason Carlotta would do the same for her brothers.

About to retreat, and wait for Maceo in one of the conference rooms, Faye froze when she heard her name. She knew she shouldn't eavesdrop, but a need to overcame her better judgement.

After several weeks in Italy she'd picked up enough Italian words to grasp the gist of a conversation, although she didn't have to be fluent to recognise the brothers' tone.

'The little whore...'

'Paparazzi sniffing around...'

'Perhaps they need to be indulged...'

Maceo's terse response produced a chilling silence she could feel even from behind the closed door. Both brothers snarled something right before she heard footsteps. She tried to retreat, but didn't get far enough. The door flew open and twin pairs of beady eyes glared at her.

Behind them, Maceo stood tall and furious. His gaze gentled a touch when he saw her, but he turned away almost immediately, raking his fingers through his hair as he strode to the window.

She entered his office, shutting the door behind her. 'Everything all right?'

'No.'

'May I ask what that was about?'

He tensed visibly, fingers massaging his nape. 'Leave it.'

She hadn't expected the harsh answer. Cold dread slithered through her stomach. 'Is it about how they treated Carlotta? Shouldn't you let that go, Maceo?' she urged softly.

He spun around, his eyes flames of rage. 'No. Because they're *snakes*. At every turn they try to undermine my position.'

'Can't you just vote them off the board?'

His jaw tightened. 'I might be the majority shareholder but I don't have the ultimate overruling authority. Not yet, anyway.'

She frowned. What she'd overheard had sounded personal. About *her*. 'So what was it about just now?' she pressed.

She sensed his withdrawal, saw the shutters coming down before he turned to his desk. 'They're making their usual threats. Wanting something for nothing.'

Perhaps it wasn't a lie, but she suspected it wasn't the whole story either. But, really, was it her business when he was visibly freezing her out?

'I'm ready to leave,' she said, changing the subject. 'I can go ahead if you want?' she suggested, hoping he'd refuse. Hoping he'd snap out of his mood so things could return to normal. But what was normal when the clock was counting down until this thing reached its end date?

'We will leave together,' he stated gruffly.

But even as he gathered his files, strode towards her and took her hand, he was a thousand miles away.

Dinner was a stilted affair, his thoughts clearly elsewhere. But all that changed when they reached the bedroom. There he focused his full attention on her. And, like the fool she was, she surrendered, allowed his searing passion to burn away her chaotic thoughts.

For a week they carried on in the same vein. Then came the added concern of her mother's suddenly frequent contact, in which she demanded to know when Faye would be returning.

Assuring her that she would return soon only highlighted how close she was to leaving Capri.

How close she was to walking away from the man she suspected she'd fallen in love with.

When her mother's calls increased in frequency the next day, Faye was forced to consider cutting her time even shorter. Perhaps going home to see her mother. Her heart eased a little at the thought that she didn't have to leave permanently just yet. She would just fly home for a couple of days.

Deciding to tell Maceo, she left her favourite position beside the pool, where she'd been toying with more new flavour combinations.

It was Saturday, but Maceo was working at home.

The first thing she noticed was the staff's tension as she passed them in the hallway.

Her second discovery was Maceo's absence from his study.

The reason for the staff's tension became clear when she heard Maceo's furious voice and saw his angry pacing a moment later as he crossed the terrace outside.

She was debating whether to retreat when her gaze fell on the papers strewn on his desk. Nausea congealed in her stomach as she saw the first of the shrieking headlines. Then the one after that. All with accompanying pictures.

One picture was of her leaving the cemetery with Maceo.

Another was of him clutching her hand as they raced towards his helicopter. A third grainy one showed them on his beach in St Lucia, clenched in a lovers' embrace that left no doubt as to their relationship.

But it was the lurid revealing headlines that rammed horror down her throat. That filled every atom of her being with utter desolation until a hoarse cry left her throat and her knees gave way.

Billionaire CEO Dates Child of Rape!
In Bed with the Dirty Laundry!

She slapped her hand over her mouth, as if that would stop the sickening feeling cascading through her. Firm hands grabbed her, attempted to right her. With a horrified shriek, she pushed Maceo away.

'Faye…' His voice was low, imploring.

She staggered away from him. As she did so her hip bumped his desk, sending papers flying to the ground. She started to reach for them but Maceo surged forward.

'Leave them!'

The peculiar note in his voice froze her. Growing colder, she peered more closely at the papers she'd dislodged. It was a report of some sort. And within the long script several familiar names jumped out at her. Hers. Her mother's. *New Paths. Luigi. Pietro?*

'Maceo, what is this?' Her shaking voice echoed her devastated soul.

His lips thinned, highlighting the whiteness around his mouth, his ashen pallor. '*Per favore.* Leave it, Faye,' he urged, his tone cajoling in a way that rattled her even more.

'No. I won't leave it. Why are you investigating me?'

'I don't want to do it like this.'

'Do what?' she shrieked. '*Tell* me!' When he didn't answer, she pointed to the newspapers. 'Did you do this?'

Anger restored his colour. 'Of course not.'

'Then who did? You're the only one who—'

'Do not even finish that sentence.'

But her pain seared too deep. 'Why not? I told Matt what happened to my mother, but this level of detail… No one knows that but you.'

Maceo's fury evaporated, leaving behind thick censure that added to the dread crawling through her.

'And you automatically assume I would betray you?'

'I don't know!'

'You should!' he sliced at her.

'Why? Because we're sleeping together?' She lashed out, her pain too huge to contain.

A look almost of hurt crossed his face before it hardened into a rigid mask. 'Because I told you I would always be straight with you.'

'Then explain why you're investigating me.'

'I'm not investigating you. I'm investigating Pietro. And Luigi.'

'Why?'

For a tight stretch he remained silent. Then, with a bleak look, he shook his head. 'Because I don't think Luigi's arrival in your mother's life was unplanned.'

Her vision wavered. She clutched the side of the desk to keep upright.

'What…?'

But she *knew*. Like a snake slithering in the dark towards her, the poisonous truth was about to sting. Change her life for ever.

'Luigi went to England purposely to find your mother— and you.'

'Explain, Maceo,' she pleaded, aware that her lips had gone numb. Her whole body had gone numb. Only a tiny sliver of her brain worked.

'Because he suspected your mother's attacker was Pietro. And in his own way he wanted to make things right.'

The sting arrived like a hot lance to her heart. Vaguely

she was aware that she was shaking her head, that every atom in her being was shaking in denial. Just as she was aware that Maceo had dropped to his knees before her and was staring at her with eyes that pitied her.

'No!' she snarled.

He lowered his head, his shoulders heaving. 'Yes.'

'Oh, my God. He lied to me,' she whispered. '*You* lied to me. About everything.'

'*No.*' The word was raw, gravel-rough. 'No,' he repeated. 'I was gathering facts. I needed to be sure before—'

'Before you splashed my family's sordid dirty laundry all over the papers?'

'That wasn't my doing. It was Francesco and Stefano. I had no idea they were doing some digging of their own. What you overheard in my office…they were attempting to blackmail me—'

'And you let them? So you could keep me onside until you got your hands on that precious share?'

His nostrils flared and she knew she'd hit the mark.

'You did, didn't you? Your precious company is worth more to you than…than anything else.' She barely stopped herself from saying *than me*.

'To have ultimate control of the company, I need to be a one hundred per cent shareholder. That's why I can't get rid of them. And yes, this isn't how I would've gone about dealing with your news. But it's not the end of the world.'

She laughed—a grating sound that frightened her. 'It's easy to say that when you're the golden child of parents who loved each other and loved you. You have *no earthly idea* what I feel.'

'Perhaps not. But that doesn't mean you should let this define you.'

'What do you expect me to do? Walk out into the street and own it?'

To her utter shock and dismay, he nodded.

'*Si*. Take the power away from them. Turn this into a positive.'

'God, you're actually serious! Do you have *any* idea how this will affect my mother?' Fresh horror shrouded her. 'Oh, God. My mother!'

He rose and held out his phone. 'Call her.'

'And say what? That I trusted the wrong person with the most devastating thing to happen to her?'

His fingers tightened around the phone. 'I will not persistently defend myself. If you won't call your mother, how will you know she's okay?'

'How do you think? By going home to her!'

He frowned. 'What are you saying?'

'That I'm leaving! Surely you can't expect me to stay here after this?'

To her chagrin, he looked utterly stunned. She walked towards the door, her feet blocks of concrete.

'Faye.'

She didn't stop. She was terrified she would break down if she did. And she refused to leave Maceo with the memory of seeing her completely defeated.

'Faye, wait. There's something else.'

Misery drenched her. There couldn't be. She knew without a shadow of a doubt that she wouldn't be able to take it. But she couldn't move. Because even drowning in utter desolation she still held out the hope of something from him. Something that resembled a reciprocal feeling of that precious knot of longing inside her that had somehow survived these devastating revelations.

Something like...hope.

Like *love*.

She held her breath as he approached. But when he arrived beside her he didn't arrive with words. Instead, he held out an envelope. One with her name on it.

Confused, she lifted her gaze to his.

'Carlotta left this for you. It's from Luigi,' he said.

Hope dissolved into despair and Faye couldn't even find the strength to be angry. 'Another lie?' she rasped.

'No. But I didn't think you were in a frame of mind to hear the truth before.'

'That's how you intend to justify withholding this from me?'

His jaw clenched. 'This is how you choose to end things, Faye? With accusations?'

'I didn't end this, Maceo. You did.'

Slowly that formidable façade locked in, his statue-like hauteur erasing every trace of emotion from his face.

'Go, then. Don't let me stop you.'

She snatched the letter. And left.

Maceo stood in one corner of the conference room, attempting to block out the buzz of excitement growing steadily behind him. Casa di Fiorenti hadn't had a new product launch in two years. It stood to reason his shareholders were thrilled at the prospect of a new range.

Alberto and his team had pulled out all the stops to preview the Arcobaleno range in only six short weeks. His ambition to push it through production in time for Christmas was well on track too.

Maceo didn't care. These days he cared very little about anything. Except for the excruciating passage of time.

Six weeks.

A lifetime since she walked out of his study. He'd laboured under the misapprehension that relocating to his office at his Rome headquarters might solve the problem of seeing her face around every corner—that returning to his penthouse apartment in the heart of his favourite city might erase the memories of her that haunted Villa Serenita.

But no.

Everywhere he went he saw her.

His staff offered pitying looks while his employees scurried away when they saw him coming. And why shouldn't they? He was intolerable to be around.

Not even the satisfaction of pushing his lawyers to find the loophole that had enabled him to finally toss Carlotta's brothers off the board had eased the savage ache inside him.

Several times he reached for the phone. Each time he lost his nerve.

Maceo laughed under his breath. He'd been through a car accident, a coma, months of intense rehabilitation, only to be cowed by the rejection of a diminutive woman with rainbow colours in her hair?

Arcobaleno.

His insides twisted at the name that suited her from head to toe. He was certain he wouldn't be able to see another rainbow without being reminded of Faye.

Should he have stopped her from leaving? How could he when she was right?

He'd withheld crucial information about who she was. He'd devastated her as surely as his own parents had devastated him. And so soon after she'd delivered him from his dark torment. For that alone he deserved this suffering.

'*Signor...?*' Alberto addressed him hesitantly. 'They're waiting for you to make a speech.'

Too bad. He was fresh out of congratulatory speeches. The only talking he wanted to do was to the woman who'd left an indelible mark on him. The woman without whom he was beginning to fear he would perish and fade away to nothing.

He stared into the glass of vintage champagne he hadn't touched, attempting to summon words that held genuine meaning. Each one felt flat and false. Hell, even the weather was conspiring against him.

In the square below, tourists milled about, huddled together or seeking shelter from the sudden downpour that had caught them unawares. Like him, they'd expected sunshine, only to be greeted with grey clouds.

He lifted his gaze, glared at the clouds. Just then they parted. By the smallest fraction. But it was enough to let through a stream of sunshine. And within that sunshine…

Maceo's heart tripped over as he caught sight of the faintest rainbow.

He didn't believe in that sort of foolishness. Yet he couldn't take his eyes off the colourful arc.

A tremor moved through him. Turning, he shoved his drink into Alberto's startled hands.

'You make the speech. You brought this to fruition.'

'It wasn't just me,' Alberto replied, a sombre look in his eyes.

Maceo nod grimly. 'No, it wasn't. And I should do something about that, no?'

Alberto was smiling as Maceo strode out of his own meeting, totally uncaring of the stunned looks he received as he walked out.

For the first time in endless weeks purpose flowed through his veins.

'Are you going to mope today as well?'

Faye looked up, startled, from the book she'd been half-heartedly reading.

'Excuse me?'

Her mother set her teacup down. 'I may be a little loopy, but I'm not stupid.'

'You're not loopy, Mum. Please stop saying that.'

Her mother gave her a sad little smile. 'We both know what I am, Faye.'

'Mum…'

Her mother reached across the small table where they were having tea and laid a hand on her arm. 'It's fine, sweetheart. You don't need to say it. You never need to say it.'

Tears that hovered just beneath the surface of Faye's emotions rose. Rapidly she blinked them away. 'I'm not sure what you're talking about.'

'You check your phone a hundred times a day. You perk up when the postman arrives and wither when he leaves you empty-handed.'

Faye started to protest, but her mother wasn't finished.

'That letter you keep in your pocket and read a dozen times a day when you think I'm not looking…'

Faye's mouth dropped open.

Her mother smiled. 'I'm not stupid,' she repeated softly. A tear escaped.

Her mother brushed it away. 'Tell me,' she invited.

So Faye told her. About Carlotta's initial contact. About Luigi's bequest. Selectively about Maceo. Even about Matt, at which her mother echoed Maceo's words so eerily, her heart lurched.

'He's a deplorable human being. Don't waste another moment's thought on him.'

But when she reached the hardest part she stopped. 'I can't, Mum…'

'It's something to do with what happened to me, isn't it?'

Miserable, Faye nodded. Then the words came tumbling out.

An apology for how she'd come into the world was written in the pages of Luigi's letter. In it, he admitted his knowledge of what his brother had done to her mother—how, several years after the attack, a family friend who'd attended the same party had divulged what he suspected had happened.

Luigi, ever the conscientious brother, had looked further into the incident and tracked down her mother. His discovery that Angela had borne his brother's child had shocked him. He'd intended to make anonymous reparation, but then he'd seen Angela with Faye in a playground.

Befriending Angela had revealed to Luigi the true depths of her fragile mental state. He'd married her out of guilt, and a desperate need to make amends, but had known deep down he couldn't provide the sort of care Angela needed.

Steering her to New Paths had been his way of helping her after he'd fallen in love with Carlotta. He had always been ashamed he'd never revealed his true identity and he begged forgiveness.

Faye's discovery that her school scholarship had been orchestrated by Luigi, and that New Paths was fully funded by a Fiorenti-Caprio foundation, had enraged her for all of five minutes before she'd dissolved into tears again. Luigi had done his best for them, and she couldn't fault him for that.

'I don't think I can quite bring myself to say his name, but I'm glad you have the answers you need,' her mother said, her eyes a forest of shadows.

It was Faye's turn to comfort her. 'I'm so sorry, Mum.'

Her mother nodded solemnly. 'I know he left us, but I'm glad you had a father figure for a while—especially when I couldn't be the mother you deserved.'

A lump clogged Faye's throat. 'I wouldn't trade you for the world.'

They stayed silent, absorbing their emotions.

'Now, the postman…' Angela pressed. 'What's that about?'

Faye blinked away fresh tears. Since her email account remained empty of anything to do with Maceo or Casa di Fiorenti, she'd taken to stalking the postman. She knew she should give up now, after six weeks of silence, and instruct a lawyer to deal with securing her inheritance. Except her inheritance wasn't paramount in her mind. What she yearned for more was something, *anything*, from the man she'd lost her heart to in Naples. Even if it was a stuffy letter from his legal team.

'You're holding back about this Maceo. Is he the one?' her mother intuited.

Faye's heart quaked even when she thought about him. 'Yes.'

'What happened?'

Misery gripped her tight. Miraculously, those harrowing tabloid exposés hadn't reached Devon. Faye intended to keep it that way.

'We rowed... I accused him of...of unspeakable things.'

'Did he deserve it?'

Faye held her breath for the longest time, then shook her head. 'I didn't wait for an explanation.'

'I suspect you *know* he didn't deserve it, or you wouldn't be feeling this bad.'

Tears of remorse slid down her cheeks as she accepted her mother's assessment. Shock and pain had stopped her from hearing Maceo out. From accepting his reasons for withholding. Six weeks of silence said she'd lost her chance.

'You may be in luck today. Here's the postman.'

Faye twisted in her seat, her heart hammering as the middle-aged man made a beeline for her. He pulled out a thick envelope and handed it over. Transfixed, she stared at the Casa di Fiorenti logo.

'Is this what you're waiting for?' her mother asked.

Was it?

Swallowing, she tore the letter open, devouring the missive from Maceo's lawyers, offering to buy her share. If she agreed to the sum, the formal signing would be in London in two days. If she didn't agree, she was welcome to commence negotiations with Maceo via his lawyers.

Despite her heart sinking at the stiff formality of the letter, her insides continued to somersault. Would Maceo be in London?

Even without knowing the answer Faye knew she would be there.

Taking a deep breath, she read the rest of the document. Her mouth dropped open when she saw how much Maceo intended to offer her. It was almost twice what his lawyers in Naples had said the partial share was worth. Whether Maceo turned up or not, she would be a fool to reject it.

She looked up. Her mother was smiling.

'Regardless of how you came into the world, you deserve

every happiness. You've settled your past, Faye. Now go and fight for your future.'

Fighting more tears, Faye leaned over and kissed her mother. Then she rose from the table.

She was going to London.

Maceo clenched his fists, impatience bristling through him as he paced his living room. He was reduced to voyeurism—a silent participant watching Faye via the monitor in his penthouse while his lawyers took their sweet time securing her signature.

He'd given them carte blanche to offer her whatever she wanted, but evidently his instruction that the transaction should be conducted in the shortest possible time hadn't quite sunk in.

He was half a second from picking up the phone when they finished. The moment they left, Bruno escorted Faye to the lift. Maceo was waiting when the doors parted on the penthouse floor thirty seconds later.

She was facing away from him, wearing a coral concoction, with bangles to match and a similar colour threaded through her hair, and he welcomed the much-needed moment to compose himself.

Then she turned, her breath catching when she saw him. *Mio Dio*, she was beautiful.

'Maceo! I thought you weren't… What am I doing up here?'

'I wish to talk to you.'

'Then why weren't you downstairs with your lawyers?'

Because I'm a damn mess.

'Because I didn't want business to muddle this.'

'And what is *"this"*, exactly?' she enquired, raising her chin.

'Would you like to come in? *Per favore,*' he pleaded.

Her gaze flicked past him into the penthouse and Maceo caught the slightest wobble in her chin. It was the tiniest chink in her armour, but he found himself praying it was a sign that all wasn't lost.

She walked past him, head held high. He followed, his heart racing as her alluring scent reminded him of its absence on his pillow.

She reached the sofa and turned to face him. 'Tell me why I'm here.'

'Because, my beautiful rainbow, I'm a desperate man, here to plead my case,' he stated baldly.

She reached out blindly, clutched the back of the sofa.

Maceo exhaled, his prayers intensifying. She wasn't immune to him.

'We said everything we had to say to one another in Italy,' she said.

'Did we? Are you absolutely certain I can't say more?'

'Depends on what the subject matter is.'

Unable to keep his distance, he took a few steps towards her. She didn't retreat. Another mercy.

'You were right, *cara.*'

'About…?' she queried, her eyes filming with a pain he would give his limbs to erase.

'About how I handled everything. Regardless of my feelings on the matter, I should've given you the information you needed for your own closure. My conceit made me believe mine was the right way. I hurt you, Faye. And I'm here to say…*mi dispiace.* I am also here to make amends.'

Something close to disappointment crossed her face. 'Is that all you're here for?'

'No,' he said. 'I am a greedy man who wants more. Much more.'

She gripped the sofa harder. 'Then perhaps this time you shouldn't quit while you're ahead?'

The thread of hope in her voice triggered his. He ventured even closer, heard her breath catch in the softest gasp. With every fibre of his being he yearned to hold her.

'I've missed you, Faye. Desperately.'

Her nostrils quivered but she remained silent.

He took that as his cue to risk everything. 'I held back about Pietro because I was ashamed. I've been ashamed of what Luigi and my parents did to cover up his activities for a very long time. Even after you showed me that there was a way forward, there was still shame. My family was responsible for letting him get away with his depravities. When you showed me his picture on the yacht, I couldn't dismiss the possibility that he was connected to you somehow. You obviously take after your mother, since you look nothing like him, but I couldn't tell you until I was absolutely certain.'

To his utter relief, she nodded. 'I was upset when I found out what you did, but eventually I understood the reasoning behind it.'

Relief smashed harder through him. 'About the letter... Carlotta made me promise to hold on to it for at least three months before giving it you.'

'Why?'

'I suspect she was hoping that what happened between us would happen. That I would meet you, see how special you are and perhaps in time it would not be too late for me. That this thing living within me now would take hold.'

She stopped breathing and her eyes latched onto his. 'What is the thing living inside you, Maceo?'

Her beautiful voice was hardly above a murmur.

'It is the need for you that never goes away. The desire to be with you every hour of every day, to make you smile, to hear you laugh, to plan a future with you by my side, bearing our children, growing old with me. It is this love I have inside for you, *amore mio*. Carlotta was an eternal optimist and I will be in her debt for ever.'

'Why?'

'Because she brought you to me. I mentioned the vow I made over my parents' grave?'

She nodded.

He reached into his pocket. 'They made a list, mapping out their lives from the night they got engaged to their old age. I was number two, right after their wedding. Casa di Fiorenti was number five. There are eighteen things on that list, Faye.' His fingers closed over the paper, pain rippling through him. 'They only made it to number seven. Because of me.'

She gave a choked cry. 'Oh… Maceo…'

'So I vowed to deprive myself of the happiness I robbed them of.'

'No… They wouldn't have wanted that for you, Maceo,' she said.

'I see that now, *amore*. You came along and I was happy to fail. Because you opened my eyes and my heart to a life beyond accumulating wealth and solitude and sacrifice. What is it all worth without someone to share it? Now I've had time to look at this list in a different light, and I can do everything in here *for* them. I know they loved me enough to wish it so. And even if I don't get to cross off the last item, and die in your arms, what I experienced with you during our time together will be enough.'

'Wow… You're giving up so easily?' she taunted, but her eyes shone bright.

Maceo laughed. 'Never. This is simply an initial skirmish. I'm Italian. I will pursue you relentlessly. Desire anything in the world and it will be yours, *tesoro*. Even Pico. Who misses you dreadfully.'

She smiled. Then sobered. 'I miss him too. But what if the only thing I truly want in the world is you?'

His world shifted beneath his feet, then righted itself in a way that made him want to shout with joy.

'What then, Maceo?' she pressed.

'Then you will have me,' he vowed on a shaken breath. 'Immediately. Now.'

Her face transformed, blooming with a smile he knew he would never forget as long as he lived. She swayed towards him and Maceo closed the gap between them, sweeping her off her feet as the sun burst through the clouds.

He froze, his gaze darting to the skies.

'What are you looking for?' she asked.

When what he searched for didn't appear, Maceo knew why. Staring into the face of the woman who held his heart, he felt joy overflow within him.

'Nothing, *amore mio*. I search for nothing. Because everything I want is right here in my arms.'

Tears filmed her eyes. 'I love you, Maceo. So much.'

Gently, he brushed her tears away. *'Ti amo anch'io, il mio bellisimmo arcobaleno.'*

Her smile widened. 'I love it when you call me that.'

'Then you should come with me back to Italy. There's a wonderful surprise waiting for you.'

The new Arcobaleno range of specially flavoured chocolates shaped like rainbows had been her idea. Maceo intended it to be one of many projects he undertook with her.

'I will follow you anywhere, my love.'

'That's good to hear. Because right now I would very much love you to come with me to the bedroom. I have six weeks to make up for, plus a lifetime.'

'I will—right after you show me that list.'

He handed it over, watched her face as she read it, then raised her beautiful face to his.

'Can we start from the beginning and work our way through it?' she asked.

A lump clogged his throat. 'As long as I get to shower you with love, live each day with you and die in your arms, you have a deal.'

Her smile filled his heart. 'I accept.'

And in that moment Maceo swore that he would never cause her to be without that smile.

* * * * *

SAVED BY
DOCTOR DREAMY

DIANNE DRAKE

CHAPTER ONE

THE NIGHT WAS STILL. No howler monkeys sitting up in the trees yelling their heads off. No loud birds calling into the darkness. Damien doubted if there was even a panther on the prowl anywhere near here. It was kind of eerie actually, since he was used to the noise. First, the city noise in Seattle, where he grew up. Then Chicago, Miami, New York. Back to Seattle. And finally, the noise of the Costa Rican jungle, where he'd come to settle.

Noise was his friend. It comforted him, reassured him that he was still alive. Something he hadn't felt in a long, long time. And when it surrounded him, it was home and safety and all the things that kept him sane and focused on the life he was living now.

When Damien had come to the jungle he'd been pleasantly surprised by the noisiness of it all. It was as loud as any city, but in a different way. He'd traded in people for animals and honking cars for wind rustling through the vegetation. Now that he was used to the sounds there, he counted on them to surround him, to cradle him in a contented solitude. But tonight was different. He felt so... isolated, so out of touch with his reality. So lonely. Alone in the city—alone in the jungle. It was all the same. All of it bringing a sense of despair that caught up with him from time to time.

This despair of his had been a problem over the years. People didn't understand it. Didn't want to. Most of the time he didn't want to understand it either, because when he did he'd overcompensate. Do things he might not normally do. Like getting engaged to someone he wouldn't have normally given a second thought to.

But Daniel understood this about him. Daniel—he was the only one, and he'd never ridiculed Damien for what other people thought was ridiculous. Of course, he and Daniel had the twin-connection thing going on, and that was something that never failed him.

Damien and Daniel Caldwell. Two of a kind—well, not so much. They looked alike, with a few notable exceptions like hair length and beard. Daniel was the clean-shaven, short-haired version, while Damien was the long-haired, scruffy-bearded one. But they were both six foot one, had the same brown eyes, same dimples that women seemed to adore. Same general build. Apart from their outward looks, though, they couldn't have been more different. Restlessness and the need to keep moving were Damien's trademarks while contented domesticity and a quiet lifestyle were his brother's. Which Damien envied, as he'd always figured that by the time he was thirty-five he'd have something in his life more stable than what he had. Something substantial. Yet that hadn't happened.

It's too quiet tonight, Damien scribbled into a short letter to his brother. *It feels like it's going to eat me alive.* He'd seen Daniel a few months ago. Gone back to the States for Daniel's wedding. And it was a happy reunion, not like the time before that when he'd been called home to support his brother through his first wife's death. But Daniel had moved on now. He had a happy life, a happy family. Lucky, *lucky* man.

*The work is good, though, bro. It keeps me busy
pretty much all the time. Keeps me out of trouble. So
how's your new life fitting into your work schedule?*

Daniel's life—a nice dream. Even though, deep down,
Damien didn't want strings to bind him to one place, one
lifestyle. Rather, he needed to do what he wanted, when
he wanted, with no one to account to. And space to think,
to reevaluate. Or was that another of his overcompensa-
tions? Anyway, he had that now, although he'd had to come
to the remote jungles of Costa Rica to find it. In that re-
moteness, however, he'd found a freedom he'd never really had before.

And remote it was. Isolated from all the everyday conveniences that Costa Rica's large cities offered. Not even
attractive to the never-ending flow of expats who were
discovering the charms of this newly modernizing Central American country.

Most of the time Damien thrived on the isolation, not
that he was, by nature, a solitary kind of man. Because
he wasn't. Or at least didn't used to be. In his former life,
he'd liked fast cars, nice condos and beautiful women.
In fact, he'd thrived on those things before he'd escaped
them. Now, the lure of the jungle had trapped him in a
self-imposed celibacy, and that wasn't just of a sexual
nature. It was a celibacy from worldly matters. A total
abstinence from anything that wasn't directed specifically toward him. A time to figure out where he was
going next in his life. Or if he was even going to go anywhere else at all.

In the meantime, Damien didn't regret turning his back
on his old life in order to take off on this new one. In ways
he'd never expected, it suited him.

*Say hello to Zoey for me, and tell her I'm glad she
joined the family. And give Maddie a kiss from her
Uncle Damien.*

Damien scrawled his initials at the bottom of the letter,
stuck it in an envelope and addressed it. Maybe sometime
in the next week or so he'd head into Cima de la Montaña
to stock up on some basic necessities and mail the letter.
Call his parents if he got near enough to a cell tower. And
find a damned hamburger!

"We need you back in the hospital, Doctor," Alegria
Diaz called through his open window. She was his only
trained nurse—a woman who'd left the jungle to seek a
higher education. Which, in these parts, was a rarity as
the people here didn't usually venture too far out into the
world.

"What is it?" he called back, bending down to pull on
his boots.

"Stomachache. Nothing serious. But he wouldn't listen
to me. Said he had to see *el médico.*"

El médico. The doctor. Yes, that was him. The doctor
who directed one trained nurse, one semiretired, burned-
out plastic surgeon and a handful of willing, if not experienced, volunteers.

"Let me put my shirt back on and comb my hair, and
I'll be right over." A year ago his world had been very
large. Penthouse. Sports car. Today it was very small. A
one-room hut twenty paces from the hospital. A borrowed
pickup truck that worked as often as it didn't.

Damien donned a cotton T-shirt, pulled his hair back
and rubber-banded it into a small ponytail, and headed out
the door. Being on call 24/7 wasn't necessarily the best
schedule, but that was the life he'd accepted for himself
and it was also the life he was determined to stick with.

For how long? At least until he figured out what his next life would be. Or if he'd finally stumbled upon the life he wanted.

"I wanted to give him an antacid," Alegria told him as he entered through the door of El Hospital Bombacopsis, which sat central in the tiny village of Bombacopsis.

"But he refused it?" Damien asked, stopping just inside the door.

"He said a *resbaladera* would fix him."

Resbaladera—a rice and barley drink. "Well, we don't serve that here and, even if we did, I've never heard that it has any medicinal benefits for a stomachache."

Alegria smiled up at him. She was a petite woman, small in frame, short in height. Dark skin, black hair, dark eyes. Mother of three, grandmother of one. "He won't take an antacid from you," she warned.

"And yesterday he wouldn't take an aspirin from me when he had a headache. So why's he here in the first place, if he refuses medical treatment?"

"Señor Segura takes sick twice a year, when his wife goes off to San José to visit her sister."

"She leaves, and he catches a cold and comes to the hospital." Damien chuckled.

"Rosalita is a good cook here. He likes her food."

"Well, apparently he ate too much of it tonight, since he's sick at his stomach."

Alegria shrugged. "He's hard to control once you put a plate of *casado* in front of him."

Casado—rice, black beans, plantains, salad, tortillas and meat. One of Damien's favorite Costa Rican meals. But he didn't go all glutton on it the way Señor Segura apparently had. "Well, *casado* or not, I'm going to check him out, and if this turns out to be a simple stomachache

from overeating I'm going to give him an antacid and tell
Rosalita to cut back on his portions."

"He won't like that," Alegria said.

"And I don't like having my evening interrupted by a
patient who refuses to do what his nurse tells him."

"Whatever you say, Doctor." Alegria scooted off to
fetch the antacid while Damien approached his cantan-
kerous patient.

"I hear you won't take the medicine my nurse wanted
to give you."

"It's no good," Señor Segura said. "Won't cure what's
wrong with me."

"But a rice and barley drink will?"

"That's what my Guadalupe always gives me when I
don't feel so well."

"Well, Guadalupe is visiting her sister now, which
means we're the ones who are going to have to make you
feel better." Damien bent down and prodded the man's
belly, then had a listen to his belly sounds through a stethoscope. He checked the chart for the vital signs Alegria
had already recorded, then took a look down Señor Segura's throat. Nothing struck him as serious so he signaled
Alegria to bring the antacid over to the bedside. "OK,
you're sick. But it's only because you ate too much. My
nurse is going to give you a couple of tablets to chew that
will make you feel better."

"The tablets are no good. I want *resbaladera* like my
Guadalupe makes."

Damien refused to let this man try his patience, which
was going to happen very quickly if he didn't get this situation resolved. It was a simple matter, though. Two antacid tablets would work wonders, if he could convince
Señor Segura to give in. "I don't have *resbaladera* here,
and we're not going to make it specifically for you." They

had neither the means nor the money to make special accommodations for one patient.

"Then I'll stay sick until I get better, or die!"

"You're not going to die from a stomachache," Damien reassured him.

"And I'm not going to die because I wouldn't take your pills."

So there it was. The standoff. It happened sometimes, when the village folk here insisted on sticking to their traditional ways. He didn't particularly like giving in, when he knew that what he was trying to prescribe would help. But in cases like Señor Segura's, where the cure didn't much matter one way or another, he found it easier to concede the battle and save his arguments for something more important.

"Well, if you're refusing the tablets, that's up to you. But just keep in mind that your stomachache could last through the night."

"Then let it," Señor Segura said belligerently. Then he looked over at Alegria. "And you can save those pills for somebody else."

Alegria looked to Damien for instruction. "Put them back," Damien told her.

"Yes, Doctor," she said, frowning at Señor Segura. "As you wish."

What he wished was that he had more space, better equipment, more trained staff and up-to-date medicines. In reality, though, he had a wood-frame, ten-bed hospital that afforded no luxuries whatsoever and a one-room, no-frills clinic just off the entrance to the ward. It was an austere setup, and he had to do the best with it that he could. But the facility's lack was turning into his lack of proper service, as he didn't have much to offer anyone. Basic needs were about all he could meet. Of course, it was his choice to trade in a lucrative general surgery practice in Seattle for all of this. So he wasn't complaining. More like, he was wishing.

One day, he thought to himself as he took a quick look at the only other patient currently admitted to the hospital. She was a young girl with a broken leg whose parents couldn't look after her properly and still tend to their other nine children. So he'd set her leg, then admitted her, and wasn't exactly sure what to do with her other than let her occupy space until someone more critical needed the bed.

"She's fine," Alegria told him before he took his place at the bedside. "I checked her an hour ago and she's sound asleep."

Damien nodded and smiled. The only thing that would turn this worthless evening into something worthwhile would be to shut himself in his clinic and take a nap on the exam table. Sure, it was the lazy way out, since his real bed was only a few steps away. But his exam room was closer, and he was suddenly bone-tired. And his exam table came with a certain appeal he couldn't, at this moment, deny. So Damien veered off to the clinic, shut the door behind him and was almost asleep before he stretched out on the exam room table.

"Like I've been telling you for the past several weeks, I don't want a position in administration here at your hospital. I don't want to be your sidekick. I don't want to be put through the daily grind of budgets and salaries and supply orders!"

Juliette Allen took a seat across the massive mahogany desk from her father, Alexander, and leaned forward. "And, most of all, I don't want to be involved in anything that smacks of nepotism." Standing up to her dad was something she should have done years ago, but first her schooling, then her work had overtaken her, thrown her into a rut. Made her complacent. Then one day she woke up in the same bedroom she'd spent thirty-three years waking up in, had breakfast at the same table she'd always had breakfast at, and walked out the front door she'd always walked out of. Suddenly, she'd felt stifled. Felt the habits of her life closing in around her, choking her. And that's what her life had turned into—one big habit.

"This isn't nepotism, Juliette," Alexander said patiently. "It's about me promoting the most qualified person to the position."

"But I didn't apply for the position!" She was too young to be a director of medical operations in a large hospital. The person filling that spot needed years more experience than she had and she knew that. What she also knew was that this was her father's way of keeping her under his thumb. "And I think it's presumptuous of you to submit an application on my behalf."

"You're qualified, Juliette. And you have a very promising future."

"I direct the family care clinic, another position you arranged for me."

"And your clinic is one of the best operated in this hospital." Dr. Alexander Allen was a large man, formidable in his appearance, very sharp, very direct. "This is a good opportunity for you, and I don't understand why you're resisting me."

"Because I haven't paid my dues, because I don't have enough experience to direct the medical workings of an entire hospital." The problem was, she'd always given in to her father. Juliette's mother had died giving birth to her, and he'd never remarried, so it had always been just the two of them, which made it easy for him to control her with guilt over causing her mother's death. Plus she was also consumed by the guilt of knowing that if she left him he wouldn't fare so well on his own. For all his intelligence and power in the medical world, her father was insecure in his private world. Juliette's mother had done *everything* for him, then it fell to Juliette to do the same.

Juliette adored her dad, despite the position he'd put her in. He'd been a very good father to her, always making sure she had everything she wanted and needed. *More* than she wanted and needed, actually. And she'd become accustomed to that opulent lifestyle, loved everything about it, which was why this was so difficult now. She was tied to the man in a way most thirty-three-year-old women were not tied to their fathers. Which was why her dad found it so easy to make his demands then sit back and watch her comply. "I just can't do this, Dad," she said, finally sitting back in her chair. "And I hope you can respect my position."

"You're seriously in jeopardy of missing your opportunity to promote yourself out of your current job, Juliette. When I was a young man, in a situation much like the one you're in, I was always the first person in line to apply for any position that would further my career."

"But you've always told me that your ultimate career goal was to do what you're doing now—run an entire hospital. You, yourself, said you weren't cut out for everyday patient care."

"And my drive to get ahead has provided you with a good life. Don't you forget that."

"I'm not denying it, Dad. I appreciate all you've done for me and I love the life you've given me. But it's time for me to guide my career without your help." Something she should have done the day she'd entered medical school, except she hadn't even broken away from him then. She'd stayed at home, gone to the university and medical school where her father taught because it was easier for him. And while that wasn't necessarily her first choice, she always succumbed to her father when he started his argument with: "Your mother died giving birth to you and you can't even begin to understand how rough that's been on me, trying to take care of you, trying to be a good father—"

It was the argument he'd used time and time again when he thought he was about to lose her, the one that made her feel guilty, the one that always caused her to cave. But not this time. She'd made the decision first, then acted on it before she told him. And *this* time she was resolved to break away, because if she didn't she'd end up living the life he lived. Alone. Substituting work for a real life.

"And it's not about going into an administrative position, Dad." Now she had to drop the *real* bomb, and it wasn't going to be easy. "In fact, I have something somewhat administrative in mind for what I want to do next."

"Why do I have a feeling that what you're about to tell me is something I'm not going to like?" He looked straight across at his daughter. "I'm right, am I not?"

Juliette squared all five foot six of herself in her chair and looked straight back at him. "You're right. And there's no easy way to put this." She stopped, waiting for him to say something, but when he didn't she continued. "I'm going to resign from my position here at the hospital, Dad. In fact, I'm going to turn in my one-month notice tomorrow and have a talk with Personnel on how to replace me."

"You're leaving," he stated. "Just turning your back on everything you've accomplished here and walking out the door."

"I'm not turning my back on it, and I may come back someday. But right now, I've got to do something on my own, something you didn't just hand me. And whether you want to admit it or not, all my promotions have been gifts. I didn't earn them the way I should have."

"But you've worked hard in every position you've had, and you've shown very good judgment and skill in everything you've done."

"A lot of doctors can do that, Dad. I just happened to be the one whose father was Chief of Staff."

"So you're quitting because I'm Chief of Staff?"

"No, I'm quitting because I'm the chief of staff's daughter."

"Have I really piled that many unrealistic expectations on you? Because if I have, I can back off."

"It's not about backing off. It's about letting go." She didn't want to hurt him, but he did have to understand that it was time for her to spread her wings. Test new waters. Take a different path. "I— *We* have to do it. It's time."

"But can't you let go and still work here?"

"No." She shut her eyes for a moment, bracing herself for the rest of this. "I've accepted another position."

"Another hospital? There aren't any better hospitals in Indianapolis than Memorial."

"It's not a hospital, and it's not in Indianapolis." She swallowed hard. "I'm going to Costa Rica."

"The hell you are!" he bellowed. "What are you thinking, Juliette?"

She knew this was hard on him, and she'd considered leading up to this little by little. But her dad was hardheaded, and he was as apt to shut out the hints she might drop as he was to listen to them. Quite honestly, Alexander Allen heard only what he wanted to hear.

"What I'm thinking is that I've already made arrangements for a place to stay, and I'll be leaving one month from Friday."

"To do what?"

Now, this was where it became even more difficult. "I'm going to head up a medical recruitment agency."

Her dad opened up his mouth to respond, but shut it again when nothing came out.

"The goal is to find first-rate medical personnel to bring there. Costa Rica, and even Central America as a whole, can't supply the existing demand for medical professionals so they're recruiting from universities and hospitals all over the world, and I'm going to be in charge of United States recruitment."

"I know about medical recruitment. Lost a top-rate radiologist to Thailand a couple of years ago."

"So you know how important it is to put the best people in situations where they can help a hospital or, in Costa Rica's case, provide the best quality of care they can to the greatest number of people."

"Which leaves people like me in the position of having to find a new radiologist or transplant surgeon or oncologist, depending on who you're recruiting away from me."

"But you're already in an easier position to find the best doctors to fill your positions. You have easier access to the medical schools, a never-ending supply of residents to fill any number of positions in the hospital and you have connections to every major hospital in the country. These are things Costa Rica doesn't have, so in order for them to find the best qualified professionals they have to reach out differently than you do. Which, in this case, will be through me."

It was an exciting new venture for her and, while she wouldn't be offering direct medical care herself, she envisioned herself involved in a great, beneficial service. And all she ever wanted to be as a doctor was someone who benefited her patients, and by providing the patients in Costa Rica with good health-care practitioners she'd be helping more patients than she'd ever be able to help as a single practitioner in a clinic. In fact, when she thought about how many lives only one single recruited doctor could improve, she was overwhelmed. And when she thought of how many practitioners she would recruit and how many patients they would touch, it boggled her mind. "It's an important job, Dad. And I'm excited about it."

"Excited or not, you're throwing away a good medical career. You were a fine *hospital* physician, Juliette. In whatever capacity you chose."

"You were, too, once upon a time, but you traded that in for a desk and thousand-dollar business suits. So don't just sit there and accuse me of leaving medicine, because I'm not doing anything that you haven't already done."

"But in Costa Rica? Why there? Why not investigate something *different* closer to home, if you're hell-bent on getting out of Memorial. Maybe medical research. We've got one of the world's largest facilities just a few miles from here. Or maybe teaching. I mean, we've got, arguably, one of the best medical schools in the country right at our back door."

"But I don't want to teach, and I especially don't want to do research. I also don't want to work for an insurance company or provide medical care for a national sports franchise. What I want, Dad, is to find something that excites me. Something that offers a large group of people medical services they might not otherwise get. Something that will help an entire country improve its standard of care."

"There's nothing I can do to change your mind?" her dad asked, sounding as if the wind had finally been knocked out of his sails.

Juliette shook her head. "No, Dad. There's not. I've been looking into the details of my new position for weeks now, and I'm truly convinced this is something I want to do at this point in my life."

"Well, I'm going to leave your position open for a while. Staff it with a temp, in case you get to Costa Rica and decide your new job isn't for you. That way, you'll have a place to come back to, just in case."

Her dad was a handsome, vital man, and she hoped that once she was gone, and he didn't have anybody else to depend on, he might actually go out and get a life for himself. Maybe get married. Or travel. Or sail around the world the way he used to talk about when she was a little girl. In some ways, Juliette felt as if she'd been holding him back. She still lived with him, worked with him, was someone to keep him company when no one else was around. It was an easy way for both of them but she believed that so much togetherness had stunted them both. She didn't date, hadn't dated very much as a whole, thanks to her work commitments, and she'd certainly never gone out and looked for employment outside of what her father had handed her.

Yes, that was all easy. But now it was over. It was time for her to move on. "If I do come back to Indianapolis in the future, I won't be coming back to Memorial because I don't think it's a good idea that we work together anymore. We need to be separate, and if I'm here at Memorial that's not going to happen."

"Is this about something I've done to you, Juliette?" he asked, sounding like a totally defeated man.

"No, Dad. It's about something I haven't done for myself." And about everything she wanted to do for herself in the future.

One month down, and so far she was enjoying her new job. She'd had the opportunity to interview sixteen potential candidates for open positions in various hospitals. Seven doctors, three registered nurses, three respiratory therapists, a physical therapist and two X-ray technicians, one of whom specialized in mammograms. And there were another ten on her list for the upcoming two weeks. The bonus was, she loved Costa Rica. What she'd seen of it so far was beautiful. The people were nice. The food good. The only thing was, her lifestyle was a bit more subdued than what she was used to. She didn't have a nice shiny Jaguar to drive, but a tiny, used compact car provided by the agency. And her flat—not exactly luxurious like her home back in Indiana, but she was getting used to smaller, no-frills quarters and cheaper furniture. It was a drastic lifestyle change, she did have to admit, but she was doing the best she could with what she had.

Perhaps the most drastic change, though—the one thing she hadn't counted on—was that she missed direct patient care in a big way. She'd reconciled herself to experiencing some withdrawal before she'd come here, but what she'd been feeling was overwhelming as she'd never considered that stepping away from it would take such an emotional toll on her. But it had. She was restless. When she didn't stop herself, her mind wandered back to the days when she'd been involved directly in patient care. And it wasn't that she didn't like her job, because she did, and she had no intention of walking away from it. But she could physically, as well as emotionally, feel the lack in herself and she was afraid it was something that was only going to continue growing if she didn't find a fix for it.

"Are you sure you want to go through with this?" Cynthia Jurgensen, her office mate as well as her roommate, asked her. Like Juliette, Cynthia was a medical recruiter. Her recruitment area was the Scandinavian countries, as she had a heritage there. And, like Juliette, Cynthia had experienced the thrill of being called to a new adventure.

"Well, the note I found posted on the internet says the scheduling is flexible, so I'm hoping to work it out that I can commute in Friday night after I leave work here, and come home either late Sunday night or early Monday morning, before I'm due back on this job."

"But it's in the jungle, Juliette. The jungle!"

"And it's going to allow me to be involved with direct patient care again. I'm just hoping it's enough to satisfy me."

"Well, you can do whatever you want, but leave me here in the city, with all my conveniences."

San José was a large city, not unlike any large city anywhere. Juliette's transition here had been minimal as she really hadn't had time to get out and explore much of anything. So maybe her first real venture out, into the jungle of all places, was a bit more than most people would like, but the only thing Juliette could see was an opportunity to be a practicing doctor again. A doctor by the name of Damien Caldwell had advertised and, come tomorrow, she was going to go knocking on his door.

"Could you get one of the volunteers to take the linens home and wash them?" Damien asked Alegria. The hospital's sheets and pillowcases were a motley assortment, most everything coming as donations from the locals. "Oh, and instruct Rosalita on the particulars of a mechanical diet. I'm admitting Hector Araya later on, and he has difficulty chewing and swallowing since he had his stroke, so we need to adjust his diet accordingly."

Back in Seattle, Damien's workload never came close to anything having to do with linens and food but here in Bombacopsis, everything in the hospital fell under his direct supervision. This morning, for instance, during his one and only break for the day, he'd even found himself fluffing pillows and passing out cups of water to the five patients now admitted. He didn't mind the extra work, actually. It was just all a part of the job here. But he wondered if having another trained medical staffer come in, at least part-time, would ease some of the burden. That was why, when he'd gone to Cima de la Montaña last week to mail his letter to Daniel, he'd found a computer and posted a help-wanted ad on one of the local public sites.

Low pay, or possibly no pay.
Lousy hours and hard work.
Nice patients desperately in need of more medical help.

That was all his ad said, other than where to find him. *No phone service. Come in person.*

OK, so it might not have been the most appealing of ads. But it was honest, as the last thing he wanted was to have someone make that long trek into the jungle only to discover that their expectations fell nowhere within the scope of the position he was offering.

"There's a woman outside who says she wants to see you," Alegria said as she rushed by him, her arms full of bedsheets, on her way to change the five beds with patients in them.

"Can't one of the volunteers do that for you?" Damien asked her. "Or Dr. Perkins?"

"Dr. Perkins is off on a house call right now, and I have only two volunteers on today. One is cleaning the clinic, and the other is scrubbing potatoes for dinner. So it's either you or me and, since the woman outside looks deter-

mined to get in, I think I'll change the sheets and leave
that woman up to you."

"Fine," Damien said, setting aside the chart he'd been
writing in. "I'll go see what she wants. Is she a local, by
the way?"

Alegria shook her head. "She's one of yours."

"Mine?"

"From the United States, I think. Or maybe Canada.
Couldn't tell from her accent."

So a woman, possibly from North America somewhere,
had braved the jungle to come calling. At first he wondered
if she was some kind of pharmaceutical rep who'd seen the
word *hospital* attached to this place and actually thought
she might find a sale here. As if he had the budget to go
after the newest, and always the most expensive, drugs.
Nah. He was totally off the radar for that. So, could it be
Nancy? Was she running after him, trying to convince him
to give up his frugal ways and come back to her?

Been there, done that one. Found out he couldn't tolerate the snobs. And if there ever was a snob, it was his
ex-fiancée.

"I'm Juliette Allen," the voice behind him announced.

Damien spun around and encountered the most stunning brown eyes he'd ever seen in his life. "I'm Damien
Caldwell," he said, extending his hand to shake hers. "And
I wasn't expecting you." But, whoever she was, he was
glad she'd come. Tall, long auburn hair pulled back into a
ponytail, ample curves, nice legs—nice everything. Yes,
he was definitely glad.

"Your ad said to come in person, so here I am—in person."

In person, and in very good form, he thought. "Then
you're applying for a position?" Frankly, she wasn't what
he'd expected. Rather, he'd expected someone like George

Perkins, a doctor who was in the middle of a career burn-out, trying to figure out what to do with the rest of his life.

"Only part-time. I can give you my weekends, if you need me."

"Weekends are good. But what are you? I mean, am I hiring a nurse, a respiratory therapist or what?"

"A physician. I'm a family practice doctor. Directed a hospital practice back in Indiana."

"But you're here now, asking me for work?" From director of a hospital practice to this? It didn't make sense. "And you only want a couple days a week?"

"That's all I have free. The rest of my time goes to recruiting medical personnel to come to Costa Rica."

Now it was beginning to make some sense. She aided one of the country's fastest growing industries in her real life and wanted to be a do-gooder in her off time. Well, if the do-gooder had the skills, he'd take them for those two days. The rest of her time didn't matter to him in the least. "You can provide references?" he asked, not that he cared much to have a look at them, but the question seemed like the right one to ask.

"Whatever you need to see."

"And you understand the conditions here? And the fact that I might not have enough money left over in my budget to pay you all the time—or ever?"

"It's not about the money."

Yep. She was definitely a do-gooder. "So what's it about, Juliette?"

"I like patient care, and I don't get to do that in my current position. I guess you can say I'm just trying to get back to where I started."

Well, that was as good a reason as any. And, in spite of himself, he liked her. Liked her no-nonsense attitude. "So, if I hire you, when can you start?"

"I'm here now, and I don't have to be back at my other job until Monday. I packed a bag, just in case I stayed, so I'm ready to work whenever you want me to start."

"How about now? I have some beds that need changing and a nurse who's doing that but who has other things to do. So, can you change a bed, Juliette?"

CHAPTER TWO

COULD SHE CHANGE a bed? Sad to say, she hadn't made very many beds in her life. Back home, she and her dad had a housekeeper who did that for them. Twice a week, fresh sheets on every bed in the house, whether or not the bed had been slept on. At her dad's insistence. Oh, and brand-new linens ordered from the finest catalogs once every few months.

That was her life then, all of it courtesy of a very generous and doting father, and she'd found nothing extraordinary about it as it had been everything she'd grown used to. Her dad had always told her it was his duty to spoil her, and she'd believed that. Now, today, living in San José, and in keeping with what she was accustomed to, she and Cynthia rented a flat that came with limited maid service. It cost them more to secure that particular amenity in their living quarters, but having someone else do the everyday chores was well worth the extra money. So, at thirty-three, Juliette was a novice at this, and pretty much every other domestic skill most people her age had long since acquired. But how difficult could it be to change a silly bed? She was smart, and capable. And if she could cure illnesses, she could surely slap a sheet onto the bed.

Easier said than done, Juliette discovered after she'd stripped the first bed, then laid a clean sheet on top of it.

Tuck in the edges, fold under the corners, make sure there were no wrinkles—

She struggled through her mental procedural list, thought she was doing a fairly good job of it, all things considered. That was, until she noticed the sizable wrinkle that sprang up in the middle of the bed and crept all the way to the right side. How had that gotten there? she wondered as she tugged at the sheet from the opposite side, trying to smooth it out and, in effect, making the darned thing even worse.

"That could be uncomfortable, if you're the one who has to sleep on it," Damien commented from the end of the bed, where he was standing, arms folded across his chest, watching her struggle. "Causes creases in the skin if you lay on it too long."

"I intend to straighten it out. Maybe remake the bed." Actually, that was a lie. Her real intent was still to pat it down as much as she could, then move on to the next bed and hope the future occupant of this particular bed didn't have a problem with wrinkles.

"You know you've been working on this first bed for ten minutes now? Alegria would have had all five beds changed in that amount of time, and been halfway through giving a patient a bed bath. So what's holding you up? Because I have other things for you to do if you ever get done here."

"This is taking a little longer because I'm used to fitted sheets," she said defensively. Her response didn't make any sense, not to her, probably not to Damien, but it was the best she could come up with, other than the truth, which was that she just didn't do beds. How lame would that sound? Top-notch doctor felled by a simple bedsheet.

"Fitted sheets—nope, no such luxuries around here. In fact, our sheets are all donations from some of the locals. *Used* bedsheets, Juliette. The very best we have to offer. Rough-texture, well-worn hand-me-downs. But I'll bet you're used to a nice silk, or even an Egyptian cotton, maybe a fifteen-hundred thread count? You know, the very best the market has to offer."

Who would have guessed Damien knew sheets? But, apparently, he did. And, amazingly, what he'd described was exactly what she had on her bed back home. Nice, soft, dreadfully expensive sheets covering a huge Victorian, dark cherrywood, four-poster antique of a bed. Her bed and sheets—luxuries she'd thought she couldn't live without until she'd come to Costa Rica, where such luxuries were scarce, and only for those who could afford to have them imported. Which her father would do for her, gladly, if she asked him. Although she'd never ask, as that would build up his hopes that she was already getting tired of her life in Costa Rica and wanted her old life back. Back home. Same as before. Returning to her old job. Taking the position as her father's chief administrative officer. Yes, that was the way his mind would run through it, all because she wanted better bedsheets.

OK, so she was a bit spoiled. She'd admit it if anyone— Damien—cared to ask but, since he wasn't asking, she wasn't telling. Not a blessed thing! "The sheet you're describing would have cost a hundred and twenty times more than all the sheets in this ward put together. And that would be just one sheet."

"Ah! A lady with a passion for sheets." Damien arched mocking eyebrows. "I hope that same passion extends to your medicine."

"You mean a lady *doctor* who's being interrupted while she's trying to do her job." She regarded him for a moment. Well-muscled body. Three or four days' growth of stubble on his face. Over-the-collar hair, which he'd pulled back into a ponytail, not too unlike her own, only much, much shorter. Really nice dimples when he smiled. Sexy dimples. Kissable dimples… Juliette shook her head to clear the train wreck going on inside and went back to assessing her overall opinion of Damien Caldwell. He was stunningly handsome, which he probably knew, and probably used it to his advantage. Insufferably rude. Intelligent. Good doctor.

"Does it bother you that I'm watching?" he asked.

"What bothers me is that you think you know all about me through my bedsheets. You're judging me, aren't you? You know, poor little rich girl. Never changed a bedsheet in her life. That's what you're thinking, isn't it?" Judging her based on what she owned and not what she could do as a doctor.

"I wasn't but, now that you brought it up, I could. Especially if you *do* own Egyptian cotton."

"What I do or do not own has no bearing on the job here. And if you want to stand there speculating on something as unimportant as my sheets, be my guest. Speculate to your heart's content. But keep it to yourself because I need to get these beds changed and I *don't* need any distractions while I'm doing it."

The ad she'd read about this job should have warned her that it came with a pompous boss because he was, indeed, pompous. Full of himself. Someone who probably took delight in the struggles of others. "And in the meantime I'm going to smooth this stupid wrinkle so I can get on to the next bed."

"Well, if you ever get done here, I've got a patient coming into the clinic in a little while who has a possible case of gout in his left big toe. Could you take a look at him when he arrives?"

Gout. A painful inflammatory process, starting in the

big toe in about half of all diagnosed cases. "I don't suppose we can test for hyperuricemia, can we?" Hyperuricemia was a build-up of uric acid in the blood. With elevated levels, its presence could precipitate an onset of gout.

"Nope. Haven't got the proper equipment to do much more than a simple CBC." Complete blood count. "And we do those sparingly because they cost us money we don't have."

"Then how do we diagnose him, or anybody else, for that matter, if we don't have the tests at our disposal?"

"The old-fashioned way. We apply common sense. In this particular case, you assess to see if it's swollen or red. You ask him if it hurts, then find out how and when. Also, you take into account the fact that the patient's a male, and we all know that men are more susceptible to gout than women. So that's another indicator. And the pain exists *only* in his big toe. Add it all up and you've got…gout." He took a big sweeping bow with his pronouncement, as if he was the lead character in a show on Broadway.

Juliette noticed his grand gesture, but chose to ignore it. "OK, it's gout. I'll probably agree with you once I've had a look at him. But, apart from that, what kind of drugs do you have on hand to treat him with? Nonsteroidal anti-inflammatories? Steroids? Colchicine? Maybe allopurinol?"

"Aspirin," he stated flatly.

"Aspirin? That's it?" Understaffed, understocked—what kind of place was this?

"We're limited here to the basics and that's pretty much how we have to conduct business every day. We start on the most simple level we can offer and hope that's good enough."

"What else do you have besides aspirin?"

"Antacids, penicillin, a lot of different topical ointments for bug bites, rashes and whatever else happens to a person's skin. A couple of different kinds of injectable anesthetic agents. Nitroglycerine. Cough syrup. Some anti-microbials. Antimalarials—mostly quinidine. A very small supply of codeine. Oh, and a handful of various other drugs that we can coerce from an occasional outsider who wanders through. When you have time, take a look. We keep the drugs in the locked closet just outside the clinic door."

"Are any of these expired drugs?"

"Hey, we take what we can get. So if it's not *too* expired, we accept it and, believe me, we're glad to get it. One person's expired drug may be another person's salvation."

"Isn't that dangerous?"

He shook his head. "I check with the pharmaceutical company before I use it. I mean, commercial expiration date is one thing, but some drugs have usable life left beyond their shelf life."

"But you do turn away some drugs that are expired?"

"Of course I do. I'm not going to put a patient at risk with an expired drug that's not usable."

"So when you call these pharmaceutical companies, don't they offer to stock you with new drugs?"

"All the time. But who the hell can afford *that* around here?" Damien shrugged. "Like I say, I check it to make sure it's safe, then I use it if it is, and thank my lucky stars I have it to use."

She hadn't expected anything lavish, but she also hadn't expected this much impoverishment. Of course, she knew little clinics like this operated all over the world, barely keeping their doors open, scraping and bowing to get whatever they had. But, in her other life, those were only stories, not a real situation as it applied to her. Now, though, she was in the heart of make-do medicine and nothing in her education or experience had taught her how to get along within its confines.

"How do you learn to get by the way you do?" she asked Damien. "With all these limitations and hardships?"

He studied her for a moment, then smiled. "Most of it you simply make up as you go. I was a general surgeon in Seattle. Worked in one of the largest hospitals in the city—a teaching hospital. So I had residents and medical students at my disposal, every piece of modern equipment known to the medical world, my OR was second to none."

"And you gave it all up for this?" It was an admirable thing to do, but the question that plagued her about that was how anyone could go from so modern to so primitive? She'd done a little internet research on Damien before she'd come here, and he had a sterling reputation. He'd received all kinds of recognition for his achievements in surgery, and he'd won awards. So what made a person trade it for a handful of expired medicines and good guesses instead of proper tests and up-to-date drugs?

Maybe he had a father who ran the hospital, Juliette thought, as her own reasons for leaving her hospital practice crossed her mind.

"This isn't so bad once you get used to it," he said.

"But how do you get used to it? Especially when it's so completely different from your medical background?"

"You look at the people you're treating and understand that they need and deserve the best care you can give them, just the way that patients in any hospital anywhere else do. Only out here you're the only one to do it. I think that's the hardest part to get used to—the fact that there's no one else to fall back on. No equipment, no tests or drugs, no excuses…

"It scared me when I first got here until I came to terms with how I was going to have to rely on myself and all my skills and knowledge. That didn't make working in this hospital any easier, but it did put things into proper perspective."

"You've gotten used to it, haven't you?"

"Let's just say that I've learned to work with the knowledge that the best I can hope for is what I have on hand at the moment, and the people here who want medical help are grateful for whatever I have to offer. They don't take it for granted the way society in general has come to take much of its medical care for granted. So, once you understand that, you can get used to just about anything this type of practice will hand you."

"Then you don't really look forward, do you?"

"Can't afford to. If I did, I'd probably get really disappointed, because anything forward from this point is the same as anything looking backward. Nothing changes and, in practical terms, it probably never will."

"But you chose a jungle practice over what you had for some reason. Was it a conscious choice, or did you come here with expectation of one thing and get handed something else?"

"I got recruited to one of the leading hospitals by someone like you. They wanted my surgical skills and they came up with a pretty nice package to offer me. Since I've never stayed in any one position too long—"

"Why not?" she interrupted.

"Because there's always something else out there. Something I haven't tried yet. Something that might be better than what I've had." Something to distract him from the fact that he'd never found what he wanted.

"In other words, you're never contented?"

"In other words, I like to change up my life every now and then. Which is why I came here to Costa Rica. The country is recruiting doctors, the whole medical industry is competing in a worldwide arena and it sounded exciting. Probably like it did to you when they came calling on you. And I'm assuming they did come calling."

"Something like that." But her motive in coming here wasn't because she was restless, or that she simply needed a change in pace. Her acceptance came because she needed to expand herself in new directions. Someplace far, far away from her father.

"Well, anyway—they did a hard recruit on me. Kept coming back for about a year, until I finally decided to give it a shot."

"So you *did* work in one of the hospitals in San José?"

"For about a month. The timing was perfect. I'd just ended a personal relationship, which made me restless to go someplace, do something else. You know, running away. Which actually has been my habit for most of my adult life." Damien grinned. "Anyway, they offered, eventually I accepted, and it took me about a week to figure out I hated it."

"Why?"

"Because it was just like what I'd left. Brought back old memories of my last hospital, of how my former fiancée thought I should be more than a general surgeon, of how my future father-in-law said that being a general surgeon was so working class. Like there's something wrong with being working class! I'd always loved working for a living but that one criticism so totally changed me, there were times I didn't even recognize myself. Tried to be what my future family considered their equal. Put on airs I didn't have a right to. Drowned myself in a lifestyle that I didn't like, just to play the perfect part." He shook his head. "I really needed something different after I got through all that. Got it all sorted—who I *really* was, what I *really* wanted to do with my life. So one day I saw an ad where a little jungle hospital needed a doctor…"

"Like the ad you placed?" He had so much baggage in his past, she wondered how he'd gotten past it to reach this point in his life. It took a lot of strength to get from where he used to be to where he was now. A strength she wished she had for herself.

Damien chuckled. "The *same* ad."

"The *exact* same ad?" she asked him.

"One and the same. No pay, hard work, long hours. Nothing like I'd ever been involved with before. So, since I'd come to Costa Rica seeking a new adventure—hell, what's more of an adventure than this?"

"Maybe a hospital with Egyptian cotton sheets?" Everyone had something to run away from, she supposed. He did. She did. It was lucky for both of them that their need to run away had coincided with a place for them to go. Whether running into each other would turn out to be a good thing remained to be seen.

"I've lowered my expectations these past few months. If I have *any* bedsheets, I'm happy."

"But they didn't train you in medical school to be concerned about the sheets."

"And they didn't train *you* in medical school how to be a recruiter. Which makes me wonder if it's a good fit for you since you came knocking on my humble little door, wanting something different than what you already had. Ever think you made the wrong choice, that you belong back in your old life?"

OK, based on the little bit she knew about him, this was the Damien she'd expected. Not the one who almost garnered her admiration, but the one who annoyed her. "I made a very good choice coming to Costa Rica, regardless of what you think!" He was beginning to sound like her father. *Bad choice, Juliette. Think about it. You'll come to your senses.* "Not that it's any of your business."

"In my hospital, it *is* my business. Everything here is my business, including you. Because you working here affects everything else around you, and I have to protect the hospital's interests."

"What's your point?" she snapped.

"That's for you to figure out. Which, I'm sure, will happen in time."

"There's nothing to figure out. I accepted a position that brings first-rate medical professionals here. It's an honorable job and I like it. It's…important."

"I'm not saying that it's not. With the need to improve medical conditions expanding, I'm sure it's becoming a very important position. But is it important *enough* to you? Or is patient care more important?"

"Why can't both be important to me?"

"In my experience, I've found that we poor mortals don't always do a good job of dividing ourselves."

"That's assuming I'm divided."

"Well, I suppose only you know if that's the case." Damien stepped away from the bed. "Anyway, your patient will be here shortly, so I'd suggest you figure out some way to expedite those bedsheets so you can go be a *real* doctor." With that, he spun around and started walking away.

"Are you always so rude?" she asked him while he was still within earshot. He was not only rude, he was also nosy, presumptuous and out of line.

Damien stopped and turned back to face her. "I do it rather well, don't you think?"

Struggling with simple bedsheets, the way she was doing right now, was almost cute. It was painfully obvious, though, that this was a chore far beyond her capabilities. Or one she'd never before practiced. Which reminded Damien of days gone by, and one of the reasons he was here in the jungle, hiding away from civilization. Juliette was obviously a rich girl, probably out on her own in the world for the very first time and, once upon a time, he'd almost married a rich girl who probably still wasn't out in the world.

Spoiled was the word that always came to mind when he thought about Nancy. It was a word he wanted to apply to Juliette as well, but the determination he could see in her stopped him short of going that far. The fact was, Nancy would have never set foot in his jungle clinic and Juliette was here, fighting to make a difference. Which didn't exactly fit his perception of a rich girl.

OK, he had a bias. He admitted it. Hated that he'd just shown a bit of it to Juliette, by raising the doubt that she could cut it here. But it was well deserved, considering how he'd endured months of spoiled behavior from a woman he'd planned on marrying. Not that Nancy had ever played spoiled rich girl when it was just the two of them. No, she'd been sweet and attentive, convincing him she was the one to settle down for. Or in *Juliette's* case, *she* was the one he needed here to help him.

But in the end, Nancy had told him he could never be enough for her. He couldn't give her enough, as her demands had grown larger. More time. More attention. More of everything. He'd tried. He'd honestly tried. Bought her everything she wanted, which put him into deep debt. Cut back his hours at the hospital to spend more time with her, which almost cost him his job. No matter what he'd done, though, it hadn't been adequate. So he'd tried harder, and always failed.

As far as Juliette working here—could that be enough for her? Or was he overthinking this thing? Truth was, he was wary. With Nancy, the vicious circle he'd got himself trapped in had played against his self-esteem and it hadn't helped when her parents told him that he'd always be struggling, that he'd never have enough to give her what she deserved. Things. Lots and lots of material things. And social status. Even with his surgeon's salary and his position at the hospital, and all the awards he'd won, they were right. At least, he'd thought so at the time.

Anyway, she'd moved out of his apartment and gone home, straight into Mommy's and Daddy's arms. As far as he knew, two years later, she was still there, dwelling quite happily as their spoiled-rotten daughter. Probably waiting for Daddy to fix her up with a man who fit the family image. A man who could give her the things Damien could not.

Which, admittedly, stung. He'd reeled from the breakup for weeks, wondering what he could have done differently. Wondering why he'd thought he was good enough for Nancy when, obviously, he was not. Wondering why he'd chosen Nancy in the first place.

So, was Juliette that spoiled? Would she spend a day or an entire weekend here, only to discover that it wasn't enough for her? Would she walk away when she realized he couldn't give her proper bedsheets, let alone a proper bed? Bottom line—he needed her here. Recruits didn't come knocking every day when he advertised. And when they did show up, they usually turned right back around and left. In fact, other than George Perkins, she'd been the first doctor in his entire year here to show any real interest in staying. And he needed her skills. But could he count on her coming through, the way he'd counted on Nancy before she'd let him down?

He didn't know, couldn't tell. Juliette was obviously of upper means and, yes, that did have a huge bearing on the way he was feeling so uneasy about her motives or dedication. But there was also something about her that caused him to believe that her upper means hadn't knocked something basic out of her. She was a hard worker and, so far, she hadn't complained about the menial tasks. Time would tell what she was really made of, he supposed. For now, he was simply trying to keep an open mind. Because for some reason other than his need of her medical skills, a reason he couldn't quite put his finger on, he wanted her to stay. Maybe for a change of scenery? Or to break the monotony? He honestly didn't know.

"You've only got just the one exam room in the clinic?" Juliette asked him, once all the beds were made.

"The clinic was originally my living quarters. One room for everything. But I built a divider so there would be a waiting room on one side and an exam room on the other. That's all there was room for."

"Then where do you sleep?" she asked him.

"In a hut next door. Another one-room setup. Not as nice as the hospital, though."

Juliette cringed. "I hate to ask, but where will I stay when I'm here?"

Ah, yes. The first test. No sheets, no bed—no room of her own. This is where it began, he supposed. Or ended. "Well, I've got two choices. You could stay here in the hospital, use an empty bed and hope we don't get so busy you'll have to give it up. We'll partition it off for you to give you some privacy. And the perk there is that the hospital has running water, a shower, a bathroom. Or, if you don't like that idea, you can shack with me. And the drawbacks there are—I don't have running water, don't have a bathroom or a shower. I have to come into the hospital for all that. Oh, and rumor has it that I might snore." He cringed, waiting for what he believed would be the inevitable.

"So if I choose your hut, I'd be what? Sleeping in bed with you?"

"No, I'm a little more gentlemanly than that. I'd give you the bed, and I'd take the floor." Said with some forced humor, since humor was all he had to offer at the moment.

"But in the same room?"

"Kind of like the student years, when you'd crash in the on-call room, no matter who was sleeping next to you. You did sleep in an on-call, didn't you?" Somehow, he could picture Juliette as the type who would lock the on-call door behind her and keep the room all to herself.

"I did," she said hesitantly. "When I had to."

"So let me guess. You didn't like it."

"It was necessary, when I was pulling twenty-four-hour shifts. But did I like it? Not particularly."

"How did I know that?" he asked, still waiting for the curtain to fall on this little act he was putting on. Who was he kidding here? Girls accustomed to silk sheets liked silk. And he sure as hell didn't have anything silk.

"You *didn't* know that," she said, expelling an exasperated sigh. "You're just into making snap judgments about me. All of them negative. Do you *ever* see anything positive in *any* situation, Damien?"

Maybe she was right. Maybe he was so used to looking for the negative that he wouldn't recognize a ray of something positive if it walked right up and slapped him in the face. Damn, he didn't mean to be like that. But something about Juliette poked at him. It was almost like he was trying to push her away. From what? He had no clue. "Look, I'll try to be more positive, OK?"

"Don't put yourself out on my account. I'm a big girl. I can take it." She squared herself up to her full five-foot-six frame and stared him down. "And I think I'll just stay in the hospital, all things considered." Narrowing her eyes, she went on, "I *hate* snoring. And, just for the record, Damien, you're not going to scare me off. I came here so I could stay better in touch with patient care, and I don't intend to back out of it, no matter how hard you're trying to push me away."

"I'm not trying to push you away," he defended.

"Sure you are. Don't know why, don't particularly care. Just let me do my job here, and we'll get along. OK?"

Well, she certainly was driven. He liked that. Liked it a lot. "Look, if you want privacy, you can have my hut on the weekends you're here, and I'll stay in the hospital."

"The weekends I'm here will be every weekend."

"You're sure of that? Because it's a long, tough drive to get here, and I don't have anything to make your life, or your work, easier when you're here."

"I'm adaptable, Damien. I'll make do."

He wanted to trust that she would. "Look, we can finish talking about your housing options later on, over dinner. But, right now, Señor Mendez is waiting in the clinic. Remember, gout? Oh, and I'm going to go make a house call. I have a patient who's a week over her due date, and she's getting pretty anxious to have her baby."

"Borrow my car. Take her for a ride on that bumpy road into town. That should induce something."

So she had a sense of humor. Even though she made her offer with a straight face, Damien laughed. "Might work better if I borrow a cart and a donkey from one of the locals."

"They actually have donkey carts here?" she asked in full amazement.

"It's called traveling in style. A modern convenience if the cart is fairly new and the donkey is reasonably young." He stopped himself short of ridiculing the kind of car she probably had back home. A sleek sports model, most likely.

Shiny and silver. Convertible. Her hair let down from its ponytail and blowing in the breeze. Nope, he had to stop this. It was going too far, almost daydreaming about her the way he was. "Anyway, I'll probably be back before you're done with Señor Mendez's toe."

"Will Alegria be able to unlock the medicine cabinet for me?"

Before he answered, he fished through the pocket of his khaki cargo shorts until he found a key. "Here, take mine. Just make sure you give it back before you leave here— when? Sunday night? Monday morning?"

"Haven't decided yet. I guess it will depend on the workload."

He dropped the key into her outstretched hand. "Well, next time I get to Cima de la Montaña I'll have a key made for you." Provided she lasted that long. In a lot of ways, he hoped she did because, in spite of himself, and especially in spite of all his doubts, he liked her.

CHAPTER THREE

"HOW WAS YOUR gout patient?" Damien asked Juliette on his way back into the hospital. She was coming out of the clinic, looking somewhat perplexed. "It *was* gout, wasn't it?"

"It was gout," Juliette confirmed. "I was concerned about his age, though. He seems too young to be afflicted with it."

"I thought so, too, but the people here live hard lives. They age faster than normal."

"And he's had a complete physical?"

"Before he presented with gout symptoms?" Damien shook his head. "Getting people around here to submit to physicals when they don't have any particular symptoms isn't easy, but about six months ago Señor Mendez did come in. Nothing out of the ordinary turned up."

"Well, I gave him aspirin like you told me to. But there was something else going on. I think Señor Mendez was high on some kind of drug. At least, that's the way he seemed. Slurred speech, slow movements. Do you know if he indulges?"

Damien laughed. "A lot of the locals indulge. I'm surprised Señor Mendez would, though. He's pretty straight. Doesn't drink that I know of. Doesn't do drugs—at least, I didn't think he did. And, even if he did, it surprises me

that he would go out in public that way because he's a very
polite, private, gentle man who spends every last penny
he has to support his family. But I guess you never know
what goes on behind closed doors, do you?"

"Is it really that common around here?"

"Ganja—marijuana—is cheap, and easily available."

"So what do you do if they come in here stoned?"

"Treat them for what they came in for, and ignore the
rest. I'm just the doctor here. I don't get involved in anything else."

"Then you won't report him?"

"If he's not bothering me, there's no reason to. My personal policy is, if someone needs help they get help, in spite
of all the external factors that might otherwise cause problems. In other words, if he's stoned, you treat him, anyway.
The rest of it's none of my business."

"That's decent of you."

"I aim to be decent to my patients. They've got enough
hardships to face in their daily lives without me adding
to them."

"But do you condone it?"

"Nope. I'm a law-abiding citizen wherever I go, and the
Costa Rican law makes ganja illegal, so I respect that."

"Then you, personally, don't indulge?"

"Never have, never will. Don't smoke, either. Drink
only in moderation. Work out regularly. Eat a balanced
diet. You know, all good things for my body." A body that
seemed to be aging too quickly since he'd come to Costa
Rica. Of course, that was about the hard work here. So
were the new creases in his face and the pair of glasses
he was now forced to wear any time he wanted to read.
Most people wouldn't consider him old, as he overtook
his thirty-sixth birthday in a few weeks. But some days

he just felt old—older than dirt. "Keeps me in good working condition."

"Well, I just wanted to let you know the condition of your patient."

"And I appreciate that. But I'm not really concerned about it. At least, not right now."

"When does that point change for you, Damien?"

"When I see someone's drug use as a potential danger to themselves or others. That's when I'll step in. But again, only as a doctor."

"We always had to note it in our chart at the hospital," she said. "And if it was too bad, we were supposed to alert Security."

"Did you ever?"

"Once. Then I had regrets, because he really wasn't that bad. But I was new, still blindly loyal to hospital policy, probably more so than to the patient. Of course, that changed pretty quickly, the more involved I became with my patients."

"So you were a true, big hospital loyalist?"

"Still am. But I'm more practical about it now. But you've got to understand that I was raised by a true hospital loyalist—the chief of staff, and those were the kinds of concerns he always brought home with him. What was best for the hospital was always his main concern, right after the kind of patient care we were giving."

"So your daddy's a big shot in a big hospital?" Given her rich girl background, that didn't surprise him.

"That's one way of putting it, I suppose. But to me he was always just my dad. A man who went to work, worked long, hard hours and came home to tuck me in every night. It never occurred to me that he was so important in terms of an entire medical community until I was probably ten or eleven and he took me to work with him to see what he did during the day."

"Did it impress you?"

"Not so much then. I think I was more impressed by all the desserts in the cafeteria than I was by my father's position in the hospital. Of course, the older I got the more I realized just what a *big deal* he was."

"But you have no aspirations for something like that for yourself?"

"I had my shot at it. Dad offered me a promotion into administration a couple of months ago."

"So let me guess. You chose Costa Rica instead. Was it to run away from Daddy?" Probably her first real act of rebellion in a very laid-out life.

"You say that like it was a derogatory thing to do."

"Was it?" he asked her.

Juliette shook her head. "I like to think of Costa Rica as something necessary in my career development. In my personal development, as well. Also, I didn't feel as though I'd earned the job. I think promoting me was simply my dad's way of ensuring that I'd stay around for a while. Or forever, if he had his way about it. I mean, my dad always wins. No matter what it is, he finds a way to win, and I was tired of always having my ideas and hopes and desires tossed into that lottery."

Actually, that was admirable. "So you *did* want to get away from Daddy." He liked the kind of spirit it must have taken for her to make that much of a change in her life—a life that was, apparently, very sheltered. Something Nancy would have never done for anyone, for any reason.

"I wanted to get away from all the usual trappings and…"

"Make it on your own merits rather than resting on the laurels your dad created for you?"

"Do you challenge all the women you come into contact with, or is it just *me* who challenges *you*?"

He thought about that for a moment, wondering if his leftover resentment of Nancy did, adversely, affect his relationships with women. Certainly, he hadn't dated since Nancy. Not once. Not even tempted. No one-night stands. No quick meet-ups at the coffee shop. No phone calls, texting or any other sort of personal communications. In fact, if anything, he assiduously avoided *everything* that came close to putting him into a relationship of any sort with any woman—young, old or somewhere in between.

"Actually, you haven't challenged me yet. But I'm sure you're waiting for the right opportunity."

Juliette laughed. "You won't see it coming," she warned him. "And you'll be caught so far off guard, you won't know what hit you."

Now, that was something he could foresee happening. Juliette had a very disarming way about her, and he had every inclination to believe that she was good at the sneak attack. Of course, he was the one who'd placed himself directly in her line of fire, and he still didn't understand why he'd done that. But he was there, nonetheless, actually looking forward to her first barrage of arrows. "Sounds like the lady has a plan."

"My only plan is to take the next patient, who's coming through the door right now." She gave him a devious smile. "Unless you're really into doing some stitches today." A snap diagnosis made with the assumption that underneath the bloody towel the mother was holding over her son's hand lay something that needed stitching. "You *do* have a suture kit, don't you?"

He turned around, also looked at the people coming through the hospital door. Diego Cruz and his mother, Elena. This wasn't the first time Diego had needed stitches, and it wouldn't be the last as Diego was an active little boy who was pretty much left to run wild through Bombacopsis while his mother cooked and cleaned and sewed for other villagers.

Elena was one of Damien's regular hospital volunteers as well, which took even more time away from Diego. "If you mean needles and thread, yep, I've got them." He waved at Diego, who gave him a limp wave in return.

"Regulars?"

Damien chuckled as he bent to greet the little boy. "One of our best. So, Diego. What happened here?"

"I fell," the child confessed.

"From the top of the gate at the church," Elena volunteered.

"Were you trying to break in again?" Damien asked him, fighting to keep a straight face.

"Only for a drink of water."

"You couldn't go home for that?"

"It was too far." Diego looked up at Juliette and turned on a rather charming smile. "And the water at the church is holy, which is good for me. It makes me grow stronger."

"Well, you weren't strong enough to keep yourself from falling off the gate, were you?" Damien took the towel off the boy's hand and had a look. It wasn't a bad cut, not too deep, but deep enough that it would take about four or five stitches. The same number of stitches he'd had in his other hand a month ago, when he'd tried to remove the log bridge that crossed the village creek, and had gotten hung up on it.

"That's because I didn't have my drink yet."

Diego reminded Damien a lot of himself when he'd been that age. He and his twin, Daniel, were always getting into some kind of trouble. Nothing serious, but usually with some consequence like a broken arm, a sprained ankle, multiple areas of stitches. "You seem to have all the answers, Diego," he said, finally giving way to a laugh.

"I try, el doctor Damien," Diego responded earnestly.

"Well, here's the deal. I'm going to go get you that drink of water, from the hospital faucet, *not* from the church. And, while you're waiting for me to bring it back to you, el doctor Juliette is going to take care of your hand. Which means you're going to get stitches like you had last month. Remember?"

Diego nodded his head. "They hurt," he said, looking up at his mother as if she was going to stop the procedure. "Do I have to?" he asked her.

"You have to do whatever el doctor Damien says," his mother told him. "He's the boss."

For a moment Diego looked defeated. Then he perked right back up. "But el doctor Damien won't hurt me much. That's what he promised me last time."

"Hey, Diego. This one could have hurt a lot more if you'd cut something other than your hand," Damien said. He raised up and looked at Juliette. "Suture material's in the third drawer in the clinic cabinet. Oh, and I do have xylocaine to deaden the pain. I keep a fair stock of it on hand, thanks to Diego, here. He's our main consumer."

"Sure you don't want to do this, since you and Diego seemed to have built a rapport?" she asked. "He might trust you more."

"No, I'll let you do it. Even at the tender age of ten, our man here has an eye for the pretty ladies, and I'm sure he'd much rather have you taking care of him. Isn't that right, Diego?"

Once again, Diego turned his smile on for Juliette. "Right," he said, scooting past his mother and stepping closer to Juliette. "El doctor Juliette is very pretty."

Damien shrugged. "Like I said…"

"OK, Romeo," Juliette said to Diego, as she took his unwounded hand and led him into the exam room. "Let's see what we can do about fixing this up."

"My name is Diego, *not* Romeo!" he said defiantly.

"Where she comes from, they mean the same thing," Damien said from the doorway.

Juliette flashed Damien a knowing look. "Where I come from, grown women never have to worry about advances from ten-year-old boys."

"Almost eleven," Diego corrected. He closed his eyes while Juliette swabbed his hand clean in order to take a closer look at his cut.

"Does it hurt much?" Juliette asked, accepting a cotton gauze pad Damien had fished out of a drawer for her.

"No," Diego said. But the slight tentativeness in his voice said otherwise.

"Diego is one tough little kid," Damien said, on his way to the closet to fetch the xylocaine. "And the shot that el doctor Juliette is about to give him won't hurt at all, will it, Diego?"

This time his tentativeness was full-blown. "No," he said, pulling back his hand slightly.

"You going to break into the church again, Diego? Because this is the second time in a month and it's not going to be too long before Padre Benicio comes after you."

Diego's eyes opened wide. "Will he hurt me?" he asked.

"No, he won't hurt you. But he'll make you do chores, like washing the windows, or cleaning up the church garden." Damien recalled how he and Daniel had been the recipient of such chores from time to time. "And if you come in here hurt again because you've done something bad, I'm going to make you pay for your medical treatment with some chores here. Like painting the fence outside, or scrubbing the floors."

"I think he means it, Diego," Juliette said as she turned to hide the smile crossing her face. "By the way, does he need a tetanus shot? And I'm assuming you *do* offer that?"

"I *do* offer that, as a matter of fact. But Diego is up-to-date. I got him a couple of months ago when he got into a fight with a fence of chicken wire." Damien liked Diego. A lot. He was a smart kid. Resourceful. Bright in school. Knew how to get along in his own little world. But he didn't have a father, which meant his mother had to work doubly hard to support her small family. That, more than anything else, contributed to the mischief that always seemed to find Diego. The kid simply had too much time on his hands.

"Hey, Diego," Damien said, suddenly finding a little bit of inspiration, "I have an idea. Are you interested?"

"Maybe," Diego said, not even noticing that Juliette was preparing the syringe to give him the xylocaine shot.

"OK, well…" Damien blinked, sympathizing with the kid while Juliette stuck the needle into his hand. The hand was sensitive and that shot had to hurt, but Diego merely flinched and bit down on his lower lip. "Want a job?"

"A job, el doctor Damien?"

"Yes, a job. Here, in the hospital."

"For real money?"

Out of his own pocket, if he had to, Damien decided. This kid needed better direction. That was something he could do, without too much effort. "Real money."

Juliette threaded the suture needle and turned Diego's hand at a more convenient angle before she proceeded to start stitching. "You could make beds," she suggested, smiling over at Damien.

"No, I have something better than that in mind," Damien responded, smiling back.

"Could I be el doctor Diego?" Diego asked.

"Not until you're older, and have had more schooling. But you could be the person in charge of el doctor Damien's files."

Juliette raised amused eyebrows. "Now, that seems like a fitting job. And a very important one."

Damien nodded his agreement. "I can teach Diego how to alphabetize, then he can keep things filed away in proper order. I mean, we do it the old-fashioned way here. Paper notes put into folders, sorted and put away in the file cabinet. Everything completely organized."

"I can organize," Diego said.

"Do you even know what organized means?" Juliette asked him.

"No, but el doctor Damien will teach me."

She looked at Damien. "He has a lot of confidence in you."

Truth was, Damien had a lot of confidence in Diego. He wanted to be a good kid, and he tried hard to do it, but too many times his circumstances simply got in his way. Damien's own father had been the influence that had kept him from becoming too out of control, and Damien hoped he could be that same influence for Diego.

"Elena," he directed at Diego's mother. "Is it all right that Diego works for me?"

"That would be very good," she said, excitement registering on her face. "He responds very well to you and maybe this will help keep him out of trouble."

"Good, then I'll make out a schedule in a little while, and maybe Diego could start working tomorrow. OK with you, Diego?" he asked, shifting his attention back to the boy.

"For real money!" Diego exclaimed, as Juliette sank her first stitch.

Damien gave him a thumbs-up.

"Maybe I'll buy a car!" Diego exclaimed, grinning from ear to ear.

"You have real money to give him?" Juliette asked Damien, after Diego had gone skipping out of the hospital, bragging to one of the volunteers on the way that he was going to have a *real* job here, at the hospital.

"I have a little bit of money put away. And it won't take much to keep Diego happy. Five hundred *colónes* a week come to little less than a dollar, and that's not going to break my bank."

Juliette was impressed. More than impressed; she was touched by the way he'd handled Diego. He was a natural with children. And his love of children shone through so brilliantly it almost surprised her, as she hadn't expected to see that from him. "Do you have kids of your own?" she asked him.

"Never married, never had children."

"Is that your avowed way of life, or just something that has occurred because of your restless lifestyle? Because, if you ever truly settled down, I think you'd make a wonderful dad."

"Not a wonderful husband, too?" he asked, grinning at her.

He did have his good qualities. Juliette was beginning to see that. But did he have enough to make him good husband material? For her, the answer was no. For someone else—it all depended on what they wanted, or didn't want, in a husband. "Since you've never been married, there's no way to tell. And, personally, I'd never get that involved with you to find out."

"Never?" he asked.

"Outside of a professional relationship, *never.*"

"That's harsh."

"But honest." She knew he was teasing her now, and that was a side of him she quite liked. Apart from his ability with children, maybe there were some other redeemable qualities in him after all.

"Said by a lady who, if I'm not mistaken, has never been married herself."

"Never married. No regrets about it, either."

"For now," he countered.

"For now, maybe for the rest of my life." She didn't think about it much, to be honest. What was the point? If it happened, it happened. If didn't, it didn't. Dwelling on the *what ifs* didn't get her anywhere.

"Because you want more than any man could possibly give you?"

"Because I want what I want, and I haven't found it yet." It was a simple statement, but oh, so true. She hadn't come close to finding what she wanted. Funny thing was, she couldn't exactly define what it was. Couldn't put it into a mental checklist, couldn't even put it down on paper it was so vague to her. Yet she truly believed that if the man who fit her undefined list came into her life, everything would become crystal clear to her. She'd know him. She'd see the qualities that, until that very moment, had been nothing but a nebulous notion.

The day passed fairly quickly, and Damien was glad to see that it was finally turning into night. People had wandered in and out all day long, none of them with serious complaints, but now he expected they would stay home, coming to the hospital only if it was an emergency. Kicking back in a chair in the hospital waiting room, he put his feet up on a small side table, clasped his hands behind his neck and stretched back, sighing. "We don't usually see too much action at night. The people here like to eat a good dinner and go to bed early."

"The *arroz con pollo* certainly qualifies as a good dinner," Juliette commented, taking a seat across from Damien. "I love chicken and rice. Probably could eat it every few days."

"Which is how often you're going to get it here. The hospital is pretty limited in its culinary offerings, and we rely mostly on what the locals donate to us. They all raise chickens, rice is cheap, so—*arroz con pollo* happens a lot."

"Maybe I can get Rosalita's recipe for it. My roommate and I trade off on the cooking chores, and most of the time I just fix sandwiches and salads. She might enjoy something different from me, for a change."

"Do you like to cook?"

Juliette shook her head. "I've always had someone to do the cooking for me. Or I ate out. But now I work such crazy hours, it's easier to stay in to eat, because when I finally do get home I'm not inclined to go back out just for food."

"So you had a maid to change your bed, *and* a cook to fix your meals. Any other servants?"

"They weren't servants, Damien. Nobody calls them that! They were just employees. People who worked for us."

"Then I stand corrected. Did you have other people who worked for you?"

"Just a gardener, and he was only part-time."

"And someone to tend your pool?"

"We had a pool," she admitted. "And someone did tend to it."

"So we're up to four people who worked for you. Anybody else? Maybe a tailor for your dad, or a personal assistant to keep your calendar organized."

"OK, so we hired people to work for us. What of it?"

"Nothing, really. I'm just trying to determine the extent of your wealth." It was late, he was tired, yet here he was, baiting her again. Something about Juliette brought that out in him; he didn't want to be intentionally cruel to her, but his need to raise her hackles just seemed to ooze out of him, no matter how hard he tried to stop.

"And here I thought you were trying to be civil with me." Juliette pushed herself up out of the chair. "Look, I'm not in the mood to go another round with you tonight. So, I'm just going out to the ward, find myself an empty bed and go to sleep. If you need me— You know what? I don't want you coming to get me. Send one of the volunteers to do it."

"It was an honest question, Juliette. I was simply trying to find out more about you." *Yeah, right.* More like he was just trying to find out how far he could push her before she pushed back. In a sense, it was vital to her work here and how much he could throw at her before she resisted him. Of course, it was also about taunting her, which was something he was going to have to quit doing. If he wanted her to come back, and he did, he needed to be nicer to her. Needed to quit testing her. Most of all, he needed to stop comparing her to Nancy because she definitely *wasn't* anything like Nancy.

"Well, I'm not in the mood for your honesty."

Damien did like the way she stood up for herself. "But honesty is one of my best virtues. I don't lie. Not about anything. And if I want to know something, I ask."

"Well, you can ask me anything you want, professionally. But my personal life is out of it because you've prejudged who I am and what I am, and I can't see you being the type who changes his mind once it's made up."

She was right about that. "OK, so let me be honest here.

I have a bias against wealthy people. More specifically, spoiled rich girls." So now she knew. In a way that was good, as it gave them a base to work from. And he really did want a better footing with Juliette, no matter how much he acted toward the contrary.

"You think I'm spoiled?"

"Are you?" he asked.

Juliette huffed out an impatient breath. "I've had advantages most other people don't have, and I'll admit that. And I'll also admit that I've enjoyed the privilege that comes from my father's wealth. So to you that may scream spoiled, but to me it says normal. Everything that I've achieved or had or done is normal to me. If you think that's being spoiled, then think it. It's not worth the effort of trying to change your mind, because I simply don't care what you think of me personally. Go ahead and label me all you want, if that's what makes you feel good. But don't waste my time pointing it out to me, because I've got better things to worry about. Like the job I intend to do here, no matter how bad you treat me."

She was red and fiery when she was angry. And sexy as hell! He liked that. Liked it a lot. "Look, I have these preconceived ideas, right or wrong, and for those, I do apologize. I'm trying to get that under control. But I also have an irascible personality that needs attention, which I haven't had time to give it."

"Irascible?"

"You know. Hot-tempered. Irritable."

"Yes, I've noticed. And you freely admit that?"

"I do because, like I said, I'm honest."

"Do you like being irascible?"

"Not so much." Especially now. But it overtook him and sometimes he couldn't control it. Like with Juliette. It was part of his restlessness, he supposed.

"Then stop it. You're a smart man. You're capable of getting a grip on yourself, if you want to. So quit acting like you're so mean because, deep down, I don't think you really are. It's only a defense mechanism, Damien. Against what, I don't know. Don't want to know. But if you keep putting people off, the way you do, you're going to wind up in a Costa Rican jungle with no friends, and no place to go. That could turn out to be very sad for you."

She was softening now, her flare of anger dying down. This smoother side of her was so attractive, all he wanted to do was stay in that place, at that time, and stare at her. But there was a part of Juliette that scared him—the part that was so easily digging beneath his surface to discover who he really was. Most of the time, he kept that face hidden. Didn't want people getting close because, in his experience, people who could find the vulnerable place had the power to hurt. Nancy had hurt him. In spite of all the things he'd seen in her, and all the qualms he'd had about marrying someone coming from an indulged, wealthy background, he'd still planned a life with her. In fact, he'd tried hard to make the changes she'd needed to see in him, changes he didn't necessarily want to make but had made, nonetheless, because that was what she'd wanted.

In essence, he'd been true to Nancy but he hadn't been true to himself. No way was he going to do that again, so it was easier to push people away before they expected something of him. "There could be worse things than ending up here without friends and no place to go," he said, even though a big chunk of him didn't believe that.

"Look, Damien. You're fighting some kind of battle here, and apparently you've decided to drag me into it. But I never fight. Not with you, not with anybody. All I want is for you to lay off the snide remarks and let me do my work. You don't have to like me, I don't have to like you. And it seems we're starting out that way, which doesn't make a working relationship easy, but since I'm only going to be here a couple days a week, our feelings about each other shouldn't get in the way. If you want to run me off, don't do it because I rub you the wrong way. Or because I'm wealthy. Do it because my work isn't good enough. Do it because I have a lousy bedside manner. Do it because I'm not as good of a doctor as you need. But don't do it because of personal issues. OK? Oh, and don't cop out to an excuse like your self-admitted irascible nature because, frankly, I don't care what you are by nature. All I want is a good supervisor. Someone who will help me when I need it, and leave me alone when I don't. And someone who doesn't ridicule me because I don't know how to make a bed."

Man, oh, man, *had* he been wrong when he'd compared Juliette to Nancy. Nancy would have never stood up to him like that. She was quiet, always ran to Daddy and Daddy did the talking. And she would have never been as passionate about anything the way Juliette was passionate about working here.

"You know. We're both tired. We've had a long day and we've got another long day ahead of us tomorrow. This is new to you, and you're new to me, both of which are going to take some getting used to. So maybe we should just stop this right here. You can go get some sleep. I'll hang around for another hour or so, do some final bed checks, turn the rest of the night over to George Perkins and go back to my hut and grab a couple hours of sleep. Then we'll regroup in the morning and see what we've got."

"Who's George Perkins?" she asked.

"My other doctor here. Plastic surgeon, good man. A little burned-out on medicine, but working his way back in."

"Burned-out?"

"He substituted work for life." The way *he* did. "Lost his wife over it, but one of the women here—let's just say that the love of a good woman has worked miracles for him. He's finding a new purpose."

"Well, here's to the good women," she said.

"They are out there, I suppose."

"You *suppose*?"

"Did I offend you again?"

"Actually, you didn't. And you didn't surprise me, either."

"Good. Then I don't have anything else to apologize for."

"Maybe, before you do, I should just go find myself a bed and stay away from you for a while."

If there was any way he could make this situation any more tense between them he sure couldn't come up with what it might be. It was as if to open his mouth was to say something he didn't intend to say. Hell of it was, he couldn't seem to stop himself. But tomorrow—ah, yes, the great unknown tomorrow. He wanted to think that come tomorrow he'd do better. Truth was, though, he didn't know if he could.

"Look, I've got a couple of room dividers stashed in the supply closet. Let me go get them and section you off from the rest of the ward. It's not much in the way of privacy, but it's the best I've got."

Juliette nodded her agreement and managed a polite smile. "Tomorrow will be better," she told him.

He hoped that would be true. "Let's keep our fingers crossed."

"So what time do you want me on in the morning?"

Damien checked his watch. It was almost midnight now, and breakfast would be served at seven thirty. "I'll have

George wake you up at six. That should give you enough time to shower and get ready."

"Get ready for what?"

"Didn't I tell you? Rosalita doesn't come in until it's time to cook the noon meal. We all pitch in so I'm putting you in charge of the kitchen for breakfast."

"You've got to be kidding!"

Damien smiled at her. "It beats bedsheets, doesn't it?"

CHAPTER FOUR

JULIETTE TOSSED AND turned for almost an hour before she finally dozed off. The bed was lumpy, the sheets scratchy and the patient down the row from her snored like a buzz saw. None of that mattered much, as her mind was focused on Damien. Images of him popped up behind her eyelids when she closed her eyes, thoughts of him sent her brain into overload, instantly awakening every synapse in her body. But why?

Well, she wasn't sure. Maybe because he was an enigma of a man. It was as if he ran hot and cold, minute to minute. Nice then cutting, all in a flash. To say the least, it was peculiar behavior. But she wasn't going to criticize him for it, even though in the span of only one day she'd become the target of his off-and-on belligerence, as if something was boiling just underneath his surface. She didn't have to look too hard to see it.

"You're Juliette, aren't you?" A man with a very thick Boston accent poked his head in around her partition. "Damien told me to wake you up if I needed help."

"What time is it?" she asked groggily.

"A little after two. And I hate to disturb you like this, but one of us has got to go down the road and deliver a baby while the other one stays here and looks after the hospital."

"Are you George Perkins?" she asked as she tried to shake her single hour of sleep off her stiff body.

"Yes," he said. "George Perkins, plastic surgeon in the States, GP in the jungle, at your service. Pleased to make your acquaintance, Juliette. Sorry this comes at such a bad time but, in my experience, most of the babies I've delivered here have preferred to make their grand entrance in the middle of the night."

Juliette switched on her bedside light to have a good look at him. He was a distinguished man with silver hair and a full gray beard. He sported a crisp linen shirt and a neatly pressed pair of khaki trousers, looking very much as if he could have stepped right off the pages of a fashion magazine. All in all, he was a good-looking gent. And he looked...happy. Something she'd never seen in her father, and had never even seen in herself when she looked in the mirror. "Damien didn't mention that I was to be on call tonight. Is it posted somewhere that I should have noticed?"

"Damien doesn't mention a lot of things. You'll get used to that if you stay with us for very long. Also, we don't post things around here because most of the volunteers barely speak English and they sure as heck can't read it. So, everything's passed down directly, from person to person. As for taking calls at night, in my current situation which, in case Damien didn't tell you, is I'm living with a very lovely village woman and I prefer working nights while Carmelita and her children are sleeping, so no one really has to take calls then, unless I'm taking a night off. I'm just hoping that you'll stand in as my backup right now because I don't want to go wake Damien up to help me. He was on thirty-six hours straight before tonight, and he needs his rest."

Juliette blew out a deep breath and sat up. "So what do you want me to do? Deliver a baby, or watch the hospital?"

"Do you like babies?" he asked her. "Because if you do, I'd rather stay here and attend to a couple of my regulars who like to come see me in the middle of the night."

"Sure, no problem." Juliette swung her legs over the side of the bed and stood up. Normally, at home, she'd be wearing pajamas. But here, in the jungle, she'd brought a pair of scrubs along as she didn't know what she'd be doing and scrubs were good everyday work clothes, as well as stand-in pajamas. "Where can I find the mother-to-be?"

"Down this road until you get to the church. Turn left at that intersection, go another block, then turn right. She'll be in the third house on the left. The best landmark I can give you is a rusted-out old pickup truck in her front yard, and the house should be well lit, as half the village usually turns out for a birth." He held out a flashlight. "No streetlights," he said sheepishly.

House calls by flashlight. Couldn't say she'd ever done anything like that before, but there was a first time for everything. So she took the light from him and switched it on to make sure the batteries were good. They were. "Any complications? Anything I should know about before I go?"

"Her name is Maria Salas, and this is her third child so it should be a fairly easy birth. She hasn't been in labor long, according to her husband, but he thinks the baby is coming quickly. Apparently, she has a history of fast births."

"Then I should get going," Juliette said, bending down to pull on her sneakers. "Do you have a medical kit with maternity supplies I can take along with me?"

"I put it by the front door before I came to get you. It should have everything you need for a straightforward birth. But if you run into any complications, have one of Maria's family members run and fetch Damien."

"Will do." Juliette pushed herself off the bed and headed

immediately toward the door. She was finally awake, still feeling a little sluggish, though, as one hour hadn't been enough to shake off her tiredness. "Should we try to get her into the hospital for this? Because I'm not sure a home delivery is the safest thing to do." Also, as director of a clinic, she'd never made a house call in her life, flashlight or not, and, while she was looking forward to the experience, it also made her a little nervous going so far outside of what she'd ever done. But that was what they did here, and she was part of it now. So it was what she did, too.

"Sure. Bring her in, if she can make it. But I doubt that's going to work out for you because most of the women here prefer home births. You know, have the baby then getting back onto whatever they were doing before it came."

That was a stamina Juliette admired. As for her, though, if she ever had a baby, she wanted it in a modern hospital with all the latest equipment. Wanted an anesthesiologist on hand to give her an epidural for the pain. Wanted fetal monitors, and heart monitors, and blood pressure monitors. Soft lights and soft music in the delivery room.

"Well, whatever happens, if she's as fast about it as you've been led to believe, maybe I'll be able to get back here in time to grab another couple hours of sleep."

"Or you can sleep in the morning, when Damien comes on."

Right. And listen to Damien taunt her about that for the next several weeks. *What did you do? Come to the jungle just to sleep?*

Juliette grabbed the rucksack by the door and fairly ran out and on down the street, flashing her light along the path, making the proper turns where she needed and continuing on until she came to the rusty old truck standing in Maria's front yard. It was surrounded by several people, who were all talking quite loudly, as if they were having a party. Indeed, half the village seemed to be there, as George had said.

"The baby's coming out now," one of the men told her. "My new grandchild."

"And it's going to be a big baby. Maria always has big babies," an older woman added.

Juliette's first thought was gestational diabetes. It was a condition that put the mother and child at some degree of risk, and usually resulted in larger than the average baby. But hadn't Damien been seeing Maria? Surely, he would have noticed such a condition and prepared for it. Also, George would have mentioned it to her. So Juliette put that notion out of her head, preferring to think that Maria had received excellent prenatal care from Damien. In spite of his attitude, everything she'd seen and read about him told her he was a good doctor. "Thank you," she said, scooting past all the gathered people and hurrying through Maria's open front door.

The lights were bright inside, revealing a clean but cluttered little house. Judging from the knickknacks, toys, books, small appliances and clothing strewn everywhere, the Salas family never came across an object of any sort that they couldn't collect. "Where is she?" she asked one of the five people huddled among the clutter.

"Back bedroom, left side of the hall. Go through the kitchen." The man pointed to a narrow pathway winding its way through a corridor of old chairs, tables and lamps.

Juliette squeezed through the maze and stopped just short of entering the kitchen. "What are *you* doing here?" she asked.

Damien, who was sitting in an old chrome chair at the kitchen table, smiled up at her. "Same thing you are, I guess."

"They came and got you, too?"

He shrugged. "I'm her doctor. Who else would they call?"

"Me."

"Not sure why they'd do that, seeing as how you've never even met Maria."

"George Perkins woke me up. Told me to get down here."

"George overreacts sometimes."

"Like sending me here in the middle of the night when I could be back at the hospital, sleeping?"

"I could be saying the same thing. But I started to realize, probably in my first couple of days here, that people's needs were always going to supersede my sleep. Comes with the territory."

"Well, that's too bad for you, I suppose."

"I'm used to it." He stretched back in his chair. "Anyway, Maria's fully dilated, fully effaced. Pushing it out as we speak."

"Then shouldn't you be in there, delivering the baby instead of sitting here, casually talking about it?" Frankly, she was shocked that he wasn't more involved at this stage.

"I'd like to be, but Maria's mother and grandmother are in there, along with her two sisters, a couple of cousins and an aunt. There's really no room for anyone else."

"You mean no room for a doctor?"

"She's already got plenty of help standing by. She doesn't need a doctor."

He was being so blithely unconcerned about this, it surprised her. "But haven't you been seeing her all along?"

"I was here earlier today, as a matter of fact. Kind of thought the baby would be coming in the next day or so."

"And yet you're sitting here, doing nothing."

"Actually, I'm sitting here, waiting to take over if she starts having problems. That's the only reason they called us in—as backups. Luckily, though, she's progressing through a normal delivery quite nicely. Oh, and I do poke my head in the door every few minutes to check on how things are going."

"So who's going to actually deliver the baby?"

"Her grandmother. She's delivered more babies than I have. I know she delivered Maria's first two. Oh, and just last week she delivered her neighbor's baby." He shrugged. "Lady's got a lot of experience, and she resents anybody barging in who doesn't belong there. In Irene's opinion, *we* do not belong there."

"Then she's a midwife," Juliette stated, relieved that someone with experience and knowledge was taking over.

"Of sorts. I mean she's not trained or anything like that. She's just always available to do something she's been doing for sixty years."

Sixty years? That alarmed Juliette. "How old is she?"

"Not sure, since she doesn't go to doctors or hospitals, and we don't have her records. But I'm guessing she's somewhere around eighty, give or take a few years."

"Eighty and still delivering babies? Why do you allow that, Damien? You're the doctor in this village. Shouldn't you have some say in the medical concerns of the people who live here?"

"Normally, I do. But when it comes to childbirth, the women here gang up on me and keep me at a distance. It's their tradition to rally around their mothers in labor and see to the delivery. They've been doing it for more years than the two of us combined have been here on this earth. So who am I to intrude?"

Juliette pushed her hair back from her face. Tonight, it wasn't banded up in a ponytail. "Do you think they'd mind if I looked in?"

"As another woman, or as a doctor?"

"Why can't I be both?"

Damien laughed. "You really can't be that naive, can you?"

"What do you mean by that?"

"These people practiced their folk medicine long before anything remotely modern came in and took over, and so many of the older ones still hold on to their old ways. They'll tolerate us when they need us, but otherwise they'll resist the hell out of what we try to offer them because they consider that an insult. People trust what they know, and resist anything new to them. The fine art of healing is included in that."

From somewhere behind the wall to her right, the quiet voices of people chattering were beginning to grow louder, and Juliette wondered if that was a sign of imminent birth. The ladies in the room with Maria were getting excited. She could almost picture them huddling around the bed, talking, as Maria was assuming the position to deliver. All so casual. "Well, resistance or not, I'm going to go take a peek."

"Or you could sit down with me here, have a nice *refresco*—" Damien held up a glass of blended fruit and ice in salute "—and wait."

"Or you could go back home and go to bed, since I'm here now," she suggested. "George said you pulled thirty-six hours straight, so I think you need the sleep more than I do."

"I appreciate the offer, but I think I'll stay since I've been with Maria through this entire pregnancy. And she did ask me, specifically, if I would check the baby after it's born." He held his *refresco* out to her. "Papaya and passion fruit. Really good. Want a sip?"

What she wanted was to go deliver a baby, but seeing as how that wasn't going to happen, she still wanted to get into Maria's bedroom and watch what was going on. Hitching her rucksack higher onto her shoulder, she passed by Damien, whose feet were now propped up on the chair opposite him, and headed on back through the kitchen. "I'll let you know if it's a boy or girl," she said before she stepped into the back hall.

"It's a boy," he called after her.

"You did some testing to find out?" Juliette asked, clearly surprised that he'd go to such lengths for someone who wanted as little medical intervention as possible.

"No tests. Just a guess. And I'm usually pretty good at guessing. Got my last five deliveries right. No reason to break that winning streak now."

"You're that confident, are you?"

In answer, he picked up his *refresco*, took a sip, then said, "Yep!"

Damn, he was sexy, sitting there in all his casual, cocky glory. She really didn't want to think that of him, and maybe her guard was let down because she was so tired but, God help her, she was beginning to like Damien. Not enough to fall for him, in spite of his somewhat unusual charm, but enough to tolerate his ways.

"Can I come in?" she asked, pushing open Maria's bedroom door.

The women in the room all turned to look at her—all but the oldest one, who was seated at the end of the bed, obviously ready to deliver a baby. "Who are you?" one of the women asked.

"Juliette Allen. El doctor Juliette Allen."

"No doctor needed here," the woman at the end of the bed said quite sternly.

"That's what el doctor Damien told me, so I'm not here as a doctor. I'm just here to watch. And if you need someone else to help…"

"Irene needs no help," another one of the women informed her.

Juliette sighed. If Damien were here, he'd be enjoying this rejection. "I won't get in the way."

"Don't get in the way somewhere else," Irene, Maria's grandmother, said. "Maria doesn't need a stranger here."

Struggling to be patient, Juliette smiled, and backed her way over to the door, where she stopped and simply stood, without saying another word. Apparently that was good enough for the women, as they turned their attention back to Maria, who was bearing down in a hard push.

"Push harder," Irene encouraged her.

"I can't," the pregnant woman moaned. "Can't push. Can't…breathe. Getting too tired."

When Juliette heard this, she was instantly on alert. "Maybe reposition her," she suggested. "Get her head up a little higher. More like she's sitting rather than laying."

Her suggestion was greeted with frowns from everyone in the room. "My grandmother knows how high she's supposed to sit," one of the younger women said, her voice curt.

Before Juliette could respond, a scream from Maria ripped through the room. "I can't do this!" she cried. "The baby's not coming."

This was more than Juliette could take, and she pushed her way through the crowd in the room and went straight to Irene's side to bend down and take a look. But what she saw was no progression toward birth. No crowning whatsoever. "How long has she been in heavy labor?" Juliette asked the woman.

"Not long enough," the woman responded belligerently.

"I *mean* in hours. How long in hours?"

"About one," one of the women called out.

"And it's been heavy like this since the beginning?" Contractions coming almost one after another.

"She always has her babies fast," Irene conceded. "But I think this one is taking too long. I'm worried I don't see the baby's head yet."

"Can I take a look?" Juliette asked, slinging her rucksack down onto the floor, then opening it up to grab out a blood pressure cuff. Damn, she wished she was back in her clinic, where she could hook up a fetal monitor, because her greatest fear right now was that the baby was in distress and she had no way to observe it.

"Maria's having trouble. So if you could move over and let me get a look at her…"

Irene hesitated for a moment, then nodded and moved aside. "You can help her?"

"I'm going to try," Juliette said, taking her position at the end of the bed. "Could you hold back the sheets for me, so I've got a little more room to maneuver?" It wasn't really necessary, but she wanted to include Irene since she was such a vital part of childbirth here in Bombacopsis, and all the women in the village respected her. There was no way Juliette wanted to dismiss Irene and diminish her in the eyes of all the people who trusted her. "And also make sure Maria stays in position?"

Irene agreed readily, and moved into her place next to Juliette, where she did everything Juliette asked.

"It's good we have you here," the old woman finally said, after Juliette had completed her initial exam. "El doctor Damien is good enough, but this should be left up to a woman."

Juliette smiled, hoping that this might be the beginning of the village accepting something they'd never before seen—a female doctor.

"Did I hear my name mentioned?" Damien asked, poking his head through the door.

"Just in that the ladies here believe this is no place for a man," Juliette returned. Then continued, "But I do need some help, in spite of that."

"What's going on?" he asked, stepping fully into the room.

"We have an obstructed labor in progress," Juliette called over the increasing noise of the women surrounding her. "In spite of Maria's strong contractions, her labor isn't progressing."

Juliette pumped up her blood pressure cuff and tried to hear the dull thudding of Maria's heartbeat after she placed the bell of her stethoscope underneath the cuff. "Her blood pressure is high," she called out. "As best as I can tell." Then she felt Maria's belly, pressed down on it to determine the position of the baby. "Baby's in normal position. But not progressing down the birth canal."

"She needs to push again," Irene shouted over the crowd.

"Pushing's not going to help now," Juliette explained. "The baby's ready to come. But it's not, and trying to push now is only going to make things worse. Put the baby at some risk."

The noise of the women was growing louder, deafening, fraying Juliette's already frayed nerves. Maria was in trouble, she needed Damien to help her with this and she couldn't even communicate with him, the ladies were so loud. Pressure mounting. Maria moaning even louder. Ladies getting frantic. More pressure—

"Damien!" she finally yelled. "Can we get these people out of here? I can't do what I need to do with everybody hovering over me, shouting the way they are." She was trying her best to shut out all the confusion going on around her, but alarm for Maria's lack of pushing out the baby was making everybody crazy, including her. "We've got a problem going on, and I can't do what I need to do with everyone hovering over me." Her own anxiety for Maria and her baby was increasing.

"Give me a couple of seconds," Damien called back to her.

She couldn't see him, as the door was at such an angle it wasn't in her line of sight. But she felt reassured just having him in the room. She felt even more reassured when each of the women started to leave the room. Whatever Damien was saying to them was working, and she was glad for that as Maria had turned a pasty white and was slowly sinking into total exhaustion.

"What have we got?" Damien asked, once all the ladies, with the exception of Irene, had exited.

"Nothing. Absolutely nothing."

"Her contractions?" Damien approached the bed and took Maria's pulse.

"Strong and almost continuous. The baby should be coming out now, and I'm getting worried that it's not."

He nodded, and immediately tore into the rucksack he was carrying, producing, in just a matter of seconds, a scalpel, a sterile drape, forceps and a handheld suction device. "Six minutes," he said, as he grabbed a bottle of sterile wash and pulled the sheet off Maria's belly.

"What?" Juliette asked him.

"I can do an emergency C-section in six minutes from the time I get her sedated. Faster, if I have to. So, stand on the opposite side of me, and let's get this thing done." Then, to Maria, "Maria! Can you hear me? It's el doctor Damien, and I'm going to get your baby out of you right now. But I'm going to have to make a little cut in your belly to do so." He looked over at Juliette. "How long will it take you to get an IV going?"

"Not long," she said, immediately plowing through her medical rucksack to find the necessary equipment. Tubing, needle, IV drip solution. "What are we going to put in it?"

"I've got ketamine."

"Ketamine?" she asked. "You didn't mention that in your drug list."

"Because it's hard for me to come by and I put the little bit I do have back for emergencies."

Resourceful, she thought. Ketamine was a valuable property. "Well, a low-dose application of ketamine will work, since this baby's going to be out of her before the ketamine can cross the blood barrier," she said, as she readied to stick the IV catheter in Maria's arm. In no time at all, the IV was started, and Juliette handed Irene the bag of drip solution to hold above the head of the bed so the medication would run down into Maria's vein, while she piggy-backed on a pouch of ketamine. As soon as the medications were both in place, Juliette opened up the port to let them pass through the tubing into Maria's body. It took only a couple of minutes for the anesthetization of Maria Salas to commence. "Ready?" she finally asked Damien, noting that he'd prepped the incision site whilst she started the IV.

"Put a clock on it," he said, poised to make the first incision through Maria's abdomen.

Juliette did, and Damien was right. Six minutes and ten seconds into the procedure and he was handing over a brand-new baby for her to check. "A boy," she said.

"I was right," Damien said, grinning. "And he's a big one. I'm guessing nine or ten pounds."

"Closer to ten," Juliette said, as she turned her attention to baby Salas while Damien finished up with Maria.

First she did the normal suctioning—mouth, nose. Then she took a towel and wrapped it around the baby, poking him gently, trying to get him to cry.

"Is he OK?" Damien asked, looking over at Juliette for a moment.

"Well, I don't have any equipment to do a proper evaluation, but he's breathing and his heart is beating."

"But he's not crying?" Damien asked.

"Not yet."

"Pinch him gently. Just a little one to see what you get." Damien grabbed up a pre-threaded suture and began to stitch up Maria's incision. But he took a second to look over at Juliette as she gave the baby a slight tweak on the bottom of his left foot. And got no response.

So she switched to tickling. Tickled a little spot on the baby's upper arm and ran her fingers down his arm lightly to his wrist, then waited for a second when he didn't respond, and tried it again. This time, baby Salas sucked in a lungful of air and let out with a royal scream.

"Good work," Damien said, without looking up at Juliette.

"How's Maria?"

"Hanging in there."

"Want me to finish closing for you?" she asked, handing the baby over to Manuela—Maria's sister—who'd snuck back into the room to be by her sister's side.

"No, I'm good. But what you can do is go outside and tell someone in the yard to run over to the hospital and fetch a stretcher. Then round up some volunteers to carry Maria over once I get through here."

"You OK?" Juliette asked before she left the room.

He finally looked up at Juliette, his brown eyes twinkling and his smile spreading from ear to ear. "I just delivered a baby. That always makes me OK."

* * *

"We do good work together," Damien commented as he and Juliette walked back to the hospital, arm in arm in the dark, leaning heavily on one another. He was tired. Almost too tired to function. But Maria and the baby were probably being settled into the hospital by now, so he had to take one more look at them before he dragged himself back to his hut for what was left of the night.

"It was a pretty slick delivery," Juliette admitted. "My first C-section since I assisted in one during my residency. Then later, in *my* clinic, I referred all my pregnancies to the obstetrics department."

"Well, around here you get to do it all. Bandage a stubbed toe, remove an infected appendix, treat malaria, remedy a bad heartburn. You know, jack-of-all-trades."

"So, I know you're a surgeon, but did you learn these other things in your training, or do you just learn as you go?"

Truthfully, it had been a culture shock coming here. No matter where he'd worked prior to this, he'd always surrounded himself with a security blanket in that he'd kept strictly to his general surgery, never wandering very far from it. Then this, where he had to wander in all different directions.

"It's been a huge learning curve. And yeah, a lot of it I do make up as I go. But the people here are patient with me."

"Do you consult outsiders? You know, friends or colleagues from your old days?"

"Not so much. We don't have great access to the outside world. Although, if I need to know something bad enough, I'll go into Cima de la Montaña and scare up an internet connection." They walked on by his hut, where he took a wistful glance at the front door, wishing he was back in there right now, sleeping peacefully in his uncomfortable bed. "And I did have several of my medical references shipped down to me, so I've always got those to fall back on, even though they're pretty outdated."

"Well, if there's ever anything you want me to look up for you, let me know and I'll do it when I go back to San José, then I'll get the answer back to you next time I come."

"Are you really coming back?" he asked her. "I mean, your first day has been pretty tough so far, and I haven't exactly been welcoming." That was putting it mildly. He'd been downright awful, which he regretted as Juliette was a real trooper. She'd come here first thing this morning, pitched right in and done everything that needed to be done. More, actually. She'd spotted the problem in Maria's labor, and the way she had assisted with the C-section was downright amazing!

"Have you been trying to get rid of me? Is that why you've been so rude? Because I thought you needed someone else here."

They entered the hospital where, down the hall in the ward, George Perkins was settling Maria Salas into bed. Irene, her grandmother, had seated herself in a chair next to the bed and was holding the baby. Maria's husband, Alvaro, was standing at the foot of the bed along with five other people Damien assumed were relatives or close friends. "I do need someone here. I just wasn't expecting…you."

"What were you expecting?" she asked him.

"I'm not sure, really. Maybe someone close to retirement age, or someone's who's basically burned out the way George was. The thing is, when you have very little to offer, you can't expect your pick of the profession to come knocking on your door. Then when you showed up here—well, you're closer to the pick of the profession, and

I simply didn't expect that. It caught me off guard. Gave me some hope I'm probably not entitled to have."

"So you immediately turned rude, because you didn't think you deserved someone like me, with my background and skills?"

"I immediately turned defensive, because I thought there was no way in hell I'd get to keep you here after you'd seen what I had to offer." It was too late, he was too tired. Otherwise, he wouldn't be standing here confessing to things that were true but would otherwise never be admitted to. In the course of one day, Juliette had softened him. Whether that was a good thing remained to be seen.

Time would tell, he supposed. "Before we go look at Maria, would you care for a cup of hot tea? Herbal, so it won't keep you awake."

"Want me to make it?" she asked him.

Damien shook his head. "A cup of tea is the least I can do for you. Oh, and Juliette, how about you take my hut for the rest of the night so you can get some sleep? I think it's going to be pretty busy, and pretty noisy, in here."

"But you need sleep worse than I do."

"I've got my exam table."

"Which is ungodly uncomfortable. No, you go back to your hut and I'll stay here."

"And here, I'm trying to be nice to you."

Juliette shook her head, then smiled. "Don't be too nice, because if you are I'm afraid I won't recognize you."

And that was the problem. He wanted her to recognize him.

CHAPTER FIVE

"IT WAS BUSY," Juliette said to Cynthia over a typical Costa Rican breakfast called *gallo pinto*, made of black beans and rice. Some restaurants made it with bacon, eggs, ham and a number of other ingredients, but Juliette preferred hers plain, as her appetite was never large in the morning. "A lot of people come in with general complaints, and that takes up most of the time. So I saw gout, bug bites, a broken finger—those kinds of things. But I also assisted in an emergency C-section, which was a good opportunity for me to learn since all my pregnant ladies at the hospital back in Indiana got referred to the obstetrics clinic."

Cynthia snapped her head up and looked across the table at Juliette. "You did a C-section? How? Because what I've been gathering is that your little hospital isn't equipped to do much of anything."

"It's not. But that didn't matter, because we did it at the patient's home." She took a sip of coffee then sat the mug back down on the table. This had become her morning routine.

A small portion of *gallo pinto* and coffee in the tiny little restaurant down the block from her flat. It was cheap, filling, and once she'd gotten used to the starchy heaviness that early in the day, she'd actually grown to like the concoction.

"It was a little dicey, since I've never assisted in a C-section outside my residency, but Damien was there and he's a skilled surgeon so Maria—the patient—was in good hands."

"Is he cute?"

"Who?"

"Damien. What's he look like? Tall, dark and handsome? Great body? Nice smile? Soft hands?"

"Whoa," Juliette said, thrusting out her hand to stop her friend. "I was too busy working to pay *that* kind of attention to him." Nice words, not exactly true, however, as she *had* paid a little attention to him. And while Damien wasn't the physical type she'd always been attracted to, something about his blatant rawness was appealing. Sexy. "Actually, he *is* tall, dark and handsome. I did notice that much." With drop-dead gorgeous brown eyes, and a beautiful smile punctuated by the most appealing dimples she'd ever seen on a man. "And I have an idea that in his real surroundings, he's probably a bad boy."

Cynthia's eyes lit up. "Maybe I'll have to go out there with you sometime. I *really* like bad boys."

"He'll put you to work," Juliette warned. "Make you change beds."

"As long as *his* bed is included in that, I won't mind."

It almost put Juliette off, seeing how her friend was reacting to a man she'd never met, let alone seen.

"He's grumpy."

"So?"

"I mean, *really* grumpy."

"Yeah, but there are ways to soothe the savage beast."

"Aren't you engaged or something?"

A dreamy look overtook Cynthia's eyes. "To my one and only. But a girl can still look, can't she?"

Actually, Juliette didn't know since she'd never been

one who was much into looking. Something else always got in the way, always took up her time and energy.

"Look, I need to get on into work. I've got a prospective GI doc coming in about half an hour, and I want to take him over to the hospital and show him around, so he'll have time to acquaint himself with the facility before his interview." She also just needed to get away from Cynthia for a little, to clear her head. To put some proper perspective on why she felt the way she did where Damien was concerned. "So why don't you finish up here, and I'll see you when you get to work."

"Do you have a thing for him, Juliette?" Cynthia asked bluntly.

"A thing?" There was no *thing* going on with her—except maybe a smidge of fascination. And that didn't qualify as a *thing*, did it?

"You know—something going on. Or maybe just a feeling. Because I think you're mad at me right now because I teased you about him."

Cynthia's reaction to Damien might have been teasing but, for a reason Juliette didn't understand, it had struck a raw nerve in her. "I'm not mad at you, and I don't have a *thing* with, or for, Damien." Said a little too vehemently, she was afraid. Which she was sure Cynthia would misinterpret.

"Well, I was just joking with you. I mean, I've got Carlos and I'm not looking to get involved with anyone else. Not even your Damien."

"He's not *my* Damien, and I'm not looking to get involved with him, either."

"Then you two didn't hit it off?"

Juliette shook her head. "He's a talented doctor, which I respect, but apart from that…" She shrugged. "He's just not my type." A sentiment that wasn't necessarily true, if she took into account all the many times she'd thought about him since she'd come back to San José just this morning. "Besides, I don't have time for a personal life. Between my two jobs, I barely have time to sleep."

"And whose fault is that? Aren't you the one who works the late hours and, as often as not, goes in early? And aren't you the one who always goes out of her way to help clients in ways not required of our job?"

What Cynthia said was true. But, in her own defense, these were the things she did to make sure the people who were trusting her to make a perfect medical match for them got everything they hoped for. She took her job seriously—as seriously as Damien took his job in his impoverished little jungle hospital. As seriously as her dad took his job in a large, university teaching hospital. "I'm just doing the best I can."

"And not enjoying your life while you're doing it. You're going to get tired of living that way, Juliette," Cynthia warned. "When I first came here, I was just like you—too dedicated. It almost burned me out. But eventually I began to back away from it and find a life outside of my work."

"You fell in love with a doctor at one of the hospitals," Juliette replied, smiling. "That'll give you a new life."

"If you let it. And, from what I can see of you, you're not letting it."

"I've barely been here a month, Cynthia. I hardly know my way around my desk yet."

"Well, keep your mind open to this jungle doctor. Your eyes lit up when you mentioned him." Cynthia shoved back from the little table for two and stood. "In the meantime, I think I'll go in a little early with you, and give Carlos a call."

"Didn't he just leave the flat like two hours ago?"

"Maybe he did, but I miss him already."

"Spoken like a woman in love," she said to Cynthia.

Of course, for Juliette, love was only an idea, a notion. Something that sounded beautiful. But she'd never been in love. Never pictured herself as someone who was lovable, as no one had ever fallen in love with her. Of course she wasn't sure she'd ever given anyone the chance. She'd been too busy, between her work and her father. In some ways, she was turning into him—always striving to take on more work, then hiding behind it in lieu of a real life. Building block upon block, which turned into a fortress. Well, she was finding herself more and more cloistered inside that fortress every day, wanting to get out of it. And Costa Rica was her out. Falling in love with someone, though, was the best out she could think of. But she didn't know if that would happen.

"Well, just give it time," Cynthia said. "Maybe you'll find the love of your life here, in Costa Rica, too."

Wishful thinking as she didn't know where to look for it. She was too inexperienced when it came to love. Embarrassed by the fact that, at thirty-three, she didn't know a thing about it. Saddened by the fact that she might have let it pass her by without even seeing it.

"Quit looking at the road, Damien," George Perkins said as he was changing a bandage on Alfonso Valverde, the local mechanic. He'd been working on a truck manifold and received a nasty burn, which he hadn't treated at the time. Now it was infected and the infection had spread from his thumb to his entire hand. "She'll get here when she gets here."

"I expected her an hour ago," Damien said, fighting to keep his eyes off the front window.

"Maybe she had car trouble. Or got swallowed up in one

of the potholes on the way out here. Or maybe a jaguar..."
George grinned up at Damien. "Or maybe she's just late."

"Or decided she didn't want to come."

"Without getting word to you?" George shook his head.
"She doesn't seem the type. Of course, I really don't know
what type she is, so maybe I'm not the one who should be
telling you to quit looking."

Fat lot of help that was! He'd spent the whole week
thinking about Juliette, planning on ways to make this
weekend better for her. Of course, he'd also spent the week
reminding himself of all the reasons he didn't want to get
involved with a rich girl again. And he stretched that involvement to include working with her.

"Well, I'm going to run down the street and see Padre
Benicio. He hasn't been feeling well for the last couple of
days and since he refuses to come into the hospital, the
hospital's going to him."

"Tell him for me that Carmelita and I want to get married in a few weeks, so he'd better get over what's ailing
him, because I don't want a sick priest anywhere near me
on my wedding day."

"It's allergies," Damien said. "He's not contagious."

"Well, I don't want him sneezing his allergies all over
my bride."

"You're actually going to go through with it?"

George taped the end of the bandage and put on his
reading glasses to make a close inspection of his work.
"I'm almost sixty, so why wait? She's given me a second
chance at life."

"Well, I wish you and Carmelita the best of luck. And,
for what it's worth, I think you're a great couple. She's good
for you." The man had so much faith in the power of love
it almost made Damien want to believe again.

"Sorry I'm late," Juliette called from the doorway. "I didn't get away from San José as early as I'd hoped to."

Without turning to face her, Damien said, "You're late? I didn't notice."

George shook his head, rolled his eyes and gave Damien a pat on the shoulder as he walked out the door. "Good luck with Damien," he said to Juliette. "He's in a mood tonight."

"Another mood?" Juliette asked.

"My mood's no better or worse than it ever is," Damien replied, slinging his medical rucksack over his shoulder.

"Something I've looked forward to all week," Juliette replied. "So, are you going out on a house call?"

"I am. And George's off tonight, so the hospital is all yours for now."

"But you're coming back, aren't you?"

"Eventually." Actually, he wanted to get back as quickly as he could, but that would make him seem anxious, maybe even desperate. So, to avoid anything that made him look the least bit interested in Juliette, he decided to take the long road home, stop at the village café for a bite to eat—he had a taste tonight for *arreglados*, a tiny sandwich filled with meat and salad—then afterward he might wander on over to see how Javier Rojas was responding to the new medication he'd prescribed for him: cyclobenzaprine, a drug used for treating the muscle spasms he was having in his back. Anything to keep him away for a while. Anything to give him time to think about some unexpected feelings he was having. Unexpected, and quick, as he'd known her only a week.

"And if I need help while you're gone?"

"Alegria's on tonight. Right now she's gathering up the hospital gowns from the lady who washes them for us, but she should be back here in about fifteen minutes."

Damn! This wasn't the way he'd envisioned the evening

starting out. Every single day this past week he'd come up with a new scenario. He and Juliette would pitch in together and check every patient in the hospital. He and Juliette would have a nice meal together before they started work. He and Juliette would simply sit down together and have a pleasant chat. The list of scenarios went on and on, yet here he was, leaving her all alone. No *he and Juliette* anything!

"So you want me to make beds again?"

"Actually, what I'd like is for you to make a bedside check of all the patients. You know, get their vital signs, assess them for whatever we're treating them for, address wounds, that sort of thing. Oh, and we've got seven patients admitted right now. Nothing seriously wrong with any of them, so you shouldn't have a tough evening."

"How's Maria Salas and her baby doing?"

"Maria's doing fine. So is Alejandro, her baby. We sent them home day before yesterday, and she's due back in here tomorrow so we can make sure nothing's going wrong with her incision." He paused, and frowned. "You know, to save her the trip over here, I might just stop by her house this evening to take a look." At the rate he was going, he'd be lucky to get back to the hospital by midnight.

"Well, it looks like I've got a busy night ahead of me. Guess I should get to work." Instead of heading into the hospital ward, though, she turned and started walking toward the clinic.

"Where are you going?" Damien asked her.

"I ran into Padre Benicio on the way in. He's got a terrible cough, and he said he's coming down with a sore throat now. So I'm going to go take a look at him. He's in the clinic right now, waiting for me."

"How'd you get him here when I've been trying for days, and he's refused me every time?"

"Simple. I asked." Juliette smiled, and shrugged. "What can I say? I have good powers of persuasion."

"That's all it took?"

"Well, that, and I also promised to pick up a book for him when I get back to San José."

"So, you're bribing a priest. Guess I never thought of that."

"Actually I didn't either, but he laid the opportunity out there by mentioning a book he'd like to have, and I grabbed it."

"Well, your new *bribed* friend has allergies," Damien said, chuckling. "He's allergic to the flowers on the trumpet tree. They produce these lovely white flowers that go perfectly with a bat's nocturnal activities. The flower is closed up during the day and opens only at night, revealing its pollen-releasing stamen, which attracts the bats. Padre Benicio is allergic to the pollen."

"You had him tested for that?"

Damien shook his head. "Nope. Just applied common sense. He's improved during the day, pretty much to the point that he functions normally. But at night all hell breaks loose with his allergies. Which means that it's related to something that comes up every night. The trumpet trees are blooming right now, and since that happens at night—" He shrugged. "Common sense."

"Ah, yes, the standard at El Hospital Bombacopsis."

"Hey, it works! When you don't have the proper equipment at your disposal, you learn to rely on your own instincts or gut reactions."

"If you trust yourself that much."

Juliette was a confident woman. Somehow, he didn't see her as someone who wouldn't trust herself.

"It's a class they should probably offer in medical school, because there are a lot of doctors, all over the world, who are treating by the seat of their pants, the way we do here."

"Well, Padre Benicio is a lucky man since his diagnosis does make common sense. Like Señor Mendez and his gout."

Damien nodded. "We do the best we can with what we've got."

"And, apparently, you've got a good gut instinct. Anyway, how are you treating Padre Benicio?"

"Diphenhydramine."

"That's it? Something over the counter?"

"It's all I have on hand, and I wouldn't have even had that if not for the generosity of someone who passed through the village a month ago and left their bottle of it behind. Unopened, and well in advance of its expiration date, in case you're interested."

"Is it working?"

Damien shook his head. "Nope. Which is why Padre Benicio calls me over to the rectory every couple of nights. He keeps hoping we've got some relief for him."

"Which you don't." Juliette frowned. "Damien, you can't just let him go untreated, especially if he's really suffering from this. And, judging from what I saw of him outside, he is."

"I'm not going to let him go untreated. In fact, I'm going into Cima de la Montaña sometime this week, and when I'm there I'll get on a computer and order something that might work better for him. Maybe a steroidal nasal spray and an inhaler for his wheezing."

"How long will that take?"

"After I get it ordered, it'll probably take a week or so to get it to Cima de la Montaña, then another few days for me to go pick it up. So probably going on two weeks, total."

"That's too long. Let me pick up something in San José

when I go back, and bring it with me next week. That'll shave off a week, which isn't great, but it's better than him having to wait for two."

She'd bring it back with her? Meaning she was coming back again? That gave Damien another week to get it right with Juliette. Another week to fret over how he was going to do that.

"Your gout is acting up again, Señor Mendez?" Juliette showed him into the clinic and pointed to the exam table. "Go ahead and have a seat, then take your shoe and sock off." Once again, the man didn't seem quite right, and her first inclination was to ask him about it. But she thought back to what Damien had said about treating the patients as they came. That was the hospital policy, so she'd follow it.

"Hurting bad tonight. I thought you could give me something for the pain so I can sleep better."

"You're not sleeping well?"

"My legs shake. They keep me up."

She wasn't getting a good feeling about this. "Can you take your trousers down so I can look at your legs?"

"Could el doctor Damien look at my legs?" the man asked.

"He's not going to be back for a while."

"I can wait," Señor Mendez said.

But *she* couldn't. She'd been on duty two hours already, and still hadn't gotten around to doing a general patient assessment. And there were other things that had to be attended to, so a shy patient was the last thing she needed right now.

"Maybe I can just rest on this table. It would feel good on my back."

"Your back hurts, too?" That plus the fact that his speech was definitely slurred tonight.

"Sometimes when I get tired. But it goes away after I rest."

"Do you ever feel any tingling in your face, or arms, or legs?" This was sounding even worse.

"Yes, but it always goes away."

"Do you get dizzy?"

"When I stand up too fast. Sometimes when I stand in one place too long."

Alarm was beginning to prickle up her spine. "I really need for you to take your trousers down. Just your trousers, nothing else." If she'd made an error in diagnosing him the first time, she wanted to be the one to correct it. "This will only take a minute."

Reluctantly, Señor Mendez slid off the end of the exam table, unfastened his belt and let his trousers drop to the floor. Juliette noticed that the man was staring intently at the ceiling. "Can you get back up on the table now?"

Exhaling a heavy sigh, Señor Mendez crawled back up on the table, and still stared upward. He clearly didn't like being in this position in front of a woman.

"I'm going to poke you in the leg, in several places, and I want you to tell me if what you feel is sharp or dull." She pulled a probe from a supply drawer and went to work. "OK, sharp or dull?" she asked, taking her first poke at the man's leg. When he responded that it felt dull, she went onto another site, then another and another, until she was pretty well convinced that he had an overall numbness in both legs. "You can pull up your trousers now," she said, as she dropped the probe back into the drawer, feeling totally discouraged by what she suspected.

"Am I sick?" he asked her.

"Do you smoke ganja?"

"No. Never."

Too bad he didn't, because she was now hoping he did.

That would have been an easy diagnosis. This, unfortunately, wasn't going to be easy. "Do you still work?"

"Every day. I work on a farm, tending the cows. Sometimes I go to pick coffee beans."

"And the tingling you get, or your occasional dizziness, does that ever stop that?"

"No. I work hard every day. But it tires me out now that I'm getting older."

"How old are you?" she asked.

"Thirty."

Younger than her! All the other symptoms, plus gout—meaning compromised immune system—Juliette felt as if she'd just swallowed a heavy lump of dough that had plunked right down in the bottom of her stomach. "Look, I'm going to give you some ibuprofen for the pain." From the bottles she'd brought to donate to the drug supply. "That should help you tonight, but I want you to come back to the hospital tomorrow. Will you do that?"

"Early, *señorita*. Before I go to work."

"That's fine. I'll be here, and el doctor Damien should be back by then." She hoped.

Actually, it was two hours later when el doctor Damien finally wandered through the door. "Anything happen while I was out?" he asked, heading straight into the exam room and dropping down onto the exam table, laying back and cupping his hands under his head.

"Señor Mendez came in for his gout again."

"What did you do for him?"

"Gave him ibuprofen and sent him home."

"We have ibuprofen now?"

"Ibuprofen and another supply of penicillin. One of my hospitals donated it to me."

"Then you come with some advantages. I'm impressed."

"Well, if a few drugs impresses you, prepare yourself

to be wowed, as I also come with a new diagnosis for Señor Mendez."

Damien frowned. "He doesn't have gout?"

"Oh, he has gout, all right. But he's thirty years old, Damien. Remember when we talked over our concern about him being too young for it?"

"Absolutely. But he denied having anything wrong with him when I did his physical. So with this gout—there's nothing else we can do except treat him for what he presented with. And hope that if he does start having other symptoms he'd tell us." He paused for a moment, then frowned. "Are there other symptoms now?"

"Now, and probably for quite some time. He has dizzy spells. His legs are marginally numb. He has slurred speech—the slurred speech I attributed to marijuana use. He gets tired too easily for someone his age, and his legs get too jerky for him to sleep."

Damien sat up and sighed heavily. "Damn," he muttered. "He never mentioned any of this. Not a word of it."

"My sentiments, too," she said, clearly frustrated by the situation.

"Well, we've got to take care of it," Damien said. "And I sure as hell don't know how we're going to go about it, since this isn't going to get fixed with a gut reaction and a penicillin pill. Any suggestions?"

"We need to get him into a hospital in San José, and I'm not going to be the one to convince him to do it. The man didn't even want to drop his trousers for me to take a look at his legs."

"Then I'll just tell him he has to go."

"And get him there, how?"

"Any number of the villagers will loan me a truck or a car."

"You mean you'd drive him in yourself?"

"I made the original mistake, didn't I?"

"It's not a mistake when a patient holds something back. We're only human, Damien. We can only see so much. And when a patient doesn't tell you what to look for, doesn't tell you what else is going wrong with him, how can you be expected to diagnose him with multiple sclerosis, or anything else, for that matter?"

"But he told you."

"I had to pry it out of him. But I'm used to prying it out of patients. That's a good bit of what a family practice is about. As a surgeon, you don't have to do that prying. The diagnosis has already been made by the time the patient reaches you, and all you have to do is patch, fix or remove something. So don't beat yourself up over this, because it was his choice not to disclose."

"Ugly diagnosis, all the same," Damien said, sliding off the exam table. "And how the hell am I supposed to treat that condition out here?"

"There are drugs…"

"Which no one can afford."

"And there are therapies we could do right here to treat some of the underlying dysfunctions that will occur. You know, exercises for cognition, various disciplines for weakness, those sorts of things."

"None of which I'm qualified to do."

"Come on, Damien. I'm trying to look on the bright side here. Señor Mendez isn't without hope."

"Hope comes in the form of convenience, Juliette. Which we're fresh out of here."

"So what do you want to do? Just sit back and watch him deteriorate because there's no hope? Oh, and feel sorry for yourself in the process because you have limitations?" She knew how he was feeling, as she was feeling the very same way. But this hospital needed Damien to function normally and, right now, she was the only one who could snap him out of his frustration.

"I don't feel sorry for myself."

"Then you're angry with yourself."

"Don't I have a right to be?"

"Damien, you chose to work in a very limited hospital. You knew, coming in, that you wouldn't have any kind of modern medicine at your disposal, yet you stayed here because you wanted to help. Give yourself some credit for that. Most doctors would have walked away because it was too difficult. But you stayed, and you do make a difference."

"Couldn't prove it right now."

"You know what? We need to pick up from right here and move forward, because that's what Señor Mendez needs us to do. No matter how he was diagnosed prior to this, and no matter how he'll be diagnosed after this, he's got a tough life ahead of him and you and George and I are the only ones who are going to get him through it."

"You say that like you intend on being in it for the long haul."

"Honestly, I don't know what I intend for my own personal long haul, but I'm in it right now and I intend on doing everything I can to help my patient. Which includes making arrangements at one of the hospitals for all the proper tests to be done. So, how are we going to accomplish that?"

Damien ran a frustrated hand through his hair. "You make the hospital arrangements this week and I'll bring him into San José next Friday, drop him off for the weekend to have his tests. Then I'll pick you up and bring you back to Bombacopsis to save you the drive, and take you back to San José Monday morning, when I go to fetch Señor Mendez."

Juliette was relieved that Damien was finally beginning to turn his inward guilt into the outward process that would accomplish what Señor Mendez needed. She appreciated the effort it took to do that.

"Look, Damien. Neither of us has really made a mistake yet. Señor Mendez is in early symptoms, and his condition might well have gone unnoticed for years. What we did was just treat what we saw, which is, really, all we can do when we don't have the proper facilities to do anything more. I feel horrible that I mistook his symptoms for drug use, but I can't let that stop me from moving forward with a different treatment. And you can't let it stop you because all you saw was gout. You diagnosed that properly."

"And you went from there and diagnosed multiple sclerosis."

"Because, in my specialty, I have to connect the dots. I look at a broad spectrum of symptoms to figure out what's going on. Relate one thing to another until I get it worked out. As a surgeon, you don't do that so much. You fix the specific thing you were called on to fix."

"But I'm not a surgeon here."

"Sure you are. Once a surgeon, always a surgeon. You were trained to think like a surgeon, and you were trained to act like a surgeon. That's what saved Maria Salas and her baby last week."

"Why are you trying so hard to cheer me up?"

"Because I have something else to tell you. Something you're not going to like. And I wanted to soften the blow."

He frowned. "What?"

"I didn't get around to doing patient assessments. I've been too busy." She knew it really wasn't a big deal, but she hoped her little distraction from Señor Mendez would defuse the moment.

"That's it?" His face melted into a smile. "You're confessing that you didn't follow my orders?"

"Something like that."

"Should I fire you?" he asked.

"That's an option. Or you could go help me do it now."

Damien laughed. "In spite of my bad mood and your naïveté, we're pretty good together, aren't we?" He stepped toward her, reached out and stroked her cheek, then simply stared at her for a moment. A long stare. A deep stare.

For an instant she thought he might kiss her and, for that same instant, she thought she might want him to. But he didn't. He simply smiled, stepped back, then walked away. And she was left wondering where a kiss might have taken them.

CHAPTER SIX

"Nice office," Damien said, twisting around to see Juliette's entire suite. It was in a newer building, in a posh neighborhood, surrounded by other posh buildings and, for a moment, he almost envied her all this civilization. But only for a moment. He'd bought into this kind of a trap once before, and learned his lesson the hard way. "And you're in charge?"

"Just the United States division. I have five people working directly for me, and the office has another couple of recruiters who have their own staff."

"I'm impressed. But you ran a family practice clinic in Indianapolis, so how does that translate into this?"

"It's where I got my administrative experience. I recruited doctors and other medical personnel to my clinic, and it was a large practice, with thirty-six doctors on staff, as well as the associated professionals needed to fill the other positions."

"Sounds like a big job."

"On top of my own practice, it was. But it was necessary to maintain the quality of the care we offered. The best care coming from the best professionals."

"So, does your position here entail a lot of paperwork?" Personally, he hated paperwork. Hated all those details that had nothing to do with the actual medicine he was practicing. Which was why his jungle hospital was turning out to be a nice relief. With the exception of charting patient notes, there was no other paperwork involved. No insurance claims to fill out, no requisitions or vouchers to deal with. No nothing. And it was nice. So nice, in fact, he wondered if he could ever go back to a proper hospital and deal with all the superfluous things outside the actual patient care.

"Paperwork!" She snorted a laugh. "About half my job is the paperwork."

"And you like that?"

"No. I hate it. But I have to do it."

So she was diligent in her job, in spite of hating part of it. That was an admirable quality, one he, himself, didn't possess.

You have a week of charting to catch up on, Damien. Fill out the correct requisitions, Dr. Caldwell. Did you forget to submit an insurance justification for the treatment you prescribed?

Yep, he sure did hate all that. "Which makes a jungle hospital seem all the more attractive."

"Who are you trying to convince?" she asked.

"Don't need to convince anybody but myself, and I'm already convinced."

"As in staying there forever?"

"I don't commit to forever. Not in anything. A couple years is about as far as I'll go." And that was a year longer than it used to be. Of course, he was getting older. Not quite so eager to pick up and move so often.

Damien walked over to a fish tank that encompassed one entire wall, and stared in at the emerald catfish, a particularly shy little creature that was trying its best to hide from him. "So, how often do you get out of here?" he asked, as he was already beginning to feel a little shut in by his surroundings, a condition, he expected, resulting from spending the past year in the wide-open spaces.

"Every day. Sometimes several times in a day, going back and forth between the various hospitals. The job keeps me on the move."

"And you like it?" He turned around to face Juliette, taking particular note of the feminine way in which she dressed—a long crinkly cotton skirt in tones of green, blue and purple topped by a gauzy white blouse. Nice look. One he wasn't used to seeing on her.

"Actually, I do. I wasn't sure about it at first, since it's so different from anything I've ever done. But once I got really involved in the work— All I'm doing is dealing with the means to provide outstanding patient care, Damien. It's really quite gratifying, especially when you get to see the results of your work the way I do."

"Meaning, you follow the people you place?"

"For a little while. To make sure they're the best fit for the job, to make sure they're adjusting to their new position."

"Then why work for me? I mean, it's a long drive, and you get no rewards for doing what you do. Wouldn't it have been easier to take a part-time position here, in San José, in one of the hospitals you work with?"

"I did try to find something here before I came to you, but nothing seemed to fit into my schedule. The hospitals all wanted more than a couple days a week from me, and several of them insisted I'd have to take calls. Which I can't do, since I have to deal with people at all hours of the day and night. Except weekends."

It seemed to Damien that Juliette's life worked out to be very tough, as she didn't have any personal time scheduled into it for herself.

"Anyway—I got Señor Mendez settled into the hospital, so I'm ready to head back to Bombacopsis anytime you're ready to leave."

"How's he doing?"

"Understandably frightened. But bearing up."

"Well, I've been talking to a couple of specialists here, and if he does come back with a multiple sclerosis diagnosis, I think there are some things we can do to treat him. It's a difficult outlook, but not an impossible one. By the way, I need to stop at one of the hospitals on our way out. Just for a few minutes. Do you mind?" She grabbed a knee-length white lab coat off the peg by the door, then slung her overnight bag over her shoulder. "I have a new recruit there, an ophthalmologist, and I want to stop by to see how she's doing."

"I can do that for you," Cynthia said, stepping into the office. Her eyes immediately went to Damien, and she opened them wide in frank appreciation. "And I'll bet you're Damien, aren't you?"

"Last time I checked," he said, extending his hand to her. "And you are?"

"Cynthia Jurgensen."

"Doctor extraordinaire," Juliette supplied.

"Well, Cynthia, it's nice to meet you. Do you and Juliette go way back?"

"We only just met when we came here. I preceded her by a while, then trained her."

"When you weren't busy swooning on the phone to Carlos," Juliette teased. Then explained to Damien, "Carlos Herrera—her fiancé."

"The cardiologist?" Damien asked.

Cynthia beamed with pride. "You know him?"

"Vaguely. I made a referral to him a few months back. Good man!"

"He's the reason Cynthia's going to stay permanently in Costa Rica." She shrugged. "What we do for love, eh?"

"And you wouldn't stay if you fell in love with someone here?" Damien asked Juliette.

"Would you?" she asked in return.

That was a good question. One he couldn't answer, as he didn't anticipate love anymore. If it happened, it happened. If it didn't, he wasn't going to worry about it. Past experience had taught him it took up too much time, and time was a commodity he simply didn't have enough of these days.

"Look, I think we need to get going. It's a long trip back to Bombacopsis, and if we need to stop at the hospital first…"

"I said I could do that," Cynthia interjected.

Juliette shook her head. "I really have to do this myself, since she's there on my recommendation."

"You just can't stay away from it, can you?" he asked, smiling.

"What?"

"The patient experience—which, I might add, implies that you're in the wrong position since for you it always goes back to the patient."

"Just like my father," she said, half under her breath. This was something she didn't want in her life—another man trying to dominate her. Her father had always dominated, and it seemed as if Damien was trying to. But she'd finally resisted her father and, compared to him, Damien was a piece of cake. So let him bring it on. She was finally ready for it!

"Did you ever consider that your father might be right?"

"I like my job finding new medical talent, Damien. And I like the hours I put in at your hospital. The rest of it's none of your business." With all the newfound con-

fidence she could muster, Juliette opened the office door
and stepped into the hall. "So, are you coming, or would
you rather stand there and think of even more ways to insult me?"

Damien chuckled as he followed Juliette into the hall.
"So, have I gone and set you off even before we start out?"

"I can resist you, Damien Caldwell. Try anything you
want, but I can resist you!"

Juliette threw her lab coat into the seat next to her, tilted
her head back against the headrest and closed her eyes.
"Finally done for the week," she said as Damien engaged
the truck he'd borrowed and began the journey back to
Bombacopsis. "And I think the people I've brought here
are, overall, working out pretty well."

"You've got good instincts."

"Thank you," she said. "That's about the nicest thing
you've ever said to me." She was starting out her weekend tired. It had been a long, grueling week—so many in-
terviews to conduct, so many contacts to make, so much
paperwork to do. Physically, her work hadn't been demanding. Not like what she was used to in her clinic back in
Indianapolis. But she was exhausted, nonetheless. Probably just emotional fatigue, high heat, high humidity, she
told herself as the noise of the cranky truck motor sput-
tered her to sleep.

"Juliette?"

She felt the gentle nudging on her arm, but resisted
opening her eyes.

"I need to make a stop in Cima de la Montaña to see if
I have any mail. Is that OK?"

Damien's voice was so soothing she simply wanted to
melt into it. "That's fine," she mumbled.

"Then I want to make a house call. I have a patient who

has just moved there from Bombacopsis, and he wants me to check his daughter. It sounds like infected tonsils. It's going to be a little delay, so I wanted to make sure you're up to it."

"I'm fine, Damien," she said, twisting in her seat to face the direction from which his voice was coming, yet still refusing to open her eyes.

"You've been sleeping," he said.

"Not sleeping. Just—resting my eyes." Too bad she couldn't rest her head on his shoulder.

"Well, your eyes have been resting a good two hours now, and you were resting so hard I began to wonder if you were sleeping, or dead."

"Two hours?" Her eyes shot open at this. "Are you serious?"

"Two hours, soft snoring, occasional mumbling."

She never took naps. Never! No matter how tired she got. For her to nap the way she had wasn't a good thing, and to do it in front of Damien? "I don't snore!" she said, sitting up straight in the seat.

"OK, so maybe it wasn't snoring so much as it was moaning."

"And I don't moan in my sleep. Neither do I mumble!"

"Well, somebody in this truck was fully invested in sleep sounds and, since I've been driving, I hope to God that wasn't me. So, are you feeling better now?"

"I was feeling fine to begin with. Just a little tired. Crazy week…"

"We all have them," he said sympathetically.

"Why are you being so nice to me?" she asked. "It's not like you, which has got me worried."

"Actually, you're the one who has me worried."

"Why? Because I took a nap?"

"Napping is fine. Fitful napping is a symptom."

"It is if you're sick. But I'm not sick."

Damien stopped the truck in front of a tiny wood-sided house and opened the driver's-side door. "Look, we've still got another hour before we're back in Bombacopsis. You look like you've been hit by a freight train, so why don't you get yourself another hour's worth of sleep?"

"A freight train? You sure have mastered the art of flattery."

"OK, maybe not a freight train. But at least a donkey cart." He grinned in at her. "Is that better?"

Juliette leaned her head back against the headrest once again, and shut her eyes. "Go do what you have to do, Damien. And if it takes you very long, you should have enough time to come up with your next round of insults. Or do you already have them stored up for me?"

He chuckled. "You do bring out the best in me."

"Thank heavens it's the best, because I'd really hate to see the worst." She settled back into the seat with a little wriggle, then deliberately turned her face away from him. "Now, go away. Leave me alone."

"Sounds like a direct dismissal to me."

With that, Damien grabbed his medical bag from behind the seat, then shut the truck door. And suddenly the truck cab was quiet. Too quiet.

"Shoot," she said, opening her eyes, and twisting around to watch him walk up the dirt path to the house, where a very anxious woman stood on the porch, wringing her hands. "Double shoot."

Reaching behind her seat, she grabbed hold of her own medical bag, jumped out of the truck and followed Damien into the house. "I may look like a donkey cart hit me, but I'm all you've got. So, what do you want me to do?"

"I knew you couldn't resist," he said, grinning.

Of course she couldn't. Not Damien. Not patient care. And this was getting very frustrating.

"Her parents are going to bring Pabla in," Damien said, tossing a handful of mail onto the seat next to him. Letters from home, advertisements that had an uncanny way of finding him even in the jungle, a medical journal, a pharmaceutical catalog. All waiting for him in his local pickup box. "In fact, they'll probably beat us there."

"Isn't there a place here, in Cima de la Montaña, where she could have her tonsils removed?"

"There's a GP here, and he's actually pretty good. Young guy, with a lot of ideals. But he doesn't do surgery. So he sends his minor procedures over to me, and anything major into San José."

"Like you're set up to do even the minor procedures."

"We do the best we can. Dr. Villalobos, here in Cima de la Montaña. George and me—and even you—back in Bombacopsis. Also Frank Evigan, a chiropractor-turned-medic who practices out of a one-room hut about an hour and a half east of us. That's the real Costa Rica, Juliette, and it's nothing like the one you live in, where you have first-rate hospitals, normal medical amenities and highly trained doctors coming in from all over the world to be part of it."

"But you stick with it, in spite of the hardships."

"Somebody has to." And, for now, he was that appointed somebody. In truth, he was glad he was. After a year, he was rather fond of his little hospital in Bombacopsis, hardships and all.

"Do you ever want to go back to a surgical practice, Damien? In society—a big city?"

"At least twice a day. I loved what I did. Loved that my scalpel could cure people. But, unfortunately, I also had a brief love affair with a lifestyle I didn't have the means to support, even at the salary of a surgeon." Which turned out to be the reason Nancy had left him. Bye-bye, lifestyle... Bye-bye, Nancy. "But, ultimately, it got me in trouble."

"How?"

"I became greedy. Wanted more than I was entitled to."

"And you recognize that in yourself."

"What I recognized was that my boat got repossessed, and my car towed off because I couldn't afford it. What I also recognized was that the condo I'd bought was far too expensive for me, and the woman to whom I was engaged was far too rich to come down to my means."

"And so it ended?"

"Because she was rich, I wasn't, and I was trying to play a part that wasn't suited for me. Bottom line—I loved it for a while, until I discovered I really didn't love it at all. That it was just me trying to face up to the fact that my life was pretty shallow—except for my work."

"So, to compensate, you were trying to come up to her standards? Is that why you hate rich girls, because you couldn't?"

"Don't hate them. Just avoid them." But, to be fair, he was in a place in his life where he was avoiding *all* women. The one he'd had hadn't wanted him for who he was, and that had hurt. What had hurt just as much was how he'd been taken in by it, how he'd been so blind to it. Now, he just didn't trust himself enough to get involved with someone else.

"Or give them a hard time."

"By that, I assume you mean the hard time I give you." It was his natural instinct taking over. He knew that, and he was fighting hard to control it as Juliette didn't deserve his leftover resentment.

"You do give me a hard time, Damien."

"But you bear up."

"I shouldn't have to, though. And that's the point. I'm a good doctor. I'm working here free of charge. People who know me will say I'm a good person. I'm a dutiful daughter. But you don't see any of this because one look at me, and one failed bed-making attempt, and *all* you see is the rich girlfriend you used to have, which equates to you as bad. And that's where it all ends for you."

"It's not you, Juliette."

"No, it's your former fiancée, and I get that. But what *you* need to get is that whatever went wrong between you and her has nothing to do with me."

She was right, of course. But that didn't change the fact that he still had his fears. Was it a fear born out of envy, though? Had he tried to emulate Nancy's wealth because he envied it? Because, if that was the case, it didn't sit well with him. Didn't say much about his character, either.

"I don't underestimate you as a person, or as a doctor," he said, giving in to the idea that he was completely wrong in all this. "And if you're intent on continuing on at the hospital—"

"Intent on continuing on?" Juliette exploded. "If I'm intent on continuing on? Who do you think I am, Damien? Someone who just flits in and out at will?"

"Well, it *is* an awfully big leap for you."

"Like it was for you? Don't you think I can measure up to you?"

"Of course you measure up to me. It's just that I thought that with the hard time I've given you—"

"And are still giving me," she interrupted.

"OK, and am still giving you. And, coming from the background you do—"

"You mean pampered and spoiled?" she interrupted again.

Open mouth, insert foot once again. He was nothing but a big blunder where Juliette was concerned, and it was beginning to worry him that he might actually drive her away. "No, that's not it. What I'm trying to say is that, in my experience, people have good intentions at the start, but they become disillusioned pretty easily. Do you know how many people have showed up at the hospital, responding to my ads, the way you did, this past year?"

She shook her head.

"Seven, Juliette. Seven. *And only one stayed.* And he stayed because, at the time, he had nowhere else to go. So why should I expect that you're going to stay, because you *do* have someplace else to go."

"Because I gave you my word, Damien." Her voice softened. "Because I'm not like the rest of them." She reached over and gave his arm a squeeze. "And one day you're going to trust that."

"What I trust, Juliette, is that I'm living in a godforsaken jungle village because it's the only place I *can* live right now. It's the only place where I can just be myself. And there's nothing else to offer here."

"You offered me a job, and that's all I wanted. It's enough, Damien." She smiled at him. "Don't make it any more complicated than that, OK?"

He didn't deserve her niceness, but he was grateful for it. More than that, he was grateful to have her there beside him. In a life that had let him down as often as he'd let himself down, he had no reason to believe that Juliette would.

"Stop!" Juliette twisted around in her seat and stared out the window. "Over there, on the side of the road. Did you see him?"

"See who?" Damien asked, as he slammed his foot onto the brake.

"I don't know. Maybe a child. Maybe a small adult. I couldn't tell. But he was huddling in the bushes."

"Where?"

"About fifteen or sixteen meters back."

Damien engaged the truck into reverse and started to back up. "Tell me when to stop."

"Right across from that tree." She pointed to a fabulously large shaving brush tree. "And I didn't get a really clear look, but I did see something—someone. I'm sure of it."

Damien stopped the truck in the middle of the road, and they both hopped out. "Over there," she whispered, pointing to a particular clump of bushes that was moving, despite the fact that there was no wind.

"Are you sure it wasn't an animal? Because we do have big cats, and crocodiles. And killer ants."

"It wasn't a killer ant," she huffed out.

"Fine, I'll go take a look. You stay here in case, well…" He shrugged.

"It was a person, Damien. I'm sure of it."

"A person who's not coming out to greet us."

"Maybe he's injured."

"Maybe he doesn't like outsiders." Damien approached the bush, looked down for a moment, then turned back and signaled Juliette over. "Or maybe he's scared to death."

Juliette looked down, and blinked twice. There, concealed in the bushes, was a little boy. Dark skin. Scraggly black hair. Huge brown eyes rolled up at them. Quivering lip. Probably aged six or seven. "He's…"

"Lost," Damien said gently. "Probably confused." He took a step toward the child, and the child hunched down into himself even more. *"Cómo te llamas?"* he asked. What's your name?

The boy didn't respond, so Damien tried again.

"Hablas español?"

The child didn't respond to that either, so Damien took another try.

"Hablas inglés?"

When a third response didn't come, Damien looked at Juliette and shrugged. "He's not admitting to speaking either Spanish or English, and he's not telling us his name, so I'm at a loss what to try next. Any ideas?"

"No. But I do know we can't leave him here like this."

"So what are we supposed to do with him?"

"Take him back to Bombacopsis with us, and ask if anyone there knows him. Or if anyone knows of someone whose child went missing."

"Or comb a thousand square miles of jungle to see if he's from an isolated family living God only knows where. Or see if we can get someone out from the Child Services Agency who will, no doubt, relocate him, put him in a group home and let him get lost among all the other lost children there. Or—we could leave him here and let his family come find him which, I'm sure, they will."

"That's not safe, Damien, and you know that! We can't leave him alone."

Damien shut his eyes and shook his head. "I know. But there's no guaranteeing that we could even get him in the truck, much less get him all the way back to Bombacopsis. He's not used to outsiders, Juliette. In fact, he's probably never even seen an outsider before."

"But that doesn't mean he's automatically afraid of us."

"No, it doesn't. But the people here aren't that trusting. At least, not until we prove ourselves to them. And he, most likely, is being raised by a family that avoids us."

"He's not running away from us, though. Just look at him. He's staying here, and I think that probably means he wants help."

"You've got some mothering instincts going, don't you?"

"That's a bad thing?"

"No, it's not. But I'm afraid it's the thing that's going to convince me to take this boy back to Bombacopsis with us, then figure out what to do with him once we get there. So, can you direct some of that mothering at him and get him into the truck, because I've got a tonsillectomy to perform, and I need to get back to the hospital as fast as I can?"

Good Lord, what was he doing, picking up a child off the side of the road? The sad truth was, there were a lot of children, on the sides of a lot of different roads. That was simply a fact of life. The other fact of life was that this little boy, if not rescued, stood a good chance of being found by someone who would force him into child labor on one of the plantations. Damn, he hated this! Hated the harsh existence that so many people were forced into.

"I can try." Juliette took a couple of steps closer to the child, then held out her hand to him. "I don't know if you can understand me," she said gently, "but I want to help you."

The boy pulled away from her, but made no attempt to run.

"I know you're scared. I would be, too, lost out here, all alone in the jungle. But we want to take you someplace safe, someplace where there are people who can help us find your family." She continued to hold her hand out to him. "We really do want to help you."

"Said to the little boy who looks too afraid to accept help." Damien took another step closer to the child and held out *his* hand. *"Permítame ayudarle."* Let me help you.

Juliette stepped back, amazed by what happened next. The child took hold of Damien's hand and stood. No hesitation, no fear. It was as if the boy instinctively knew he could trust Damien. "Looks like you two are forming a bond," she said.

"OK, now what?" he asked, standing alongside the road, hand in hand with the little boy.

"We take him with us, like we discussed."

"Like *you* discussed," Damien said, leading the boy over to the truck. "I didn't discuss it."

"Your gruff side isn't working on me right now, Damien. I can see right through you, and what I'm seeing is a big softy."

"What you're seeing is total confusion. I don't know what to do about the kid."

"What I'm seeing is a man who's stepping up to something even though he's not sure about it."

Well, that much was true. He *wasn't* sure about it. Had never thought about taking on the responsibility for a child, never even for the short term. Didn't want that obligation because he was always sure there was someone else who could do it better than him. Daniel could do it better. He saw that with Maddie. Juliette could do it better. He saw that with this little boy. So, as for him stepping up to anything—best-case scenario was someone in Bombacopsis would know the boy and, by evening, Damien would have him reunited with his family. Worst-case scenario—well, Damien didn't want to think about that one. Didn't want to think about how happy Juliette looked sitting in the truck next to the boy. Didn't want to think about how that mothering instinct in her had turned him on.

Nope. He didn't want to think about any of that. In fact, all he wanted was to get back to the hospital and get on with Pabla's tonsillectomy. "Do you think he's hungry?" he asked Juliette. "Because I have a candy bar in my medical bag."

She smiled at him. "Yep, a big, *big* softy."

CHAPTER SEVEN

"IN THE EXAM ROOM?" Juliette shook her head in amazement. "You're going to perform a tonsillectomy in the exam room?"

Damien looked over his shoulder into the waiting area, to check on the little boy they were calling Miguel for a lack of a real name, and shrugged. "I have an exam room, hospital ward, a storage shed out back and a one-room hut in which I live. Which one of those places do you think I should turn into an operating room?"

"OK, so I'm overreacting. I get it. But Damien, you need a real surgical suite if you intend on doing surgeries here. Even minor ones."

"How about I add that to my list of needs, not to be confused with my list of wants, not to be confused with my list of desires. Which you'll find in the filing cabinet, filed under *nonexistent*, since I don't even have the means to buy the paper to write that list on. The government doesn't fund me here, Juliette. The people who use my services do, when they can afford to. And when they can't they cook me food and wash my clothes and clean my hut. They're also the volunteers you see doing odd jobs around the hospital."

"But you do have some income, don't you?" She knew

that El Hospital Bombacopsis operated on a shoestring, but she'd never known just how short that shoestring was.

"Some. And I have my own personal money, which is seriously on the decline since it's all about expenditures now, and no income."

He was using his own money to fund the hospital? She knew Damien had it in him to be noble, but she was only now coming to realize just how noble he was. "Have you ever thought about trying to find a benefactor? I know that can't happen in any of the villages because the people are usually too poor, but you could go into San José, or even back to the United States. I'm sure someone somewhere would be willing to donate to your hospital." She'd seen generosity at work all her life, seen what it could do. So why couldn't some of that generosity she'd come to count on go toward this ragtag little operation?

"And what would I have to offer them in return? A plaque over the door dedicating the building to them—a dedication that most of the people here won't be able to read? Or maybe I could name one of the beds after them? I mean, people who donate money do so for a reason, and we're fresh out of reasons here. There's no glory in it, no bragging rights, no visibility. So why bother?"

"That's a little jaded, isn't it?"

Damien shrugged. "It's all I've ever seen."

"So it gets back to your aversion of the wealthy." A very limiting aversion as she knew people out there who would donate simply out of their need to make a difference and their desire to see less fortunate people receive good medical care. Her father was one of those people. She'd watched him write checks for worthy causes all her life.

"Well, if you happen to run into one of them, tell them my door is open to them 24/7. But don't hold your breath, Juliette. This hospital's been operating hand to mouth for ten years, and none of them has ever shown up yet. And I'm not expecting that they ever will, even though your naive view of the world is telling you just the opposite."

"My view of the world is based on what I know—based on generosity I have seen all my life." And sure, she hadn't traveled as much as Damien had, or seen as much as he'd seen, but she trusted that people were basically good—something Damien apparently didn't trust, and that made her feel sad for him. To have so much to offer, and to keep it buried away under such deep resentment—it was a waste. "And I know people, Damien. Generous people I can contact in due course."

"You know people who keep themselves locked into a tight little clique. And I'm not criticizing you for that, Juliette, because I don't think you've ever had the opportunity to spread your wings and see what's out there in this world."

"But you have?"

Damien nodded.

"And what you've seen—it's all ugly?" Had the man never witnessed true generosity and goodness? Or was he just too wounded to accept that it could exist?

"Not ugly. Just harsh. And not as giving as you seem to think it is."

"Maybe that's because you've never taken the time in the right places to find beauty and happiness, and optimism. But I know it's out there, Damien. I've seen the good in so many people. You just have to look for it. Expect it."

"Like I have to look for donors for the hospital, and expect that out of the goodness of their hearts they'll want to help us here?" He shook his head. "I've gone knocking on dozens of doors, asking for donations, only to have them slammed in my face. Asked pharmaceutical companies for donations and been denied. Approached medical equipment companies for anything they want to get rid of and, as you can see from what we have around here, failed miserably at that, too. I've turned up too many rocks, Juliette, and I know what's underneath them—nothing!"

"Yet you're here, doing good, in spite of all your rejections. Going into debt, taking a physical beating, getting lashed emotionally more than you'll ever admit, and you dare to tell me there's no good?" She shook her head and smiled at him. "Nope. You're wrong about this, Damien. I'm looking at good right now, and you give me the hope that there's so much more of it out there to be found. All you have to do is look for it. And that doesn't mean just turning up rocks to see what crawls beneath them. Although I'm sure if you turn up enough rocks you're bound to find something good there, too."

"What in the world did I do to deserve little Miss Optimism?" he groaned.

"You ran an ad, remember? And if you didn't want optimism you should have stated, *Optimists and believers and people who have a general sunny outlook needn't apply.*"

"That's exactly what the ad said when I applied," George said as he walked into the hospital. "Which is what got him *me.*"

"And I'm glad to have you," Damien reminded him, smiling.

"Good thing, since I'm not leaving." George patted Damien on the shoulder as he walked by him and entered the exam. "Now, what about this tonsillectomy?"

This was an interesting dynamic, to say the very least, Juliette observed. Not just Damien and George, but the whole hospital and all its workings. And the more she was here, the more she was growing to like it.

"So while you two are operating, what do you want me to do?" she asked. "Oh, and, Damien. I'm not giving up on you and the whole donation thing. You *need* an operating room, and there's going to be a way to get it." Even if she had to fund it herself, which was actually an appealing idea.

"You're not going to be here long enough for that to happen. In fact, I probably won't, either."

"We'll just see about that," she said cheerfully.

"Stop that!" Damien said.

"What?"

"Being so damned optimistic."

"You afraid it's contagious?" She took the stethoscope off his neck and put it around her own. Damien responded by heaving out a defeated sigh, but the twinkle shining in his eyes spoke of something other than defeat. Juliette wasn't quite sure what she was reading there, but she liked it, whatever it was. "Now, tell me what I need to do."

He bent down and whispered in her ear, "I'm not taking your money," he warned, then straightened back up.

She smiled up at him. "Who said I was offering it?"

"Your eyes."

"You read all that in my eyes?"

"I read all kinds of things in your eyes," he said with a seductive arch of his eyebrows. "And I meant what I said."

"So what if I march in here with a brigade of contractors ready to build you a proper OR?"

"How well do you withstand punishment?"

A slow smile crossed her face. "What kind of punishment are you offering?"

"Juliette, I mean it..." he said, squaring his shoulders, trying to put on a rigid face. And failing.

She laughed. "Just tell me where you want me to work. OK?"

He shook his head in surrender. "Do you always win?"

"I don't know. I've never really tried. But I'm liking the feel of this."

"And I'm not."

"Then we agree to disagree. Good!"

"You're incorrigible," he accused, finally giving in to his own smile.

"I'm working really hard at it, so I hope so. Now, about my assignment…"

"Fine. You win—*this round.* But only because I need to get to work. So, for you—take care of Miguel for starters. Make sure he gets fed. Get him washed up, get his hair combed. Padre Benicio's going to come and take him to the festival so people there can see if they know him."

"And if no one does?"

"Then we give him a bed for the night, and approach the problem from a new perspective in the morning."

"If I'm attending to Miguel, who's going to look after the patients in the ward?"

Damien grinned. "You are."

It sure sounded as if it was all adding up to a busy night. Owing to the fact that she was already a little draggy, she wasn't sure how far her limited reserve of energy was going to take her. But she'd be darned if she'd let it show to Damien. For a reason she didn't understand, it was important that he saw her as capable in everything she attempted. His opinion of her mattered more than she wanted it to. "Then I guess I've got my work cut out for me, don't I?"

"Did I mention that you also need to supervise Diego? He's coming in tonight to do some filing for me since his mother is going to be out, delivering meals to some of the village's shut-ins."

"Two little boys, several sick people—anything else? Any beds that need changing? Or windows that need washing? Floors needing a good scrubbing?"

Damien chuckled. "Well, you might have a few inebriated partygoers wander in later on. This is the first night of Festival del Café, a celebration of the good fortune they receive from their coffee crops. Singing, dancing, food, beer—they really know how to put on a good party and usually we get some of the casualties of that *fun*. But don't worry, I should be done with my tonsillectomy before anything gets too out of hand."

Juliette shook her head. Well, so much for the little nap she'd hoped to sneak in sometime during her shift. "Fine, I'll get myself ready."

"You don't sound so enthused."

"I'm just…just worried about Miguel," she said. "That's all." That plus a definite lack of sleep these past few days.

"Well, just keep your fingers crossed that someone at the festival knows him."

An hour later she was still keeping her fingers crossed, as Padre Benicio took hold of Miguel's hand and escorted him out of the hospital.

"Where's his *madre y padre*?" Diego asked. He was currently working in the G section of the file drawer, putting away folders and sorting the ones that were already in there.

"We don't know. That's why he's going out to the festival tonight. To see if anyone there knows who he is."

"Doesn't he know who he is?" Diego asked in all seriousness.

"He hasn't talked since we found him, so I have no idea if he knows who he is or not."

"Will he come here to work for el doctor Damien, the way I do?"

She wondered if Diego was fearful for his position here. He had such an affinity for Damien, much like the way Miguel did, that she suspected Diego was scared to death of being replaced. "I'm not sure what we're going to do yet, Diego. Right now, we're just hoping to find his parents." She was happy both boys responded so positively to Damien. And Damien was so kind to the boys, even though he tried to hide it. It was a side of him that made him sexy and likable and all kinds of other good things she didn't want to acknowledge.

"That would be good," the boy said. "Very good."

An hour after that, though, *very good* hadn't panned out, as Padre Benicio returned to the hospital with Miguel in hand. "No luck," he said to Juliette, who was in the middle of doing routine patient assessments.

Huddling over a patient who was being treated for general flu symptoms, she looked up at the priest and took her stethoscope earpieces out of her ears. "No one?" she asked him.

Padre Benicio, an older gent with a round belly, thinning brown hair and kind gray eyes, shook his head. "No one has heard about a missing child, either. And I talked to everybody in the streets."

"Well, I appreciate what you've done." What she didn't appreciate, though, was the outcome as her heart ached for the little boy. "So, what do you think we should do next? Does the church have some provision to take care of lost children?"

"In Bombacopsis, no. I could keep him in my cottage, if that would help you for a little while, but I think you're going to have to go to Child Services in Cima de la Montaña to see what they suggest."

She already knew what they'd suggest. Damien had pointed that out so clearly. "Or we can keep him here at the hospital for a few days and hope that someone from outside Bombacopsis comes in and recognizes him." How Damien would feel about this, she didn't know. But she suspected he'd be agreeable, in spite of the protest he might put up. "Leave him here for now, and I'll talk to Damien once he's out of surgery. If he doesn't want to keep Miguel here, one of us will bring him to you later on tonight."

"Do you understand any of this?" Padre Benicio asked Miguel.

The boy looked up at him but didn't answer, and Juliette sighed a weary sigh. "He hasn't said a word since we found him."

"I'm sure he'll speak when he's ready, won't you, Miguel?" Padre Benicio said, as he let go of Miguel's hand and backed toward the hospital door. "In the meantime, I'll be at the festival if you need me."

If she needed him. Truthfully, she didn't know what she needed. Miguel's parents, a nap, a few extra hours in the day to accomplish everything she needed to...

"No luck," she said to Damien, once she noticed that he'd emerged from the exam room. "Looks like Miguel's ours to take care of for the time being."

"What it looks like to me is that you need to take a break. You look exhausted." He held out his hand to Miguel, who scampered across the corridor to take hold of it.

"It's nothing that a good cup of coffee won't fix."

"Well, if I thought that was true, I'd send you down to the festival to get one. They serve extraordinary blends at several of the roadside vendor stalls. But I think your tiredness goes beyond that."

"Are you diagnosing me?" she asked him, touched that he was noticing her so closely.

"Just worrying about you. You're running yourself into the ground, and I think you need to go over to my hut, where it's quiet, and take a nap."

"You know what they say..."

"That you'll sleep when you're dead?"

She nodded. "I'll be fine, Damien. But I appreciate your concern." This was a nice moment between them and she didn't want it to end, but Miguel needed to get settled down for the night, and she wanted to get onto the rest of her patients. So, reluctantly, she turned her back on Damien and returned to the ward, to the patient who was suffering complications from an infected puncture he'd got when, trying to grab its fruit, he fell out of a milk tree.

As Juliette lifted the bandage on her patient's right leg, she caught a glimpse of Damien standing in the doorway to the ward. He was staring at her. Holding on to Miguel and staring. It made her nervous, caused her to become self-conscious. So she tried her best to turn her back to him, but she knew he was still staring. She could feel it igniting a flame up and down her spine.

So what was *this* all about? She'd encountered all kinds of people before, in all kinds of places, but none of them had ever affected her like Damien. None of them had ever made her go weak in the knees or caused her pulse to quicken. None of them had ever distracted her so much. And she was distracted, make no mistake about that. In fact, she was so distracted she almost put the soiled bandage back on her patient's leg. Almost—but she caught herself before she did. Chastised herself for the absent-mindedness. Berated herself for the straying thoughts that were trying to grab hold of her.

The thing was, she wasn't even sure she liked Damien. That caused her the most concern. The man was affecting her in odd ways, ways she couldn't anticipate, and there were moments she couldn't even stand being in the same room with him. Of course, there were also moments when she wanted to be in the same room with him, in the same space, breathing the same breath. And those moments were seriously overtaking the other moments.

So maybe she did need that nap. Maybe it could cure her of whatever was ailing her. Only problem was, she wasn't sure there was a cure for *that—if that was, indeed what was happening.* Or if she even wanted to be cured if it was.

Pabla was sound asleep when Damien went to check on her. Doing nicely after her tonsillectomy. Juliette was in the bed next to the girl, sound asleep, as well. As much as he needed her help with the influx of partygoers from the festival trooping into the waiting room, he truly didn't want to disturb her. But George had gone home after the tonsillectomy, Alegria was off for the night and, with the exception of Miguel, who was bedded down in one of the ward beds, the patients already admitted and Diego, who was busy taking the names of potential new patients coming into the hospital, he was all by himself. And, from the looks of things, this was going to turn into one hell of a busy night.

"Juliette," he said quietly, still on the verge of not disturbing her.

"Do you need me?" she asked, looking up at him groggily for a moment, then bolting straight up in the bed. "I didn't, did I?" she asked, rubbing her eyes, then her forehead.

"What? Take a nap?" The expression on her face was frantic, almost like a deer caught in the headlights. For a moment, all he wanted to do was reach out, take her hand, pull her close and hold her. Reassure her. But, of course, he didn't. Urges like that had no place here. No place in his life, either. If he did allow them to take hold of him, though, it would have been with Juliette. Right here. Right now. In his arms. Loving the feel of it. Savoring the emotional foreplay. Nice thoughts, but too distracting…

"I didn't mean to, Damien. I'm sorry." She pushed off the edge of the bed, stood and tugged her scrubs back into proper place. "I sat down, thinking I'd rest here next to Pabla for a minute, just to keep an eye on her, and I must have…" She looked over at the young girl who was sleeping peacefully in the next bed. "How long was I asleep?"

"About an hour."

"Why didn't you wake me up?"

"I assumed you needed the sleep. It happens, Juliette. We all get to that point where we just break down. I figured you'd reached that point." He reached over and squeezed her arm. "And you looked so peaceful I didn't have the heart to wake you up—until now, when I need your help."

She looked up at him. "Damien, I don't put in nearly as many hours as you do, and most of my work isn't that physically demanding. I shouldn't have been so exhausted."

He chuckled. "Why not? You're only human, like the rest of us."

"But I didn't come here to sleep. I'm still up to pulling off a few straight shifts without…" She frowned, and drew in a deep breath. "Maybe I'm getting too old to do this, and I'm just kidding myself thinking I still can."

"Juliette, are you feeling all right?" Something about her seemed a little off this evening, and he worried that her hours here at Bombacopsis were proving too much for her to handle. It was a different kind of medicine than she was used to, in a harsher environment than she'd ever dealt with. He'd had to make some physical adjustments when he'd first arrived or he'd have burned out too quickly. Better nutrition. Sleeping whenever he could. Asking for help when he needed it rather than plowing through by himself.

Maybe that was all Juliette needed—some adjustments. He hoped so, anyway.

"I'm fine. Better now that I've wasted half the shift sleeping."

"Don't beat yourself up. I had a med student once who sat down on the side of the patient's bed to take an assessment, and fell asleep right there. When the nurse on the floor called me down to have a look at what she'd just found, I walked in on my med student all cozied up with his patient, snoring away like he didn't have a care in the world."

Juliette laughed. "What was the patient doing?"

"Looking stricken, and fighting not to get pushed out onto the floor."

"Well, if you ever catch me literally falling asleep on my patient, do me a favor and fire me on the spot so I don't have to go to the trouble of resigning."

Damien stepped closer to her and put his arm around her shoulders as they headed to the desk at the entry to the ward. They stopped for a second, Damien picked up the clipboard listing all the patients waiting to be seen and, with his arm still around her shoulders, they continued on toward the waiting room. "Are you good to take on a few patients? Because the festival is ending for the night and we've got them lining up for us now."

"What are the chief complaints?" she asked.

"Nothing serious, as far as I've seen. Mostly cuts, scrapes and bruises from too much merrymaking."

She stopped, then looked up at him, clear confusion written all over her face. "How?"

"Too much booze leads to shoving and hitting. Or people falling down or stumbling into things. Like I said, nothing serious. But what you get are a lot of the men who don't want to go home in their condition, don't want their wives or families to see what they've been up to, so they come here first. It's sort of a village tradition, I've been told."

"How long does this festival last?"

"Two nights."

They started to walk again. "Well, sounds like a fun evening."

"Diego's giving them all numbers as they come in. How about you take the evens and I'll take the odds? And we'll both keep an eye out for serious problems that need to be seen immediately."

"So you've got an eleven-year-old boy on triage?"

"Almost eleven." Damien chuckled. "And I'm betting this isn't exactly the way your father would run a hospital, is it?"

She laughed. "Damien, this isn't the way *anybody* would run a hospital." In spite of that, she was growing to love it here, every underfunded, understaffed minute of it.

"Miguel is not his name," George Perkins announced, stepping into the exam room. Juliette was busy on one side of it treating a patient for minor abrasions, while Damien was treating a head bump on the other side. "He's Marco. Marco de los Santos. He's seven. And he has a little sister, Ivelis, who's four."

Damien snapped his gloves off, tossed them in the trash and escorted his patient to the door; his patient reached into his pocket, grabbed out a few *colónes*, enough to total about twenty cents in US currency, and handed them to Damien in exchange for his medical care. *"Gracias,"* the man mumbled, then hurried on his way.

Damien turned to George. "So you've found the family?"

"Not exactly," George said. "I found someone at the festival who knew who Miguel—Marco—was. Told us where to find his family. Actually, his grandmother. In the jungle, in a pretty isolated little community. Marco and Ivelis have lived there with her since their mother died a couple years ago, according to the neighbor. Anyway, I took a couple guys from town out there and found…"

"His grandmother?"

George nodded, but the expression on his face told Damien there was more to the story. "So what's the bad news?"

"I think you found Marco on the road because he'd gone looking for someone to help his grandmother."

"She's sick?"

"She's dead, Damien," George said, practically whispering, so not to be heard. "Little Ivelis was sitting in a chair next to the bed, while her grandmother was laying there…"

"Dear God!" Juliette gasped. "That must have been horrible for the poor child."

"So what did you do with Ivelis?" Damien asked.

"Brought her back to Bombacopsis with me. Carmelita is looking after her now, but we really can't keep her since there's not enough room in our cottage, not with Carmelita and me, and her three children."

"And the grandmother?" Juliette asked.

"Padre Benicio is going to see to a proper burial. He's also going to make arrangements for the children."

"What kind of arrangements?" Damien asked.

"They've got no one. At least that's what the neighbor said. So the *padre's* going to talk to someone in Child Services in Cima de la Montaña this coming week and—"

"And they'll get lost," Damien snapped. "Separated from each other, and lost!"

"You can't be sure of that, can you, Damien?" Juliette asked, helping her patient down from the exam table and showing him to the door.

"No, I can't be sure of anything. But what I know is that there are so many abandoned children in Central and South America that all the protective agencies are too over-run to be effective. And what I know is that so many of the children who go into protective care don't fare well, especially older children like Miguel—Marco."

"But what else can you do?" she asked him. "Could Padre Benicio find them an adoptive family? Would Child Services allow that?"

"They'd love it. But it's an almost impossible task. Adopting out one older child is difficult, and to ask some-one to take in two of them—there are too few resources to conduct that kind of a search for anybody who'd be willing to do that. And it would have to be done from here, because Child Services are so busy just keeping these kids alive from day to day, they don't have time to do much else."

"Which is why so many of these children are put into the fields to work," Juliette said, discouragement thick in her voice.

Damn, he hated this. Hated it to hell, as there was no real solution here for Marco and Ivelis. If only he'd just kept on going when Juliette had told him to stop, he wouldn't have known that these two children existed. Wouldn't have become involved in their lives. Ignorance would have been bliss for him in this whole situation. But not for Marco and Ivelis. And that's where his mind stopped and stayed—on the children. *Damn!* He *had* to find a way to help them.

"You'll figure it out, Damien," Juliette said, squeezing into the doorway next to him once George had left. "And you'll do the right thing by those children." She reached up and brushed his cheek. "I know you will." Then she scooted on by.

Damien watched her for a moment, the trace of her fin-gers still lingering on his cheek. How was it that someone he'd known for so short a time had made such an impression? But Juliette did make an impression, and it left him feeling—nice. Even happy.

"So tell me, Juliette, what's the right thing? Because I don't know," he said, following her through the ward, both on their way to do general assessments.

"I wish I could." She stopped, turned around to face him, then laid a reassuring hand on his arm. "I really wish I could."

He looked down at her, smiled wearily. Then kissed her. At first on the forehead. Then on the tip of her nose. Then full on her lips. A gentle kiss. A kiss of warmth and subdued passion. A kiss of need. It was a short kiss, though. Come and gone before he even realized what he'd done. But it left him feeling…stronger. And that was all he needed right now. Strength. Juliette's strength.

"I wish you could, too," he said, pulling her into his arms, and holding her tight to his chest.

CHAPTER EIGHT

THE WEEK HAD turned into a busy one for Juliette. She'd taken on twelve new placements, as well as spent time checking into various avenues of funding for Damien. Plus she'd met with a pharmaceutical representative who'd given her enough antibiotic samples to keep Damien's stock in decent supply for a few weeks. On top of that, she'd worried endlessly about Marco and Ivelis and what was going to happen to them. It was frustrating spending a whole week not knowing.

Given all the worrying, as well as all the other efforts expended on El Hospital Bombacopsis's behalf, she was coming to realize that she was getting too involved there. Too invested. But she couldn't help herself as the more she did, the more she wanted to do. To impress Damien, though? That thought had crossed her mind and she'd swept it aside as quickly as it had entered. Apart from Damien and any feelings she might be having for him, Juliette did like her short stay there every weekend. Liked the people. Especially liked the work.

Of course, there *was* that kiss. One simple kiss they hadn't talked about. One simple kiss that had caused her a week's worth of distraction. A kiss she could almost still feel on her lips.

"It's getting rough out there," she told Cynthia, as she

packed an overnight bag to throw into her car for her weekend trip to Bombacopsis.

"The work, or your feelings for that gorgeous Dr. Damien?"

"Neither one. It's the involvement with the people. It's like I'm turning into a permanent part of the whole operation."

"Isn't that what you wanted?"

"I wanted some patient interaction, on a limited basis. I didn't want to get myself involved in day-to-day lives, and look at me. I've packed the whole backseat of the car with supplies I've managed to scrounge up for them." She sighed. "And I want to spend more time there than I have to give them."

"Is that a bad thing?"

"I don't know." Maybe she belonged back in direct patient care on a full-time basis after all. Maybe both her father and Damien had been right about her all along. Two dominant men, both tugging at her life. She was trying to resist, but not sure she really wanted to anymore.

"Did you know that Damien is in town right now?" Cynthia asked her.

"He is?" That surprised her. Hurt her a little, too, as he hadn't thought to confide his plans to her. Not that he should have. But it would have been nice. Might have signaled something more than their brief kiss being only a whim. "Why?"

"He referred a patient to Carlos, and he came in to have a consult. I'm surprised no one told you about it."

"It's none of my business what goes on out there during the week." Brave words, to cover the fact that she was bothered.

"Yet when you leave here this afternoon, your car will be packed full of things that will be used to take care of matters you state are none of your business. And you spent hours on the phone this week, looking for contributions. How does that make sense, Juliette, if it isn't your business?"

"Damien does what he does, I do what I do. We meet up on the weekends and work together, and that's as far as it goes." The problem was, he was taking up too much space in her thoughts now. Encroaching in places she'd never thought could be encroached upon. Putting notions into a head that had been previously blissfully notion-free.

"But you do have a working relationship, so shouldn't that count for something?"

"He didn't want to see me, Cynthia. Or else he would have let me know he was here." Truthful words, but they stung, nonetheless. She was getting in way too deep. Sinking down into the bottom of an undefined process that appeared to have no way out. Was she falling in love with him? In love for the very first time in her life?

"Look, I've got an appointment in twenty minutes. It should take me about an hour and after that I'll be back in the office for a couple hours. So if you're here when I get back we'll talk, and if you're not I'll see you when I get back Monday. Oh, and tell Carlos I said hello, and ask him if he could please do something to secure the towel rod in the kitchen."

"You should invite Damien to stay sometime. Maybe *he* could fix your towel rod."

"Except Damien and I aren't like that."

"You should be," Cynthia said, as she followed Juliette out the front door. "And you could be if you wanted to."

"You don't know that." Juliette turned to make sure the door was locked, then headed down the hall to the elevator in a casual stroll, Cynthia at her side. "Besides,

Damien and I aren't really existing together under normal circumstances."

"Couldn't you make them normal?"

Could she? Honestly, Juliette wasn't sure what constituted normal with Damien. Wasn't sure he'd ever reveal that side of himself to her. Wasn't sure she'd recognize it if he did.

"Lunch?" Damien had promised himself he wasn't going to do this when he'd come to San José, and here he was, doing it, anyway. So what the hell was he thinking? Why was he trying to turn a perfectly good professional relationship into something else? "I was in the neighborhood, so I thought I'd stop by and ask."

Juliette spun around in her desk chair to face Damien. "I wasn't expecting you."

"I wasn't expecting me either, but here I am." Approaching something he wasn't sure he should approach. "So, since it's lunchtime, I thought…" He shrugged.

Something about seeing her away from the hospital—she looked different. Not as confident as he normally saw her. Not as happy. And the stress he saw on her face—he'd never seen that in Bombacopsis, even when they'd performed a C-section bedside. "Are you OK?" he asked.

"Why wouldn't I be?"

"I don't know. Maybe because you look tired."

She smiled. "I'm fine. Just preoccupied."

"Do you want me to hang around and drive you to Bombacopsis later on?" He knew it was a feeble attempt to get some alone time with her, but it was the best he could come up with.

"If you did, you'd have to drive me back Monday morning, and that would put you on the road for half a day, coming here, going back to the hospital. So, as much as I appreciate the offer, I'll be fine driving out later on. Oh, and thanks for the lunch offer. It would have been nice, but I've got an awful lot to do between now and when I leave later today. But next time you come to San José—"

He was disappointed, but he wasn't surprised. Had he wanted a date with her, he should have asked properly rather than simply showing up and expecting it.

"Damien, why didn't you tell me you were coming?"

"Probably because we don't have to account to each other for anything. That's part of our relationship." A lame excuse, if ever there was one. He hadn't told her because he didn't know how to face her. And he didn't know how to face her because he wasn't sure about his emotions anymore. Or his dwindling resolve.

"What relationship, Damien? I work for you and, apparently, that's as far as we go."

"Is this about me kissing you?"

"It was just a kiss, Damien. Kisses happen all the time for no good reason."

"So you think I kissed you for no good reason?"

Juliette shrugged. "I don't know. But in my experience I don't take those things lightly. Maybe in your experience you do. But it's bothered me all week, because I've wondered if you have something more on your mind than only a professional relationship."

"Is that what you think we're doing? Forging a personal relationship?" In his mind, he believed that was exactly what they were doing. In a most awkward way. In a way that couldn't possibly work out for either of them as they were both headed in such different directions.

"Is it?" Juliette shook her head, and rubbed the little crease forming between her eyes. "Look, I have a lot of work to do before I leave for Bombacopsis, and I don't need to be distracted by this awkward dynamic we always seem to have between us."

"In other words, you're asking me to leave." Something he couldn't disagree with, considering the circumstances.

"Yes, I am."

"But you'll be in to work later on?" OK, so he knew he was on the verge of driving her away, but it was as if every time he got near Juliette he felt the need to retreat from her. Problem was, his way of retreating was all tied up in pushing her away. And he really didn't want to do that. But something always took him over, forced him into doing things he didn't want to do, saying things he didn't want to say. Was it simply that he expected Juliette to do the same thing to him that Nancy had done? Was he really *that* unsure of himself?

"I made a commitment to help you at the hospital, and I'll honor that, unless you say otherwise. So yes, I'll be there."

He was glad. Glad she could get around him. Glad she persevered in spite of his efforts to keep his distance. "I appreciate what you do, Juliette," he said, heading to the office door.

"Not enough, Damien. You don't appreciate it enough."

"You're right. I probably don't."

"And that's your problem, not mine."

It *was* his problem. Especially since thinking about Juliette had started keeping him up at night.

The three-hour drive seemed to take forever this evening, and when Juliette reached the edge of Bombacopsis she'd never in all her life been so happy to see anyplace as she was this one. First off, she intended to apologize to Damien for making it sound as if he had to account to her for his activities. He didn't. And she didn't want him thinking that she expected it. She also wanted to apologize to him for misinterpreting their relationship when, clearly, he had no intention of having anything other than a professional one with her.

Of course, that meant she'd have to quit reading more into it than was there. The kiss meant nothing. The personal interactions meant nothing. She was a colleague to him and she'd have to accept that, despite her growing feelings, or she'd have to leave. But she didn't want to leave.

This was where her inexperience in love was showing, and it embarrassed her.

Proceeding slowly down the main road, dodging potholes and barefoot children darting back and forth across the road, she looked to see if Marco and Ivelis were among any of them. But they weren't. She'd meant to ask Damien about them earlier, but her muddled thoughts had gotten in the way. So now she'd spent the better part of her three-hour drive imagining ways she would approach Damien and, alternately, worrying about the kids.

"Where are they?" she asked immediately upon entering the hospital. "Marco and Ivelis? Have you sent them to Child Services?"

Damien, who was busy rummaging through the file cabinet next to the single dilapidated desk in the exam room, turned to look at her. "They're with George and Carmelita right now. They've been looking after them during the day, when I'm working, and I've been looking after them at night, when George is working. It's not the best situation, but it beats having them locked up in an institution."

"Child Services are good with that arrangement?"

"Child Services are good with anything that doesn't add to their list. The kids are eating, they're being schooled at the church with the rest of the village's children, by Padre

Benicio, and they have a roof over their heads—that puts them way ahead of the game, considering how things could be turning out for them."

"But it's only temporary, Damien. In the long term, what's going to happen to them?"

He shrugged. "Out here, you take it one day at a time. You know, get through the day and hope you make it to the next and, when you do, figure it out from there."

Would Damien actually take on the responsibility of tending to these children in the long term? Feed them, clothe them, continue them on at the school? *Love them?* In spite of his casual exterior, she saw a man who had great compassion, especially for children, so she was encouraged to believe that this could turn into a permanent situation. Damien as Dad. In an unexpected sort of way, it seemed to fit him.

"Look, Damien, I'm sorry for how I acted earlier. You're right. We don't have to account to each other for anything outside this job. But I was a little hurt. I mean, I'm not making a lot of friends in San José. Not enough time. And I suppose I thought we were becoming friends, then when you didn't tell me you'd be there, that just pointed out to me how wrong I was. I presumed too much."

"First, you didn't presume too much. We're friends, and I should have told you I'd be in town. That's what friends do, but I'm not very good at it. And second, I can't have a permanent relationship with you, Juliette," he said, quite directly. "Something other than friendship. If you thought I was leading in *that* direction, I'm sorry. I didn't intend that."

"Because I'm wealthy," she stated.

"No. It's because I'm not available. I came here to avoid those kinds of trappings, and I can't afford to get entangled again. I need space to sort my life. Space to figure out where I'm going and how I'm going to get there. Space to come to terms with what I've done in my past so I'm not doomed to repeat it in my future. Nancy, my biases, my envies—all the things that, for a time, turned me into someone I didn't want to be."

"And I take up your space?"

"In ways you probably wouldn't even understand."

"So that's it? We can be friends and colleagues. But that's all?" She wasn't surprised by the direction this conversation was going, but she didn't like it. Didn't like knowing that these strange, new feelings she was having were letting her down.

"Honestly, I don't know." He sighed heavily. "I didn't want you to make a difference in my life, other than in a professional way. But you're doing that, and I don't know what to do about it because it wasn't in my plan. I mean, I felt guilty as hell about not letting you know I'd be in San José, and I intended to do that because I was trying to distance myself from whatever it is we're doing."

"Because?"

"Because I'm trying *not* to fall in love with you."

Could that mean he *was* falling in love with her?

"Falling in love with me would be bad?" If this was the way love started, it was a lot more difficult than she'd ever imagined it to be.

"It's very bad because I don't want to get hung up on someone. I don't want to feel guilty when I decide to avoid a situation or don't meet personal expectations. I don't want to be distracted from the things I'm trying to accomplish both professionally and personally."

"I distract you?" This was leading to something depressing. She could feel it coming. And it scared her because the side of Damien she was seeing right now, the brutally honest side, was the one she desperately wanted in her life. But it frightened her because his truths were turning out to be painful.

"When I let you."

"Which leaves us what? Anything? Or do you intend on running another ad to replace me?" In and out, just like that. It was almost too much to comprehend. "What do you think?"

"What I think, Juliette, is that I'm better off alone. It suits me. Keeps me out of trouble. Keeps me from putting myself in the position that I might not do the best work I can do."

"Then that's the answer, isn't it? I'll go, and you can find somebody else to replace me. Someone who won't mess with your mind the way I, apparently, am." Better to do this now, before she got in any deeper. But she certainly hadn't counted on how much it would hurt. And it did hurt. And now she was feeling light-headed and dizzy. Nauseated. Headachy. "Well, if it's OK with you, I'll stay on until my replacement arrives." Stay on to endure more of an emotional beating. Because she did have her obligations here, and she wasn't going to let him defeat that in her. Not while she had a shred of pride still intact. "So go ahead and assign me my work for the evening, and I won't bother you."

"Juliette, I—"

She held out her hand to stop him. "Look, Damien. All I want is to do my job, and skip the rest of this. OK? Just let me work." Which was all she should have ever done in the first place. But, stupid her, she'd stepped in too far.

"Fine. I have two patients down in the village I need to see, and I want to drop an inhaler refill off to Padre Benicio. Alegria is here, tending to some basic chores, and what I need you to do this evening is to admit Senõra Calderón when she shows up in a little while. She was complaining of symptoms that lead me to believe she might be diabetic, but when I tried to admit her earlier she insisted on going home and bathing first. So she should be back here anytime. Do an A1C—I have the test kit in the medicine cabinet. Also a general assessment for any signs of neuropathy, and take a comprehensive medical history. I mean, you know all this already, so I really don't need to tell you what has to be done. By the time you're finished, I should be back, and I'd like for the two of us to inventory our supplies—"

Business as usual, she thought. That was all she was to him—business as usual.

"—and then, after that, I want to check our medicines. Which should pretty well take us on into the night."

Couldn't he simply ask her not to go? Couldn't he say something to encourage her? Something? *Anything?* This was awkward. She felt it. He felt it. But there was nothing they could do about it. She was developing feelings for him, and she had no idea what he was developing for her, he was so back and forth about it.

"Anyway, I'll be back in a while." That was all he said. Then he walked out the door, and Juliette walked into the exam room, feeling numb.

Damn, he was stupid. She'd done all but admit to him that she loved him, and here he'd gone and thrown it right back in her face. How stupid could any one man get?

"Have you ever done something you knew you didn't want to do, but you did it, anyway?" he asked Padre Benicio.

The *padre* chuckled. "Too often, I'm afraid."

"I've got something good happening to me, and I know it's good, and I know I want it, but I'm doing everything I can to stop it because I don't know what kind of future

I have. Whether it's here or someplace else. Whether it's as a jungle GP or a big-city surgeon. And if I don't know these things about me, how can I offer anything to anybody else?"

"Whose best interest do you have at heart in this?"

"Everybody's—nobody's. I don't know."

"Then maybe you should reevaluate this good thing that's happening to you and try to figure out if you want it badly enough to sort the rest of your life. Ask yourself what you're really afraid of. Because the jungle is a good place to hide, Damien. It has a way of sorting things for you, if you're not careful."

The *padre* was right, of course, as Damien wasn't sure he even knew how to go about *starting* to put his life in order, let alone proceeding through and finishing it. He was scared of changing his life, scared of changing himself, scared of coming to terms with what he *really* wanted. Which was Juliette. And now she was leaving. He'd pushed her too far. Pushed her in a direction he didn't want her taking. And he was the only one who could rectify that.

"Look, I've got to go try to straighten something out before it's too late." He prayed that he wasn't.

Hearing the approaching footsteps, Juliette looked up to greet her patient and was surprised to see Damien standing in the exam room doorway. "You just left," she said, trying to sound even when everything inside her was fluttering and flustering.

"I came back because I shouldn't have walked out and left things hanging between us, the way they are."

"You said what you wanted to say, Damien. What else is there?"

"That I don't want you to leave. That I look forward to Friday evenings, knowing that you're on your way here.

That I don't know what to do with our friendship and I want you to try to help me figure it out."

This wasn't what she'd expected from him. Not at all. And she wasn't sure what to make of it. Wasn't sure of the way he swung back and forth.

"You know, I've never had a relationship other than friendship before."

"Never?"

She shook her head. "I've had casual dates, nothing serious, and no, I'm not a virgin. But anything that went beyond casual—" She shrugged. Life just hadn't permitted anything else for her, between her work commitments and the fear of what losing her might do to her father. Yes, dutiful doctor, dutiful daughter—all of it had caused her to miss out and now, here she was, practically clueless. "I don't know how to help you figure it out, Damien. If you want something more, you've got to figure out how to do it. And if you decide you really don't want anything other than what we've already got, that's fine. I'll accept it." Even though it would break her heart. "But the one thing you have to know is that if we go any further, I don't expect to be hurt."

"I wouldn't hurt you intentionally."

"But there are so many unintentional things you do. And sure, you have regrets and apologize, like you're doing now. But some things can't be undone. When you say the words, they can't be unsaid. Apologies may be accepted, Damien, but words still linger." OK, so she was putting it all on the line now, but what was there to lose except a little self-esteem?

"I didn't come here to fall in love, Juliette. I came to escape it. Had one serious experience with it, and it didn't work. And it scares me to think that I could go and do it again."

"I didn't come here to fall in love, either. I came to escape my father's dominance. I don't want to be dominated, don't want to be around anyone who believes he or she has that right."

"So where does that leave us?" he asked.

"It leaves us as two runaways with strong ideas of what we don't want, trying to define what we do want." And that pretty well summed it up. "We don't have to date, Damien. We don't have to get physical. We don't have to admit our feelings toward one another. But what we do have to do is realize that our friendship isn't just casual, nor is it just professional. If you can live with that—if *I* can live with that—then I can stay here. But if we can't live with what's apparently going to go unspoken, then I'll have to leave." It surprised her that she'd summoned the courage to say these things to him, but they needed to be said. And so far Damien hadn't made any effort to say them himself.

But she felt good about clearing the air. It gave her hope that even if she couldn't move forward with Damien, someday she might be able to move forward with someone else. Although she didn't think she'd ever find anyone who could compare to him. It was a thought that made her feel as if she'd just said her last goodbye to her best friend.

"I don't know what to say, Juliette. I mean, I appreciate your honesty. And I appreciate you."

He looked as if he were at a loss for something to latch on to. An explanation, a hope. It was something she'd never seen in him before.

"I don't want you to leave. I just don't… I just don't know how to handle you being here. So for right now, how about we let this blow over and see what happens in the future. OK? You know, get past it, and see what we've got left."

"So what do you want from me, other than work? Or do you even want anything?"

"Damned if I know," he said, slamming his fist into the file cabinet so hard the sound resonated out the door and down the hall. "I had this plan. I was going to come here for a couple of years, get away from all the trappings that almost ruined me before, try to find my worth again. All of it just me, by myself. I mean, who the hell ever goes to the jungle to hide and comes across someone like you?"

She laughed. "It goes both ways, Damien. I didn't expect to come to the jungle to find *you*."

"But here we are. And this *thing* between us is driving me crazy because I don't even know what it is."

He *did* know what it was. She was sure of it. But he was dancing all around it, coming so close, then backing away. And it was frustrating that he wouldn't, or couldn't, admit it. Not to her, not even to himself. As much as Damien had tried pushing her away, he was pushing himself away even harder.

"Then, by all means, distance yourself, Damien. Think as much as you want, and I'll stay out of your way so you'll have even more time to think." She didn't want to be cross with him, but his hot-and-cold switch was confusing her so much she didn't know how else to react. This *thing*, as he called it, was getting complicated—for both of them.

"You want me to take them back to the hospital and get them something to eat?" Damien asked George. "I hate dumping all this responsibility on you and Carmelita." The more he was around the children, the more he wanted to be around them. It was yet another new facet to his ever-baffling life.

George looked over at the two, who were playing in the churchyard, keeping a distance between themselves and the other children who were there for school. "We're good for dinner. How about we let them stay for that and I'll bring them back to the hospital in a couple of hours?"

Damien sighed. "I might be back by then, if I don't feel the sudden urge to get out of there and take another walk." Although walking, as he was doing now, wasn't a solution to what was bothering him. And what was bothering him was—him! He was disgusted with himself. Didn't know where all this uncertainty came from, as it was something new to him. Normally when he was interested in a woman he'd ask her out. They'd dine, dance, maybe make love at the end of the evening. Then he'd call her again, or he wouldn't. Whatever struck his fancy at the time. Of course, there was Nancy, and he'd thought she was the keeper.

But, in recent days, he'd even wondered about that. Wondered if his real motivation in that relationship was to prove to himself that he was worthy of climbing into higher circles, worthy of being embraced by the likes of Nancy's ilk more so than by Nancy, herself. Which made him pathetically lacking in character, and full of self-doubt. And it wasn't a stranger to him. He'd felt it recently when he'd gone to Daniel's wedding and saw what a wonderful life his brother had made for himself in the wake of a tragedy that many men would never overcome. He'd seen happiness and contentment and joy—things he'd never seen in himself. Things he'd never thought he could have, given his lifestyle choices. Things that made him desirous of something he didn't know how to get.

Home, family, all the trimmings—in other words, maturity. It was bound to happen at some point in his life, but he wasn't prepared for it the way it hit him. He'd actually looked forward to scaling back on his lifestyle, not running around so much, driving a family SUV rather than a sports car, maybe even mowing the yard on Saturday mornings.

Yep, that was him. Craving the domestic after living the high life. But he'd picked the wrong person, and had actually convinced himself for a while that Nancy would do well living that life. Apparently, he'd been seeing things in her that just weren't there, though. Deluding himself. Which was why he'd come to the jungle. After Nancy, he'd needed to get away—from what he'd been, from what he'd hoped to become. Just get away from it all. Isolate himself from everything and try to figure out what was real in his world, because for so long nothing in his past had been.

"Are you and Juliette disagreeing again?" George asked, his eyes twinkling.

"Juliette and I aren't anything!"

"Maybe that's the problem," George said as he signaled Marco and Ivelis over to him. "Maybe you and Juliette should be doing something. Talking at the very least. Taking a walk together. Holding hands. Gazing into each other's eyes. You get the point anyway. I'll bring the kids back down to you later. Good luck with Juliette, by the way."

Talking? Walking, holding hands, gazing? Yes, good luck, but to whom?

Juliette looked at the results of the A1C test she had given Senõra Calderón and cringed. She was reading way above the normal for diabetes, which was a pretty good indication that the woman was afflicted. Damien had called it right and she wanted to consult with him to see what could be done to treat the woman, given that resources for diabetic treatment out here in the jungle were very limited. But he'd been gone for over an hour now, and she was beginning to wonder if he was coming back.

"I'd like to admit you to the hospital tonight, and have el doctor Damien talk to you when he returns."

"You can't talk to me? Because I like seeing a lady doctor."

That was flattering, especially in a village where old-school values prevailed and outsiders were viewed as intruders. Most notably, female outsiders. "El doctor Damien is going to be your doctor, not me, since I'm only here two days week. Which is why I want you to see *him*."

"Then I'll come back tomorrow when he's here. Right now he's at the Bombacopsis Taberna drinking *cerveza*, and he didn't look like he was going anywhere for a while." Senõra Calderón hopped off the exam table and went on her way, walking right by George, as he brought Marco and Ivelis into the hospital.

"Are you OK?" George asked Juliette on his way in the door.

"Just tired. Nothing big. What's the Bombacopsis Taberna?"

"The Bombacopsis Tavern."

"And *cerveza* is…?"

"Beer." He smiled sympathetically. "But he limits himself to one, just in case you were wondering. Oh, and Damien knows the kids are here."

"You talked to him?"

"Briefly, on my way here. He should be back anytime."

She wasn't going to hold her breath on that one. "So what am I supposed to do with them in the meantime?"

"Find them a bed and let them go to sleep. That seems to be the usual routine."

"That's a heck of a way for a child to live, isn't it?" Even though this arrangement was better than what they might have ended up with, she wanted better for them. Wanted them in a happy home. Normal life. Normal family.

"Damien means well, and I know he's trying to do right by them. And he *has* been building a partition in his hut so the kids can have their own room there. It's just that these things don't get done too quickly when your resources are limited."

Was Damien actually setting himself up in a family situation? She liked the idea of that. Liked it a lot. The light on him, bit by bit, was shining much brighter. And it notched up even more thirty minutes later, when he entered the hospital ward and went straight to the beds she'd sectioned off for the children. He stood there looking at them, while she stood there looking at him. The tender expression for them on his face—it made her heart melt. Made her heart swell at the same time. For this was the real Damien. The one who kept himself hidden under so many layers of uncertainty. The one he probably didn't even know existed. The one she'd gone and fallen in love with. And yes, it was love, in spite of all its obstacles.

CHAPTER NINE

RUBBING HIS EYES and shaking himself, trying to stay awake, Damien took one last look into the waiting room and finally, after sixteen hours of back-to-back patients, it was empty, except for Juliette, who'd taken a moment to sit down and rest. She'd apparently fallen asleep. But who could blame her? She needed it, and that was really all he wanted for himself, as well. Several hours of uninterrupted sleep.

To sleep, perchance to dream... Dreaming that impossible dream... Dreaming dreams no mortal ever dared...

Damn, he was getting punch-drunk now. He shook himself again. Harder this time, trying to throw it off. But random thoughts were running rampant through his brain, which meant he was no good for anything. Especially not for anything as far as the hospital was concerned. So as soon as George came in to take over the shift, he was going to go back in his own hut. Take the rest of the afternoon for himself—no children, no patients. Nothing but perfect peace and quiet. And sleep.

But first he had to tend to Marco and Ivelis. He'd walked them down to the church for morning school earlier, and now it was time to take them back to the hospital for lunch. When he arrived, Padre Benicio was standing in the doorway, waiting for him, holding the children's hands. Just seeing them there—it caused a lump in Damien's throat. He wanted so badly to have more time with them. Desperately wanted to take Marco out to play ball, and Ivelis to one of the local women who cut hair. Wanted to read to them. Sit down to a quiet meal with them and ask them about their day. Wanted to…be a father? *Did he really want to be a father?*

No. He couldn't—*could he?* He thought about that for a moment. Thought about all the changes he'd have to make to accommodate children in his life. About how much he enjoyed having them around—and what might happen to them if he didn't allow them to stay. That was the thought that sobered him. Made him sick to his stomach because he knew what was waiting for orphans like Marco and Ivelis, and it was bleak. How could he let those children step into the kind of life that awaited them outside Bombacopsis? Which meant—well, it meant a lot of things. Changes in his life. Changes in his outlook. Changes in ways he couldn't even anticipate.

Could he do it? Could he take on two children when he refused to take on a real relationship with Juliette? How did any of that make sense?

"Any new developments with the children?" he asked Padre Benicio.

"Nothing's changed. They don't talk, don't go outside to play when the other children do. They don't do anything. So I was wondering, do you think it's time to take them somewhere and have them examined? See if there's something psychological that can be treated? I know I'm not a doctor, but I am concerned that they might have a condition of some sort."

Damien shook his head. "The only condition they have is an overwhelming sadness for the loss of the only security they had in this world. I imagine they're scared to death and they're drowning in everything that's going on around them."

"They need a family, Damien. Two parents together, or a mother or father, separately. Someone to look after them properly, and not do what we're doing here—trotting them from place to place, person to person. Dropping them into situations they couldn't possibly understand."

"I know that and, believe me, I'm looking at ways to take care of them." One way, actually, and he wasn't yet sure about it. Wasn't sure about anything.

"Damien, Child Services isn't going to list them as a priority now, since they already have a roof over their heads, they're being fed, bathed and schooled. As far as the child authorities are concerned, these children are in a good situation. They're not going to change that, since they've got so many other children to deal with who are in horrible situations."

"I know," he said. "Their prospects aren't good."

"Unless they stay here, with you."

He shook his head. "I've been thinking about it. But sometimes I'm barely able to make it on my own as an adult, and I certainly shouldn't be dragging two children along into that. They're great kids, but they deserve better than me." That much was true. They did.

"They deserve to be happy, Damien, however that happens. And whoever that happens with. And I don't think what you consider to be a lack of stability would matter at all as long as you love them."

"Look, Padre. I'm doing the best I can, with what I have. It's not good enough, but it's all I can do. And I'm well aware of my limitations." The biggest one being how turning himself into a single dad scared him to death. As much as he cared for those kids, he didn't know if he could do justice by them.

"We all have limitations, Damien. But the real measure of a person comes not in what he knows he can do, but in what he doesn't know he can do and still does in spite of himself. Think about that for a while. And, in the meantime, I'm going to go find a nice *casado* for lunch, then I'll come down to the hospital to get the kids and take them back to the church for afternoon school." He tipped his imaginary hat to Damien, and scooted out the door, leaving Damien standing there, with Marco on his left side and Ivelis on his right.

"Well, let's go see what Rosalita has fixed for your lunch." He extended a hand to each child, and the three of them wandered off toward the hospital, looking like a perfect little family.

"Juliette?" Damien gave her a little nudge. She was still asleep. Three hours now. And she was sitting up in one of the chairs in the waiting room, looking totally uncomfortable. He should have insisted she go to bed hours ago, but he hadn't had the heart to wake her. Now he wished he'd found that bed for her, as he could practically feel the stiff muscles she'd have when she did wake up. Which would be in about a minute since he wanted to make sure she got something to eat before Rosalita got busy with dinner preparations.

"Wake up, Juliette. We need to get some food in you." And he needed her company, if only for a few minutes. Missed it when he didn't have it.

"Not hungry," she mumbled, turning away from him without opening her eyes. "Let me sleep another few minutes."

"After you've eaten." He nudged her gently again, then

frowned. Stepped back. Took a good hard look at her. And his face blanched. "Juliette, do you understand what I'm saying to you?"

"Yes," she said, dropping her head to the left side, resting it on her shoulder. "And I'll get back to work in a minute."

"Juliette, listen to me. I want you to look at me. *Open up your eyes and look at me.*"

"They're brown, Damien. Dark brown. Nothing extraordinary." She opened her eyes wide for him to take a look. "See?"

Damien uttered an expletive and immediately reached down to feel her forehead. Then uttered another expletive. She was burning up! Fever, fatigue... "Do you have a headache?" he asked, grabbing his stethoscope out of his pocket and positioning it in his ears.

"Only because I haven't had enough sleep lately," she said, finally starting to rouse, starting to stand. But Damien pushed her gently back into her chair.

"Stay there while I listen," he instructed, sticking the bell of the stethoscope just slightly into the top of her scrub shirt.

"What?" she asked, her face beginning to register slight alarm. "What are you looking for?"

He held his finger up to his lips to shush her. Then listened, first to her lungs, then her heart, then her lungs from the back. "Any joint pains?" he asked when he'd finished his cursory exam. "Or vomiting?"

Now she looked totally alarmed. "What aren't you telling me?"

"Any joint pains or vomiting," he repeated, trying to sound as calm as he possibly could, when nothing inside him felt calm.

"No, and no. Now, tell me!"

"Before you came to Costa Rica, what were you vaccinated for?"

"Typhoid, Hep A and B, malaria…"

"And you're up-to-date?" He looked down at her. "With everything?"

"What's wrong with me, Damien?"

"I need blood tests to confirm…"

She bolted up out of her chair, but was struck by a sudden, severe dizziness, and almost toppled over. Toppled into Damien's arms instead and, rather than pushing away from him, stayed there as he wrapped his arms around her close. "Is it malaria?" she asked, her voice now trembling.

"Your eyes are jaundiced, Juliette. And the rest of your symptoms…" Damn, he hated this. Her onset was too fast. Her symptoms growing too severe far too soon before they should have. Nothing about this was as gradual as he'd seen before, and that worried him. Malaria was bad enough, but with this kind of reaction to it— "And you're showing all the usual symptoms." Of all the diseases he'd treated here, he hated malaria the most.

"I can't have malaria, Damien. I was vaccinated!"

Worldwide, malaria killed nearly half a million people every year and infected over two-hundred million.

Soon after he'd arrived in Bombacopsis, a small outbreak of it had taken eleven villagers. It had swooped in and killed them before he'd even known what was happening. But he didn't want Juliette to know that. Didn't want her to know that, right now, he was scared to death for her. "I'm afraid you do have it, sweetheart," he whispered gently, stroking her hair. Wiping the fever sweat on her face onto his shirtsleeve.

"Damien…" She nestled tighter into him.

"Shh," he said tenderly. "I'm going to take care of you."

"But if the vaccine didn't work…"

Then there was a good chance the limited antimalarial drugs he had on hand might not work, either. It was unthinkable. But he had to face it.

Damn, he wanted to take her to San José, put her in a proper hospital, hold her hand while she got cured there, but he was sure she couldn't make it that far. Especially now that she was starting to tremble in his arms. Hard trembling. Paroxysms. Soon to be a spiking fever, plummeting in the blink of an eye to a below-sustainable life temperature, then spiking back up and plummeting back down again. Over and over until coma. Then death—

No! That wasn't going to happen. He wouldn't let it. "It will work," he said, hating himself for giving her an empty promise. "I'll take care of you, Juliette. Whatever you need, whatever I have to do, I'll take care of you."

"Promise?" she whispered.

"Promise," he whispered back. But she didn't hear him as she'd slumped even harder against him, exhaling a long sigh.

Juliette remembered being swept up into Damien's arms, then being carried across the hall and placed gently down on the exam table. Remembered the tender way he'd examined her, started her IV, sponged her down with cool water, removed her fever-drenched clothing and put her into a hospital gown. She even remembered him carrying her out to a bed in the ward, and pulling the protective screens around her for privacy. After that, though, she remembered nothing. It was all a blank. A vague cloud in her mind that concealed something she couldn't find.

"How long have I been out?" she asked, as Damien appeared at her bedside, preparing to change her bedding.

"You're awake!" he said, his voice sounding almost excited.

"I think I am. Not sure, though." She reached up to brush the hair back from her face and saw the IV running in her right arm. Saw the old-fashioned green oxygen tank sitting next to her bed. Saw the darkness coming from the window above her head. "Is this still Sunday?" Sunday night. Late. Yes, it had to still be Sunday, as she remembered working earlier.

"It's Thursday," Damien said, setting the bed linens down on a chair. "Thursday night, almost midnight."

"No," she protested, shaking her head. "It's Sunday. I'm just tired from overworking."

"You're tired because you have malaria, sweetheart. And the last time you worked was four, almost five days ago."

Nowhere in her mind was she prepared to process this. Nowhere in her mind was she prepared to accept it. "Damien, I don't see how…" She shook her head. "You've got to be wrong. I haven't been sleeping for four days!"

"No, you weren't sleeping. Not exactly, anyway."

"I was unconscious? In a coma?"

Damien nodded, then sat down on the edge of her bed, and took hold of her hand. "You have malaria. An advanced case of it. And you collapsed Sunday night."

"But I remember Sunday night, and I wasn't feeling that bad." Medically, she understood this. Understood the gravity of it. But emotionally—she couldn't grasp it. She hadn't felt sick. Just tired. Down-to-the-bone tired. Nothing some proper rest wouldn't have cured. Malaria, though? "I don't recall that I had any symptoms."

"You didn't. Not up until just a few minutes before you collapsed."

"And you've been treating me with?"

"Quinine and doxycycline."

The same combination they would have used in any

hospital in San José. But they'd had such a limited supply on hand. How had he sustained her for so long on what they had? "How?" she asked.

"I have my ways," he said, offering no further explanation, dipping his hand into his pocket to finger the exorbitant bill that came with an overnight express delivery out in the middle of a jungle. A bill he'd paid himself as the hospital had no funds for it.

But she wanted to know what they were. Not that it made a difference to her one way or another, but that was what her mind was fixed on now. She was fighting to make sense of things she couldn't... But the drugs—they made sense to her. She understood them, even though she understood little else. "Where did you get them, Damien?" she persisted.

"Why is it so important to you?" he asked.

"I don't know. I'm...confused. I can't think. Can't focus. But the drugs you used—I remember them, and I remember you didn't have enough of them. I wanted to bring you some. I remember that. I put it on my list of things I wanted to find for the hospital."

"You have a list?" he asked.

"Things you need." Things that she couldn't remember yet. But she did remember there was such a need here. A need she'd wanted to fix for some reason that had also vacated her memory.

"You never told me."

"I didn't?"

Damien shook his head.

"I should have. Don't know why I didn't." Was she involved here in something more than merely being a doctor? Juliette studied Damien's face for a moment. Was she involved with *him*?

"It'll come back to you, Juliette. In time. Your brain is

suffering a trauma right now, with the malaria, but you're getting better."

"I hope so," she said, as her eyelids began to droop. "I really…" She didn't finish her sentence. Couldn't finish it, as she dropped back off to sleep.

So Damien waited until he was sure she wouldn't wake up, then changed the bedsheets underneath her, and kissed her on the forehead. "You've still got a way to go, Juliette," he whispered, as he pulled a sheet up over her frail body. "But you're going to make it. I promise, you're going to make it." Wishful thinking? Empty promise? He didn't know, as she was clearly not out of the woods yet. But hearing the words, even though he'd been the one to speak them, made him feel better.

Damien searched for twenty minutes before he found Marco and Ivelis. Twenty long, panicked minutes. Padre Benicio had brought them home from school, left them outside the hospital to play, and when Damien had gone to call them inside they were nowhere to be found. Frantically, he'd searched the property, looked in the supply shed, run to the church to see if they were there. But no one he'd asked knew where they were, no one had even seen them, leaving Damien to wonder if they were trying to get back to their home. Trying to get back to that one place where they felt secure.

He'd been so preoccupied with Juliette these past few days—caring for her, holding her hand, talking to her even though she was unconscious again. He hadn't meant to neglect the children, but he had, and he felt guilty as hell. Now, he was nearing nausea, he was so worried, as he headed back to the hospital. To think Padre Benicio had actually suggested to Damien that he keep the children!

How could he, when he couldn't even keep an eye on them for a few minutes?

"No luck," he told George, as he entered through the hospital's front door. "I'm wondering if they're trying to go home."

George gave him a sympathetic smile. "There's something you need to see," he said, pointing into the ward. "Or two young people you need to see, rather."

"But I searched the ward first," Damien said, clearly perplexed.

"Not all the ward, you didn't."

"Then they've been here all along?" His heart felt suddenly lighter.

"Like I said, there's something you need to see." He gestured for Damien to follow him, and he stopped at the end of Juliette's bed, on the other side of the partition. "Take a look."

Damien pushed one of the partitions aside and there, standing next to Juliette's bed, were Marco and Ivelis. Just standing there, looking down at Juliette. Not moving. No facial expressions. Nothing. It was a curious sight. But a nice one. Juliette surrounded by children. It suited her, and he only wished she'd wake up again so she could see what he was seeing. "Thank you," he whispered to George, as George backed away then returned to the clinic.

Damien stepped closer to Juliette's bed, and stopped next to Marco. But he didn't say a word. Instead he just put his arm around the boy, and held out his other hand to Ivelis, who clasped on immediately. And they simply stood there together. For how long? Damien didn't know. A minute? An hour? An eternity? It really didn't matter, as he was so relieved that everything else around him faded into a blur and all his concentration was on this, right here, right now.

"Por qué la señora duerme tanto?" a tiny voice finally asked. Why does the lady sleep so much?

It was Marco asking. A voice of concern where previously there had been no voice.

A lump formed in Damien's throat, causing his own voice to go thick. *"Porque ella está muy enferma."* Because she's very sick, he answered, trying hard not to show how affected he was by one simple sentence. But he was affected, and it was strange that he would be, as he was trying hard not to care for these children. To be custodial, yes. But to care—

"Cuando ella va a despertar?" When will she wake up?

Damien bit down on his lip.

"No sé. Realmente, no sé." I don't know. I really don't know. Words he almost choked on.

Marco accepted this, and nodded. Then he reached out and took hold of Juliette's hand. But only for a moment before he turned and walked away from the bed, and Ivelis let go of Damien's hand and followed him.

And neither Marco nor Ivelis spoke during dinner. Or afterward, when they did their drawing assignment for school. Or later, when they went to bed.

But Damien didn't speak either as, for the first time in his life, he felt overwhelmed. Too overwhelmed to function. Too overwhelmed to speak. Too overwhelmed to make sense of anything. Except this. Seeing Marco's little hand in Juliette's—this was what Damien wanted. All of it. The whole picture. Everything he'd never wanted before. And everything he so badly wanted now, yet still wouldn't admit, for fear he couldn't have it.

"Where is she?" the booming voice demanded from outside, on the doorstep.

Damien, who was just then exiting the clinic, spun

around to the door to face the man. "Who?" Actually, he did know. Who else would have trekked out into the middle of godforsaken nowhere in crisply pressed khaki pants and a blue cotton dress shirt to find Juliette, other than her father? Asking Padre Benicio to go to Cima de la Montaña to contact the man was one thing, but standing here now and facing him—it put fear in him. A new fear. A different fear. The fear that he would take Juliette back with him. That he would never see her again.

"My daughter, Juliette. Tell me this is the place, because I've had a hell of a time getting out here, and I hope I don't have to continue searching for her."

"She's here," Damien conceded, pointing to the open ward behind him. "First bed on the right."

"I don't understand," Alexander Allen said, still keeping his distance from the door. "What was she doing here? I'd been led to believe she was working for a company in San José, so how the hell did she end up here, with malaria?"

"How she ended up here is that she answered my ad. I needed another doctor to help me in the hospital, and Juliette was the one who came out here to do that. As for the malaria—this is Central America. People here get bitten by mosquitoes. Mosquitoes carry the parasite and Juliette was one of the unfortunate ones who had a vaccination against it that didn't work. Look, she's sleeping right now. In fact, she's slept for the past several days. A fitful sleep, sometimes so close to the verge of consciousness you think that she's simply going to open her eyes and smile as if nothing was wrong. So she might wake up if she hears your voice. Come in and talk to her." God knew he'd been talking, and talking, and getting nothing back from her.

"Has she been conscious at all, from the start of this?" Alexander asked.

"Briefly. I explained what was happening to her and

how I was treating her, and I guess that's all she needed to hear because she went back to sleep and hasn't woken up since."

"What's her prognosis?" Alexander asked, sounding very stiff about it.

"Physically, she's stable."

"Her vitals are maintaining?"

"Pretty much. No major problems."

He nodded, as if taking it all under consideration. "And prior to her collapse, she was showing no symptoms?"

"She was tired, but around here we all get tired, so it didn't seem unusual."

"But you continued to allow her to work, even though you knew she was tired." Stated, not asked.

"That's just one of the facts of life in this hospital. We always work under difficult circumstances. Juliette knew that before she accepted the position, and she was good with it."

"Why this hospital, though? That's what I don't understand. She chose to work here when she could have had her choice of any proper medical institution in the world. So, what is it I'm not seeing?"

He wasn't seeing Juliette. Not at all. But Damien wasn't going to step into that mess. It wasn't his place. So, instead, he ignored the question, as it was Juliette's father's to answer.

"Juliette was sleeping lighter than she has been when I looked in on her a few minutes ago, so go on in and…"

"You're not worried that she's still unconscious?" Alexander interrupted.

"Worried as hell." Beyond worried. But that was something Alexander Allen didn't have to know. "But she's getting the correct medication, and we're taking good care of her, and waiting—which is all we can do."

"I want her transferred to another hospital. To *my* hospital."

"Against medical advice, Doctor. Juliette's in no condition to travel anywhere."

"With all due respect, she's not in any condition to stay here, either. In case you haven't noticed, her illness is not manifesting itself in the normal way, which means something, or someone, is going wrong. My intention with this, Doctor, is to save my daughter's life, *not* to spare your feelings."

The thin thread of civility between them was nearing its snapping point. And Damien was nearing his own snapping point. With the exception of the past few minutes, he'd spent most of an entire shift sitting at Juliette's bedside, holding her hand, wondering if someone else could do better by her. Wondering if, somehow, he'd gone wrong. Doubting himself. Doubting his decisions. And now, here was her father, practically throwing all Damien's doubts in his face. Accusing him of not being good enough, the way Nancy's father had done.

"Then we agree on something, since my intention is to save Juliette's life, and I don't give a damn about my feelings because they don't matter in this." His impassive facade was beginning to slip, and he wasn't sure what to do to put it back in place. Wasn't sure he even wanted to. Not for *this* man.

For the first time, Damien realized just why Juliette had been so keen to get away from her father. And Alexander Allen's wealth had nothing whatsoever to do with Damien's mounting hostility toward him. Which, surprisingly, was a step in a completely different direction for him. It made Damien wonder if it was not the wealth he hated so much as the way some people acted because of it. That eye-opener gave him a whole new perspective of

Juliette. Caused him to see something in her that he'd refused to see before. The fact was, she wasn't spoiled, as he'd first assumed. She wasn't caught up in the trappings of wealth, but she was trying to escape the way her father was caught up in them. And he owed her an apology for that, and for all the other wrong assumptions he'd made. When she woke up—

"There's a chair next to Juliette's bed." One that was probably warm from all the hours he'd spent in it. "Please feel free to stay as long as you wish. We don't have visiting hours here. Oh, and if you'd like something to eat or drink, just ask. I'll be in and out for a while, as will my nurse, Alegria, and a couple of our volunteers."

With that, Damien turned and walked back into the empty clinic, and shut the door behind him, then slumped against it. He was so sick with worry over Juliette he could barely function, and part of him wanted her father to take her back home with him to get her other help. But part of him feared that once she was gone from Bombacopsis, he'd never see her again. That was the part he feared most. Because he loved Juliette. Pure and simple. He'd gone and done the thing he'd promised himself he wouldn't do and he was about to lose her, without ever having told her how he felt. That was the worst part—he'd never told her.

CHAPTER TEN

"YOUR FATHER WAS here today, Juliette. Did you hear him?" It was dark now, and Bombacopsis was staying away from the hospital. No minor complaints coming across the threshold, no major complaints in queue. They were staying away out of respect, and Damien appreciated that as he didn't want to leave Juliette's side. He also didn't have it in him to do any doctoring. Something about seeing Juliette lying there, so pale, so helpless—slipping away from him. "He's staying with one of the families in the village tonight, even though I don't think he's happy about the arrangement. But it was the best we could do for him.

"The hospital's quiet, too. No patients at the moment. Oh, and you'll be happy to hear that there are no other cases of malaria in the village. We asked people to come in to be checked, and George went out door-to-door the other day, and we're all good. So when you wake up and get back to work…" Wake up? Back to work? The words were so painful to say, he almost choked on them. "When you wake up and get back to work you won't have to be treating a crisis." Damien raised his hand to his forehead and rubbed the spot just above his nose, directly between his eyes, the spot where a relentless throb had set in and wouldn't let go. She'd been like this a week now and he felt so helpless. So damned helpless.

"Marco and Ivelis are fine. They've been in to see you every day, and Marco is actually beginning to talk a little bit. Not Ivelis, though, although sometimes I think she's right on the verge. Padre Benicio is keeping them up with their schooling, and he says they're both very bright. Apparently, Marco is good with numbers. Oh, and Ivelis— she's a budding artist. Draws lovely pictures. Anyway, they're staying with George and Carmelita until you get better. It's a little crowded but, with help from so many of the locals, it's working out. Everybody in Bombacopsis is concerned about you, Juliette."

Small talk. It was all just small talk, and he felt awkward about it because he wanted to tell her that he loved her. But he wanted her to hear it. Wanted to see her reaction when he said the words. Wanted her to laugh at him, or fight him, or kiss him. Wanted to look into her eyes to see if they reflected any love for him.

"Your dad's a formidable man, but you already know that, don't you. I hope you don't mind that I had him called to come see you. But I thought he needed to be here. Also, just in case you don't know where you are when you wake up, it's probably going to be back in Indianapolis. Your dad is making arrangements to have you transported there. He doesn't think we're doing enough for you here."

Damien took hold of Juliette's hand, and kissed the back of it. And he fought back the lump in his throat that was threatening to explode, because Juliette needed him to be strong right now. Strong enough for the both of them. "And I don't want you to go, Juliette. I don't ever want you to go. Which is why I need for you to wake up and tell me what *you* want. If you do that, sweetheart, I'll fight for it with everything I am. I promise."

"You don't have the right to keep her here," the voice from behind him said.

Damien twisted to see Alexander Allen looming over the foot of his daughter's bed. "But do you have the right to take her back to a place she doesn't want to go?"

"Legally, yes I do."

"What about morally? Have you ever, once, done anything for Juliette that she wanted, and not what you wanted for her?" He didn't want to have this argument with the man. Especially not with Juliette here. Whether or not she could hear, he didn't know. But he wanted to believe she could. Wanted to believe that his words were getting through to her on some level and making a difference. "Have you ever listened to her, Dr. Allen?"

"My whole life. And even though you think I'm being an ogre, all I want to do is what I believe is right for my daughter."

"What's right for Juliette is to wait until she wakes up to make the decisions herself."

"And in the meantime?"

"We talk to her and give her a reason to want to come back to us."

"That's not exactly a medical cure, is it?" Alexander Allen said. But his voice wasn't stern. Now, it was full of worry, and fear. The voice of a loving father.

"When she found out her vaccination hadn't worked, she was afraid the antimalarials we might give her wouldn't work, either. And I promised her they would." And she'd trusted him. Damn it, she'd trusted him!

"You had no way of knowing."

"But I shouldn't have promised."

"I'm sure my daughter needed to hear that promise from you." He stepped up to the bed and squeezed Damien's shoulder. "Look, son. I know you care for her. I think you might even be in love with her. But right now, I want to take her home. I've got an expert there—he's expecting her."

"Her body is weak, Dr. Allen. She's been unconscious for quite a while now and her overall condition may be stable, but the physical strain of putting her through what it would take to get her transported may be more than she's able to withstand." That, and the fact that he simply wanted her here. Wanted to be the one to take care of her. "In the end, I just want to do what's best for Juliette, and I think staying here's what's best."

"We both want what's best for Juliette, Dr. Caldwell. In my medical opinion, she's fit to travel. So, tomorrow morning, I'm returning to San José to arrange for an ambulance to come get her, and I'm also going to hire air transport to get us back to Indianapolis. If all goes as I hope it will, Juliette and I will be leaving the day after tomorrow. So spend your time with her now. Say what you have to say to her. I won't interrupt that. But do know that I'm taking her home with me, and I'm not going to be persuaded to change my mind."

Damien didn't respond to that. How could he? What was there to say?

"Remember when you first came here," Damien said to Juliette a little while later, after her father had gone. "And you promised that someday, someway, you were going to challenge me, and I wouldn't see it coming? Well, this is the challenge, Juliette. But I did see it coming when I sent for your father. I knew what he would do. The thing is, I think I know what you'd do, too. And you're going to have to wake up and do it, because I can't do it for you. Do you hear me, Juliette? Squeeze my hand if you hear me."

But she didn't squeeze his hand, and he was crushed. "OK, if you can't squeeze my hand, can you wiggle your toes, or open your eyes? Anything to give me a sign?" Yet still no sign, and he was crushed again. Maybe later—

Damien stretched his shoulders and rolled his neck to fight back the stiffness settling into his muscles, then he took a drink of water from the cup sitting on the bedside stand, and exhaled a deep breath. Bent down, kissed Juliette on the forehead, then tenderly, fully on her lips. "Did I ever tell you about the time my brother Daniel and I burned down the next door neighbor's shed?"

And so it went into the night. Damien talked until he was hoarse, while Juliette slept.

"You look terrible."

Damien bolted up in his chair, blinked open his eyes and looked around. He must have dozed off for a moment. And now he was a little off on his orientation. It was daylight, but barely. He'd been sleeping for—what? Maybe two hours. Then something—a voice? Had someone spoken to him? Was that what had startled him out of his sleep? Or was he dreaming it?

It sounded like Juliette but, looking over at her, he saw that her eyes were still closed.

"Morning, Juliette," he said, standing up to stretch his body. He looked a mess. His hair was in disarray. His scrubs wrinkled beyond recognition. His normal three-day stubble gone way beyond that. He needed to grab a shower, wash his hair, shave, put on some fresh clothes, grab a bite to eat since he couldn't remember the last time he'd been anywhere near a plate of food. Yes, he had a long list of things he needed to do, but hated to do, as they would take him away from Juliette longer than he wanted.

Damien bent down, kissed her on the forehead and took hold of her hand. "Juliette," he said, "I've got to go make myself presentable. But I won't be gone long. I promise.

And while I'm gone, I'm going to have Alegria come in and bathe you, and change your linens—just so you'll know what's going on around you. Also, it's Friday morning, and you've been sleeping for eight days now." He'd oriented her first thing every morning, but he'd never, ever used the words *coma* or *unconscious*. *Asleep* sounded much more gentle—much more hopeful. And he needed some hope here. Desperately needed some hope.

Before he left Juliette, Damien pushed his chair back to the wall, then took a look out the window directly over Juliette's bed. It was beautiful out today. Sunny. Cheery. For a moment he thought about carrying Juliette outside, to let some of that sun sink into her body. Maybe she would feel its warmth. Maybe she would taste the difference between the stale hospital air and the fresh air out there. Of course, it was only a thought. A rather silly one at that. Fresh air and sunlight didn't cure malaria or, in Juliette's case, the toxic side effects of the drug used to treat malaria.

Bending down to kiss her once more before he left, he pushed the hair back from her face. "This won't take me long," he said, then turned away from the bed and headed to the opening between the two partitions set at the end of it.

"Could she comb my hair?"

Damien spun to face Juliette. But her eyes weren't open. "I'll ask her," he said cautiously, even though his heart was about to leap out of his chest. "Anything else you want?"

The reply came, but it seemed to take forever. "Water," she said eventually. "Dry throat."

Damien bit down hard on his lower lip, trying to control his emotions. "A few sips. It's been a while since you've had anything in your stomach, and I don't want you cramping up."

"I'm a doctor." Finally, she opened her eyes. "I know that."

"Juliette…" Damien choked out, stumbling back to her bedside and pulling her up into his arms. "We were so afraid… I was so afraid…" He moved back away from her. "Do you know how long you've been out?"

"You've been reminding me every day."

"You've heard me?"

She let out a weary sigh, and nodded. "I heard you sometimes." Then she closed her eyes and snuggled her head against his arm. "And like I said a few minutes ago, you look terrible."

She held out her hand to his, and he took hold. "Don't leave me yet, Damien. Please, just sit with me for a while."

"For as long as you want," he said, bending down to kiss her hand. "For as long as you want."

"You *know* my dad wasn't too happy about my staying here," Juliette said. She was sitting outside in the sun today, three days after she'd awoken, and she was greeting the many visitors who'd casually dropped by to say hello, bring her flowers or simply hang around hoping to help her out in any way they could. She was truly touched by the sentiment, and shocked to discover how highly regarded she was in Bombacopsis.

Damien, who'd pulled out a chair next to her, and was taking in the sun as well, smiled lazily. "He'll get over it."

"I'm glad he was here, though."

"I was afraid you'd hate me for sending for him."

Juliette laughed. "No. He needed to be here. It would have hurt him if you hadn't sent for him, and I really don't want him hurt. He loves me, Damien. And maybe he's a little too overprotective, but that's just the way he is."

"I know your dad means well, Juliette. I think he'd

move heaven and earth to take care of you. And while we didn't necessarily agree on what was best for you, I think he's a good man."

"He *is* a good man," she agreed. "And a good doctor." She was touched by Damien's kind words, especially since her father and Damien had been on opposite ends of the debate on how to best take care of her.

"Well, all I know is, we both agreed that we wanted what was best for you, even though we wanted it done differently."

"Wouldn't it have been easier on you to let me go back with him?"

"No," he said quite simply. "I wanted you here."

But why did he want her here? Why wouldn't he just say the words? She knew he loved her. There was no doubt in her mind. But she wanted him to tell her, and she was afraid he never would. Yet she'd felt his kisses when she was somewhere smothered deep in her fog. Felt his hand holding hers. Heard the words, but never the right words. The words that would have soothed her heart.

"Well, it's a good thing I woke up and made the decision for myself."

"But staying in Costa Rica is going to be very difficult for you, especially now that you don't have a job here."

"Can you believe they'd do that to me?" she asked, sounding more angry than hurt.

"I don't think it was nice of them, but I can believe it. People look after their own best interests, and your employers needed to move on at a time when you couldn't. Would I have done that to you? No, I believe in loyalty. But you were apparently working for someone who didn't." Her company had laid her off days ago, after he'd sent Padre Benicio to call Cynthia and ask her to explain Juliette's absence to her employer. The director of her office had sent an impersonal note explaining his circumstances and said, if Juliette recovered sufficiently, she could reapply should another position come open. But, as he'd explained, he had too many medical professionals waiting in queue, and they had to be attended to immediately.

"Well, it stings. And more than that, it leaves me stranded here needing to find work or else I'll be forced to leave in ninety days, thanks to the visa requirements."

"And ninety days to find work may be unrealistic, considering that you'll still be recovering from your malaria and the hospitals here might not be so eager to take you on due to your medical situation. But maybe going home is what you need to do, considering how badly you responded to standard malaria treatment."

It almost sounded as if he wanted her to leave. Between losing her job, and now this...

"There are other cures, Damien. A whole host of other drugs I can try. And I still have the hospital here, if you'll let me work." Would he let her, though? Over the past couple of days, she'd given it a lot of thought then reconciled herself to the fact that here, with Damien, at this little hospital, was where she was happiest. What she didn't know, however, was if her being here made him happy. But since the rest of her world seemed to be crumbling at her feet right now, it seemed like the perfect time to find out if this little piece of it was, too.

"Will you let me stay and work for you?"

"But how would you support yourself since I can't pay you?" he asked.

This wasn't what she wanted to hear. No, what she wanted to hear was him telling her how thrilled he'd be to have her stay, that he wanted it more than anything. That they could have a bright future together here. He hadn't said any of that, though. Hadn't even sounded close to anything hopeful. "Remember—I'm rich. I don't need for you to pay me."

"Could you actually work under these conditions, Juliette? I know you can do it for a couple days a week, but do you even realize what it's going to be like if you're here every day, all day? And there's no phone connection. No internet—"

And again, nothing hopeful. "I'm well aware of what you don't have here, Damien." This hurt. When she'd thought he loved her—had she mistaken that for something else? Something she didn't understand? Had she truly believed everything had changed between them when nothing had? Nothing at all?

Suddenly, Juliette felt tired. Overwhelmed. Sad. Didn't want to sit outside anymore. Didn't want to talk to Damien. Didn't even want to see him. Wanted to get away from him before the tears came. "I need to go back to my bed and rest," she said, scooting forward in her chair, ready to stand up.

Damien sprang immediately to his feet to help her, but she held out her hand to stop him. "I'm fine," she snapped. "I can do this by myself."

"You've only been awake three days, Juliette, and you're still weak." In spite of her protests, he stepped forward to take her arm. But she shook him off.

"I *said*, I can do this by myself." Brave words, even though her legs were still weak, and her back still ached from too much time flat in bed.

"Damn it, Juliette! What the hell's wrong?"

"Wrong? Do you want to know what's wrong, Damien? You're what's wrong. And I'm what's wrong."

"Why are we fighting?"

"Because that's what we do. We have since the first day I stepped into the hospital, and while I'd thought we'd gotten past that, apparently I was wrong." She took two steps toward the front entry to the hospital and her legs gave out on her, causing her to lurch forward. But Damien was there to catch her before she fell, and for a moment she clung to him, wishing that his desire to hold her came from something more than simply trying to keep her from hurting herself.

"Juliette, I—" he started, his voice almost in a whisper.

Why didn't he just tell her that he loved her? That would make everything right. But he was running out of chances, and she was running out of hope. Whatever was holding him back was still hanging on, and she didn't know how to break through it. Not even her near-death had broken through it.

"Look, Damien. I can't get out of here on my own yet, but I've decided to talk to Padre Benicio, to see if he can find someone to help me get back to San José. I'll have my dad help me from there. I think that's best for every-body concerned." For everybody but her. But falling in love with a man who kept himself hidden from love was impossible to deal with. She wasn't strong enough, now. Her defenses were gone. And, for the first time in her life, she found herself totally without direction.

It was time to go home.

"I think you should stay here for a while. The children need you—"

The children, but not Damien. "The children will be fine. They've got you, and you're turning into a great dad." She did hate to leave Marco and Ivelis. In fact, the idea that she'd never see them again was tearing her apart. It was amazing how quickly she'd come to love them. But they were great kids. So full of life and eagerness. So adaptable to their new situation. So easy to love. Ju-liette's throat tightened when she thought about walking away from them, but she couldn't allow the emotions she knew would come from that sad scene to stop her from doing what she had to do. The children would get along without her and, as much as Damien loved them, he would eventually adopt them. Maybe he didn't know that yet, but she did.

"But they huddle around you every minute they can."

Juliette smiled. "And they adore you, Damien. The thing is, I can't stay here only because the children need me, especially when I know they've got a wonderful life ahead of them."

"I want to keep them, Juliette, but I don't know how. They need more than I can provide them."

"Do you love them?" she asked.

He nodded. "It snuck up on me, but yes, I do."

He could admit his love for the children, but not for her. It hurt. "Then that's all they need. The rest will work itself out. See, you *need* to be a father, Damien. And once you realize that, you're going to discover some happiness you never thought you could have." But what he wouldn't realize was that he needed to be a husband. It was too late for that now, and she had to leave before her emotions affected the children. "Look, I won't be going for a couple days, because I'm not up to the travel yet, so I'll have plenty of time to say my proper goodbyes to Marco and Ivelis. And I'll be gentle about it, Damien, because I don't want to hurt them."

"You won't be coming back again, will you?"

His face was shielded from her, but she wanted to think it was covered with sadness.

"I think it's time for you to run your ad again. Now, if you'll help me back to bed, I really do need to rest." And fight back the tears that wanted to flow. And pray that her heart wouldn't hurt any more than it did at this moment.

* * *

Damien looked at the truck parked outside the hospital's front entrance, then turned his head away. He didn't want to see it, didn't want it to be here. But it was, and there was no denying the fact that Juliette was about to climb into that truck and leave his life for good. He'd struggled with this for two days now. Struggled from the moment she'd told him she was going until this very second. Why was he letting her do this? Why wasn't he trying to stop her?

Because she deserved better than this. And *this*, he was coming to realize, was where he was going to stay because, for the first time in his life, he fit. Anyplace else, he floundered. Either way, it wasn't enough to offer her.

Did he want her to stay? More than anything. Did he want to work with her and love her and marry her and raise an army of kids with her? He did, so much so that when he thought about life without her he couldn't breathe. Yet he couldn't ask. Didn't have that right because he knew that to have Juliette here would be to deprive her of a life where she truly belonged. Yes, she was a rich girl. And yes, she was used to privilege. But she wasn't spoiled by it. He'd been so wrong about that. So terribly wrong. But it was a wrong he couldn't right because, if he did, she would fall into his arms and tell him how much she loved him and if she did that he'd never be able to let her go. And, for Juliette's sake, she had to go.

"You know you're going to have to do something about this, don't you?" George said. He was standing in the clinic door, watching Damien purposely turn his back to the hospital entrance.

"About what?" he said, even though he knew exactly what.

"How stupid can any one man be, Damien? You love

her, she loves you—admit it to yourself, you damned fool, then admit it to her, and the rest will be easy."

"Easy?" Damien spun to face the man. "This isn't easy, George. And it can't be easy, no matter what I do. Juliette belongs in a different world, and in time she'll remember that. Then she'll resent me for telling her that I love her because that's what would hold her here. And I don't have the right to hold her because all I'll ever be able to give her is a run-down, underfunded little hospital and a hut with maybe enough room to add another room or two."

"The village will build you a proper house, Damien, if that's what's concerning you."

"Hell, they can build me a mansion. But that's still not good enough."

"What's 'good enough,' Damien, is what she wants. Have you ever asked her what she wants?"

Damien turned to look out the front door. The damned truck was still there, still waiting. Still breaking his heart. "Nobody has," he whispered. "Not her father. Not me."

"You're right," Juliette said, exiting the hospital ward. "Nobody has."

George walked over to Damien, squeezed him on the shoulder, then retreated back into the clinic and closed the door.

"Why is that, Damien?" Juliette asked. "Why didn't you ask me?"

"Because I was afraid you'd tell me."

"Do you really not want me here that much?" she asked.

"No. I really *do* want you here that much." This was, perhaps, the most honest thing he'd ever said to her. Maybe the most honest thing he'd ever said to anyone.

Juliette stepped up to him, her face to his back, but maintained a few inches of separation between them. "Then ask me, Damien. Ask me what I want."

He wanted to, but did he really have that right? "If I ask you, then what?"

"Then I'll know that, for the first time in my life, someone values me for who I am and not for who they want me to be."

Damien swallowed hard, then turned to face her. She was so close to him he could smell the scent of her shampoo—the shampoo she always brought with her for her weekends at Bombacopsis. The shampoo he'd grown to love. "What do you want, Juliette?" The most difficult words he'd ever uttered.

"I want to stay here, work in a little hospital where daily hardship is normal. Where I'll have to scrape for drugs and bandages. Where I'll have to make beds. And love a man who spends too much time worrying about the things he can't give me to fully understand what he *can* give me. Raise two lovely children who need both a mother and a father, and maybe add a couple more to the mix. Live in a hut, or a cottage, or a mansion or anywhere the man I love lives."

"And give up everything you've ever known?"

"Yet have so much more than I ever expected to have. See, Damien. The thing about falling in love is, it changes everything. Several weeks ago, when I first came here, I wasn't sure I wanted to stay. And, to be honest, I had to do some pretty stern talking to myself to get me back here that second weekend. I loved the work, but I wasn't particularly anxious to work with you. But, you know, falling in love replaced all that. It changed me so much that by the third week I was actually looking forward to seeing you. I'd spent my whole week away from you wanting to see you. And it wasn't only you. I wanted to be part of the work here. It made me feel vital, and necessary. Back in Indianapolis, I was…replaceable. Any number of people could have stepped into my job at a moment's notice, and my absence there would have never been noticed. But here—it's the first time I've ever been necessary for who I was and not for who my father was, or who he wanted me to be. Being necessary—that's the highest calling a doctor can have. And you know what, it doesn't matter that I can't just send someone down the hall for a CT scan or an endoscopy, and all I may have available to fix a serious gash is a simple stick-on bandage. What matters—the *only* thing that matters—is that you and your hospital allow me to be the doctor I always knew I could be." She reached up and stroked his cheek. "What I want, Damien, is the rest of my life with you, but I'm not sure you want the rest of your life with me."

"Do you know what you're saying, Juliette? Do you understand what a life with me will be like?"

"It'll be difficult. It will lack the advantages I'm used to. It will be nothing that I'd ever planned for myself. And it will be wonderful because I'll be facing the challenges alongside the man I love, if the man I love loves me enough to want me there." She looked deep into his eyes to see if the answer showed, and what she saw was a softening she'd never seen before. Tenderness. Love.

"The man you love does love you. But he's terrified that the life he's offering you won't be good enough. That, in time, you'll grow to resent it, and him." He sighed deeply, lamentably. "And I couldn't bear that, Juliette. Knowing that I couldn't give you enough to make you happy—"

"Damien, I know what will make me happy. For the first time, I truly know. And it's not going to change because all I want from you is to have you love me."

"Juliette, I do love you. More than I can express. But I can't give you…Egyptian cotton bedsheets. In fact, I'll be damned lucky to give you a proper bed."

"Do you think I really care about Egyptian sheets, or proper beds? I'm not that shallow, Damien. Are you still hung up by my wealth?"

"I know you're not shallow, and I got over my rich girl lunacy shortly after I met you. But to love you is to *want* to give you everything. That coming from a man who has nothing."

"A man who has nothing? How can you say that, Damien?"

"Because it's true."

"What's true is that, to me, *everything* is waking up every morning and seeing the man I love lying there next to me. *Everything* is raising two wonderful children with the man I love and someday giving him another couple. *Everything* is working by his side, fighting the odds with him and knowing that, together, we can't be beaten. *Everything* is who you are to me, Damien. Don't you understand that? *You* are everything."

"Juliette, I... I..." Words failed him, but his actions didn't as he lowered his face to Juliette's, and sealed their unspoken vow with a deep, eternal kiss. A kiss that Juliette melted into and knew that there she would find the rest of her life.

Damien and Daniel Caldwell looked the handsome pair, standing outside the village church in their matching suits and matching ties, mixing and mingling with the few remaining wedding guests. If it weren't for the fact that Damien's hair was long and his face scruffy with stubble, a look she adored on him, and Daniel was clean-shaven with short hair, they were absolutely as identical as Damien had told her they were. Same bright eyes, same dimples to die for, same smile. Zoey, her new sister-in-law, was a lucky woman to have Daniel, and Juliette was a lucky woman to have Damien.

Juliette looked out into the garden, where Marco and Ivelis were playing with their soon-to-be new cousin, Maddie—Daniel and Zoey's daughter—and Diego, who'd seemed to latch on to their lives and wouldn't let go. Marco's and Ivelis's adoption wouldn't be final for a while, but they were already a family, in spite of the children's legal status. And what an amazing family it was—a joining of what, at times, seemed almost insurmountable odds.

"You know this means you're a grandfather now, don't you?" she said to her dad.

Alexander Allen cleared his throat, straightened up rigidly. "I'm too young to be a grandfather," he said, trying to sound stern. But there was no real sternness there. Not from the man who'd packed an entire suitcase full of toys for his new grandchildren.

"Well, Grandpa, like it or not, that's who you are now. And, for the next two weeks, you're going to have an awful lot of time to perfect it." When her father assumed temporary medical duties at the hospital and also took over the care of Marco and Ivelis, while she and Damien slipped away to Hawaii for a honeymoon.

"I did tell you that I'm having a few supplies delivered here because I refuse to work under such primitive conditions. Oh, and antimalarials. I'm having every kind on the market shipped down here so you'll have them on hand, since you insist on living here with the mosquitoes."

"Bring in whatever makes you comfortable, because Damien and I expect you to come visit us several times a year, and when you're here you know you *are* going to be expected to work with us."

Alexander finally conceded a laugh. "I was right, you know. I always did say you'd be a great administrator. Just didn't expect it to be in—" he spread his arms wide to gesture the entire village "—this!"

"Well, get used to *this*, because it's now your home away from home. In the meantime, the village is throwing us a festival and Damien and I need to put in an appearance."

"Only an appearance?" Alexander questioned.

"Only an appearance," Damien confirmed. "They tend to overindulge a little during their festivals around here, and Juliette and I need to go back to the hospital and get ready to take care of about half the villagers who'll eventually come in sometime later on." He took hold of his wife's hand, then leaned down and kissed her on the cheek. "It's just one of the things we do around here."

"Mind if I join you?" Alexander asked. "My doctoring skills may be a little rusty but, since you really don't have anything to treat people with, I don't suppose anybody will notice."

"I'm in, too, bro," Daniel said, stepping into the mix with his wife. "And I'm serious about what I said. Zoey and I will be down here a couple times a year to help you out in the hospital."

"So I might as well get started tonight, too," Zoey said cheerfully. "If you could use a nurse on duty."

"We can always use a nurse on duty," Damien said.

In the distance, Juliette heard the sounds of the festival and smiled. This was going to be a great life. "Well, why don't you three head on over to the hospital, while Damien and I arrange for Padre Benicio to look after our children tonight, and we'll join you shortly. Oh, and scrubs are in the storage closet."

As Daniel, Zoey and Alexander set off together, Damien and Juliette stood in the road and watched after them for a bit. "This is good, Damien," Juliette said, turning to face him, and raising her arms to twist around his neck.

"Very good," he agreed, tilting her face up to his. "Very, *very* good."

And there, in the middle of the road, in a remote jungle village in the middle of Costa Rica, to the sound of revelers celebrating her marriage to Damien, Juliette kissed her husband with the first of a long lifetime of soul-shaking kisses. For the first time in her life, Juliette truly knew where she was meant to be.

* * * * *

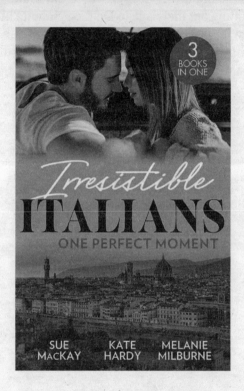

LET'S TALK

Romance

For exclusive extracts, competitions and special offers, find us online:

f facebook.com/millsandboon

𝕏 @MillsandBoon

◎ @MillsandBoonUK

♪ @MillsandBoonUK

Get in touch on 01413 063 232

MILLS & BOON

THE HEART OF ROMANCE

A ROMANCE FOR EVERY READER

MODERN
Prepare to be swept off your feet by sophisticated, sexy and seductive heroes, in some of the world's most glamourous and romantic locations, where power and passion collide.

HISTORICAL
Escape with historical heroes from time gone by. Whether your passion is for wicked Regency Rakes, muscled Vikings or rugged Highlanders, awaken the romance of the past.

MEDICAL
Set your pulse racing with dedicated, delectable doctors in the high-pressure world of medicine, where emotions run high and passion, comfort and love are the best medicine.

True Love
Celebrate true love with tender stories of heartfelt romance, from the rush of falling in love to the joy a new baby can bring, and a focus on the emotional heart of a relationship.

Desire
Indulge in secrets and scandal, intense drama and sizzling hot action with heroes who have it all: wealth, status, good looks…everything but the right woman.

HEROES
The excitement of a gripping thriller, with intense romance at its heart. Resourceful, true-to-life women and strong, fearless men face danger and desire - a killer combination!

To see which titles are coming soon, please visit

millsandboon.co.uk/nextmonth